Skeletons

Written by Tracey Dowtin

To you, my friends, family, team, Diva Dolls, extended family and supporters, there's no limit to what you can do in life. The sky is the limit and it's your time to bring your vision, goals and dreams to pass. Never allow anyone or anything to hinder you from walking in your destiny. Find the strength and courage you need and reach deep inside to pull your dreams out. IT'S YOUR TIME!

BAILEY

Chapter One

Bailey sat at her desk with her face pressed firmly in both hands and thought. *Lord, what am I doing and what have I gotten myself into? I've made the biggest mistake ever and I can't undo what's been done. If I could only turn back the hands of time, I'd have never done this. I can't stand living this lie and I've* got *to get myself together. I'm headed for total self-destruction. If I know this, why can't I be a woman about the situation and be honest with her? Do I not know what I really want or what I need to do? If I don't get it together and quick, this shit is going to blow up in my face and it's not going to be pretty.*

I know deep down inside what's in my heart, where I want to be, and who I want to be with. Unfortunately, in a situation like this, I can't just follow my heart. I have a lot of factors to consider so I have to use my brain. I'm so afraid of hurting my family and losing everything I've worked so hard to build. But at the end of the day, I know that whatever I decide, someone is going to get hurt. I hate to think what Noah would do if he found out about my little indiscretion. I'd hate for him to find out from someone else. That *wouldn't be good. I knew in the beginning I had too much to lose when I started this shit. My husband is going to leave my ass. I don't know how much longer I can hide this from him. Hell, you only live once so why can't I have the best of both worlds? Is it selfish of me to want it all?*

As Bailey sat at her desk pondering over what she needed to do, she switched gears and reflected over the conversation that she and Maisha had had the night before. "I need you to make a decision, so what are you going to do?" Maisha had asked.

Bailey put her head back down on her desk and her assistant called her. "I know you're busy but Maisha would like to see you."

Damn, I just got to work, I'm not ready to start my morning off with this bullshit. "Can you tell her I'm busy right now?" Bailey asked.

"She said it's really important," Rachel said.

"Okay."

Maisha walked into Bailey's office and looked at her. "Good morning, how are you?"

"I'm good but things could be a whole lot better."

"I know you're not happy with him so why the fuck you continue with this pretense is beyond me. Why are you lying to yourself and wasting your time with him?" Maisha asked.

"It's too damn early in the morning for this. I can't deal with this right now."

"That's part of the problem too. It's always about you and what you want—what about the rest of us? Or do we live just to serve you?"

"We're at work right now and this is neither the time nor the place for this conversation."

"Then answer this, why are you stringing me the fuck along as if I'm a goddamn violin that you play whenever it's convenient for you?"

"I'm not going to answer that question. We'll talk later," Bailey said.

"Oh I forgot, the queen only does what she wants whenever the hell she wants and how she wants."

"You really need to cut it out. You're blowing this shit all out of proportion. I'll have a conversation with you, just not right now and in the office."

"If not now, then when?"

"I'll stop by your house later on."

"Bailey, you can't keep dodging this topic, it needs to be addressed now, not later."

Rachel popped her head round the door. "I know you're going to be busy with the end of month reports and don't want to be disturbed, but don't forget you have a conference call in fifteen minutes."

"Thanks, Rachel, the call had actually slipped my mind," said Bailey.

"Noah also called and wants to meet with you at your earliest convenience, he said it's really important," Rachel added.

"Okay, let me know when he gets in."

Rachel nodded and shut the door behind her.

"Why the hell is it so hard for you to decide? You're happier with me! I treat you like the queen you are, I love your children, and we have a great time together. More importantly our relationship is not based solely on sex," Maisha said.

The women had had this secret friendship for two months now. Maisha was becoming extremely impatient and was tired of going back and forth with Bailey's indecisiveness. "I thought you were going to leave him?" she asked.

"Let me correct you, we're not in a relationship, we're friends. You're a lesbian and I was bi-curious, you helped with my curiosity, we had fun, and that's that. I never told you I would leave my husband," Bailey said.

Regardless of the realization that her illusion of living happily ever after together was a fairy tale, Maisha had assumed they were in a relationship and would be together.

"I'm not walking away from my marriage for you, I can't hurt Noah like that," Bailey said.

"Every time I kiss your lips, suck your pussy or fuck you, don't you think that hurts him? We'd be better off having a threesome, it's me he tastes every time he kisses you anyway," Maisha pointed out.

"Do you have to be so crass? Not only would that hurt him, it would devastate him!"

"What about my hurt? Do you not care, do you not love me?"

"I do care about you, but as a friend. The chances of us being in a committed relationship will never happen, not in your wildest dreams."

"Never say never."

Bailey chuckled and said, "Trust me, it ain't happening."

"That's a fucked-up thing to say."

"Sweetie, I'm just keeping it real. If I've misled you in any way I sincerely apologize. You were the one who assumed I was ending my marriage. I never said anything remotely like that," Bailey said.

"So, in other words, I'm just a piece of ass to you?"

"When you weren't acting crazy, you were a great person to be around."

"Can you think about it? I know we could be happy together. Just let me show you."

"Can we finish this conversation later? Again, this is not the place for this."

"There you go, brushing me off again like I and my feelings don't mean a damn thing," Maisha said, near tears.

"You're reading too much into the situation. I feel like I can't talk to you because you're being irrational," Bailey said, unmoved.

"You're acting like a damn man and you're a cold-hearted bitch. You don't give a damn about nobody and you don't care who you hurt," Maisha yelled.

Noah walked into the office, demanding to know what Maisha was shouting about. He said he could hear her hollering from the other end of the hall.

Maisha sat on the sofa and crossed her arms. She hoped Bailey would finally stop the lies and end the marriage once and for all.

Bailey looked at her husband and said, "We're just having a disagreement over the monthly financial statements."

Noah co-owned the company with her; her statement made him inquisitive and he wanted to know more. "I thought you were supposed to be on a conference call ten minutes ago?" he asked.

"Oh shit! Maisha, we'll have to discuss this later."

As Bailey gathered the necessary documents and information for her call, Maisha walked over to Bailey and said, "This is bullshit and I'm not going to deal with it anymore!" She walked out of the office and slammed the door.

"Baby, what's going on with her? She's been difficult to deal with for the last couple of weeks," Noah said. "She's been short, snappy, unprofessional and extremely disorganized. One of our clients even called about her attitude during a meeting last week. I want to remind you that this is the woman in charge of overseeing our company finances. I can't afford for her to fuck up our money. I suggest you speak with her, or if you're not comfortable doing that, the human resource director can speak with her."

Bailey shrugged. "I don't know what's going on with her. I think she's a little stressed about some personal issues."

Noah looked perplexed. "No, not Maisha. She always handles everything so well. Whether here or there, personal issues should be left at the door and not brought into my office. If she can't separate the two and doesn't get her shit together, friend or not, she needs to find another job."

"You're being a little harsh, don't you think? We all have good and bad days and everyone is different. You never know what someone's going through or their breaking point. We're all human, but we deal with situations differently. She's here every day, works hard and is very dedicated to our company. She could be like the person I fired a couple of weeks ago. You remember? He came to work every day but only to surf the Net and sit on Facebook all damn day. But I *will* speak to her."

Reassured that his wife would take care of the situation, Noah gave Bailey a hug and a kiss then said, "I have to leave for a 9:30 a.m. meeting in Virginia, but I'll see you at 12:30 for the meeting with Wiley & Smirch Management Group."

"Ok, sweetie, I have to get on this call. I'll see you at the meeting. Drive careful, love ya."

"Love ya too," Noah replied as he walked out of Bailey's office.

Bailey didn't know what to do. She was at her wits' end. She knew how Maisha felt about her, but Bailey did not reciprocate those feelings. She and Noah had been married for twelve years and ending her marriage wasn't an option. She refused to lose her best friend, business partner and the love of her life.

She picked up the phone to call Maisha but before she could dial the last number, Rachel walked in. "If you're looking for Maisha she'll be working from home the rest of the day."

Bailey just looked at her then said, "Are you serious? It's only 10 a.m. Why did she even bother to come in?" *I guess I really do need to have that conversation with her after all. In spite of our intimate friendship, she still shouldn't fuck up her job.* "I'll be leaving shortly, I have something I need to take care of," she told Rachel.

As Bailey approached the elevator, she called Maisha from her cellphone. "Where are you?"

Maisha answered in a sarcastic tone, "I'm almost home. Why?"

Bailey informed her that she was on her way and asked, "Do you need me to pick up anything?"

"No, I'm good!"

Within ten minutes Bailey was ringing Maisha's doorbell. Maisha came to the door and said, "Damn, did you fly here?"

Bailey didn't utter a word. She grabbed Maisha and kissed her. Then she guided Maisha upstairs to the master bedroom.

Maisha said, "So you've nothing to say about what happened at the office?"

"Yes, I have a lot to say about what happened at the office as well as your work performance the past several weeks. I also want you to know if you don't get your shit together, Noah's going to fire you. But right now, it's not the time."

Bailey led Maisha to the bed, undressed her, then slowly and passionately began kissing her neck. She softly grabbed her breasts and began a gentle sucking of her nipples.

"Bailey, not now, we need to talk, this shit has to be sorted out!"

Bailey continued to lick Maisha's nipples and sucked them again. She then started working her way down, leaving none of Maisha's stomach untouched. Bailey opened Maisha's legs, kissed her intimately, then slowly licked and sucked before inserting two of her fingers and enjoying the feel and the touch.

She kissed her way down Maisha's inner thighs, then worked her way back up before grabbing her ass, pushing her pussy closer to her face and sucking on her clit. Maisha groaned loudly and Bailey sucked faster, bringing her to climax. "Now we can talk!"

Maisha sat up, looked at Bailey and said, "What the fuck? You have got to be kidding me, we're not finished yet!"

"That was mid-morning delight. Besides, I just needed you to calm down a little before we had this conversation. You were so tense and worked up earlier, now we can talk. I'll meet you downstairs after I wash my face," replied Bailey.

"Fine, give me a second, and I'll be down."

When Maisha reached the last step, she looked at Bailey. "Before you get started, if this is the same conversation we've been having for the past several weeks, then save it." Maisha walked to the dining room table. "I'm getting tired of discussing the same topic and nothing has changed. From the looks of things you want your cake and eat it too. If you love your husband so much then what are you doing with me? Why are you cheating? Why won't you let me go? What's holding you back?" Maisha threw question after question at Bailey. She was extremely irritated and needed Bailey to make a decision.

"You and I are good friends but I can't offer you anything else. I never told you anything different," Bailey said. "The only thing I'm trying to hold on to is our friendship and a damn good employee."

"That's all I am to you? Just a friend and employee?"

"There's no other title I can give you," Bailey said.

"Well damn, I feel like I was just stabbed in the heart."

"You knew in the beginning it wasn't going anywhere. Sometimes we just can't control our feelings as much as we'd like to. Shit happens."

"You're right, we can't control our feelings but you act as though I was a bad mistake."

Bailey relocated to the dining room and sat at the table. "I never said you were a mistake. I keep telling you to stop putting words in my mouth. I'm very capable of speaking for myself."

"Just so you know, I have and will always fight for what I want. Regardless of whom or what it is. So if I have to fight for you I'm more than happy to do so," said Maisha.

"But you can't fight for me, Maisha, I'm not yours."

"Don't get it twisted. I'm going to fight for you. And I'm going to enjoy every minute of it."

"From day one I've been saying the same thing over and over. We're cool and all, but ruining my marriage was never in the plan."

"You ruined your marriage when you started sleeping with me. Yeah, I might have pursued you but you acted on it. You didn't have to give in to temptation but you did. At first you acted like you weren't interested but I knew the entire time that you wanted me. I could tell by the way you looked at me. That's why I was so persistent. I knew with all certainty that it was only a matter of time before I got you. It didn't matter to me that you were married. I damn sure didn't care that your husband's my boss. I saw something I wanted and I went after it. I want you—all of you. I don't understand why you don't get that."

"I do get it but I'm not available to you. Granted, I can't undo what's been done but we have to move past this."

"I love you to death but in all honesty I don't believe you know *what* you want. If you don't want me then I have to try and accept that. It's not going to be easy but I'll get over it. I think it would be best for you to fall back. Search your heart. Work out what it is you actually want. When you figure it out then get back to me. I really think it would be beneficial for the both of us if we take a break until you figure out what you want to do," Maisha said.

"I can do that. A break sounds good right about now," Bailey said.

"Now you're being nonchalant about the whole situation. As if you really don't give a fuck one way or another."

"Don't get me wrong, I do care about you but I'm not in love with you. I need for you to understand that I have a lot going on right now. I have a lot on my plate. I don't share everything that happens in the world of Bailey with you. I do have other stuff going on in my life besides you. For me you were the outlet I needed away from everyone and everything else. I have other significant issues that are the center of my attention. My family, my businesses, meetings out of my ass, employees, to name but a few."

Bailey got into her truck, thinking about the past two months. *I had ample time to end the friendship. While I'm taking a break maybe she'll lose interest and move on.* She started the truck and fastened her seatbelt, then remembered she was supposed to have accompanied Noah to a meeting on the other side of town an hour ago.

She pulled out her phone and called him. "Sweetie, I'm on my way."

"Where are you? You know you're late for this meeting."

"Yeah, I know. I'm on my way, give me fifteen minutes."

As Bailey drove and listened to the car radio she felt as though a weight had been lifted. *I'm so glad Maisha suggested me taking time to think. But there's nothing really for me to think about. She needs to move on and I need to focus on other pertinent issues at hand. I hope she'll find someone else to occupy her time, and focus less on me.*

Bailey finally arrived at the meeting and pulled into the parking garage. When the valet stepped out of the booth she handed him her keys. Before she could get the parking ticket, her phone rang.

"Bailey, there's no need to come to the meeting, it's over," Noah said abruptly.

"Over? I'm in the parking garage, I'm on my way up."

"Don't even worry about it. Even though this meeting was spontaneously scheduled, between your two assistants and a goddamn phone there's no reason why you couldn't be here on time. What were you doing that was so fucking important you had to miss this meeting? You know better than anyone else the significance of this project. Not only could we make a lot of money with this deal but also open up hundreds of jobs. In addition, it would give our company great exposure. I'm starting to think that maybe you have too much on your plate or you're starting to not give a fuck. I'll just see you when I get home tonight."

"But Noah . . ."

"Bailey, I don't want to hear it. I'm a little pissed off with you right now. Like I said, I'll see you when I get home tonight."

"You're not giving me a chance to say anything."

"You're right. Goodbye!" Noah yelled.

Well I'll be damned! Noah's never spoken to me like that before. What's gotten his boxers in a bunch? In all honesty he has every right to be pissed with me, but damn. Today hasn't been a good day for me and it's only 1 p.m. I think I've done enough damage, so I'll call it a day. I'll pick my babies up from school early. They'll be totally surprised and we'll hang out the rest of the day, shop and have dinner. I guess I should call Nina or Rachel to let them know I'll not be back in the office.

"Good afternoon, thank you for calling Jones Management & Investments, this is Nina, how may I direct your call?"

"Hi, Nina," said Bailey.

"Hello, Bailey."

"I'm calling to inform you that I'll not be back in the office today. There's also a possibility that I'll be out the remainder of the week. I'll touch base with you and Rachel tomorrow and let you know."

"Are you guys going on vacation or something?" Nina asked.

"No, I have some things I need to take care of."

"Is everything alright, are you sick?"

"Everything's fine."

"Will Noah be out too?"

"Most likely Noah will be in the office. I've been so busy lately and haven't spent much time with my babies."

"Oh, okay. I can't remember the last time you were actually away from the office. Especially for three whole days, I thought maybe you were a little under the weather or something."

"As we speak I'm on my way to pick up the girls from school. Today seems like a good day to hang out with them and have a little fun. The sun is shining and surprisingly it's almost seventy five degrees."

"I know the girls are going to enjoy that. Where are you going?"

"I was thinking a little shopping, dinner and maybe to the movies. Spring's creeping up on me so I haven't had a chance to buy their spring and summer clothes."

"I know, time's ticking away and I haven't done any shopping either. I normally order the majority of my stuff online, but this year my funds were a little tight," said Nina.

"I know how that can be. It's been a rough year for a lot of people. But things will get better," Bailey reassured her.

"I hope so."

"Where are you divas going shopping?" Nina inquired.

"Knowing TyShae, her first stop will be Old Navy. Tyanna really doesn't care as long as it's pink and cute," Bailey said.

"I know that's right. Are you going to keep them out of school the next three days?" Nina asked.

"I'm not sure about that. Noah would have a fit."

Nina laughed and said, "I can hear him now asking you if you've lost your mind."

Bailey chuckled. "Is your husband still out of work?"

"Yes, ma'am."

"What type of work does he do? Maybe we have a position for him."

"Well . . . um . . . he didn't actually lose his job because of the layoffs or the recession. He got fired because his urine was dirty."

"Oh, I see, well, maybe he was using whatever for medicinal purposes," Bailey joked.

"That's the story he told Human Resources. They told him to bring in a doctor's note. After two months without one, they finally let him go. Truthfully I was a little embarrassed to tell you about that. I darn sure didn't want to ask for a job for him."

"Nina, you know I have an open door policy and you can talk to me about anything. I guess it depends on the reason he got fired from his last job, but everybody deserves a second chance."

"True but I didn't want his behavior to reflect badly on me. That's why I don't recommend my friends or family for any open positions that we have," Nina said.

"Just because he's your husband doesn't mean you'd be held accountable for his behavior or actions. He'd be treated like everyone else. Background check, drug test, reference verification. He wouldn't be exempt from any of the pre-hiring norms."

"Thank you and I appreciate that, but he still hasn't gotten his act together. Now he's supposedly so depressed that he can't work."

"Why's he acting like this and where's he getting all of this stuff from?" Bailey asked.

"I don't know where this crap is coming from. He told me he's been working all of his life and he needs a break."

"How old is he?" Bailey asked.

"He's only thirty."

"Are you serious?"

"He called EAP and got the number for a psychiatrist the other day. So I thought well, his crazy ass is finally getting the help he needs. This asshole gets mad with the doctor and storms out. Then he comes home like nothing had happened. I wasn't only embarrassed but I was appalled, flabbergasted, pissed, all of that and then some rolled into one. I sat there with my mouth wide open because I couldn't believe it," Nina said.

"I hate to ask this question but what did he do?"

"The doctor started off asking him some generic questions. Trying to figure out and determine the reason for the visit. He blatantly told the doctor let's cut the bullshit. I'm here for one reason and one reason only. All I need for you to do is fill out the paperwork so I can get a check," Nina said.

"No—he didn't!" Bailey said.

"Yes the hell he did! After the doctor told him he couldn't do that he got angry, picked up the man's side table and tried to throw it."

"Okay, so what happened?"

"Do you mean after the paramedics brought him round with the smelling salts?"

"What?"

"You heard me right, the paramedics were called and they had to use smelling salts. Lo and behold, he'd knocked out his own dumbass self. When he picked up the table and tried to throw it, it hit him on the back of his head and he went down. He was out cold. I didn't know whether to laugh, cry or run. After that, the doctor called the police and he was arrested for disorderly conduct. They couldn't charge him with assault because the only person he assaulted was his own damn self!"

Bailey started laughing hysterically and said, "You know what, I don't think we have any positions for him. Clearly there's something wrong with your husband and he needs help."

"I know something's wrong with him. He is stone cold crazy," Nina whispered.

"I see you have something on your hands."

"Yes I do. He's worse than both our children put together."

"I'm shocked and really don't know what to say."

"I never know what I'm going to face when I get home from work," Nina confided.

"Well, what's going on in the office? It should be quiet since so many people are attending that conference."

"Yes, it's pretty quiet. Some people came back here since they had like a two-hour lunch break."

"I'm impressed we have such a great team of people. Well, at least the conference hotel is within walking distance of the office," Bailey said.

"And that's a good thing. People don't have to worry about parking or traffic. Besides, I think most of them came back to the office because we still have a lot of food left over from Rachel's engagement party yesterday."

"I'm so glad the food won't go to waste."

"Even after we all took bags of stuff home I still can't believe how much was left. I packed up a couple more bags today. I also took some to the other offices. I hate to see food wasted," Nina said.

"Before you leave and if there's more food left, just throw it away. There can't be much more left anyway."

"Not a problem."

"I'm pulling into the parking lot of the girls' school. I'll speak to you in the morning. Please lock up my office and, since nothing is really happening, you and Rachel can leave for the day. Also, send an all-staff email that the office is going to be closing early. Please let everyone know that I won't be available for the remainder of the day. I'll be checking my emails but not until later on tonight," Bailey said.

"Okay, sounds good. Have an enjoyable day with the babies. Give them my love and I'll talk to you tomorrow," Nina said.

"You too."

Within moments of ending her call with Nina, Bailey received a call from Noah.

"Yes?"

"Did you ever think that maybe you should consult with me before you closed our office for the day?" Noah asked.

"No, not really, the thought never crossed my mind. Why? Even if the office is closed that doesn't mean you can't enter or exit. You do have keys, correct?"

"Bailey, not only are we partners in marriage but we're also partners in business. I just don't know what's going on with you. Lately you've been acting as if I work for you when that's not the case. I could understand it if you didn't know my schedule or the meetings that I have, but you do. The next time you want to make an impromptu decision, just let a nigga know first. I have some people coming into the office this afternoon. Now I have to play doorman because the office will be closed," Noah said.

"Apparently you're still pissed off with me and I understand that. I can't listen to you bitch at me right now. So, like you said several times earlier, I will see you tonight," Bailey said.

"Where are you?" Noah asked.

"Right now I'm standing in the front office of Middlebrook Preparatory School."

"Why, is something wrong, are the girls alright?"

"Yup, they are fine. I made another impromptu decision after our last call. I decided that I wanted to spend some time with my daughters. Is that okay with you?" Bailey asked.

"No, that's not okay, not in the middle of a school day. So you decided to take them out of school for that. Couldn't you have spent time with them over the weekend?"

"Nope, I wanted to do it today. Uh-oh my bad, I didn't consult with you first. Oh well," Bailey said.

"Bailey, that's the bullshit I'm talking about. I'm not going to argue with you right now. I don't have the luxury of leaving work in the middle of the day for fun time."

"And you're saying that I do. You must have me mixed up with someone else. Like you, I too work close to seven days a week."

"I have no clue what's going on with you or why you're acting a little uncanny today. You keep doing unnecessary stupid shit," Noah said.

"You haven't given me a chance to explain. You're the only one that's doing any talking."

"From last night to this very moment you had sufficient time to talk to me about any and everything. You find the time to discuss your friends and the dense shit that goes on with them."

"Babe, you are blowing this out of proportion. Can we discuss this later on?" Bailey asked.

"I have to go." Before Bailey could say anything else Noah hung up the phone. She thought to herself, *If Mr. Man wasn't pissed earlier he is now. To make matters worse I keep adding fuel to the fire. Oh fucking well, what's he going to do about it?*

"Hi, Mommy, why are you here?" TyShae asked.

"Because, baby, I have a surprise, we're going to have a fun day. We're going shopping and to dinner," Bailey explained.

"But we're in class right now."

"Yes, baby, I know," Bailey said.

"Is Daddy going too?" Tyanna asked.

"No sweetie, Daddy's at work. Is there any place special you girls would like to go?" Bailey asked.

"Anywhere as long as it's with you," TyShae responded.

"Um, I want to go to the movies to see that movie about the little girl and her magical puppy. And then I want to go and buy a magical puppy," Tyanna said.

"What's the name of the movie, sweetie?" Bailey asked.

"Mommy, I don't know."

"A magical puppy, I think we should speak to Daddy first about a magical puppy. Daddy has allergies so a puppy may not be a good idea," Bailey explained.

"But, Mom, it's magical and can make Daddy's algeries go away," Tyanna protested.

"Allergies, sweetie, it's called *all-er-gies*," Bailey said.

"Okay, I'm calling my daddy and he'll let me get the magical puppy so he can feel better," Tyanna said.

For the next few hours, Bailey and the girls shopped, went to dinner, the movies, got their nails and feet done and went to buy a puppy. The highlight of Bailey's day happened to be shopping for the puppy, buying puppy supplies and apparel. Bailey figured since Noah was already pissed, bringing home a dog couldn't do much more damage than had already been done.

As Bailey drove up the driveway of her home she hated that the day had come to an end. She'd had a nice day with her daughters as they shopped and had dinner. She knew Noah wouldn't go to sleep until the issues of the day were resolved. As the garage door opened she didn't see the car that Noah had driven that day parked in the garage.

Hmmm that's weird, it's almost 11 p.m., where's Mr. Man? He didn't call to say he was going anywhere.

Bailey woke the girls up from their tired slumber and got them into the house. As Bailey struggled with getting the sleepy girls, the puppy that wouldn't stop whimpering, and all the packages in the house, her phone rang. Since her hands were full she was unable to answer the call, so Bailey decided to finish unloading the truck and get the girls settled before returning the call.

After three trips to the truck, giving the girls a bath, putting them to bed and getting the puppy situated, Bailey decided to make herself a cocktail. She undressed quickly, put on her robe and, with a drink in one hand and her phone in the other hand, went downstairs to her office. Nine missed calls and seven voice messages: Noah, Noah, Mom, Noah, Kya, Deion, Noah, Momma T, Brandi. Bailey looked at the clock located in the corner of her mahogany desk. *Oh goodness, it's midnight and it's too late for me to return calls. I'll call the girls in the morning but let me call Mr. Man now.*

Bailey picked up her office phone and dialed Noah's number.

"Hello!" Noah yelled.

"Babe, where are you?" Bailey asked.

"Yeah, I really can't hear you, let me call you right back!" Noah yelled.

"Excuse me? Call me back, whatever, Noah. Just keep doing you!" Bailey yelled. Ten minutes later and Noah still hadn't called back. Bailey picked up the phone and called him again. This time, his phone went straight to voicemail. Bailey pressed the redial button—again: voicemail. After two unanswered calls she decided to call once more. Still no answer. Bailey decided that after the continuous arguments with Noah throughout the course of the day maybe he needed to blow off some steam so she decided to let him be, for now. Noah must need some time away from Bailey since he was normally home no later than 6:30 p.m.

Bailey fixed another cocktail, grabbed her work tote, and repositioned herself on the sofa in her office. She then turned on the seventy-inch smart TV that was diagonal to the sofa. *It's almost 12:30 a.m., I've had a very long day, I don't feel like reading through these Requests for Proposals tonight. But I need to determine which of these contractors to hire. Instead of procrastinating I should have read them several weeks ago. I wonder why Mr. Man didn't take on this tedious and daunting task. Wow, there are thirty five RFPs and Eugene has already read through them and typed up summaries. That helps me out tremendously. But, depending on his notes, I might have to revert back to the RFP. Hopefully his notes are good and there'll be no need to read over all the RFPs. I need to hire someone by Friday, which is three days away.*

By the time Bailey got to the second page of the first RFP, she'd drifted off to sleep.

Bailey felt someone tugging at her robe and she opened her eyes.

"Mom. Mommy. Mother. My tummy's hurting and Diva won't stop crying," Tyanna said.

"Huh?"

"My tummy is hurting and Diva is in my room crying and she won't stop. She woke me up," Tyanna repeated. Bailey looked at the clock: it read 4:36 a.m.

"Sweetie, your puppy misses her mommy, that's why she's crying. Eventually she'll get used to us and she'll stop crying. Your tummy is probably hurting because you ate too much junk while we were out," Bailey explained.

"But her crying is making me sad."

"Don't be sad, sweetie. Come on, let me put you back to bed. I'll give you something to make your tummy stop hurting."

"Mommy, where's my daddy?" Tyanna asked.

"Sweetie, your daddy's upstairs in the bed."

"No he's not. I looked in your room before I came downstairs. Can I get in the bed with you?" Tyanna asked.

"Sure you can," Bailey said. As Bailey and Tyanna walked up the steps, she heard the recorded voice of the alarm system, "Front door open."

"Tyanna go and get in Mommy's bed, I'll be right up," Bailey said.

"Can I turn on the TV?" Tyanna asked.

"Yes, Ty," Bailey replied. She watched Tyanna go up the stairs then proceeded to go back down. Before she could get to the foyer, she noticed Noah coming down the hallway out of the kitchen with a glass of water.

"Hey," Noah said.

"Hey. Hey! Is that all the fuck you have to say? Noah it's 4:51 a.m., where the fuck have you been all night?" Bailey asked.

"I was out."

"Out, what the hell? What do you mean you were out?" Bailey shouted.

"Yes, out, and please stop repeating the first word of everything I say. You're starting to sound like a goddamn mocking bird."

"You know what, babe, I can't do this right now. Like you, I too have had a very long day and I'm going to bed. You've been arguing with me all day. No matter what my behavior was, that doesn't give you the right to ignore me. Then you come in the house at 5 a.m. as if you're a single man. You act as though you've done nothing wrong. You said you were going to call me right back, and you never did. Then your phone kept going straight to voicemail. What's up with that?" Bailey asked.

"I called you several times and you never answered the phone," Noah said.

"The first time you called was around the time the girls and I got home. I had to get them out of the truck, give them a bath, put them to bed, and then I had to make three trips to the truck to get the bags and other crap out. So forgive me for not noticing that you'd called. Instead of calling my phone why didn't you call the house phone?"

"Can we continue this discussion upstairs?"

"No we can't, Ty's not feeling well and she just got in our bed. Knowing her she's sitting in the middle of our bed watching television. I hope she won't be awake the rest of the night."

"Me too, I have a conference call at 7:45 a.m. After I shower I want to get a little sleep," Noah said.

"So we'll have to discuss the bullshit from earlier later on. By the way, Ty was looking for you a little while ago. Just be prepared for the questions she's going to ask. I don't think you'll be going to sleep anytime soon," Bailey said.

Noah headed to the bathroom to take a shower while Bailey got into bed. He looked in the bed and noticed Ty was asleep.

"I guess I don't have to worry about answering her questions. She's sound asleep," Noah said.

"I guess not. You should be worried about the twenty questions I have for you."

As Bailey enjoyed the last and final stage of sleep, the telephone woke her.

"Hello," Bailey whispered.

"Hey girl, are you asleep?" Kya asked.

"What else am I supposed to be doing this time of morning? What time is it?"

"How about working, it's 11:39 a.m. Are you sick?" Kya asked.

Bailey slowly whispered, "No."

"Are you going into the office today?"

"I hadn't planned on it. Let me call you when I get up."

"Okay, enjoy your much needed rest. Call me when you get yourself together. I have something to tell you," Kya said.

"Okay," Bailey said.

"Don't forget, Bailey, it's really important. It's about last night."

"Look, I heard you, Kya. I'll call you later."

"Ewwwww. You're a grouchy bitch when you don't get rest," Kya said as she hung up the phone.

Bailey pulled the blanket over her head and drifted back off to sleep. TyShae entered her room.

"Mommy, Diva went to the bathroom."

"That's good, sweetie," Bailey whispered.

"Mommy, she went in the family room," TyShae said.

"Okay, go and tell your daddy."

"Okay, Mommy. Go back to sleep. I'll check on you later," TyShae said. Then Bailey felt something pulling the blanket off her head,

"TyShae, I heard you, I'll clean up the mess," Bailey said.

"Baby, when were you going to tell me that we had a puppy?" Noah asked.

"Noah, please. No drama, issues or arguing before noon. I'm not even out of bed yet."

"I wasn't going to start an argument, I just wanted to know. Is it safe to assume since we overslept and you're still in bed, the girls aren't going to school and you're not going to work?"

"Yes, that's safe to assume. I was actually going to keep the girls home the rest of the week," Bailey said.

"For what?"

"So we can hang out and do stuff."

"Babe, you want to keep them home for three days just to hang out? No, that's not happening. I can see one day but not three," Noah said.

"Okay, whatever."

"I'm going to work from home today. Did you have a chance to review the RFPs?" Noah asked.

"No, I didn't," Bailey said as she pulled the blanket back over her head.

"You do remember that you have to make a decision by tomorrow?"

"Yes, Noah, I'm aware of that. But since you won't let me get any rest I guess I need to get out of bed and get my day started. After I shower I'll start reading through the freaking RFPs. Did the girls eat breakfast?"

"Yes, I think I slept for about an hour and a half and then Ty got me up. She informed me that the dog needed to go out. After that I couldn't get back to sleep so I did some work and cooked breakfast. Eugene called my phone looking for you; he said if you needed help with the RFPs he could stop by."

"I should be okay. Before I fell asleep last night I had a chance to review his summaries. He did one hell of a job. Maybe he doesn't want to get fired again. In all actuality all I need to do is review his summaries. I should be able to make a decision from those. Hopefully it shouldn't take more than two hours for that process. I have some other tasks that I need to take care of as well. Did you want to do something with the girls today or are you too busy?" Bailey asked.

"Work is work but family comes first. I always have time for my family. What did you have in mind?"

"I don't know. Let's ask the girls what they'd like to do. We still need to talk about last night."

"I know, babe."

"I also spoke to your mom yesterday," Bailey said.

"What did she want? I hope not money. I'm not giving her any fucking money."

"Babe, she didn't call about money. She only wanted to know how we were doing. I told her I was keeping the girls out of school for the next couple of days. She asked were we going out of town or something. I said we're spending some quality family time together, that's all. She asked if the girls could come and spend the night with her."

Noah looked at Bailey and said, "Did you tell her hell no?"

"I didn't tell her no. I did tell her that Tyanna is having a sleepover this weekend. I mentioned that the girls will have to be home by 6 p.m. on Friday at the latest. But it's only one night, what's the harm?" Bailey asked. "Do you want to drop the girls off while I go through the RFPs? Afterwards, we can go to lunch and spend the rest of the day doing nothing."

"Um, no. When you get back from dropping the girls off then we can go to lunch. I'll wait right here until you get back," Noah said.

"Okay, I'll drop them off in a couple of hours and I'll start my daunting task of going through the RFPs. Oh, and before I forget, I think Brandi is interested in starting a foundation for teenage girls. Since she and Derick just purchased a new home she might need some money. Is that alright with you?" Bailey asked.

"Is what all right with me? Brandi starting a foundation or us loaning her the money to start the foundation?"

"You know what, babe, she hasn't asked for any money. In fact, she actually hasn't said much of anything. She was sharing her thoughts and ideas with me. I was reading between the lines considering I know about her finances. You know she isn't comfortable with asking people for help. I did share with her my viewpoint on starting and running a debt-free business. She was in agreement and she feels the same way I do. Should I ask her if she would like for us to help?"

"Why don't you try to get a little more information before volunteering the money? You know I'm game for helping people out. However, I don't want to jump into something without having all the facts. This sound like it could be a great cause if it's run properly. Besides giving her the money there could be other ways that we could help her. I need to know all of the logistical information first," Noah said.

"Okay. Brandi and I are going to a fundraiser for breast cancer next Saturday. I think I'm supposed to pick her up and I'll speak to her about the foundation then. If not maybe both you and I can meet with her one day next week," Bailey said.

Even though Bailey and Noah had spent the majority of the previous day arguing, they had managed to pick up and act as though nothing had happened. Besides having a rule of not going to bed angry they also had the twenty-four-hour rule. If the situation or issue wasn't discussed and rectified within twenty four hours then they weren't allowed to bring it up after the twenty-four-hour time limit. For the most part those rules had been helpful to their marriage. Noah was the type of man that never raised his voice; if his voice elevated then you knew he was really pissed off. Bailey, on the other hand, was different. She was quick-tempered and wore her feelings and emotions on her sleeve. When she was pissed you knew she was. When she was happy you knew, and when she was getting ready to curse you out, you definitely knew. Nonetheless, the older she had got the better she was able to handle her anger. She learned a long time ago that you picked your battles and that all disagreements did not have to end in a heated argument.

By the time Bailey got downstairs to her office her phone was ringing.

"Yes, ma'am," Bailey said.

"You didn't call me back," Kya said.

"Kya, I did have to wash my ass first, I haven't even gotten to my office yet. Let me get a cup of coffee and I'll call you back in a couple of seconds."

"Okay, but hurry up. It's important."

Bailey couldn't help but wonder what was so urgent that Kya couldn't wait for her to return the call. Since Kya always had a story to tell, whether baby daddy drama or some other gossip, Bailey wasn't that eager to listen, mainly because her deadlines were quickly approaching. But Bailey, being the type of person that always had time for her friends, knew that if she didn't call Kya back, Kya would continue to call.

After Bailey got her coffee and a cherry croissant from the kitchen, she sat at her desk and returned Kya's call.

"Yes, ma'am, what's the problem?" Bailey asked.

"Remember the other day I told you I opened a Facebook account?" Kya asked.

"Yes."

"Well, guess who I found?"

"Um, your daddy," Bailey said jokingly.

"No girl, Steve," Kya said.

"Steve. Who the hell is Steve?"

"Steve. Remember we dated briefly several years ago during one of mine and Jeff's off seasons."

"Ohhhhh, Steve. I do remember him but I wouldn't say that the two of you actually dated. It was more of a brief encounter that consisted of unadulterated fucking."

"Okay, well, maybe we didn't date but I found him," Kya said.

"Mommy!" Tyanna shouted.

"Hold on, girl. Yes Ty," Bailey said.

"Diva's under the bed and won't come out!"

"Okay, sweetie, ask your sister to get Diva," Bailey said.

"Okay!" Tyanna shouted.

"Okay, I'm back," Bailey said.

"What the hell is going on at the Jones household today? You and Noah are home from work and the kids are out of school. Is it a fucking holiday and no one told me?" Kya asked.

"Girl, you're crazy. Let's just say that it's too much to get into right now. But finish your story."

"Where was I? Oh, so, anyhoo, after I sent Steve a friend request he quickly accepted then sent a message to my inbox. We exchanged numbers and for the past couple of days we've been chitchatting here and there. We arranged a time to meet and have lunch. I just didn't have time because I was running around like a chicken with my head cut off for your gala. I actually invited him to the gala the other night but he had a prior commitment and couldn't attend. I started to think he was full of shit. Whenever we'd set up a time to meet, he always had something else to do or something pressing came up. But he'd always call me and be very apologetic so I didn't trip. Anyway, I told him that I'd be staying at the hotel overnight and he could stop by, we could do drinks and dinner."

"*Ewwww*, you freak!" Bailey said.

Kya laughed and said, "I told him we could meet after I finish with this gala. Once my staff left, I went to my suite to freshen up a little."

"Right."

"Girl, I had to touch up my makeup and spray on a little smell-good. Then I went downstairs to the lobby to meet him but I didn't see him."

"He stood you up?" Bailey asked.

"Hell, no."

"Oh. I was about to say," Bailey said.

"I pulled out my phone to call him when I felt a tap on my shoulder. I turned around and I thought I was going to hit the goddamn floor."

"Why? Was he big and fat, receding hairline and dressed like Mr. Brown? What was wrong with him?" Bailey asked.

"Honey chile, everything was perfect! He looked good, from head to toe. Well, all that I could see looked good anyway. He gave me a hug and I felt like I was going to melt right in his arms. And it wasn't one of those church hugs either. I put it all up in there too. I tried to cave in his chest with my boobies. We walked over to the bar but they were just closing. I then suggested that we go to my suite because I had a well-stocked bar and we could order room service."

"Uh oh, I know where this is going."

"Bailey all I'm going to say is *wowwwwww*!" Kya shouted.

"No bitch, that's not all you're going to say," Bailey said.

"I thought I had great sex before but this was the best ever! Don't get me wrong. The conversation and reminiscing about the past was also good. But it was what took place after the conversation ended. He fucked me all over that suite and I just could not hold back.

Maybe this was long overdue. Whew! I so needed that. That was the fuck of the year. Not to mention he ate me as if it was his last meal. We fucked so much that I couldn't even walk the next day. My pussy was still throbbing and it felt like I couldn't stand on my legs."

"Damn girl, what the fuck were y'all doing?" Bailey asked.

"What *didn't* we do?" Kya shouted.

"Well, I hope with all of that fucking going on, condoms were used. He did have some helmets for the soldier, right?" Bailey said.

"It's not like it was planned and the gift shop was closed. Where were we going to get rubbers that time of night anyway?"

"Girl, I'm going to beat the *shit* out of you!" Bailey yelled.

"I only expected drinks and dinner. I didn't know it was going to happen."

"Someone could have gone to a gas station, 7-Eleven or a fucking twenty-four-hour Walmart," Bailey yelled.

"You can't be serious."

"Yes, I am serious! You have no excuse whatsoever for not using protection."

"Can I at least finish the story before you start fussing and shit?" Kya asked.

"Sure, go ahead."

"I have *never* in all of my life fucked all night long. I guess there's a first time for everything. You would have thought that it was the last day on earth and this was our final task. Around 6 a.m., we were just lying there talking about life in general."

"Oh yeah. What did you discuss after your fuckfest?" Bailey asked.

"We talked about the past and what happened with us. I mentioned that tomorrow is not promised and you should live everyday like it's your last. Then I told him that people come into our lives for a reason, a season or a lifetime," Kya said. "He agreed, then said that sometimes we may not see the significance of the person in our lives but they were put in our lives for a specific reason."

"Those are very true statements. More importantly we sometimes don't understand why certain people are in our life," Bailey said.

"He also shared some of the things that he went through with his ex. I shared some of my issues about Jeff. But I didn't say too much, I picked and chose what I told him. Then he told me that he always cared about me. He said he'd have married me a long time ago. He also said he thought we'd have been great together but I went back to Jeff. He said he never forgot about me and always prayed for another chance to cross my path. He felt if he could get another chance with me, things would be different the second time around."

"Of course he'd say that. He was all up in the coochie and he wanted some more," Bailey said.

"No, he's not like that."

"How the hell do you know what he's like? Okay, sweetie, let me say this again. You haven't seen this man in a very long time. When you dealt with him in the past, it was very brief and even then you only fucked. You find him on Facebook, chit chat and have about eight hours of uninterrupted sex. Don't you think it's a little too soon to be talking about a relationship or hearing wedding bells?" Bailey asked.

"It appears as though we both are on the same page. A person is put in your path for a reason and tomorrow is not promised, Bailey. Life is too short so I'm going to make it sweet and enjoy it. I thought you of all people would understand."

"Sweetie, I totally understand where you're coming from. More importantly you deserve happiness. You deserve to be treated like the queen you are. You deserve a good man. You're my friend and I love you to death, but I don't want to see you hurt. You've endured enough hurt in one lifetime at the expense of men. I don't think after a couple of conversations and sex you should start making wedding plans with this man."

"All I'm saying is that Steve and I share some of the same feelings and concerns about life, we have so much in common, and he's a good man. I was just wondering if this could possibly lead to something more. Everyone can't have the perfect relationship like you and Noah. As much as I would love to I can't live vicariously through you," Kya said.

"Girl, Noah and I don't have the perfect marriage. We have issues like everyone else and you know that better than anybody. But we work through those issues. Let's not forget that little indiscretion he had some time ago. He's my husband and I love him, I'm his wife and he loves me. Life isn't about what you go through, it's about how you handle things. Marriage is a full-time job and there are no days off."

"I'm just going to see where this friendship goes and I'm not going to rush into anything. Besides, if it's meant to be, it will happen."

"That's totally understandable. Have fun. But I suggest before you open a new chapter you close the existing one. Hint, hint, Jeff," Bailey said.

"Jeff and I are done, finished, it's a fucking wrap."

"And I've heard that several times throughout the years. That's what you normally say when you're pissed with him. So I'm supposed to believe this time you are serious. Sure, Kya, I hear ya," Bailey laughed.

"No, seriously, this time I'm not going back to him. He got too much shit with him and I don't have time for it," Kya said.

"Let me make one other suggestion. Before you dive into something new, please get rid of the baggage you're carrying around. Once you let go and heal, you can move forward, to something better."

"I gotcha, sis. Your points are well taken. I will get rid of the baggage. I'm going to pack it up and take it to the incinerator to burn. Yet I still don't have any regrets or reservations about the other night or the morning after. It was fucking off the chain up in that suite. If only walls could talk."

"Okay, I got it, and I don't need a mental picture either. I'm still fucked up with you about not using protection. You lost a few cool points with that one," Bailey said.

"Girl, I never got a chance to finish the story. There's more."

"I have to get some work done, and I need to take the girls to my mother-in-law's house. So save the rest for later. I'm sure you'll have more to add by then."

"Stop playing, she wants to be a grandmom this week? Ain't that some shit, as long as she had money in the bank and was doing well no one ever saw her. She was on top of the world and you couldn't tell her shit. I still can't believe she lost everything and because of that young boy. All of a sudden she moves back to the area and wants to play Grandmom."

"Please don't get me started on her. Because you know she's running around with her hands out. I haven't mentioned it to Noah but she asked if I could loan her some money," Bailey whispered.

"Girl, she is a shitty damn mess. How much money did she ask for?"

"$25,000."

"Get the shit outta here. She asked for $25,000 like it's $25.00?"

"My point exactly. I told her I need to talk it over with Noah first."

"You know he's not going to approve that one," Kya said.

"Yeah, I know. That's why I haven't mentioned it to him yet."

"Why does she need so much money anyway?"

"She said she can't access her money because her accounts are frozen."

"Oh. Are they still investigating her from those embezzlement charges?"

"You got it. Noah said he wasn't going to give her any more money. He told her if she was woman enough to take money that didn't belong to her then she should be woman enough to figure out how to pay her bills."

"Is her boyfriend still locked up?"

"Yes. They were able to prove that he actually had something to do with it. But the details pertaining to my mother-in-law were sketchy. Her bank records showed where she made several large bank deposits. When she couldn't account for the money, that's when things went bad. She's still a little salty that Noah didn't tell the District Attorney that he gave her the money," Bailey said.

"Girl, your mother-in-law is a mess! You have got something on your hands with that one. Good luck."

"Girl, let me get off this phone and get some work done."

"Call me when you take a break, or later on tonight.

"Okay, sweetie, and stay out of trouble."

"Who me? I never get into trouble."

"Whatever, girl, we'll talk later," Bailey said as she hung up the phone, shook her head and thought, *I can't believe that damn girl. She's almost as bad as me. I guess they're right when they say birds of a feather flock together.*

To prevent any further interruptions, Bailey decided that it would be best if she dropped the girls off next. She picked up her phone and sent a text to her mother-in-law: DO YOU STILL WANT THE GIRLS TO SPEND THE NIGHT? IF SO, WHAT TIME CAN I DROP THEM OFF?

Within a matter of seconds, her mother-in-law responded and wrote, ANYTIME IS GOOD. WHEN THE GIRLS GET HERE WE'LL RUN TO THE STORE TO GET A FEW ITEMS FOR SNACKS AND DINNER.

Bailey replied, I'LL BE THERE IN ABOUT AN HOUR. She got up from her desk and went upstairs to put on some sweatpants and tennis shoes, then got the girls and their overnight bags together.

"Come on girls," Bailey said.

"Can we take Diva with us?" TyShae asked.

"No, not this time, sweetie, maybe next time when Diva's fully trained."

Noah walked his wife and daughters to the door and said, "Behave and don't give Grandmom any problems."

"We won't," Tyanna said.

"See you in a little while," Bailey said.

"Okay," Noah replied.

When Bailey returned from dropping off her daughters, she went into her office and started working. Noah walked in, sat on the sofa, and asked, "Babe, did you know that Maisha called in sick for the second day in row?"

"Yes, I knew about her calling in."

"Why didn't you say anything?"

"Because I knew how you'd react."

"And how did you think I'd react?" Noah asked.

"You would have said fire the bitch. I'm tired of her bullshit," Bailey said.

"Well, you're wrong, I would have said, fire that trifling bitch. Did you know she's a lesbian?"

"Yes I know she's a lesbian, and what does that have to do with anything?"

"One doesn't have anything to do with the other, I was just saying. What's wrong with her besides her being crazy as shit? Why does she keep calling in?" Noah asked.

"I guess she is sick, Noah, I don't know. I haven't spoken to her. You have the option of calling her and finding out," Bailey said.

"As long as she has a doctor's note when she returns."

"Do we have to talk about this now, can't we enjoy the peace and quiet? The girls are at your mom's house and we can just chillax. I think she wants to keep them until Saturday."

"Is that all we can do?" Noah asked.

"No. We could have done more but you're on punishment right now."

"For what? I didn't do anything."

"Okay, you're starting to sound like your daughters. Do you need me to refresh your memory?"

"Naw, you don't have to. If that's the case then you should be on punishment too. If my memory serves me correctly your actions yesterday were indescribable," Noah said.

"Maybe you should go finish your paperwork and leave me alone. Let me get back to work," Bailey said.

"How do you expect me to work like this?"

"Like what, babe?" Bailey asked. She glanced at Noah as he stood from the sofa.

"My dick is so hard that my stomach hurts. It's so hard that I can break glass with it," Noah said.

"Whatever," Bailey said.

"No, I'm serious. You keep prancing around wearing a little ass wife-beater and some boy-cut underwear. How do you expect me to act?"

"When your punishment is revoked, then I got you," Bailey said.

"Why can't you get me now? Are you really going to make me wait?"

"We haven't even discussed anything from last night. Not to mention that your black ass was out all fucking night long. And there's nothing open after midnight but legs and liquor stores. What the shit was that about?"

"I was pissed with you. What's that saying you're always using? I was pissed beyond pissedosity." Noah laughed.

"See, you're playing, I'm serious, Noah. Is this how we're going to start handling our disagreements? Whenever one of us gets angry, you're telling me it's acceptable to hang out all night long and ignore our phones, then come home and act like nothing ever happened. I guess it's all right to act as though we're single occasionally. Alright, I got it."

"Babe," Noah said.

"What? How can I help you?"

"You can help me by coming to see what I want."

"Boy, you're really working my nerves today. You know I have all of this work to do. I'm sitting right here, what do you want?" Bailey asked. She walked over to the sofa where Noah was sitting. "What do you want?"

"I have some work you can do. Look at what you do to me," Noah said.

"You did that to yourself," Bailey said. He grabbed Bailey's hand and placed in on his groin.

Bailey snatched her hand away and said, "Stop! I have shit to do."

"You're right, we do have work to do," Noah said. He stood up and pulled down his basketball shorts.

"And what are you going to do with that?" Bailey asked.

"What would you like for me to do with it?"

"Put it away."

"I don't know why you keep playing hard to get. That doesn't really suit you," Noah said.

"I'm trying to prove a point and right now you're not making it easy," Bailey said.

"Okay, you've proved your point. I understand you're pissed because I went out last night and came home late. I apologize for that, please forgive me."

"Those aren't the only reasons, but you're on the right page."

As Noah kissed Bailey, he grabbed her hand and placed it back on his dick. This time she didn't pull away. As Bailey stroked him back and forth, Noah groaned every couple of seconds. Bailey pushed Noah onto the sofa and removed his shorts from around his ankles.

"Don't move or use your hands, let me do all the work." Bailey spoke softly in Noah's ear. She then opened his legs, knelt down between them, and started to fondle him. She moved in closer, put her mouth on his dick and began to suck, using her left hand to caress and massage his balls. She moved her mouth up and down, over the top, slow then speeding up, licking his dick from the tip of the head down to the base. As she held him, her hand squeezed and released, and she continued to suck while moving up and down.

Bailey took a firmer grip and began to jerk him gently as she sucked each of his balls. As Noah continued to moan and grow more aroused, Bailey realized how wet she was. She gently kissed, then licked, and sucked his balls. She grew excited and couldn't wait any longer to bounce on her husband. Bailey stood, removed her tank top and shorts, then gently sat on Noah's dick.

"*Ahhhhhh,*" she sighed.

"Babe, you're so wet," Noah whispered.

"I know, this is what you do to me," Bailey murmured. With her arms around Noah's neck, she started to ride slowly as if she was a cowgirl in a rodeo. Up and down, back and forth, fast then slow, gentle then hard. Noah grabbed Bailey's ass and squeezed it tight as she continued to rock.

He lifted Bailey off, stood up and positioned Bailey on her knees. Then he pushed his way into her, gliding in. In response, Bailey groaned and whimpered. With Noah's hands planted firmly around her waist he began slowly to fuck her.

"Is this what you want?" Noah asked.

"Yes, babe, fuck me," Bailey whispered. The tighter he held onto her waist the harder his thrusts.

"Babe, your pussy is so good and it's so wet. You keep coming all over me."

"Fuck me harder. I want you to fuck me harder," Bailey said.

Noah placed his hands over Bailey's shoulders and said, "You're going to make me come." The harder he fucked, the tighter she squeezed around him and the louder she moaned. "It's so good! I'm going to come," Noah whispered.

Bailey held on to the back of the sofa and yelled out, "Harder . . . harder . . . fuck me harder."

"Oh baby, bounce that ass on this dick . . . oh, this pussy is good . . . you're coming again . . . baby, I'm coming!" Noah exclaimed.

Afterwards, Bailey and Noah changed their position on the sofa. As Bailey lay in Noah's arms, she whispered, "I'm still mad at you."

Several minutes later, as Bailey got up from the sofa to go into the kitchen, her phone rang.

"Hello," she said.

"Are you busy, can you talk?" Maisha asked.

"Right now is not a good time. Can I call you back later on?" Bailey asked.

"I'd rather talk now but I guess it'll have to wait. Where are you? I know you're not at work because I called Rachel," Maisha said.

"I don't think I owe you any explanations. I'm busy right now. I'll call you back later."

"Can you come over?" Maisha asked.

"No, not today."

"Why not?"

"I'm hanging up. Tootles," Bailey said.

"Okay, before you hang up let me ask you one question. What attracts you to me? Why are you attracted to women?" Maisha asked.

"That's two questions. I can't get into that discussion right now."

"Well, think about that and call me back. I want to hear your responses. I'll talk to you later."

As Bailey walked back into her office, she noticed that Noah had drifted off to sleep.

"Babe, go upstairs and get into bed," Bailey said.

"Okay, wake me up in about two hours." As Noah approached the door he turned and asked, "Are we still going to lunch or would you prefer dinner?"

"We can go to dinner. That would be nice."

"All right. I need to lie down for about an hour or two. I'm a little tired," Noah said.

"I just bet you are. That's what happens when you stay out all night. Is there something you need me to take care of?" Bailey asked.

"Yes, those RFPs."

"As soon as I take a shower, I'm on it. Enjoy your nap."

Bailey patiently waited for Noah to go upstairs before calling Maisha, making sure he was out the way before making the call.

"That was a quick turnaround time," Maisha said.

"I couldn't talk to you in front of my husband. You must be feeling much better. I thought you were supposed to be sick," Bailey said.

"I am sick. You damn sure didn't call to see how I was doing."

"How are you feeling?" Bailey asked.

"I think I may have a stomach virus."

"Did you go to the doctor?"

"No, not yet, but I have an appointment tomorrow. Why haven't you called me?" Maisha asked.

"I really didn't have anything to say. If I'm not mistaken you told me to call you when I figured out what I wanted to do," Bailey said.

"So you haven't figured it out yet?"

"No. There's really nothing for me to figure out. In all actuality I haven't thought any more about it."

"Apparently you really don't fuck with me, huh?" Maisha asked.

"I've never said that. Your problem is that you want more than I'm willing to give. I've already explained to you that ending my marriage isn't an option. These conversations are becoming redundant."

"Can you answer my questions then?"

"What would that prove?"

"I just want to know."

"I wouldn't say that I'm attracted to women. I've never thought of them that way. It was because of you that I became curious. You would make cunning comments every chance you could get. The day you told me that if given the opportunity you could make my body feel better than any man had ever done, that you would explore places of my body that had never been touched, I wanted to know how that was possible. Not only was I inquisitive but I also wanted to experience that feeling. I'm a very sexual person by nature. You never know what you like until you try it at least once. So I did. Now I can add that to my list of things accomplished," Bailey said.

"So I was just an experiment. Besides sex you really had no other use for me."

"Please don't put words in my mouth or twist my words around. I didn't and probably would never have pursued you. In the beginning before we actually had sex I said no strings attached."

"Other than a fuck here and there you don't want more from me?" Maisha asked.

"No I don't," Bailey said.

"You just used me?"

"Um . . . no. For one, even though I knew you were bisexual I've never thought of you that way. For two, how could I possibly commit to you when I'm married? If it wasn't you then maybe someday it would have been someone else. It's not like I was walking around thinking about or planning secret rendezvous with women. You just happened to be the one at the time," Bailey said.

"Wow. I really thought we were better than that. Does your husband know you're a lesbian?"

"I'm not a lesbian," Bailey said.

"Does he know you're bi?" Maisha asked.

Bailey chuckled and said, "He knew about the one unexplainable encounter that I had before he and I started dating."

"If I tell him about us how do you think he would respond?"

"It would shock the shit out him. Especially if he knew it was you."

"He wouldn't be upset?" Maisha asked.

"I can't answer that. Only he can answer that question."

"Okay, now I'm a little confused. You had a sexual experience with me the first time. But you did it more than once. So you must have liked it."

"I enjoyed the experience as well as the time that we spent together. It's not like you and I would be locked in the bedroom for days on end. Yes, we had sex three times but we did more than that. Now and again we hung out together. Movies, shopping, dinner, lunch, plays . . . we managed to do a lot in three months. I enjoyed every minute of it. You're a nice person but you're not being realistic about the situation," Bailey said.

"What attracted you to me?"

"There was no attraction. It was more about companionship than sex. The more I got to know you for yourself, the more I became attracted to you. Your level of confidence and persistence definitely got my attention. You're also very good-looking and smart. You have a good head on your shoulders. I knew that what I was doing was wrong and I knew that it could be damaging. For a lot of inexcusable reasons I didn't use good judgment."

"Thanks for the compliment. In other words are you saying you have regrets?" Maisha asked.

"No, sweetie, I don't live my life with regrets. Even if I make mistakes occasionally I never regret anything that I say or do."

"Well, I regret that we hooked up."

"If that's how you feel that's your choice. There's nothing I can do to change that."

"You have really hurt me and I can't just turn love on and off like that. Maybe you can but I can't," Maisha said.

"The part that's not sinking in your head is that I didn't intentionally hurt you. And no I can't just turn love on and off," Bailey said.

"How would you feel if I tell Noah about our affair?

"I would be very angry and that still wouldn't make me want you. If anything I would have nothing to do with you at that point. If you had or have any thoughts of ruining my marriage you might as well cancel them out. You know what, the longer we discuss this issue the more I think you should quit your job."

"So you're ending our friendship and firing me?"

"I don't have any problem whatsoever continuing our friendship. You just need to know that we won't have sex again. I'm almost confident that you won't be able to handle the situation," Bailey said.

"I can't lose my job over this bullshit. I have bills to pay."

"Sweetie, you should have thought about that before you fucked the boss."

"I had no idea things would be this way. I thought you were different from the other women I've dated," Maisha said.

"We never know how things are going to turn out. We both took a huge risk. Because things didn't turn out the way you wanted them to you're having a hard time. It's not that serious. If you think you're mature enough to work there then you have nothing worry about. But please don't think just because we fucked a couple of times that you'll receive special treatment," Bailey said.

"I hate when people string me along as if my feelings don't matter."

"Stop saying you didn't know because you did. Apparently, you must have thought you could change my mind with time. You knew how I felt. I wasn't stringing you along and there is no reason why you should feel that way."

"So what am I supposed to do now?" Maisha asked.

"I suggest you count it as a loss and move on."

"You're really a bitch when you want to be."

"Sweetie, this conversation is going nowhere. We're going back and forth about something that won't change. I can't sit on the phone with you all day while you try to figure this out. What more can I do?" Bailey asked.

"I honestly think that you're afraid," Maisha said.

"Afraid of what?"

"You're afraid to be with me. You're afraid of what people might say. You have this illusion of your perfect little family as if it's a goddamn Norman Rockwell painting. If you're so in love with Noah then why were you with me?" Maisha said.

"We dealt with each other for about three months give or take. We had sex three times. I hate to tell you this but it really meant nothing."

"I can't believe you. You act as though you don't give a shit about me," Maisha said.

"There's nothing left for us to discuss. I didn't want to end things this way but I have no choice. You forced my hand."

"We'll see about that."

"Is that a threat?" Bailey asked.

"No, it's a promise," Maisha said as she hung up the phone.

At least that's over. I no longer have to worry about having that discussion, Bailey thought.

Three hours later and Bailey was finished with her work. *Whew! I'm finally done with those damn RFPs. I can get Noah up and we can't start getting ready to go out.* As Bailey got up from the desk the telephone rang.

"Hello," Bailey said.

"May I speak to Bailey?"

"Speaking."

"Do you know where your husband was last night?"

"Excuse me?"

"I said do you know where your husband was last night?"

"Who is this?" Bailey asked.

"Don't worry about who this is. You should be worried about who your husband was with." Before Bailey could say anything else the caller hung up. By the time she reached the door of her office the phone rang again. Bailey walked back to her desk and looked at the caller ID. Private name, private number. She answered the phone and didn't say anything.

The caller then said, "Tell Noah that my pussy is still sore from last night."

"What? Who the fuck is this?" Bailey asked. The caller hung up.

With her heart pounding and feeling perplexed, Bailey went upstairs to her bedroom. She didn't know if this was a joke or if the caller was actually telling the truth. Because she didn't know who this woman was, she didn't want to mention this call to Noah prematurely. Especially if the information wasn't true. Unsure of what to do, she entered her bedroom, and noticed that Noah was already awake and in the shower. She opened the shower door.

Noah looked at Bailey and said, "Why did you let me sleep so long? I needed to make some calls." Even though Bailey was angry, shocked and pissed she said nothing to Noah about the calls.

"Do you want me to get in the shower with you?" Bailey asked.

"That would be good. Come on in." As Bailey was taking off her robe, the telephone rang again. Bailey walked over to the nightstand and answered it.

"Some things never change," said the voice at the other end. "Noah still likes it rough. It was such a pleasure seeing him last night."

"Who is this?" Bailey asked.

"Ask your husband. He'll tell you all about me."

"Look, bitch. Don't call my damn house again. You better hope that I don't find out who the fuck you are," Bailey said as she slammed down the phone.

"Babe, come on. I have something for you," Noah shouted.

"You can go ahead. I had a shower earlier. Not really in the mood for another one right now."

"Are you sure?"

"Positive,"

"Okay, I'll be right out."

"Babe, would you be angry if we didn't go out tonight?" Bailey asked.

Noah walked toward Bailey as he was drying himself off. He threw her a glance and said, "Yes I would. Why? Have you decided against going out?"

"Yes"

"Why, what's wrong? You were so eager to go out today."

"I have a really bad headache. Let's just stay in tonight."

"Then what's for dinner? Do you want me to go and pick something up?" Noah asked.

"Yes. That'll be fine," Bailey said.

"Is there anything in particular you want for dinner? You know how picky you are."

"It doesn't matter. You know what I like and dislike."

"I'll go and get the food after I put something on."

"That's fine, I'll rest until you get back."

While Noah was out picking up dinner, Bailey couldn't help but think about the calls. *Who the hell was calling my house playing on the damn phone? I didn't entertain stupid shit like this when I was in school. I'm damn sure not going through it in my thirties. I know it's not Maisha because she knows we'd recognize her voice. All I want to know is what grown-ass woman calls and plays on somebody's phone. I guess I'm going to have to get the number changed. Once I do that I'll only give the number to a few select people. I really can't believe this shit. This has really fucked me up.*

Bailey grabbed her phone off the nightstand to call Kya.

"Hey," Kya said.

"Hey, girlie, what's up?" Bailey said.

"Nothing much, I'm about to leave work. I have to go out to Arlington and pick up some supplies. I really don't want to, the traffic's going to be a mess."

"Oh, okay. I was just wondering if you were going to be in my area. I was going to ask you to stop by."

"Do you need me to stop by? Because if you need me, just say the word."

"No. Go ahead and take care of your business. I just wanted to talk," Bailey said.

"What's wrong?" Kya asked.

"You're not going to believe this bullshit."

"What?"

"Someone is calling my house playing on the fucking phone."

"Get the fuck out of here! Stop playing."

"I'm not playing. I'm very serious. They called here twice today, but that's not the worst part," Bailey said.

"I didn't think it could get much worse than that."

"When I spoke to you earlier, I never got a chance to tell you about last night. Noah didn't come home until five this morning," Bailey said. "Hello . . . Kya, are you still there?"

"I'm sorry, I was trying to talk but nothing came out. I'm speechless and I can't believe this."

"Well believe it, sweetie. I spoke to him once for maybe four seconds. He said he was going to call me back but he never did. Then I kept calling and calling but he didn't answer his phone. Sometimes it would go straight to voicemail. Then he came stepping in the house like everything was all fucking hunky-dory."

"I don't know what to say. Where did he say he was?"

"He supposedly went out because he needed to blow off some steam," Bailey said.

"Out where? Was he at the club with Jeff?" Kya asked.

"That's the same fucking thing I said when he told me he was out. I don't know if he was with Jeff or not," Bailey said.

"You know Joi works at the club now she's a bartender. She's there a couple of nights out of the week."

"Joi!" Bailey shouted.

"Yup."

"Why are you just telling me this?"

"I just found out today. I called the club looking for Jeff a little while ago and she answered the phone. Since her voice wasn't familiar I asked who it was," Kya said.

"So Jeff didn't tell you?" Bailey asked.

"Hell, no! He didn't say one goddamn word."

"How long has she been working there?"

"Two weeks now."

"Is that right? Oh, okay I see what's going on," Bailey said.

"Sweetie, I know what you're thinking but don't even think it."

"Oh, I'm thinking it. If he's not hiding something then why the fuck didn't he mention that? Why the hell would Jeff hire her knowing who the bitch is?"

"I'm not going to justify why Noah didn't say anything. But I will say this, Jeff don't have the sense that God gave him. I know for a fact that Noah isn't stupid enough to cheat again especially with that bitch," Kya said.

"Kya, you have to expect the unexpected and never put anything past anybody. We can't say what people will or will not do. Besides, he's a man and they think with their dicks. Let me rephrase that, they let their dicks think for them."

"True. True. But we're talking about Noah. He wouldn't hurt you like that."

"Yeah well, whomever the bitch was that called, she said that she was with him last night. And I don't mean sitting around drinking tea and eating crumpets," Bailey said.

"All I can say is, wow. I don't know what else to say. I hate to ask you this, but do you actually think he's cheating on you?"

"I don't know. I don't know what to think. In all actuality I have no clue where Noah was last night. He didn't answer his phone. He never called me back and he came home at 5 a.m. So what am I supposed to think?" Bailey asked.

"What the fuck is really going on? Noah can't be cheating."

"I'm not going through that bullshit again."

"Where is he?"

"He went to pick up some food. We were supposed to go out to dinner. I'm not in such a festive mood right now. I'm sure you can imagine. After those phone calls I no longer wanted to go out. I told him I had a headache," Bailey said.

"Are you going to confront him?"

"Sweetie, right now I really don't know what I'm going to do. I don't even want to think about this shit. But I know I have to."

"It's going to be okay," Kya said.

"I know it will. Speaking of the devil . . ."

"Is he back?"

"Yeah, I just heard the alarm."

"At least we're going away soon. Just what the doctor ordered, a relaxing spa weekend for us both," Kya said.

"I don't know if I want to go now," Bailey said.

"Listen, you cut that shit out. You're going and we'll have a great time. Whether you're at home or if you're at the spa you can't stop someone from doing what they really want. If he is in fact cheating he'll manage to find a way."

"Thanks, Kya, for your insight. That really makes me feel worse."

"I'm sorry, sweetie, I was just saying. I don't know whether Noah's cheating or not. Don't just give up on the things that you like to do. Why start hanging around the house like an old maid? What's that going to prove?"

"Okay, I'll go, regardless of how I might feel. I'm not going to have any fun," Bailey said.

"Whatever, girl, you're going to have a blast and you know it. I already packed my damn bags and they're sitting at the front door. I'm ready to go."

"I was just messing with you. I just wanted to see what you were going to say. We'll have a wonderful time and I definitely need to get away. I also have some other stuff that I need to discuss with you. *That* conversation we'll need to have over drinks," Bailey said.

"Oh goodness, what did I do now?"

"Surprisingly it wasn't you this time. We'll have that convo later. Noah just brought my dinner up. I'll give you a call tomorrow."

"Okey-dokey. Don't hurt him too bad."

"Hmmm . . . I'll try not to," Bailey said. She sat up and repositioned herself on the side of the bed. "Babe, you know we still need to discuss last night."

"Okay, did you want to wait until later on?" Noah asked.

"Nope, now's a great time."

"Okay."

After Noah placed the food on the desk, he sat on the side of the bed next to Bailey.

"Where were you last night? Why were you so busy that you couldn't call? And why did you come home so late?" she asked.

"I hung out with Jeff at the club and for some reason my phone was acting weird."

"You mean to tell me you couldn't use the phone in Jeff's office, you couldn't at least tell me that you were going out?"

"I didn't think to use the phone in Jeff's office. But I should have called and told you I was going to hang out," Noah said.

"But you still haven't answered why you came home so late this morning," Bailey said.

"After the club closed I just hung around with Jeff and a couple of the fellas."

"The club closed at 2 a.m. So you and the guys were just sitting around shooting the shit until about 4:30 a.m.?"

"Yes."

"Yeah okay, whatever you say."

"I apologize and I know I was wrong."

"I hear you."

"Do you forgive me?" Noah asked. Before Bailey had a chance to respond, Noah gently kissed her on her lips and said, "I love you."

"Okay, me too," Bailey said.

"That's different. You can't tell me you love me back?" After a couple of seconds Bailey still hadn't responded and Noah said, "I guess not."

"Let me ask you this question. Why the fuck didn't you tell me that Joi worked at the club?" Bailey asked.

"Because I knew how you'd respond."

"Noah, you don't know shit and you can't speak for me. You probably got the bitch the job."

"I don't have anything to do with the people that Jeff hires. I was shocked too."

"So this was just a coincidence. Is that what you're telling me?"

"Yes."

"Are you cheating on me, Noah?" Bailey asked.

"What? Why would I do something like that?"

"I don't know, you tell me. But you still haven't answered the question. In case it went over your head, I asked, are you are fucking cheating on me?"

"No, I'm not cheating on you."

"I guess it's also a coincidence that some bitch has been calling my house playing on my phone. The same bitch that said she was with you last night. The same bitch that went into explicit details about how you fucked her. I guess that's a goddamn coincidence too."

"What are you talking about?"

"You heard what the hell I said. Are you fucking someone else? Don't keep acting like you don't hear me and you can't comprehend what I'm saying. Don't play games with me, Noah. I'm not in the mood for this bullshit right now."

"I told you I wasn't fucking anyone else. But you're going to believe whatever you want," Noah said.

"I'm damn sure not going to believe that everything happens to be a coincidence. Who the fuck do you think you're talking to? Do I look like some dumb bitch that just fell off a banana boat? I'm going to say this and I will only say it once. I will not deal with you cheating on me again. So if there is somewhere else you want to be then get the fuck on."

"Babe, you are totally overreacting and blowing this out of proportion. I'm not cheating on you."

"I've said what I have to say," Bailey said.

"So now you're mad with me. And for nothing."

"First of all I don't get mad, dogs get mad and I'm not a freakin' dog! The reason I'm pissed with you is because I'm not buying this bullshit that you're trying to sell me. I don't know who you think I am. You know what? I'm done with it. I'll find out who the stupid bitch is, trust me. By tomorrow morning I'll know everything I need to know about her. I'll know where she lives, works and her telephone number!"

"How would you do that?"

"If you're not doing anything and have nothing to hide then why the fuck do you care?"

"I was just asking."

"Since the ignorant whore called more than once I put a trace on the phone. Therefore, this time tomorrow I'll know all about the whore. So, if there is something you need to tell me I suggest you do so now. Otherwise, if I find out you've cheated on me it's a wrap. We are fucking over. A done deal! I refuse to waste my time with someone who can't treat me right. I'm not doing it. I'm not the one for that bullshit!"

"Babe, I wouldn't hurt you, I swear. I wouldn't risk what I have with you for a quick fuck. I wouldn't jeopardize my family like that. You know me better than that," Noah said.

"I thought I knew you two years ago too. You had a lot to lose back then but you let your dick get you caught up. Apparently you didn't give a shit about me and my daughters then so why is now different? We didn't make you cheat. You did what the fuck you wanted because that's what you wanted to do. Leave me and my children out of your bullshit."

"I thought you forgave me and we moved on. You're the one that always says leave the past in the past. There's nothing we can do to change what's happened."

"You can't let the past be the past when it comes back to haunt you. Right now it feels like the past just took a big bite out my ass."

"Babe, do you trust me?" Noah asked.

As Bailey relocated to the chaise she looked at Noah and said, "Noah, please do not go there with me. You know what? I can't do this, not right now. This conversation is over. Just leave me alone." Bailey got up from the chaise, went to the closet, and grabbed some clothes. She removed her robe and put her jeans on.

"Where are you going?"

"I can't do this right now. I just can't. I just need some air, Noah. Just leave me alone." As the tears began to roll down her face, Noah walked toward her.

"Where are you going?" he repeated.

"I don't know," Bailey whispered.

"I don't think you should leave. You're upset and you shouldn't drive like this. Let's just eat dinner and sit and talk."

"Noah, I'll be fine. I don't have anything else to talk about. I'm all talked out." Bailey walked out of the room with Noah following her down the steps. As she collected her coat, Noah grabbed her arm.

"Noah, just let me go. I just want to get some air, please."

"Babe, I love you so much and you know this. I don't want to fight. Can't we just talk?" Noah asked.

Bailey looked at Noah and said, "We just did. Now let go of my arm."

While Bailey sat in her truck she cried more when she thought of the possibility of her marriage ending. It wasn't only because of Noah's infidelities but hers with Maisha as well. Once she pulled out of the driveway she had no clue where she was going. After dealing with Maisha and then Noah she felt like she'd had all she could take for one day. For the next couple of hours she drove and enjoyed the peace and solitude. For her, silence was also comforting. After people shouting at her for the past week all she wanted was to be alone. She reached for the phone to call Kya and noticed that her phone wasn't in the holder or in the front seat. Since she was driving she was unable to reach the back seat to search further.

After a while Bailey pulled over into a gas station. She looked in the back seat of the truck and realized she'd left her purse at home. Damn, no phone or wallet. She grabbed some change from the coin holder then walked to find a pay phone. As Bailey lifted the receiver she became aware that the phone was broken. *Oh well, I guess I won't be calling Kya. There's no point in driving all the way to her house in case she's not at home.* Bailey walked back to her truck and just sat there. After ten minutes, the gas station attendant came out.

"Are you okay? Do you need some help?"

"Yes, I'm fine. I'm trying to figure out where to go."

"Are you lost? I can help with directions."

"No, I'm fine. Thanks for asking," Bailey said.

"Okay, let me know if you need anything."

"Thank you."

After sitting in the gas station parking lot for forty five minutes, Bailey decided that wasn't where she wanted to be. She knew her mother was out of town and she wouldn't have to worry about the questioning.

After driving for an additional hour Bailey arrived at her mother's house. Much to her surprise, when she pulled up she noticed Kya's car sitting in the driveway. Bailey got out of the truck and walked over to Kya's car.

"You're a hard person to find," Kya said.

"What are you doing here?" Bailey asked.

"Your husband called me looking for you. Sweetie, he sounded worried."

"And I should care because?" Bailey asked.

"He said you left the house without your phone or purse. He was also concerned because you left very upset."

"I just needed some air. How did you know to come here?"

"Because we've been friends for over twenty years and I know you. Whenever you need to run, your mom's house is the place you run to. And you're a big-ass brat so I knew you wanted to get in your mama's bed."

"Okay. Maybe you know me too well. Did you tell Noah you were coming here?"

"No, I told him that you'd be fine and to give you a little space right now."

"Good. I'm glad you told him that. I don't want him coming here looking for me."

Kya grabbed Bailey's hand and said, "It's going to be okay. You can handle whatever's thrown at you. You always have and you always will. Don't crack on me now. We need you. You hold all of us together. We rely on your strength to get us through all of our bullshit. God knows I couldn't handle my drama without you."

"Kya, there's so much going on right now I can't even think. My thoughts are all over the place and I can't get it together. I don't know whether I'm going or coming."

"Let's go in the house and talk. I think I need a drink and I have to get you something to eat."

"How long have you been here? And where's Lexi?"

"I've been here for an hour and a half and I dropped Lexi off at my sister's house."

"How did you know I didn't eat?" Bailey asked.

"Noah told me."

"What else did he tell you?"

"He pretty much told me everything."

"I hope that you are not here on behalf of Noah?"

"Girl, just sit your ass down and relax your nerves. I'll be right back."

"Where are you going?"

"To the kitchen to get your mama's takeout menus and some ice for the cocktails."

"But I'm not hungry," Bailey said. While Kya was rummaging through the kitchen drawers for takeout menus, Bailey picked up the phone. Before she had a chance to dial the numbers she quickly slammed it back down.

"Do you feel like Italian, Chinese or pizza?" Kya shouted from the kitchen.

"None of the above," Bailey said.

"Do you want an egg and bacon sandwich then?"

"No, Kya."

"Chips and dip?"

"Nothing, just a nice stiff drink."

"You haven't eaten all day and you can't drink on an empty stomach," Kya said.

"Just bring the chips, pretzels and dip."

As Kya returned she said, "Did you call Noah?"

"No, I was but I decided not to," Bailey said.

"Come on, sweetie, don't act like this. At least call him to let him know that you're safe. Don't make matters worse by being stubborn. You know how you felt last night when *you* couldn't find *him*."

"I'm not calling."

"Would you like for me to call?"

"I don't want him to know where I am but that's up to you. If you want to call then call."

"What do you want to eat?" Kya asked.

"If you say one more word to me about food, I think I might hit you. I don't want anything to eat right now. I'm not hungry, I lost my appetite several hours ago."

"Okay, Moo Shoo Shrimp and spring rolls it is. Would you like anything else?"

"Please don't order anything. I'm sure there's plenty of food in Mama's kitchen."

"I need for you to put something in your stomach. If you don't eat then you can't have any cocktails," Kya said.

"Okay, then order the damn food. I'll eat it later on."

Once Kya placed the takeout order, she kicked off her shoes, made cocktails then repositioned herself on the sofa.

"So what's going on, Mama?" Kya asked.

"I don't know where to start, there's so much to tell. I don't want to talk about all of that crap right now. Let's talk about something cheerful. Why don't you tell me about you and Steve? How are things going?"

"I don't want to talk about Steve. I'd rather talk about what's going on with you. You keep saying there's a lot going on. Besides the situation with Noah, is there other stuff too?" Kya asked.

"Yeah, there's quite a bit. I just need time to process all of it then I can talk about it."

"I know you and you'll hold all this shit to yourself. Then you'll begin to back away from everyone slowly until you've figured it out. But that's not going to solve anything. Right now I think it's a little premature to be so angry with Noah. I understand the circumstances and the events from today and last night are a little far-fetched. He said he's not cheating, what more do you want?"

"Sweetie, something just doesn't feel right. I can feel it in the pit of my stomach. It's like déjà vu. The way that I'm feeling now is the same way I felt two years ago," Bailey said.

"Do you think you could be going over the top a little? You don't have any concrete information that Noah is dipping out on you. I could see it if he was like Jeff but he's not. Noah's a good man."

"This time I'm not going to sit around. I was able to put a trace on our house phone so I'll definitely find out who she is."

"How the hell did you do that?"

"Three little buttons on the telephone keypad. Just like we pay for voicemail you can also pay for call trace," Bailey said.

"If it is Joi calling your house, then what are you going to do? Are you going to leave Noah?"

"I'm very much in love with my husband, but I can't deal with constant cheating. At this very moment I can't say what I'm going to do. I honestly don't know."

"You and Noah have a great marriage. You have the model marriage. It's better than for most people I know. I'm familiar with the ups and downs you've had, but some way and somehow you and Noah always bounce back. The things you go through are tedious compared to the nightmares that most of us go through. I could only hope and pray when I do get married that I can model your relationship," Kya said.

"I don't think you want to do that."

"Why not?"

"Because we're not perfect people, nor do we have a perfect marriage. There's a lot of stuff that goes on that I don't share. You don't know everything. Some things you have to keep to yourself. Everything is not for everybody," Bailey said.

"We've been friends for a long time and we've never kept anything from one another. We discuss everything."

"Don't be so sure."

"Okay then, what is it? Is there something you'd like to tell me?" Kya asked.

"No, not right now, when the time's right."

"I think this is a perfect time. But first let me top up our drinks."

While Kya was refreshing the drinks Bailey went into the kitchen to get more snacks. In the kitchen the phone rang.

"Do you want me to answer that?" Kya shouted.

"No, it can go to voicemail. Everyone knows my mother's out of town."

After Bailey finished putting together a tray of fruit and snacks she went back into the living room.

Once she repositioned herself on the floor Kya asked, "Okay, so what's really going on?"

"Have you been with a woman before?" With a puzzled look on her face, Kya looked at Bailey and smirked.

"That has got to be a rhetorical question right?"

"No, that wasn't a rhetorical question. Have you ever been with a woman or thought about it?"

"No, I like dick too much and there's nothing that a woman can do for me. Why did you ask me that question? Have you?"

"Yes," Bailey said.

"Get the hell outta here, stop joking."

"I'm not joking."

"Get the fuck out of here! When? With whom?"

"Recently," Bailey said.

"How recent? A couple of years ago, a month ago, when?"

"The past three months . . . I've been having sex with Maisha," Bailey said.

After taking a long swallow of her drink, Kya gasped and said, "Shut the hell up. Ha, ha . . . are you punking me or something? Okay, you got me. That was a good one."

"No, I'm serious. I've been sleeping with Maisha."

"Bailey you play too much. You need to stop it."

"I'm not playing," Bailey said.

"Are you serious? How long has this been going on? Damn bitch, you keeping secrets and shit. How did this happen?"

"It started three months ago but she's been saying slick shit to me for over a year. The more comments she made the more curious I became. I got tired of the comments and one day I took her up on it. For the past several days I've been trying to break it off with her. Today I was finally successful."

"Why didn't you tell me this?" Kya asked.

"Tell you what? That I was cheating on my husband with Maisha, who happens to be a woman that works for me?"

"Yes. You could have said something. No wonder you've been so stressed and a little difficult for the past couple of weeks."

"I have been a little all over the place lately. I probably would have been okay but Maisha started tripping. Then I was still trying to take care of home and work. But this week has really been a nightmare. It seemed like everything that could go wrong did."

"You said she was tripping. Does that mean she didn't want to end the relationship?" Kya asked.

"That's the thing, it wasn't a relationship. I told her that from the get go. No relationship. No strings attached, just sex. Now she tells me she's in love with me and wants me to be with her. She actually expected me to leave Noah."

"Damn, oh my goodness! Are you going to fire her?"

"I had no intention of firing her. But if she keeps getting on my nerves then yes, she'll have to go. I was trying to avoid a potential lawsuit and not have my personal life on display."

"And a whole lot of embarrassment. Oh well, it is what it is," Kya said.

"I wasn't really worried about being embarrassed. That part I could deal with. No matter what you do, people talk about you regardless."

"Do you think she's going to tell Noah?"

"I have no idea what she's going to do. Lately she hasn't been mature about the whole situation," Bailey said.

"Well. What do you expect? The girl did tell you that she's in love. Damn, you must have put that thang on her and now she's addicted to your woman juice," Kya said jokingly.

"Girl, stop."

"No. I'm serious. You're making the girl go crazy. You might have to fire that ass or else you'll have a real-life fatal attraction on your hands. I don't think she's just going to let you go."

"So not only am I stressing about home and work, I got Psycho Suzie on my ass," Bailey said.

"Literally she's on that ass. Sorry, I'm just kidding but I couldn't help it. Before Psycho Suzie tells Noah, will you?"

"I wanted to tell him but after today and last night I don't know. I have a lot on my mind right now. I just wanted a little time to sort all of this out."

"Omg, I just had a thought, what if you come home one night and find a large pot on the stove with that cute little puppy boiling? OMG!" Kya yelled.

"Bitch, you got jokes."

"No for real, you don't know what Psycho Suzie is capable of. Hell hath no fury like a woman scorned."

"Whatever, Kya. She might be stupid but I don't think she's stazy."

"Stazy, what the fuck is that? Is that some lesbo-freak nasty term?" Kya asked.

"No girl, stupid and crazy," Bailey said.

"Oh, okay. Girl, you know sometimes I'm a little slow, you got to break shit down."

"Yeah, I know."

"Riddle me this, and I know this is going to sound crazy, but I'm going to ask anyway. Could it really be considered cheating even if it was with a woman?" Kya asked.

"Um . . . yes. Cheating is cheating. Why wouldn't it be considered cheating? It would be considered cheating if he knew about it," Bailey said.

"I was just wondering. Maybe he won't be too upset about it. It's not like he's going to be threatened by a woman. Hell, isn't the fantasy of most men to have two women?"

"Yeah, when the man is a part of the equation and the women aren't fucking on the side without him involved."

"Maybe he'll be alright with it," Kya said.

"He may not be threatened by her but his ego might be a little fucked up. He might have felt better if I was cheating with a man. How would you have felt if Jeff was cheating on you with other men?"

"I'd be fucked up. My self-esteem would be a mess, and I might question my womanhood. A bitch might need a little bit of therapy after that."

"Okay then. No matter how you look at it I was wrong," Bailey said.

"Well, I hope fucking that crazy bitch was worth it."

"It was all right. It's not like we were fucking every chance we got. We only had sex three times."

"That's all?" Kya shouted, surprised.

"Yes, ma'am. Why are you so surprised?"

"Because I know you, you love sex. You love great sex. You love experimenting and trying new things. You're a sexual beast! If it's something you like then you damn sure do it more than three times."

"That's all true but I think it was more about being curious. I can say I tried it and it was ummmm . . . very good, but not good enough for me to leave dick alone. That's just one more item I can add to the list of things accomplished," Bailey said.

"Damn, boo, you that beast! You've always been a risk taker, even when we were kids. If there was something you wanted or wanted to do, no one could stand in your way. Your ass would just jump out there and deal with the ramifications later."

"Very true! However, at the end of the day I'm a married woman with a family I love very dearly. I couldn't keep creeping around like that. I had to put an end to that shit before it got bad or before I started enjoying it a little too much."

"Let me ask you another question. What the hell were you thinking?" Kya asked.

"I can honestly say that I wasn't thinking. I jumped in head first."

Kya started laughing uncontrollably. "Girl, stop with the metaphors and shit. You unquestionably jumped in head first, isn't that the way it's done with women? Head first, fingers next?"

"I'm going to beat the shit out of you. It's really not funny. You're on joke time and I'm being serious," Bailey said.

"Okay, let me get myself together. But if you think about it, this shit is funny as hell! I'm going to have to make another cocktail on that one."

"If I was thinking with my brain then I wouldn't be in this situation. Because if I was, then I wouldn't be worrying about Psycho Suzie."

"In all seriousness, I'm not shocked that you tried something different. I'm more shocked about who you tried it with, a crazy bitch that works for you. Now that's classic. But it could have been worse. You could have been fucked some man, got pregnant or got a damn disease. Girl, it's all good. You only live once, right?" Kya said.

"Right, but I hope my husband is as supportive when he finds out."

"Don't tell him."

"What do you mean don't tell him?"

"Like I said, don't tell him. If Maisha doesn't say or do anything stupid then you don't say a word."

"In other words you want me to live a lie. You want me to walk around like nothing has happened? Then in all fairness how can I be angry with him if he's cheating?" Bailey said.

"You have every right to be angry with him if he's cheating. This wouldn't be the first time. And if he's cheating with Joi, that's the second time around with her. At least as far as we know."

"I don't know, Kya, that's a double standard. Two wrongs never make a right."

"I agree but what if he's not cheating and you tell him about your little three-second fling with Maisha. Do you want your marriage to end?"

"No," Bailey said.

"Okay then. Don't say a damn thing. You don't have to worry about me saying anything either. We'll take this shit to our graves. With all that you've done for me, this is the least I can do for you."

"Sooner or later I *will* figure out what to do. Hopefully sooner rather than later."

"I just told you what to do, keep your fucking mouth shut," Kya said.

"I hear ya, girl."

"You know what, out of every bad situation something good happens."

"I can't wait to see the good that's going to come out of all of this," Bailey said.

"Me neither. If I was you I wouldn't stress too much about Maisha. Just let it roll off your back. For one she's not crazy enough to do anything stupid. Secondly, jobs are a little scarce these days and I doubt that she wants to be in the unemployment line. But if you think about it she actually sexually harassed you. She's the one that kept propositioning you and trying to get the va-jj," Kya said.

"But she didn't force me to do anything. I did it of my own accord. It's not like she said fuck me or else."

"Yeah, I know. Bottom line, there's nothing she could do to you."

"You never know, Kya."

"Unless you got some skeletons in your closet and she's the only one that knows. What could she possibly do? Not a damn thing."

"No. No skeletons in the closet, this is the only one—at least the only one that I'm aware of. Oh, I almost forgot the time you and I tried it. But hell, we were too fucked up to remember if anything actually happened," Bailey said.

"Exactly. No more engaging in sexual escapades with your staff. No more coochie for you, missy," Kya said teasingly.

"Well, there you have it, that's my drama in a nutshell. I know we're supposed to go to the spa in a couple of weeks. I think I'll fly out the previous Monday. I really want to be alone to clear my head."

"That sounds good but what about TyShae and Tyanna?" Kya asked.

"They have their father at home. He can take care of everything until I get back. I'll spend some time with my babies this weekend. I almost forgot that I'm going to have a houseful because of Ty's sleepover."

"Maybe you should cancel it," Kya said.

"No. She's really been looking forward to it."

"Do you want me to go to the spa a bit earlier with you? I can send Lexi to my mom or sister's house for the week. I don't have a lot going on at work this week and I don't have any catering events either."

"No, sweetie. I'll be fine, I'm a big girl. A little peace, quiet, solitude, rest and relaxation are just what I need right about now," Bailey said.

"Okay, you know I don't mind going to keep you company."

"I guess we need to figure out something for Brandi's thirtieth birthday," Bailey said.

"Yeah, she does have a birthday coming up in a couple of months. The big 3-0! I have a few ideas of things to do: Vegas, St. Croix, the Turks and Caicos or Aruba," Kya said.

"They are all good choices, but do you really think Brandi will want to go to Vegas?"

"She just might, she wanted to go out for drinks the other night."

"Are you serious? Not the church lady!"

"Yes, the church lady. We ended up going to the café for tea and coffee instead," Kya said.

"Anyway, if Brandi is game for going to Vegas then that's what we should do. We can go for the weekend. Maybe we should check with her husband to see if he already has something planned."

"Unless he's taking her to Vegas, we can still go. I don't think he's going to be throwing a big soirée or anything."

"He just might, it is her thirtieth and that's a milestone event," Bailey said.

"From what I was told all he does is work. From morning to night—work, work, work and more work. He's worse than you and I put together."

"Who told you that?"

"Brandi told me," Kya said.

"They did just purchase a home. Maybe things are a little tight over there. Maybe we should give her money for her birthday."

"How about you just pay for her plane ticket, room and food? That way all she'll have to worry about is gambling or spending money."

"Kya, do you think I'm a bank?"

"Yes, I do," Kya said.

"I like how you threw in I can pay for her plane ticket, room and food. How about you, Deion and I will pay for her plane ticket, room and food?"

"Damn, I thought I'd try. That's fine, the three of us can split the tab."

"Thank you," Bailey said.

"We can talk about it more another time."

"Her birthday's in a few months. We might want to make the reservations now. Let's just ask her and then go from there."

"Okay. I hope you don't mind but I told Brandi to give you a call about this foundation she wants to start."

"She and I are attending a fundraiser for breast cancer on Saturday," Bailey said.

"I hope not this Saturday," Kya said.

"Oh shit! Ty's sleepover is Saturday. Dammit! Maybe you or Deion can go in my place. I have to be there for the sleepover. I'll give Brandi a call tomorrow. I hope she won't be disappointed that I'm not going. Maybe she can stop by the house tomorrow before the slumber party to talk," Bailey said.

"That will be good. From the sound of things she's adamant about starting this foundation. Shockingly, Derick isn't being supportive of her plans."

"So that means she needs some money?"

"Correcto," Kya said.

"Did you volunteer us to loan her the money?" Bailey asked.

"Yes I did. I told her you're the only person I know with money."

"If I'm giving her the money for her foundation then we need to cancel all these trips. I don't understand you. You and Deion are financially stable as well. Why is it that you're so quick to volunteer my money?"

"That's because you have more money to spare."

"But you don't know that. I have more overheads too. Any minute my husband is going to tell me I spend too much," Bailey said.

"He's been telling you that shit for years. You don't listen anyway."

"I figured you told her to ask me for the money. Noah and I have already discussed it. I just need a little more information before I can put money into her business."

"I know that's right. You just can't be giving money away willy-nilly."

"Do me a favor," Bailey said.

"What's up?"

"Do not tell anyone else to ask me for money. Got it? Bailey and Noah's bank has closed."

"Okay. Damn. I can go to the breast cancer event on your behalf. It's not like I have anything better to do. However, I don't have anything to wear. Can I get something from the boutique?"

"Oh my goodness, I knew that was coming. All those clothes that you have. I can't make any damn money with you keeping on getting shit," Bailey said.

"I pay for stuff. I may not pay full price but nevertheless I pay."

"Bitch, you don't pay for shit. After you get your outfit for this fundraiser, you're officially cut off. Don't call the boutique or come by."

"Can I get shoes and a purse too?"

"Now you're pushing it," Bailey said.

"I might as well go all out. This is a big event and I cancelled my plans to go for you."

"You didn't have any damn plans, you're such a liar."

"I'd appreciate if you'd call the boutique and tell those people I'm coming to get an outfit. Every time I go that little girl is always gritting on me. Acting like I did something to her. The next time she looks at me like that I'm going to knock the shit out of her," Kya said.

"They hate when you come into the store."

"Why's that?"

"Because they know they're not getting a commission," Bailey said.

"Oh well. It's not my fault that my best friend is the owner."

"I suggest that you enjoy this outfit. You're not getting anything thing else for a very long time."

"What the hell ever, you always say that shit."

"Anyhoo, what's going on with Deion? I haven't spoken to her since last week. I saw that she called me the other night but I didn't have a chance to call her back," Bailey said.

"She and I went out the other night. She was a little teed off with me," Kya said.

"What did you say to her?"

"I expressed my concern regarding her behavior. I'm really concerned about her. I told her she needs to stop opening her legs for every Tom, Dick & Larry."

"What behavior, Kya? What are you talking about now?" Bailey asked.

"I know I'm not a doctor or anything but her sexual behavior just isn't normal. I confronted her about it."

"Okay . . . and?"

"And she pretty much told me to mind my fucking business," Kya said.

"Really? Why would you say something like that to her? Did she ask your opinion about her sex life or did she open the door for that conversation? You really have to be careful what you say to people. If they don't invite you into their business then watch what you say."

"Neither! I was just expressing my opinion. Hell, we've been good friends with Deion for years so why couldn't I say what I felt?" Kya said.

"Yes, we have known her for a long time but our relationship didn't become buddy-buddy until recently. She was always a little distant," Bailey said.

"And I have no understanding of that. It's like she's always backing away from us, like she really doesn't want to be friends. She's been a little stand-offish lately. Oh well, it is what it is. I'm too old to care whether or not somebody doesn't want to be my friend. Fuck, life goes on."

"Yeah, I know. But I noticed a couple of months ago how she never wants to participate in anything or go out. Maybe she's busy with work or something. Hell, she could have some shit going on that we don't know about. Some people do keep their business to themselves."

"That I do know."

"What made you think her sex life isn't healthy? Maybe she just loves sex," Bailey said.

"Bailey, the shit she does can't be normal. She sleeps with men before she gets a chance to know them or their last name. Not only that, but who knowingly sleeps with married men? She's slept with all of her bosses. Not to mention some of the other men she works with. She also has a whole hell of a lot of one-night stands. That shit isn't normal."

"I admit it's so hard to ignore things when the people we love show signs of self-destructive behavior. If she does in fact have a problem then she has to own up to it. You, Brandi or I could tell her all day every day that something's wrong. But if she doesn't think anything is wrong herself, she'll be defensive and pissed off."

"What are we supposed to do, just sit by and let her destroy herself? Look how many times she got fired. It's not because she's a bad employee. It's always because she screwed the boss," Kya said.

"Maybe there's a different approach to dealing with this. Personally, I've never encountered anyone with a sexual addiction. Therefore, I don't know what we should do," Bailey said.

"I'm going to give her a little more time to get it together. If she doesn't, I'm going to have to do something."

"What the hell can you do, Kya?"

"I don't know yet but I'll figure it out. I have to gather all the facts and look it up on the Internet."

"Sweetie, what is it that you're going to look up?"

"Sex addicts, nymphomaniacs, and I'll see if they have SA. If they have NA they damn sure will have SA," Kya said.

"I'm only telling you to be careful with what you say to her and how you're saying it. You know how Deion can be."

"Yeah, and you know how I can be too," Kya said. "It's getting a little late, shouldn't you be getting home?"

"No, I'm going to stay here tonight. I've been drinking and I don't want to drive," Bailey said.

"Bitch, you had one drink and you've been babysitting the one I made an hour ago."

"Shouldn't you be getting home?"

"I've been drinking too. The last drink I made I believe was number five. There is no way I'm going to get on the highway like this," Kya said.

"You must be getting up super early in the morning. You have to go home, shower and get ready for work. Then you have to get back in traffic to go to the office."

"I'm way ahead of you, I'm going to take a sick or personal day tomorrow. Hell, I need a mental health day."

"You still have to get up early enough to call in. At the rate you're going with those drinks, you're not going to be able to get up at all."

"I'll set the alarm on my cellphone, or I'll text them tonight," Kya said.

"As long as you have it figured out. Please don't expect me to get up at the crack of dawn to wake you. I needs my beauty sleep," Bailey said jokingly.

"You needs to call your husband so he can know you're alright."

"You needs to stop working my nerves about that. I'm going to call him."

"When, Bailey? We've been here for hours. Okay, I'm not going to say anything else. He's going to be pissed. That's all I'm going to say. Just call and say I'm okay and since it's late I'm staying at my mother's house. It's best to call so he won't be worried and assuming the worst. I know how that can be."

"I'll call him before I go to bed," Bailey said.

"I'm hopeful that everything will work out between you and Noah," Kya said.

"Are you really?"

"Yes, I am."

"I don't want to get back on the Noah situation. I don't have anything else to say about that topic right now," Bailey said.

"Your tenacity gets on my nerves. If it was about me you'd have a lot to say. Because it's you, you'd rather not discuss it."

"It hurts to imagine my marriage could possibly be over. I guess that's why I don't want to talk about it. Besides, at the moment I don't have enough proof that he's cheating. Until I do, I'm not going to work myself up. I'll wait. Everything in the dark comes to light sooner or later."

"Okay. I think I'm about to call it a night," Kya said.

"Good! Take your drunken ass to sleep."

"Excuse me! I am not drunk. I'm a little tipsy that's all."

"Okay, not drunk. Every time you get up I watch you do the two-step with one foot."

"Whatever. I'm feeling good but not drunk. I hope your mama don't have a lot of junk in the guest bedroom. I also need to call my sister and check on Lexi. I'm going upstairs now, I'll see you in the a.m."

"Okay. Goodnight. After I call Noah I'll probably call it a night too," Bailey said.

Once Kya went upstairs to bed Bailey finally finished her drink. She sat there for a while pondering over the day's events. After tidying the living room Bailey took what was left of the uneaten snacks into the kitchen, grabbing a bottle of water out of the refrigerator and two aspirins out of the cabinet. She went back into the living room and sat on the sofa. *What am I going to do? Is the love that Noah and I have worth salvaging? What happened to us? I definitely have a part in this mess too. My hands aren't exactly clean. I guess I need to call Noah and let him know that I'm okay.*

Bailey picked up the cordless phone and dialed her number. After the first ring Noah picked up the phone.

"Hello," Noah said.

"Hey," Bailey said.

"I see you're at your mom's house. I called there a couple of hours ago but no one answered."

"Yes, I am. I heard the phone ringing but didn't answer it. I figured it was someone calling for my mother. I was just calling to let you know that I'm okay."

"Thank you. I was worried about you. Especially because of the way you left here. Then I noticed that you left your phone and purse here. Are you coming home?"

"No. Since it's late I'm going to go ahead and spend the night here," Bailey said.

"I figured that. It's too late for you to be driving on the highway by yourself."

"Why aren't you asleep?"

"How could I possibly be asleep when I didn't know where my wife was?" Noah asked.

"Now you see how I felt last night. At least I'm calling you. You didn't even have the courtesy to call me and say anything."

"I see how you felt. Babe, I apologize and it won't happen again. I promise."

"Okay Noah, I hear you. But don't make a promise that you can't keep. I didn't call you to start that back up or to argue. I just wanted you to know that I was safe," Bailey said.

"Are you going into the office tomorrow?" Noah asked.

"No, I'm not. I forgot Tyanna's having a sleepover. I need to go to the store and pick up some stuff for it. Of course I have to come home first to get my purse and phone."

"Do you want me to go with you?"

"No. I can take care of it. I'll see if Kya can go with me. Don't you have to go into the office?" Bailey asked.

"I can take a day off. I'd love to go with you. But if you don't want me to go I understand. I just thought you might need some help getting everything together."

"Thanks for offering but I'll be fine. Have you spoken to the girls tonight?" Bailey asked.

"Yes, I spoke to them earlier. Ty called me fifty times to remind me to walk her dog. They asked where you were. I told them you were out with your friends. I couldn't tell them I didn't have any idea where you were. Each time Ty called back she asked if you were home yet. The last time she called was about an hour ago."

"Why were they up so late?"

"Ty said that they were watching movies with Grandma."

"Did you speak to your mother?" Bailey asked.

"No, I didn't. What are you doing?" Noah asked.

"I'm walking up the steps so I can get in the bed. It's been a long day and I can't wait to get in."

Once Bailey got upstairs she looked in the room and checked on Kya. *Yup she's drunk, she's lying diagonally in the bed and fully dressed. Her head is going to be killing her in the morning.*

"Damn!" Bailey said.

"What's wrong?" Noah asked.

"I don't have anything to sleep in. I'm going to have to go through my mother's dresser to see if I can find a t-shirt or something."

"You don't like sleeping with clothes on anyway."

"Very true but I'm not at home. Besides, Kya's here."

"Oh, I didn't know Kya was there."

"Yeah, my girl's here. She was sitting in the driveway when I pulled up."

"Where is she now?" Noah asked.

"Right now she's in la-la land, she's asleep," Bailey said. "Why wouldn't you think she was here? Didn't you speak to her?"

"Yes I did, but I didn't know she'd go looking for you. She didn't mention that."

"I guess like you she was worried about me but she chose to find me."

"I wish you were here with me," Noah said.

"I'll see you tomorrow or should I say today after you get home from work," Bailey said.

"I might just stay home so I can hang out with you."

"That's your choice. But I told you I'll be fine."

"Maybe we can go to breakfast or something in the morning."

"I don't know, I have a lot of things to take care of."

"That's why you should let me help you," Noah said.

"By the way, did you remember that I'm going on the spa trip with the girls next weekend?"

"Yeah, I remember. Why, have you decided to cancel?"

"Actually I decided that I'm going to leave on Monday instead of Friday," Bailey said.

"What? Why are you doing that?"

"Because I want some time alone, I have a lot on my mind and I need to get things in order."

"I really wish you'd think about that. What are we going to do without you here?" Noah asked.

"You'll be fine. I'll be back before you know it. I'll give Mrs. Jenkins a call tomorrow to see if she can pick up a lot of the slack. Hopefully, she'll be able to stay at the house. That way you can go to work and not stress about the girls. They both have doctor's appointments, dance class and some extra-curricular stuff at school. If you need additional help you can always call your mom, Brandi or Kya."

"Why are you doing this?"

"Doing what?"

"Why are you leaving? It feels like you're running away from me."

"Noah, I'm not running away from you. I just want some time alone. That's all. Before I leave I'll make sure everything's taken care of."

"Why can't you leave for the spa as originally planned? The girls and I have never been away from you that long. What are we going to do?" Noah asked.

"You'll manage. It's not like I'm going to a desert island. I'll have my phone and computer with me. You can call me or we can Facetime or Skype," Bailey said.

"What about work?"

"I have a couple of meetings. I'll have Nina reschedule them. My schedule next week is pretty clear."

"Aren't the girls out of school next week for spring break?" Noah asked.

"No. That's the week after next. I think they should spend their spring break with your mom," Bailey said.

"Are you asking me or telling me?"

"It was just a thought. We haven't made any plans to go anywhere. Was there some place that you wanted to go while they're on spring break?" Bailey asked.

"I thought maybe we could go down to Charleston. I want to check on the house and see what needs to be done."

"I don't think there's anything that has to be done. The contractors supposedly finished everything three months ago."

"When are you going on vacation with your friends?" Noah asked.

"In June, the girls and I haven't figured out the exact date yet."

"Okay, it's late and I need to try and get some sleep," Bailey said.

"If you can't sleep call me back."

"Okay."

"I love you."

"I love you too, Noah."

After what appeared to be a long night of restlessness Bailey decided to go home, take a long, hot shower and get in her own bed. Instead of parking in the driveway Bailey pulled up in front of her house. She assumed since the girls weren't home and Noah was at work that she'd be able to relax. By the time she walked up the driveway her front door opened.

"Good morning," Noah said.

"Hey. Good morning," Bailey said.

As she entered the foyer Noah asked, "How are you?"

"I'm good, just a little tired. Why aren't you at work?"

"I thought I was going to hang out with you today. Aren't we going shopping for Tyanna's sleepover and birthday gift?"

"I thought last night I made it perfectly clear that you didn't need to go."

"I know I don't need to go, I *want* to go with you," Noah said.

"Well, I'm not going. I spoke to Mrs. Jenkins this morning and she's going to pick up the items for the sleepover. So, I'm going to take a shower and get in the bed for a while."

"Is something wrong? Do you feel okay?"

"I have a slight headache and I'm a little nauseated. I also didn't sleep too well last night. I think I'm just a little overworked, stressed and need some rest. So you can go ahead to work. I still have a couple of days before the slumber party. I could always go out later on tonight or tomorrow to get Ty's gift."

"What if I want to hang around the house with you today? Is that okay with you?"

As Bailey walked up the steps to their bedroom, she said, "That's up to you. If that's what you want to do." She reached the bedroom, undressed and put her robe on. "Did I get a phone call this morning?"

"Yes, you had four. Eugene, Nina, your mother and Rachel called. Eugene asked if you needed help with the RFPs. Rachel and Nina wanted you to give them a call about your schedule for today and your mom wanted to know if everything was okay. She said one of her neighbors called her and said you were at her house all night."

"Damn. I guess if I was sneaking over, her nosy ass neighbors would have busted my ass," Bailey said.

"Yeah, I guess so."

"Do you know where my phone is?"

"Yes, it's in the same place that you left it last night, downstairs in the living room."

"I'll get it later," Bailey said.

"Do you want me to go and get it?"

"No, I can get it later on. I just wanted to see if the phone company called with the information that I needed."

"What information?" Noah asked.

"The information on the person that was calling the house last night."

"Oh, okay."

"If they don't call by the time I get up I'll ring them again."

"Do you plan on staying in the bed all day?" Noah asked.

"No, not really. I still have work to do. Once my headache subsides I have calls to make and some documents that I need to review."

"Do you feel like discussing last night?"

"What about last night? I thought we already discussed everything. You're not cheating and I need to get away to clear my head. What else is there to discuss?"

"I wanted to discuss the Joi situation. I have something to tell you," Noah said.

"Babe, can it wait until later on? I'm really not feeling too hot right now."

"No, I think we should talk about it now."

"Noah, can I at least rest for about an hour? My head's pounding, I'm nauseated and every time I get up it feels as though I'm going to pass out."

"Maybe you're pregnant. Do you want to go to the doctor?" Noah asked.

"I'm sure whatever's wrong with me, it'll pass. There's no need to go to the doctor."

"Could you be pregnant?"

"I could be a lot of things but pregnant isn't one of them," Bailey said.

"How could you be so sure?" Noah asked.

"I'm not 100 percent sure and anything is possible. I'm just saying I don't think that I'm pregnant. I'm pretty sure that sterilization op was effective!"

"Well, I hope you're pregnant. Maybe that will slow you down some. That'll keep you from running around so much like a chicken with your head cut off. Your schedule would have to be altered."

"I thought you knew," Bailey said.

"Knew what?"

"That I'm a renaissance black woman. I can do all things."

"Ah, but I thought you knew," Noah said.

"What?"

"That you have a loving and caring husband so you don't have to do all things by yourself. But okay, renaissance black woman, I still think we should get that checked out."

"Well, you don't have nothing to worry about, I'm not pregnant," Bailey said.

"I'd feel better if you went to the doctor to find out."

"Okay, I'll make an appointment. But trust me, I'm not pregnant. Can I rest now?"

"Yes, but we really need to talk," Noah said.

"Babe, what's so important that it can't wait until later on? All I need is a couple hours of rest. Then we can talk."

"It can wait until later. Would you like me to fix you something to eat or get you a ginger ale or something?"

"A ginger ale and some painkillers would be fine," Bailey said.

As Noah went to the kitchen he heard Bailey's phone ringing. By the time he went into the living room it had stopped. As Bailey wasn't feeling well, he decided not to disturb her but to turn her phone off, knowing that people could leave her a message. He went into the kitchen and grabbed a ginger ale as well as the pills. By the time Noah got back upstairs, Bailey was wrapped up under the blankets and sound asleep. Noah placed the drink and painkillers on the nightstand, closed the curtains, turned down the television and closed the balcony door. He thought Bailey was indeed unwell or very tired. She didn't even hear him in the room so he decided to get on with some work.

As Noah walked downstairs the house phone began ringing. He walked into his office and answered the phone.

"Hello."

"Where's your wife?" Joi asked.

"What are you doing calling my house?"

"I'm calling your house because you're not answering any of my calls or texts. How else am I supposed to reach you?"

"How did you get my number?" Noah asked.

"Why does that matter? You need to be careful where you put your phone. Maybe you should try locking it so no one can access your information," Joi said.

"Look, don't call my damn house anymore. Whatever happened last night was an accident. I don't know what you're thinking but it won't happen again."

"An accident. An accident? It wasn't an accident. So every time we fuck it's an accident? You fuck me because you want to."

"Listen Joi, I love my wife and kids and I'm not leaving them for you or anyone else. So whatever it is that you're thinking about, you might as well get it out of your head. There will never be an 'us'."

"You think so. Well, make sure you tell wifey that I'm prego," Joi said.

"Why are you telling me? It damn sure isn't mine," Noah said.

"Of course it is."

"I'm not the only one you're fucking."

"That's very true. However, you're the only one I'm fucking without a rubber," Joi said.

"I don't have time for your goddamn games. What is it that you want? Money?"

"So now you're treating me like a whore!" Joi yelled.

"Joi, listen, I really don't give a fuck about you. You were just another piece of ass to me. Just something to do at the moment."

"What the hell ever. I know you want me and you care about me. If you didn't want me you'd have ended all communication two years ago but you didn't."

"I thought we were friends but I guess not," Noah said.

"You're a really great friend. When I moved back to town you got me a job and a place to stay and you provided the dick when I needed it. I'm so glad to have a friend like you," Joi said.

"Look, I hope things work out for you. I gotta go, I have shit to do."

"Noah, don't act like you don't give a fuck about me. Because clearly you do! I don't know why you keep stringing your wife along. Either you tell her or I will. She needs to know about us and our baby."

"Don't ever call my house again."

"I'm going to give you a little more time to tell her. But trust me, if you don't tell her I will!"

"Just like everything else this call is over," Noah said as he slammed down the phone.

For the next several minutes Noah sat at his desk with his head in his hands. *Fuck! What the hell did I get myself into? I have to tell Bailey what I did,* he thought. *There's no way that she'll forgive me this time. I've really fucked up.*

After the call with Joi, Noah couldn't focus on work. The more he tried to clear his mind of Joi's phone call, the more he thought about Bailey's reaction. Noah decided to go and check on her. As he got to the top of the steps, he saw Bailey walking down the hall.

"Babe, where are you going? You should get back to bed," Noah said.

"I was reaching for the ginger ale and knocked it over. I was going to get another glass."

"Go and get back in the bed. I'll get you something to drink. Are you sure you don't want to go to the doctor? You really look sick."

"No, not today. If I'm still not feeling well tomorrow I'll go," Bailey said.

"I really think you should go today."

"I'm fine. It's probably just a stomach virus or something I ate."

"Okay, babe. But if you're not better tomorrow you're going to the doctor."

As Noah helped Bailey back into the bed the phone started ringing again. Bailey reached for it and Noah said, "Let it go to voicemail. You don't need to talk to anyone right now. Try to get some rest."

He grabbed the phone and said, "Hello."

"So you want to play games. Okay, I got something for that ass," Joi said.

"I'm sorry you have the wrong number." Before Noah hung up the phone he turned the phone off.

"Who was that?" Bailey whispered.

"It was a wrong number."

"Okay, wake me in an hour. I want to call and check on my babies. I haven't spoken to them since I dropped them off yesterday."

"The girls are fine, they called this morning. Momma was taking them out to lunch and then the movies. You just worry about you right now. I'll call and check on the girls a little later," Noah said.

Before he could leave the room Bailey sat up and asked, "Where are you going? Can't you do your work up here?"

"I was going to get you something to drink. I'd rather not disturb you since you're not feeling well."

"Can you get in the bed with me?" Bailey asked.

"Yes, I'll come and get in the bed with you. Let me get you something to drink first and I need to call Nina or Rachel."

"You can call them later on."

"Okay, but I still need to go and get you something to drink," Noah said.

"That can wait until later on too. Just get in the bed with me," Bailey said. As Noah climbed in the bed, Bailey repositioned herself and then laid her head on his chest. "I miss my babies. I think I want them to come home today."

"Okay, I'll go and get them later on," Noah said.

Within a couple of minutes, Bailey drifted off to sleep.

For hours Noah lay there and tried to think of the best possible way to handle the situation. He didn't know if he was more afraid of telling Bailey or of her actions after he told her. Either way, the outcome did not look good. They'd always said that divorce was not an option for their marriage. He hoped and prayed that Bailey still felt that way, but knew he had no one to blame but himself if she didn't. He decided he needed to man up and tell his wife what he'd done.

He looked at the clock and realized that neither of them had eaten anything all day. As Bailey continued to sleep, Noah got up and went down to the kitchen. He pondered whether to cook or order out and decided on a pizza. He hoped Bailey would be all right with that, or he'd have to order something else. After Noah called the pizza place, he went into his office to grab his wallet. Whilst there he decided to check his emails. There were twenty from Joi. He selected all of them and hit delete, wondering if and when the girl would just stop.

Before Noah had a chance to check the remainder of his emails, he saw Bailey walking past his office.

"Babe!" Noah shouted.

As Bailey turned and entered Noah's office she said, "I didn't see you sitting there."

"What are you doing?" Noah asked.

"I was looking for my phone."

"It's upstairs on your dresser."

"Okay. Thanks. Are you doing some work?" Bailey asked.

"I was going through my emails."

"Anything interesting?"

"No, not really."

"I guess I should cook us something to eat. What are you in the mood for?" Bailey asked.

"I wasn't sure how long you'd be asleep so I ordered a pizza from Ledo's," Noah said.

"Did you order me a salad too?"

"Yes I did. I figured you didn't want to go out or cook."

"Good call!"

"Are you going back to bed?" Noah asked.

"No. I feel a little bit better. I need to take a shower. Maybe later on I can get some work done."

"I think you need to take it easy. Why don't you use today as a rest day? If you feel like it tomorrow then you can do some work."

"Babe, you know what, that sounds like a good idea. I can just chill, do nothing and watch television."

Noah knew he needed to speak to Bailey about Joi, but he didn't want to have the conversation right away. He was hoping Bailey wouldn't bring it up either.

"I'll let you get back to work and I'm going to take a shower. How much longer are you going be down here?" Bailey asked.

"Probably until the food is delivered then I'll be back up."

"Okay. Would you like to join me in the shower?"

"If you wait until the food's delivered. I don't want to miss the delivery guy."

"Maybe I'll wait. I'll just go upstairs and check my messages," Bailey said.

Shortly after the food came Noah went upstairs. Bailey was already in the shower. Noah began taking off his clothes as he moved toward the bathroom. He opened the shower door and stepped inside.

"I was just about to get out," Bailey said.

"I thought you were going to wait for me. I see you must have changed your mind."

"No, I didn't change my mind. I thought I'd get in so I could wash my hair." Bailey stepped to the back of the shower and turned her back to Noah. He put his arms around her and whispered in her ear, "I love you."

Bailey said, "I love you too."

Noah grabbed Bailey's washcloth and began washing her back. After he'd finished, Bailey stepped back so the water could rinse away the soap. Noah walked closer behind her and put his hands around her waist. He began to kiss her ears softly and worked his way down to the back of her neck. He put his hands on her breasts and gently fondled them, then gently entered her. She let out a sigh and placed her hands on the wall of the shower. Noah gently stroked her pussy in and out and Bailey lifted her leg and placed it in the corner. She could feel the pulsating throb of Noah's dick with each stroke.

Bailey placed her hands on Noah's hips and squeezed ever so tight as he slowly fucked her. While she continued to moan, Noah bent Bailey slightly over and grabbed her hips. In and out . . . gentle then hard . . .

With each stroke Bailey's whimpering grew louder. She placed her hands back on the wall and Noah used one hand to play with her clit and held onto her waist firmly with the other. As Noah started to fuck his wife harder he began to come.

A while later, Bailey finished showering, went into the bedroom and sat on the side of the bed. Several minutes afterwards Noah finished his shower and joined her in the bedroom.

As he was drying off, he looked at Bailey and asked, "What's wrong? You have a very weird look on your face."

"Nothing's wrong, I'm good. So do you want to have that important discussion before or after we eat dinner?"

"We can wait until later on," Noah said.

BRANDI

Tracey Dowtin

Chapter Two

"Good morning, Sherman & Tate Real Estate. This is Brandi Knight, how may I help you?"

"Hi sweetheart, I was calling to let you know I'm going to be home a little late tonight. I have a meeting," Derick said.

"Again? Another meeting? This is the third spur-of-the-moment meeting this week. They're really working the crap out of my baby. I thought we were going to dinner at Southern Komfort, that new soul food restaurant."

"I know, honey, but this meeting is extremely important. One of the board members has just flown in. Since he's not going to be available for a while we need to iron some things out."

"Why? What's going on?" Brandi asked.

"I'm not certain. I think the company is about to go through some significant restructuring. Hopefully whatever changes that are made, they'll be for the better this time around. I'll make it up to you, I promise. We'll go to dinner Friday night or maybe to that jazz club."

"Okay, Derick. Maybe Bailey and the girls are available for dinner. I'll call them to see. If not I'll hang around the house as usual. I guess I can find something to do."

"Okay, well I have to go now. I'll talk to you later on," Derick said.

"Okay. Make sure you grab something to eat."

"Will do," Derick said as he abruptly hung up the phone.

After Brandi got off the telephone with Derick she decided that, before she met with her new client, she'd go and get a salad from Subway. She was out of the office a little longer than anticipated. By the time she returned, her 3 p.m. appointment was waiting.

"Brandi, Mr. Wilborough is waiting in the conference room for you," Patricia whispered.

"All right, let me put my salad in the refrigerator. Could you let him know that I'll be right with him? Did you offer him tea, coffee or something to drink?" Brandi asked.

"Yes, I already took care of that."

Brandi quickly placed her salad in the refrigerator and her purse in her office. She went into the conference room, spotting a well-dressed, caramel-complexioned man standing in front of the conference table. He stood about 6'5" and had a fresh, tapered haircut with a beard and goatee, and wasn't wearing a wedding ring. Brandi immediately thought he'd be the perfect man that Kya needed in her life. An intelligent, intellectual, stylish, professional man that didn't have his pants hanging off his ass.

"Hello, I'm Brandi Knight. Sorry to keep you waiting," Brandi said as she extended her hand.

Chase extended his hand too, and said, "Hello, I'm Chase Wilborough III. At last we meet. More importantly, it's nice to put a face to all of those emails at last." They both chuckled.

"That's true, we've only been emailing each other off and on for eight months now. Okay, should we get started? I have several property listings I'd like to show you," Brandi said.

"Okay, I'd also like to add another home to the list. On my way here I rode past this gorgeous Victorian home on Capitol Hill. They were just putting the For Sale sign up," Chase said.

"All right, let me go and pull the information on that property and I'll be right back."

As Chase waited for Brandi to return with the details, his phone rang. "Chase Wilborough," he said.

"Hey, this is D, what's up? Are we still on for tonight?"

"Yes, is 8:30 p.m. good for you?"

"That's fine, I have enough work to keep me busy until then. I'll call you when I'm on my way."

"Okay babes, I look forward to seeing you. It's long overdue and I miss you like shit," Chase said.

"Me too."

As Brandi re-entered the conference room Chase was ending his call.

"How many properties are we going to today? I have a prior obligation at 8:30 p.m.," he said.

"Well, according to your specific requests, I have a total of six properties. If we leave shortly we can see at least three today. I know you were adamant about what you wanted so this can be somewhat time consuming."

"Sounds good, are you available to go to the other properties on Saturday?" Chase asked.

"I normally don't work on Saturdays but if we can get an early start that would be great," Brandi said.

"How about I call you Friday evening for confirmation?"

"Sounds like a plan. Let's get going, I don't want us to get caught up in traffic."

"I think it's a little too late for that. Traffic is already backed up," Chase said.

There was little conversation in the first few minutes en route to the first property. Chase's phone rang every couple of minutes and in the interim he was typing and texting.

"I see that you're a very busy man. A fashion stylist and personal shopper for celebrities. That's got to be exciting," Brandi said.

"It is but I have a few bad days here and there. We all have a few challenges with our jobs. I'm sure you can relate. It's hard to please some of our clients," Chase said.

"I remember during our initial conversation, you mentioned you're always on the road. Why do you need a house here, if you don't mind me asking?" Brandi questioned.

"That's easy. Me, my belongings, the inventory and my team. Those are the only reasons I'm looking for a house. I've managed to outgrow the loft that I have now. I need a lot of space."

"The first house that we're going to see would be perfect for you. It has a very large square footage with the amenities you requested including office space on a separate floor. You would definitely have your own space so you can separate yourself from your team if and when needed."

"Good, because I need to find something really quick. Hopefully I can find a house where I won't have a lot of work or renovations to do. Right now, my team and I are stepping over each other because of the limited amount of space. It would be great if this new house had a separate entrance, a kitchenette and a powder room as well. Preferably all on one floor. That way I wouldn't have to worry about the clients, staff or vendors walking through my home. We'd have everything that we need on one level," Chase said.

"I know a great contractor with reasonable rates. Not to mention that his work is exceptional," Brandi said.

"Okay, I'll keep that in mind. God knows I'm tired of them messing up my house and leaving the kitchen a damn hot mess."

"How do you get your clients?" Brandi asked.

"WOM," Chase replied.

"WOM, is that some sort of referral service?"

Chase laughed then said, "No. My business has been built exclusively on word-of-mouth."

"And how long have you been in business?"

"Fifteen years now."

"Do you style common folks like me?" Brandi asked.

"I sure do. I'll give you some of my business cards. I like styling professional women more than celebrity women anyway. To me, the professional women appreciate your hard work and efforts more than celebrities do. Excuse my language but those bitches are a trip."

"One of my closest friends owns a boutique for men and women. When I have an event to attend or I need something classy and elegant, that's where I get my attire," Brandi said.

"What's the name of the boutique?"

"Sheer Elegance," Brandi said.

Chase looked at Brandi and said, "Are you serious? Stop playing! That's Bailey and Noah's shop. I'm in there at least three times a week."

"If you're there that often, I'm surprised we haven't run into each other."

"No, I would have remembered. I might forget other stuff, but faces, never," Chase said. "Besides, when I go I'm normally there before the sun comes up."

"Then that's why we're never run into each other. Because of my work schedule, I only get a chance to go after hours. Sometimes I call Bailey and say I have an event to go to and I need an outfit. All I tell her is where I'm going and what type of event it is. She'll send someone to my house with a complete outfit. The dress, handbag, shoes and all of the accessories. Even down to the bra and britches," Brandi said.

"That's Bailey for you. Were you at the grand opening?"

"By the time I got there, everything was winding down. My husband was fired up too. He said I made him dress up in all his good clothes and I didn't even see him."

"Bailey's my girl and we go way back. She and Noah are good people and they always look out for folks too," Chase said.

"Wow! It's a small world."

"Too damn small."

"That's why you should never say anything bad about anyone, you never know who you're talking to," Brandi said.

"Right, that's so true. You could be talking about someone's mama, sister, daddy, husband or whomever. You just never know. My motto is, if I have something to say about you, I'll tell you to your damn face. You don't ever have to worry about someone saying that I said anything. If I don't have anything good to say about anybody I don't say a damn thing. One of the things my mama taught me, besides fashion of course, is that a dog that brings a bone will certainly carry one."

As Brandi chuckled, she said, "Your mama taught you well."

"I would love to style you. Just call me and we can make a day out of it, a full makeover from head to toe. Clothes, hair, nails, makeup, the works."

"Maybe I'll schedule a time prior to my birthday."

"When's your birthday?"

"June eighth," Brandi responded.

"Ahhhh, a Gemini. Two personalities but very sweet people. A Gemini will give you the clothes off their back if you needed them."

"And that's the truth."

"Just give me a call to make sure I'm in town and like I said we'll make a full day out of it. Do you drink?" Chase asked.

"I might have a cocktail here and there but I'm not really a drinker," Brandi said.

"I've heard that before. Anyway, I'll make my specialty cocktail that's out of this world. I'll also make us some lunch."

"Sounds good, I look forward to it."

"Make sure you bring Miss Bailey with you. Cocktails, food, friends and fun. We're going to have a blast," Chase said.

Brandi smirked and asked, "Do you need me to bring anything?"

"No, girl. Just bring yourself and my girl Bailey. I'll take care of everything else."

Conversation flowed between Brandi and Chase as they looked at various houses that evening. They laughed, joked and talked about a lot of topics. For Brandi, Chase wasn't narcissistic or superficial like the majority of her clients and she appreciated that. That made him much more pleasurable to work with. Brandi quickly recognized that he was down-to-earth, kind-hearted and had a great sense of humor. He also said whatever was on his mind and didn't bite his tongue. There was definitely no sugar-coating how he felt. Brandi thought he was almost a replica of Bailey, just a male version. She decided the only way she'd know the answers to her questions was to ask rather than assume. She wanted to tell Chase all about Kya but she needed to ask a few questions first to see if she could make a love connection.

"Chase, are you single and looking for a friend or are you married or attached?" Brandi asked.

"No, I wouldn't say I'm single. I'm seeing someone right now. If everything works out, hopefully I won't be living in a big house all alone. Why are you asking?"

"I don't normally do this but I have a good friend that I would love you to meet."

"Thank you but no thank you. I'm going to see where this relationship goes. I definitely don't play the cheating game," Chase said.

"I hope your relationship works out. But if it doesn't, please let me know. You'd be a good man for my girlfriend Kya," Brandi said. Chase laughed hysterically. With a puzzled look on her face, Brandi asked, "What's so funny?"

"Thanks for the compliment but I don't do women, honey, I only do men. Or should I say, I get done by men."

Brandi's jaw dropped as she stood there in shock.

"You do who . . . you do what . . . you do huh?" Brandi asked.

"Yes, girlfriend, you heard me right. I'm strictly dickly. I like the same thing that you like. The last time I was with a woman I was fourteen years old and playing hide and go get it. After that, I've never looked back and I've never touched another woman."

"Wow. I'm totally in shock. I don't know what to say."

"It's okay, most people can't believe that I'm gay but I am," Chase said.

"Excuse me for my ignorance but you don't look or act like a gay man. I didn't know."

Chase chuckled and said, "How are we supposed to look and act? Am I supposed to be the three F's?"

"The three F's, what's that?"

"Fruity, flamboyant and feminine."

As Brandi stumbled over her words she said, "No, that's not what I meant. You just don't look or act like a gay man."

"Explain to me how does a gay man look or act?" Chase asked.

"Like a woman I suppose. But then again I really don't know. It's not like I have any gay friends or relatives. None that I know about so I really don't know how gay men act, talk, dress or anything else."

As Chase laughed, he said, "It's okay, it's not that serious, I know what you mean. What works for some doesn't work for others. We're not all ostentatious, loud and dressed like a bunch of crayons just exploded all over our clothes. Just because we like the same things women like doesn't mean we have to dress or act like women."

"I mean actually you look like a supermodel. Everything looks perfect about you, like you were hand-carved."

"Thank you for the compliment but looks can be deceiving."

"If I wasn't married and a little on the coy side, I'd have tried to give you my number. Wow, you learn something new every day," Brandi said.

"Yes, that's true. We're supposed to learn something new every day, but not all of us do."

"It's 7:15 p.m. and now that I've made myself look like an idiot, I have to get you back to your car. I don't want you to miss your appointment."

"It's all good. Girl, don't worry about it, it was nothing. As we work together more you'll find out that I'm an open book and don't mind sharing anything. Some people say I'm a little too open but who gives a shit? I'm me and will continue to be me and whoever don't like it knows what they can do."

"I know that's right," Brandi said.

"I couldn't care less what people say. I'm happy and confident within my own skin, with my life and where I'm going. I'm ecstatic about the steps that my God has ordered for me as well as my purpose in life."

"Preach, brother, very well stated and so true. If more people felt like that then the world would be a better place."

"What people need to realize is that happiness isn't determined by what other people think we should be doing, where we should be going and who we should be doing it with," Chase said.

"All very true indeed. And just like blessings, happiness is something you have to reach up and grab."

"Folks just don't get it. People or things don't make you happy, they fill a temporary void and contribute to your happiness."

"If people stopped running around meddling in other folks' business or trying to please others they'd be better at living their life."

As Brandi pulled up beside Chase's car, Chase said, "Well, Ms. Brandi, I enjoyed our short time together. The next time I'll make sure I'm free all day. I'm definitely going to keep you busy."

"Sounds good and I look forward to our next meeting. Have an enjoyable evening," Brandi said.

"You too and try not to work too hard, you'll age faster."

"Okay, I'll speak to you in a couple of days."

After dropping Chase off, Brandi arrived at her house around 8 p.m. When she walked through the front door, all she saw was a house filled with moving crates, boxes and clutter everywhere. *I know I should be packing but that's not going to happen tonight. I had a long day and I'm not up for it.*

It wasn't just the packing that Brandi wasn't in the mood for; she really wasn't up for being home alone tonight. Over the past couple of weeks it appeared as though the only time she saw her husband was in the mornings when he was getting ready for work. Lately Derick had been working extremely long hours and throughout the weekends. By the time he got home, it was so late that Brandi would already be in bed. They had an occasional conversation through the day but they hadn't spent much time together.

I'm not going to watch that DVD that I got from Red Box, nor am I sitting in the house tonight. Who's most likely to go out with me tonight? Bailey's probably spending time with her family. Deion's probably doing God knows what. Kya's probably catering an event or too tired from catering an event. Maybe if she isn't too exhausted she'll hang out with me. Ultimately, the only way I'll find out is to call and ask.

"Hi, sweetie, how are you?" Brandi asked.

"I'm good," Kya said.

"What are you doing tonight?"

"Nothing much, just hanging around the house with Lexi."

"Did you cook?"

"Girl, no not tonight, I didn't feel like cooking tonight. I ordered some food from the carry-out. With the amount of money I paid for the food I could have gone to the grocery store and spent less money on the ingredients. These carry-outs are getting ridiculous with their prices. Since the recession, they've raised the price of the food by $2.00 per item. The minimum delivery amount is no longer $10.00, it's now $20.00. They also add in tips and gratuity as if they're a restaurant. Girl, when they told me the amount for my four items, I said what the fuck? Clearly you must have added someone else's order to mine."

"But why didn't you cancel your order. Did you still get the food?" Brandi asked.

"Yes, I ordered the food anyway and it was delicious. It was an expensive order but it was worth it, I really and truly did not want to go back out. Lexi wanted to go to Ruby Tuesday's but I told her wait until later on. Then she asked if we were still going out because she no longer felt like it. Like she was going to be the one driving and fighting through traffic. I just looked at that damn girl and shook my damn head. Then I placed an order for the carry-out. So now I have leftovers for my midnight snack. But anyway, what's up with you, mama? What have you been up to lately?" Kya asked.

"Nothing much, I just got home from work. All I've been doing lately is working and going to church. I'm also trying to get ready for us to move in a couple of weeks."

"We told you we would come over and help you. But you said no. You didn't need the help."

"I know, we really don't have a whole lot to do. I'm donating the majority of our stuff to the Salvation Army. It's so time consuming because I'm going through everything and discarding a lot of stuff."

"Whether here or there, we still can help."

"Now that I think about it, if I had some help I might have finished by now. Maybe you and the girls can come over next week," Brandi said.

"We can pack, talk shit, and order something to eat. It'll be fun. The four of us always have a great time together."

"So, tell me more about the foundation that you'd like to start. What type of foundation will it be? Have you already done all of the research and started your business plan?"

"I've done some research. I believe in my heart this is what I'm supposed to do with my life. Help people. I'd like to help teenage girls with issues like: bullying, good health, obesity, self-esteem, preparation for womanhood, sex education, proper etiquette, hygiene, how to be a lady, etc. I also want to be able to provide them with mentors. I feel like a lot of teen girls from the inner city go in the wrong direction because they don't have the right people in their corner and to guide them. Or should I say they have the wrong people in their corner? Anyway, I feel like this is my way of giving back."

"So does that mean you're going to quit your job?"

"I'll probably quit my job but not in the beginning. I would love to put my undivided attention and time into my foundation."

"That's great, Brandi. I'm so proud of you. You know you'll be rewarded greatly for all of your selflessness."

"I'm not doing this because I want to be rewarded. Since I was younger I always wanted to help other people. Despite some of the things that I've been through I've been so blessed. Therefore, I know that I need to be a blessing to others. I may not have a whole lot but I have more than most people."

"You're such a good person, I need to be more like you when I grow up. I really think this foundation is a fabulous idea," Kya said.

"Kya you're a good person too. You do a lot for your friends and for people in general. I hope you know that God has something great in store for you."

"I hope so," Kya said.

"Even though you can be a little crazy, you have a good heart," Brandi said teasingly.

Kya chuckled and said, "Crazy is my middle name. What can I do to help you?" she added. "I would definitely love to help you. I have two card indexes on my desk with contacts that may be of some assistance to you. You're more than welcome to go through them and pull some names. Between me, Bailey and Deion I'm sure we can hook you up with some of the right contacts. I briefly spoken to Bailey about your idea. She is looking forward to sitting and chatting about your foundation."

"She and I are going to a fundraiser on Saturday, I was going to chat with her then."

"Bailey hasn't called you?"

"No, why?" Brandi asked.

"She won't be able to go to the event with you. It's Ty's birthday and she's having a sleepover."

"The event must have slipped her mind. I'll find someone else to go in her place."

"The event didn't slip her mind, Ty's sleepover slipped her mind. She was all prepared to go to the event with you," Kya said.

"It's so weird how Bailey forgot about the sleepover but remembered the event. That girl is working too hard. She needs a break or a vacation."

"Yes, that's Bailey. She's going to work herself to death. She definitely needs to slow down. Don't worry about finding someone to go in her place, I volunteered."

"And you're going?"

"Of course I am."

"I guess I'll have to find another time to chat with her."

"You should give her a call or stop by. She's been home for the past couple of days," Kya said.

"Is she sick or something? That's not like her to take time off."

"She had some things she needed to take care of. But she's definitely looking forward to having that conversation with you."

"Okay, well I'll call her to see if I can stop by tomorrow," Brandi said.

"Where are you getting the start-up money? Are you taking on loans or using your own money or do you plan on getting it all from Bailey and Noah?"

"That part, I really need to think about a little more. Since we purchased the new house in Fort Washington, I no longer have the start-up funds. My savings account is on B.E., beyond empty. Derick strongly suggests not acquiring any more loans right now. Especially since we just got the new house."

"But your man works at a bank. I know there are some resources or start-up funding he can tap into," Kya said.

"He suggested waiting for a little while."

"That doesn't make much sense to me, but it is what it is. Like I said before, I guess you have no other choice but to ask Bailey. She's the only person that I know besides a bank that got money coming out of the ass."

"I know Bailey is really my only option at this point. I also thought about asking my mother. But the shaky relationship I have with my mother means that's not a choice. If you ask her for anything she wants to know why you need the money, when you intend paying it back and why you're asking her for the loan. Then she waits about a week or two and calls and asks more questions. So, to avoid going through an interrogation and the third degree with my mother, Bailey sounds like the better choice after all. I know I would have to pay Bailey back but right now I don't want to bite off more than I can chew. Even though it'll be a foundation, I know I could possibly get government grants and funding. But right now I'm worried more about the start-up capital. Another thing I could do after we're somewhat established is do direct mail campaigns and have fundraising events to solicit donations."

"I think fundraising, financial solicitations and direct mail campaigns are a good start. Do you think you could make enough money to fund your services and programs? I know it's a good cause and a lot of individuals and corporations would be more than happy to donate. I don't want you always worrying about the money part of it. You're going to have enough on your plate. You never know, maybe people would make significantly large donations. A loan from Bailey and possible grants could keep you afloat for a long time if not indefinitely," Kya said.

"You're right and it's worth a shot. I wish my husband was as supportive of my idea as you."

"Once you have all the pieces together he'll jump on the bandwagon. Most people are like that when you present business ideas and ventures to them. I'm sure he knows this isn't some fly-by-night idea. You never know how something is going to work out unless you try. People might have a lot to say but until you put your plan into action you'll never know. Don't let anyone even attempt to knock your idea out of the box or steal your shine. If this is what God is leading you to do, then that's all the support you need."

"I'm being very optimistic and I know everything will work out for the best," Brandi said.

"If you decide to have a gala, I'd be more than happy to cater the event for you," Kya said.

"What? Are you kidding me? That would be very expensive and I can't ask you to do that."

"You didn't ask, I offered, and there's a difference between the two. Besides, what kind of friend would I be if I didn't help you?"

"Kya, I really appreciate that but the costs of the food and your time would be too much to ask. The food alone would be a major expense."

"Girl, don't worry about it. I'll hire additional staff and everything will be fine. You'll have one banging-ass event."

"Wow, I don't know what to say. Thank you so much and I'm going to pay you back, I promise."

"Girl, really, it's nothing and this is my way of giving back. Now, shut your ass up talking to me about nothing."

"Thank God for good friends. I love you, girl," Brandi said.

"I love you more. But I'm going to suggest that you hurry up and speak to Bailey. You know that Bailey loves to help others, especially when it's for a good cause."

"Will do."

"What do you have planned for this evening?" Kya asked.

"I actually called you to see if you wanted to go out tonight. I'm tired of sitting in the house and I'm not in the mood to pack, which means I'll be sitting in the house bored out of my mind."

"Go out? You? Are you serious? Not the church lady—you never want to go out!"

"Girl, I'm human and I'm far from being perfect. I could definitely use a diamond martini right about now."

"Where's Derick?" Kya asked.

"He's at work."

"He's at work at 8:30 at night? I thought banks closed at 5 or 6 p.m. I guess that's the price you pay for such a demanding job."

"Derick really hasn't gone into specifics. He keeps telling me they're making lots of changes."

"Oh, okay, I guess he gotta do what he gotta do. Are you sure everything's alright over there? You sound kind of sad today," Kya said.

"Yes. Everything's good. I guess I'm just tired and a little concerned about my husband. But, like you said, he's doing what needs to be done. But I feel so bad for him because he's always tired and it seems like he's working around the clock. Some nights by the time he gets home it's the next day before you know it. A lot of the time, after he takes off his clothes, eats dinner and showers, all he wants to do is go to sleep. I know he's burning the candle at both ends, I wish I could ease the burden. But there's nothing I can do as far as his work goes. Not only is he exhausted but also stressed and cranky lately."

"I hope everything's okay with his job and they're not about to do layoffs. If that's the case no wonder he's been stressed out and cranky."

"I totally understand but I wish he didn't have to work so much. I barely get to spend time with my man. That's why I've taken the lead on the moving and packing situation. I know he doesn't have the strength, time or energy. I try to deal with stuff pertaining to home."

"And he's not saying anything. I find that weird. Most people talk about the BS of the job as well as their annoying co-workers. Perhaps he doesn't want to worry and stress you."

"I can respect that but I think I'm a little overwhelmed too."

"Have you found tenants for your house?" Kya asked.

"I'm trying my best to find tenants. I don't want to put just anyone in the house. I've been getting a lot of calls but I can't show this house right now because it's a mess. I should have waited to list it until after we'd moved and had a chance to do some work and renovations," Brandi said.

"Maybe you can pull the listing, and when the house is done being renovated, relist it."

"You know what, Kya, I don't know why I didn't think of that. I'll do that first thing in the morning. Girl, I really have to start getting some of this stuff off my plate."

"Maybe the two of you should just go on a damn getaway. A couple of days away will make a hell of a difference,"

"You may be right, a getaway is probably what we need. But I'm going to have my own getaway soon. We have the spa trip coming up. Derick is too busy to do anything or go anywhere these days."

"By the time we get back from the spa you'll feel refreshed and renewed," Kya said.

"I sure will. I'm looking forward to that trip. I've already packed my bags."

Kya laughed and said, "You sound like me, my bags have been sitting at my front door for weeks now."

"You know what, Kya, we've managed to get on another topic and you still haven't answered my question. Remember, the purpose of this call was to see if want to go out tonight or am I going to have to watch *Breakfast at Tiffany's*?"

"Even though I'm tired I'd love to go out with you. I most certainly don't want to watch *Breakfast at Tiffany's* again but that's my relaxation movie of choice. Just know the only reason I'm going is because you rarely want to go out. First, I need to find a sitter for Lexi. Keep your fingers crossed, I'm going to see if my sister can keep her tonight," Kya said.

"I thought you had a babysitter on speed dial?"

"I do but she's studying this week for finals or something. Hopefully, my sister will be able to watch Lexi. Let me get her, get me and Lexi ready, then I'll be ready to go."

"All right. Call me and let me know."

"I'll call back in a few."

As Kya dialed her sister's number, she also started packing Lexi's overnight bag. "Hey sis, what are you doing?"

"Hey, Kya, what do you want now?" Karen asked.

"Can you watch Lexi tonight?" Kya asked.

"No problemo, do you want me to come over?"

"That will be good."

"I'm down the street from your house. I'll be there in a couple of minutes. Did you cook?"

"Nope."

"Let me stop and get something from Popeye's, then I'll be there. I'll see you in twenty minutes."

Kya called Brandi and said, "It's a go. My sister will be here in a couple of minutes. I'm going to get in the shower then slip something on."

"I also have to shower and get dressed. I can be at your house in about an hour or hour and a half," Brandi said.

"Okay, see you when you get here. By the way, if no one answers the door use your key."

"Okay, see you soon."

After getting off the phone with Kya, Brandi called Derick and, much to her surprise, he answered on the first ring.

"Hello, my love, what are you doing?"

"Is that a rhetorical question or are you being funny? I'm trying to get some paperwork done," Derick said.

"Derick, it was actually a rhetorical question. I know you're busy. I was trying to lighten the mood a little. Are you going to be home soon?"

"In all likelihood I doubt it. Maybe another couple of hours or so if I can finish up what I'm doing, why?"

"I was going to go out with Kya," Brandi said.

"Going out with Kya for what, and where are you going?" Derick asked.

"I don't know where we're going, but I want to go and have a drink. I'm a little tired of sitting at home like an old maid and working like a Hebrew slave. I'm twenty nine not ninety nine."

"I know how old you are, but you never want to go out. Especially to a club," Derick said.

"I know but it's a first time for everything, I'm bored."

"Baby, there's plenty of stuff around the house that you could be doing. We only have about three more weeks to move into the new house and it doesn't appear as though you've made any progress."

Brandi chuckled. "A lot of work *I* could be doing, but what about us? There's no I in team, and the last time I checked we're a team. But it seems like you're married to your job these days. That's part of the reason why I've taken over this moving preparation. I work a full-time, demanding job just like you do. Not to mention the majority of my evenings are spent at the church. I guess if I wasn't the one packing this stuff up then we wouldn't have made as much progress as we did. But I guess you haven't noticed," Brandi said.

"Look, sweetheart, right now is definitely not the time for this. The sooner I finish up here, the sooner I can get home to you."

"Okay, fine. Lately whenever I need to talk to you about anything pertaining to our relationship, the house or anything else, it's never the right time. But whatever, I really didn't call to distract you from your work or get on your nerves. I was just calling to let you know that I'm going out."

"Listen, have a good time with your girlfriend and be careful out there," Derick said.

"Yeah, I sure will."

Her mood was a little altered when she hung up, but she refused to sit in the house. She finished getting ready and left for Kya's house.

By the time Brandi arrived at Kya's, Kya really wasn't in the mood for the club scene and she suggested that they go to the movies or to the café. As much as Brandi wanted a diamond martini she decided a cup of tea or a latte would suffice.

"Thanks for coming out with me, girl. I really needed to get out of that house. It felt like the walls were closing in on me," Brandi said.

"Anytime. I know you have a lot on your plate right now. Is this move the reason you've been a little distant lately?"

"Kya, not only do I have a lot on my plate but also a lot on my mind as well."

"I knew something was wrong but you're different from Bailey, Deion and I. We tend to wear our feelings on our sleeves and talk about whatever's bothering us. Not you, you tend to back away and shut down when something's going on. For that reason I didn't want be intrusive. I knew sooner or later you'd discuss whatever's bothering you," Kya said.

"There are some things that I've been holding inside. Besides a couple of my relatives, Derick is the only other person that knows. For weeks I've been trying to talk to him but he's always working so I hold it all in."

"It's not good to hold everything in, you have to talk to somebody, Brandi."

"I've been walking around for years with all of this stuff, I just didn't know how to release it," Brandi said.

"You know, it's okay to be vulnerable sometimes. No one would think any less of you because of your problems or whatever the case may be."

Brandi looked at Kya with tears in her eyes and said, "I just don't know where to begin."

"What's wrong?" Kya asked.

"I really don't know where to start."

"If you open your mouth the words will come out."

As tear fell down Brandi's cheek, she looked at Kya and said, "I was molested by my father from the age of ten to sixteen. Everything was just swept under the rug and I've never really healed from that."

Kya's mouth dropped open and then she asked, "The pastor of the church?"

"No, no, no, he's not my biological father, he's my stepfather," Brandi said.

"I never knew that."

"Throughout all these years I never went to therapy or talked to anyone. I guess you can say the issue went unresolved. I try to deal with it the best way I can."

"Does your mother know?" Kya asked.

"I've never said anything to my mother about it and she's never said anything to me either. I know she had to be aware of it, though," Brandi said.

"How can you be so sure that she knew? What type of mother would knowingly let something like that happen to her child?"

"My mother. She had to have had an idea of what was happening. I don't understand why she never did anything to stop it."

"Sweetie, I wasn't there and I'm so sorry this happened to you. I can't grasp how you can be so sure that she knew. Nor can I justify why she did nothing about it," Kya said.

"When I turned seventeen, I decided that I couldn't take it anymore. I called my aunt and asked her if I could come and live with her. My aunt didn't ask any questions. All she said was, "Pack your shit and I'm on my way." After my aunt and I got all of my belongings into the car, my mother came up to me, hugged me and whispered in my ear, "Baby I'm sorry, please forgive me." I pulled away from her and got into the car. That's how I know with all certainty that she knew."

Tears flowed from Kya's eyes as she said, "I'm sorry this happened to you. You're a good person and you didn't deserve that abuse." As Brandi pulled some tissue out of her purse Kya added, "I bet she sits on the front pew of the church acting like she's holier than thou."

"Kya, besides my aunt, the women in my family are really screwed up. I don't totally blame them, I blame my grandmother. It was the way that she raised those five girls. I don't know how my aunt escaped the madness but she's totally different from my grandmother, mother and other aunts. My aunt would tell me stories of her childhood and the things that my grandmother would say to her. She said my grandmother always instilled in her daughters that a black man has got the weight of the world riding on his shoulders and sometimes you just got to let him be. A woman needs a man to survive, without a man she just ain't shit, it's the man that holds everything together. She also instilled within her daughters that a woman gotta know her place in the relationship, and that's behind the man. It's all right for men to cheat here and there but she never strays away from home, you just have to deal with it and stand behind your man. So, I'm sure with those types of horrible family morals, and even with her suspicion of the molestation taking place, my mother believed that she had to stay no matter what. If my father hadn't left my mother, she'd still be with him till this day."

"Brandi, forgive me for what I'm about to say, and excuse my language but your grandmother is ignant as shit! Not ignorant, downright ignant! No wonder your family's all fucked up. I can't even fathom that someone actually believed all of that bullshit. Girl, I just can't believe her crazy ass raised her children like that."

"It's not like I talk about my family a lot. If I hadn't moved to live with my aunt I'd be a worse mess than I already am," Brandi said.

"Is your grandmother still alive?" Kya asked.

"Yes she is. She calls me once in a blue moon. She never has any real conversation and she only calls for money. If I tell her I don't have any money then she'll say just buy me a bottle since you don't want to give me the money."

"Clearly grannie got some issues going on. What's sad is that she's been like that her entire life. I guess she's set in her ways and she'll never change."

"I actually think she gets worse the older she gets," Brandi said.

"As far as the situation goes with your dad, for you, it's never too late to get the help you need. I have a client that's a therapist, I'll call her tomorrow and schedule you an appointment."

"I never said anything because I was so embarrassed, and I thought it was my fault," Brandi said.

"Don't say that. It wasn't your fault and you're going to get help, sweetie. Does your brother know?"

"No, I never mentioned it to him. He just assumes that I resented our mom because of dad leaving. I've never corrected him and left it at that. He was very young when it happened and once he got older I never had the nerve to tell him."

"In due time you'll be able to tell your brother. He's not going to love you any less," Kya said.

"To this day I still have nightmares. Sometimes I don't want to go to sleep because I'm so afraid," Brandi said.

"If there is ever a time that you need to talk, you call me. Any time day or night. I'm here for you, sweetie. Not only me but you have Bailey and Deion too. We're girls and we look out for each other, you know that."

"That means so much to me. Besides you and the girls, the only real family that I have is my aunt, my brother and Derick."

"Whatever happened to that son-of-a-bitch father of yours?" Kya asked.

"From what I was told he left home for work one day and never returned. A couple of years later my mother was served divorce papers. Apparently he met someone younger and wanted to marry her."

"Ain't that some shit. She lost her husband and her child. The man that she stood beside, or behind all of those years just left her ass. Karma is a bitch but I guess she's happy now. I bet her conscience is eating her ass up. There's no way possible she sleeps peacefully at night. She needs help too, maybe she'll consider going to therapy with you."

"She still had my brother to take care of so she couldn't give up. I guess she had to do what she had to do, in order to survive. We've never really had a mom-and-daughter type of relationship. We don't see each other much and we definitely don't talk that much. My stepfather occasionally calls and invites us to dinner, his church, or other events but we never go. The closer I got to God, the more I realized that I had to forgive her and I did. I know I have a lot of healing to do. One day I'll be able to move on but I'm not ready for family vacations just yet," Brandi said jokingly.

"Thank you for sharing with me, I know that took a lot of courage. Remember from now on the key word is healing. It may be a little rocky in the beginning but you can do it. You won't have to take this journey on your own. You have a group of supportive people in your corner and we love you dearly," Kya said.

"Just by talking and sharing this with you I feel like a weight's been lifted off my shoulders. I feel like I can breathe again."

"I don't mean to change the subject but Bailey's going to kick ya ass. She's going to be furious."

"I know, I should have told all of you before. But I will share with Bailey and Deion as well."

"Would you like to order another cup of tea or get something to eat?" Kya asked.

"It's getting late, I think I should be getting home," Brandi said.

"You're right, time is really going quick. I almost forgot you have to drop me off. So we should get out of here." As they both got up from the table, Kya grabbed Brandi and gave her a hug.

"Thanks girl, for listening," Brandi said.

"No, thank you for sharing."

A couple of minutes later, as Brandi pulled in front of Kya's house, Kya said, "If for any reason you need to talk, call me and it doesn't matter what time it is. Drive carefully and get home safe."

"Okay, I'm going to go home and do a little packing before I go to bed. I'll give you a call in the morning."

Once Brandi arrived home she noticed that Derick had been home, showered and changed. *Maybe he went out to grab something to eat,* Brandi thought. After she changed into her comfy pajamas she poured a glass of wine then started packing. She decided to call Derick again. His phone rang three times then went to voicemail.

"Sweetie, I'm home. I see that you've been here, but left again. Where are you? Call me," Brandi said. *I'm up like I have nowhere to go in the morning. Geesh, I really could use a day off. I'll try to wait up for Derick to get home before I go to bed.* Shortly thereafter the telephone rang.

"Hey, baby, I saw that you called," Derick said.

"Yes I did. Where are you?"

"I ran out to pick me up something to eat. I'll be home in a few minutes."

"I was wondering if you were still in the office, it's 11:45 p.m.," Brandi said.

"No, I left the office a while ago. I'm not far from the house, I'll see you soon."

"Okay."

Brandi continued packing as she waited for Derick to come home. An hour later and he still hadn't arrived, so Brandi decided to get into bed. *Hopefully I'll be awake when he gets in, I really need to talk to him.* By the time Brandi placed her head on the pillow, she heard Derick coming up the steps to the bedroom.

A couple of seconds later he came into the bedroom and said, "It's really a mess down there. You have got to do something with all of that shit. I almost tripped and fell over one of those crates or boxes, or whatever the hell you have in the middle of the floor."

"If you haven't noticed we're in the process of moving. And I'm trying to pack up all of this stuff as fast as I can. Unfortunately, I'm only one person," Brandi said.

"Why haven't your girlfriends helped?" Derick asked.

"How does it look with my friends helping and you haven't lifted a darn finger? I don't feel right asking them. Why can't you help? This is your house and your belongings too. You can't expect for everyone else to do your job."

"Brandi, I'm a little too busy to be packing."

As Derick undressed, Brandi sat up in the bed.

"Derick, I can't remember the last time that we actually had sex. If I'm not mistaken it's been almost a month since the last time you touched me. You don't even kiss me anymore."

"Here we go with this again. I don't feel like talking about this right now."

"You never want to discuss anything."

"Brandi, what is it that you feel like you need to discuss? Get it all out tonight because I'm tired of you nagging me. I also get tired of hearing the same shit over and over."

"You can start by answering the question," Brandi said.

"We haven't had sex lately because by the time I get home from work I'm too tired. The majority of the time, when I get home you're already asleep and I don't want to disturb you."

"There are other times that we can have sex. We're not only limited to sex at night. We can have sex during the day, in the middle of the afternoon, and on the weekends. It's whenever the mood hits you. There are twenty four hours in a day. You make time for whatever or whomever else that you want to. When we first got married we were having sex all of the time."

"That was before I became branch manager of the bank. My schedule was very different then. I thought you understood that," Derick said.

"I've understood everything that you've said for the past several weeks, sometimes it feels like you shut me out and are pushing me away. Are you not attracted to me? Is it because I've gained a little weight and I've gotten fat?" Brandi asked.

Derick sat next to Brandi on the bed and said, "I haven't noticed that you've gained any weight. You still look the same to me. When we started dating you were a size twelve and the last time I checked you're still a size twelve. Please tell me how that's fat. It's all in your head. What's up with you? Why is it that every time you do a self-evaluation you make the problem my fault?"

"I'm just trying to figure out what's wrong with us."

"There's nothing wrong with us. I just work a lot that's all. Brandi, I have other shit on my mind these days besides fucking you!" Derick yelled.

"I can't believe you just said that to me. Am I not worthy of you fucking me?"

"I didn't mean to say that."

"Well, you did, and it's a little too late to take it back," Brandi said.

"All you manage to talk about is what I don't do. If you're not getting what you need from me, then leave."

"You're right, we don't have a problem, *you* do. I don't know what's going on with you but something's going on. I would hate to think that your job is starting to affect our marriage."

"My job isn't affecting our marriage, you're just tripping or something. You've been really emotional lately. Maybe you should talk to someone about your problems," Derick said.

"For weeks I've been trying to talk to *you* about my problems. About our problems. But I guess there are more pertinent things that you're worried about."

"I don't have any problems, this is all in your head. You're not happy with your life that's your problem not mine."

"Derick, I do all I can for our marriage. But if I listen to you, I don't do a damn thing. You make it seem like my contributions to our marriage and household are undersized and insignificant. Like all of the responsibilities should fall on me."

"What problems do we have?"

"Financial, communication, time, should I go on?"

"Again, I'm good. You need to stop telling our business to your girlfriends. They're filling your head with this nonsense. The more y'all hang out the more foolishness you come up with. Brandi we don't have any problems. Financial, you said, are the bills getting paid?"

"I don't discuss these issues with my girlfriends. Yes, I agree the bills are getting paid: because I'm paying all of them. The only bill that you've paid within a year around here is your car note. You claimed that you were saving your money for the new house and still haven't put any money into it. But I haven't complained. I still pay the bills and do what I can for the house. I keep going and I keep pressing. Hoping the day will come for you to act like you appreciate me and the things that I do."

"Okay, so you've paid a few bills. Big deal. You're the big time realtor, you can handle it. I simply asked you last year to give me time to save more money. So I can take care of some things."

"If I'm not mistaken, it was the commission of my last three sales that got us into the new house. I'm literally busting my butt so we can stay afloat and I need help. You're my husband and I shouldn't have to ask for help to pay *our* bills," Brandi said.

"Yes and I know that. I do what I can when I can. My money is tied up right now. How many times are you going to throw that in my face? You're the one that wanted a larger house. I'm content with this house. What's your point?" Derick asked.

"My point is I would like for you to take time to help me. Not only that, I would love for you to spend some time with me. I would love for you to hold me, and touch me the way you used to. It would be nice if you would at least make love to me from time to time."

"After the smoke clears on my job, you'll have me all to yourself. As far as the bills, I'll help as soon as I can. I've already said that."

"In other words, once everything is okay on your job then you'll fuck me. Then you'll reconvene with your husbandly duties and assisting financially in our household. But everything in our personal life is dependent on your job."

"Yes. That's an accurate statement."

"I thought during the fourth year of our marriage we were going to have a baby. I guess that'll have to wait too," Brandi said.

"We can't afford a baby right now. I think we should wait a little while longer."

"No matter what I ask you, that's always your response. It's almost like you're programmed to say that one sentence. Why don't we have any money, when we're living off of my income? It's like you woke up one day and decided to no longer pay bills. Ah, I'm sorry you did pay your car note this year."

"Maybe if you were a little understanding things would work out in your favor," Derick said.

"I've been extremely understanding. But why does everything have to be one-sided? I understand wholeheartedly that you're working extremely hard but so am I."

"It's not always going to be like this. I anticipate that things will be changing significantly within the next couple of months. Trust me."

"From the time we started dating up until a few months ago you were totally different. You were supportive, you were attentive to me and my needs, you listened and you cared about me and my well-being and you did things around the house. Now you're just focused exclusively on you and your job. What type of partnership is this?" Brandi asked.

"It's me doing what I need to for us and our family. We have to work for whatever we want. We can't just do what we want nor do we have money like Bailey and Noah."

"Bailey and Noah go to work every day like we do. Remember, no one gave them anything. Whatever they have, they worked for it, together and as a team. Whenever we have a conversation about money you always bring the two of them up. They don't have anything to do with this. But I'm glad you mentioned them, I'm going to borrow some money from them."

"I don't know how much wine you were drinking, I don't know what you were smoking, but you've lost your goddamn mind. Why do you need to borrow money from them?" Derick asked.

"I need the money to start my foundation and I know they'll help."

"No. You can't borrow that kind of money from them. I can't let you do that. You know how I feel about shit like that. I don't want them in my business."

"Well, Derick, I don't have any other choice. I really want to start this foundation but I don't have the means to do so. It's not like I'm asking them to give me the money, I'm going to pay them back."

"You heard what I said. Do not ask Noah and Bailey for shit. Money can ruin a friendship. What if you can't pay it back when it's expected, then what?"

"Noah and Bailey aren't like that. I'll continue to sell real estate, and that way I can pay them back. Eventually I'll quit my job so I can focus more on the foundation."

"Quit your job! Have you lost your damn mind? We're a double-income family, not one!" Derick yelled.

"Lately, we've been a one-income family because you've decided to save everything you make. I haven't lost my mind but eventually I'll quit my job."

"I think we need to talk about this a little more. I'm tired and you're talking crazy. Let's talk about this over the weekend."

"No, let's talk about this now," Brandi said.

"Brandi, we can't afford for you to quit your job. We just bought a new house, you want a baby, and you want to start a foundation. We have to save for all of that first."

"How about we use some of the money that you've been saving?"

"Hell, no. That money is tied up right now."

"Tied up in what?" Brandi asked.

"Listen, stop asking me about that money. We don't have the funds to do all of this crap and we need to wait until the right time. Now isn't the right time."

"I disagree with you. We can do it all and have it all. Remember, anything is possible with God. I prayed about it, I claimed it, and now it's time for me to put my plan into action. If I make one step God will make two. Everything will work out. You just need to work your faith," Brandi said.

"I'm working my faith but you want to do too much too soon," Derick said.

"Who are you to put a timeframe on when I should do things? Derick, you're my husband and I love you but I serve God. This wasn't placed in my spirit for nothing. How do you know this isn't God's will for me? You act like you're afraid to share me with the rest of the world. I'm your wife but I still have to carry out God's plan and purpose for my life. The way I am now is the way that I was before you met me, and when you married me."

"Yes I know that, but you're not being realistic. I'm just asking you to be patient and to wait. Why are you rushing into everything? We haven't discussed this foundation that you want to start."

"Maybe that's because every time I bring it up you don't want to talk about it."

"Sweetheart, there's a lot going on with my job right now. I don't know if I'll still have a job next week or not. I didn't want you to worry so I didn't say anything. That's the reason I keep asking you to wait," Derick said.

"I wish you'd have said something sooner. But I'm not worried. I know who my provider is. I know who I serve. God is good all of the time and I trust in his timing. There is nothing that mankind can say or do to me. Just pray and give it to God. Whatever is His will, Derick, not mine or yours," Brandi said.

"Yes I know."

"He doesn't work according to your time. He works according to His time."

"After we bought the new house I started stressing a little bit. I was hoping that we didn't get in over our heads. I don't know the fate of the bank, whether we're shutting the doors or if we're merging with another bank. Instead of trying to do everything at one time, do it little by little," Derick said.

"I hear you, and I hear your concerns, but I'm going to move forward with the foundation. I don't know what will happen if I don't try. I don't know about you but I walk by faith and not by sight. I hope that you'll support me with my dream of starting the foundation."

"You're being stubborn and you're not listening to me. Good luck with your foundation but when it fails, don't say a damn thing to me. I tried to warn you. I'm tired and I'm going to sleep now."

"My foundation will be prosperous and successful. I can see now that I won't have your encouragement. But that's fine, I'm still moving forward with my plans. Goodnight," Brandi said.

The following morning, when Brandi awoke she realized that Derick had already left for the office. As she got ready for work she reflected over the conversation the night before. She couldn't pinpoint why Derick was acting strangely lately. She decided to try and smooth things out by surprising Derick and taking him to lunch. She had an appointment at noon, but she knew that Derick normally ate lunch at 2 p.m. That would give her just enough time to get to the bank before Derick left.

Before I leave the house I need to call Bailey. I really need to start putting everything together for this foundation. After Brandi located the cordless phone, she called Bailey at home.

"Hello," Brandi said.

"Hey Brandi, how are you?" Noah asked.

"I'm good, is your wife around?" Brandi asked.

"She's in the shower. I'll tell her to give you a call as soon as she gets out."

"Okay. How's everything with you?"

"Everything's good, I can't complain."

"That's good. Can you tell Bailey to call me at home? I'll be here for another thirty minutes."

"Okay."

While Brandi waited for Bailey's call, she made herself a cup of coffee. As she sat at the kitchen table, she looked at her calendar for the next couple of days. *Since I don't have anyone scheduled after today, I'm going to take the next couple of days off. Besides packing I can take care of some of the tedious tasks on my to-do lists. I hope within the next couple of days I can sit down and talk with Noah and Bailey. I'm really eager to get this foundation started and I'm going to need some help. I hope Derick will change his mind. Maybe once I present my business plan to him he'll feel differently about the foundation.*

As Brandi started jotting down her notes and tasks for the foundation, the phone rang.

"Good morning, Ms. Lady," Bailey said.

"Good morning," Brandi said.

"How the hell are you?"

"I'm good, I'm just trying to make it."

"I know what you mean. So what's up?" Bailey asked.

"I wanted to sit down and talk to you as well as pick your brain," Brandi said.

"Is this pertaining to your foundation?"

"Yes, it is."

"Kya mentioned to me that you wanted to start it. She told me I should expect your call."

"Yes. This is sort of a dream of mine. The only thing is, I want to get things started right away. Are you available this week?"

"Yes, ma'am. I've taken a couple of days off. Would you like to swing by my house today so we can discuss starting your business?" Bailey asked.

"Oh, okay. I can stop by this afternoon after I leave work."

"Sounds good. We can figure out how much money you'll need to get things started. Then we can go from there. Have you already written your business plan?"

"No, not yet. I don't even know where to start with a business plan. That's like a foreign language to me."

"Don't worry about it. I have the perfect person that can help you with this process. He actually works for me," Bailey said.

"I really appreciate that. I think I'm going to need all the help I can get."

"And you'll have all the help you need."

"I have to get out of here so I won't be late. But I'll give you a call when I'm on my way."

"Okay, have a wonderful day and I look forward to seeing you this afternoon."

Shortly after Brandi got off the phone with Bailey she left for work. As she drove through the city she couldn't help but think about Derick. She wondered if the stress from his job was the reason he was acting differently. She wanted to call and share the news with him that the plans for her foundation were happening. Then she remembered that he wasn't supportive or happy about her new endeavors. *I'm hoping that Kya was right about what she said last night. Once Derick knows all the information regarding the foundation then his attitude will change and he'll jump on the bandwagon. I hate that everyone else is so excited and supportive but he isn't. The only thing I can do for my husband is to pray for him. Hopefully and prayerfully everything will work out for the best with his job. That will be a tremendous burden lifted from his shoulders. And we need to do whatever has to be done in order to reignite the spark in our marriage.*

Brandi arrived at the office earlier than usual. After the morning staff meeting she sped through her paperwork and calls; she was thrilled about surprising Derick at his office with lunch. Shortly after noon Brandi left her office and stopped to buy the lunch. En route she called Derick's phone to find out his schedule for the afternoon. The first time she called, his phone went to voicemail. On her second attempt Derick answered.

"Hey, what are you doing?" Brandi asked.

"I'm working. What else would I be doing?" Derick asked. Brandi could hear the irritation in Derick's voice and thought maybe he was having a bad day.

"I was just calling to see what your schedule's like this afternoon."

"I have a couple of meetings. Why?"

"No reason, just asking. What time does your meeting start?"

"The first one for the afternoon starts at 2 p.m. Why are you asking so many questions?"

"Because that's the only way to know anything—I have to ask. Well, I'll let you get back to work. Give me a call later on or whenever time permits."

"Okay," Derick said.

A couple of minutes later, Brandi pulled into the parking lot of Derick's bank. As she drove around the lot she didn't see Derick's car. *I hope I didn't miss him and he's not at lunch. I should have told him I was on my way here.*

After Brandi gathered the food that she had purchased from Panera Bread, she went inside the bank. Since it was early afternoon, it was crowded. Brandi proceeded to the back of the bank where the offices were located. As she walked down the hall she ran into one of Derick's co-workers.

"Hello, John," Brandi said.

"Hello Brandi. What are you doing here?" John asked.

"I came to surprise Derick with lunch."

"Derick isn't in the office today. He called this morning and said that he wasn't feeling well."

Without looking unaware, Brandi acted as if she had forgotten.

"Oh, that's right. I don't know what I was thinking. I have a lot going on these days. I don't how I got sidetracked and let that slip my mind. I guess I better get home to that sick husband of mine."

"Yeah, you better. He sounded really bad when I spoke to him earlier. Keep us informed about how he's doing," John said.

"I sure will."

Before Brandi got to her car she pulled out her phone and called her house. *Okay maybe I'm losing my mind. I spoke to Derick a couple of minutes ago and he said he was at work. I know I'm not crazy and he did say that.* Brandi then tried calling Derick on his own phone. When it was answered, a male voice she didn't recognize said, "Mr. Knight's office, how may I help you?"

"Hello," Brandi said.

"Hello, how may I help you?"

"I must have dialed the wrong number, I'm sorry," Brandi said as she hung up. A couple of seconds later she called Derick's phone again, but this time no answer. Brandi immediately became distressed, confused and worried. She didn't know if Derick was okay or if he had lost his phone. *He couldn't have lost his phone. Whoever answered the phone made reference to my last name. I don't know what the hell is going on. Instead of going back to the office I'm going home to see if he's there. Maybe he got hurt and someone answered his phone on his behalf.*

As Brandi drove to her house she kept calling home and Derick's phone. She was unsuccessful in contacting him. This made her more worried. As she tried to focus on the road, she didn't want to think the worst but couldn't help it. *I hope he's all right and he wasn't in an accident or something.*

By the time Brandi got home she had tried to calm herself down. *Maybe I'm overreacting. Let me get myself together.* As Brandi parked her car she didn't notice Derick's car parked anywhere on their block.

She entered her house, and could smell the scent of Derick's cologne in the living room. As she walked into the kitchen she called out Derick's name. Brandi placed the food she'd purchased on the kitchen table, then went upstairs. She continued to call Derick's name but he still didn't answer.

Once Brandi got to her bedroom she noticed that the bed was disheveled and the pillows were on the floor. *I know I made that bed this morning after I got out of it. So Derick was home but where is he now? I know he left the house this morning before I did. But when did he come back home? If he was sick and couldn't make it to work then why didn't he call and tell me? Even after I spoke to him he said he was at work. I know I'm not the smartest person but I'm not the dumbest either. None of this is making any sense to me. Derick definitely has some explaining to do.*

She walked over to the nightstand, picked up the cordless phone and dialed his phone number again, this time blocking her number from view. Surprisingly Derick answered on the first ring.

"Hello."

"Hey, where are you?" Brandi asked.

"I'm at work, where the hell else would I be? I just left the office and I'm going to grab some lunch before my meeting," Derick said.

"Is that right? Where are you going, maybe I can join you for lunch?"

"I don't think that would be a good idea. I'm with a lot of people from my office as well as a board member. We're going to have a working lunch." Before Brandi said anything else, she hesitated because she could hear the background noise of the car radio as well as someone talking.

"Who's that?" she asked.

"Who's what?"

"The person in the background speaking."

"Oh, those are my co-workers," Derick said.

"Derick, we need to talk."

"I'm almost certain that you know right now is not a good time."

"Yes, I know that. We'll talk later. Enjoy your lunch. I have to go," Brandi said.

Brandi decided to leave the bed the way she found it. She also decided not to go back into the office and called them to say she'd be out for the remainder of the day. She then grabbed her lunch and headed out of the door. Once she was in the car she called to see if Bailey was at home.

"Hello," Bailey said.

"Is it okay with you if I come to your house now?" Brandi asked.

"Sure. I'm just finishing up some work. Is everything okay?"

"I really don't know."

"What do you mean you don't know?"

"I'm not at work right now so I thought I could hang out with you for a while. I should be there in about thirty five minutes or so," Brandi said.

"Okay, see you when you get here."

While Brandi was driving down the beltway, she received a text from Kya: I SCHEDULED YOUR APPT FOR TOMORROW AT 10AM WITH MICHELLE JONES. LET ME KNOW IF YOU NEED ME TO GO WITH YOU. CALL ME LATER.

Brandi almost felt as though she was in a daze. No matter how she tried, she couldn't understand why Derick lied about his whereabouts. *Why did he lie about being at work? Where and what's he doing that he needs to lie? We've always been honest with each other so I can't understand why the lies all of a sudden.*

Before Brandi arrived at Bailey's house she tried to regain her composure. *I don't know if this is worth mentioning to Bailey or not. Considering I don't know what's really going on it might be best not to say anything. I keep trying to come up with reasons for why he lied to me. But in all actuality I can't justify his actions.* As Brandi pulled in front of Bailey's house, Bailey came outside and greeted her with a hug.

"Hey, girl, you got here quick," Bailey said.

"The beltway was clear and I think I might have been speeding," Brandi said.

As they entered the house Brandi's phone started ringing. When she glanced at the screen, she saw it was Derick, and declined the call.

"Are you not accepting calls today?" Bailey asked.

"No, not at the moment."

"What if it's important or an emergency?"

"Oh well," Brandi said.

"Let's go and sit in the family room. I've been in my office all morning and I could use a break."

"I have some sandwiches and salads from Panera Bread," Brandi said.

"Do you need something to drink or anything from the kitchen?"

"Yes, can you make me a flirtini?"

Bailey turned to look at Brandi and said, "Excuse me, a flirtini, in the middle of the day?"

"I'm in need of one bad. Why is there a certain time of the day that I should have a cocktail?" Brandi asked.

"Sweetie, you can have a cocktail whenever you like. I was just a little shocked because you normally don't drink and when you do it's a glass of wine. Is there a reason for the afternoon cocktail?"

"Bailey, there are a lot of reasons for the cocktail."

"Girlie, my schedule is clear for the rest of the day. Kick your shoes off and get comfortable. We have all night to talk and drink. If you're unable to drive later, I'll just send your ass back to Southeast in a taxi or call Uber car service."

"That's fine with me. Just keep the cocktails coming."

"Oh, my. Let me go to the kitchen and get some ice, I'll be back in a few. Do you need anything else while I'm in there?"

"No, not right now, I'm good."

When Bailey left the room Brandi turned her phone to silent. She also checked to see if she had any additional missed calls. Before she began her conversation with Bailey she thought it would be best if she called Derick to tell him her location. As Brandi dialed Derick's phone her heart began pounding faster. *Why am I so anxious and frightened? Maybe subconsciously I know he's not going to tell me the truth. I really don't need to get into a long, drawn-out conversation about his lying. I'm only calling him and telling him where I am.* At the third ring Derick picked up the phone. Before Derick said anything Brandi could still hear a lot of background noises. Derick finally said, "Hello."

"Hey, I was just calling to tell you that I'm not at work."

"Oh yeah? Where are you and why aren't you at work?" Derick asked.

"I should be asking you those very same questions," Brandi said.

"What do you mean by that?"

"Because I know you're not at work and I know you called in sick. I also know that you were at home."

"I was at work today," Derick said.

"Really Derick? I'm going to need for you to stop lying. I went to your job today. I actually wanted to surprise you with lunch, that's why I called you earlier. Shortly after we got off the phone I was there but you weren't. Then I looked like a damn fool when I asked for you and I was told that you were off sick."

"That's not true, somebody was lying. Who told you I wasn't there?"

"You're right, someone was lying but it wasn't your co-workers. It doesn't matter who said what. Apparently you had something more imperative to do today besides going to work."

"Brandi, I'm at work."

"I think we should end this call now. You insist on lying to me and I'm not going to listen to it. I'll see you later on."

"Wait a goddamn minute! Who the hell do you think you're talking to? You must have me mixed up with one of your girlfriends. Where the hell are you?"

"Right now, that's not important. I'll give you a call later on, Derick. Enjoy the rest of your day doing whatever you're doing," Brandi said angrily.

"I'll deal with this bullshit when I get home tonight," Derick said.

Brandi was so angry and irritated with Derick's lies, that instead of saying anything else, she pressed the "end call" button on her phone.

Before Brandi had a chance to put her phone back in her purse, she noticed that Derick was calling back. She declined the next five calls. After each one she noticed she had a new voice message. *I'll listen to those later on. There's nothing he can say to me right now that I actually want to hear. He had a chance but he insisted on lying.*

Bailey walked in the family room and said, "Here's your cocktail but eat your lunch first. I can't have you getting sick on me."

"Thanks, girl, you don't know how bad I need this cocktail," Brandi said.

"Okay, church lady, what's up with you? I hear you want to start a foundation."

"Yes I do and I need to borrow a little money from you to get started."

"Noah would like for me to get all of the logistical like the business and strategic plans before we commit to loaning you the money. How soon do you want to get the ball rolling?"

"Yesterday," Brandi said.

"That soon?"

"Yes. I'll start looking at locations for commercial properties, and see if there's something I can move into right away that wouldn't require a lot of work. Or I could lease some space. I also need to get this business and strategic plan stuff rolling."

"Are you able to stop by my office on Monday? If so, I'll introduce you to the guy I'm going to ask to help you with your business and strategic plan."

"Yes, I can be there first thing Monday morning."

"For the next couple of days, why don't you start jotting down your mission, your vision, and the goals of your foundation? With a little more information and a brief conversation, Eugene will be able to incorporate your ideas into the business and strategic plan. He's good like that," Bailey said.

"Are you serious?"

"Yes, I'm very serious. He'll spend probably thirty minutes with you. He'll ask you a couple of key questions and by the end of the week, your plans will be completed."

"Wow, he can really complete them that quick?"

"Yes, ma'am. I'll tell him to make this his priority for next week. Trust me, you might only have a few tedious changes, if any. I also know a couple of people that could help with the writing of grant applications. All I need to know is how much start-up money you think you'll need. Think about everything from the furniture to the software. I might have some checklists and other documents in my office that could guide you. Are you sure you want to start a foundation right now?"

"Yes, I'm positive. I've never been so adamant about doing anything in my life," Brandi said.

"Okay, that's all I needed to know."

"I want you to know that I'm going to pay you back every cent and with interest."

"Right now, all I need you to do is to meet with Eugene and get your plans on paper. As far as the money goes, don't stress about that. That will be the least of your worries. I just had a thought. We have some office space in one of our buildings. The tenants that were going to move in decided that the space was too much for them. The location was recently renovated. I'll have Eugene show you the space," Bailey said.

"How much would my rent be?"

"Just go and see the space first. You may not be interested. But, if you are, I'll make you a deal you won't be able to resist. We'll discuss that later. Now, is there anything else we need to discuss pertaining to your foundation?" Bailey asked.

"I don't know what to do. I'm excited but apprehensive at the same time."

"Girl, don't worry or stress yourself out. We'll all do our part to help you. Trust me, you're not going to do this alone. We got your back."

"I have the greatest friends. I don't know how I'm going to return the favor," Brandi said.

"All we need for you to do is help those young girls. Do everything you can for them not to be a statistic. Make sure they stay on the right path. Make them good, upstanding citizens. Help them. That's how you can repay us," Bailey said.

"And I'll do that. If I have to work twenty four hours a day, I *will* make it happen. I promise you."

"Okay, so what else is going on? Do you need any help packing and moving?"

"Girl, I need a lot of help. It's so time-consuming."

"The girls and I decided that we're going to hire a moving company for you. They'll be there Saturday morning for their instructions. They've been given clear guidance, they do everything! You won't lift another damn finger. They already know that you have specific instructions as far as what you're taking and the items that are being donated. What else?" Bailey asked. As Brandi sat there with her mouth open, tears fell from her eyes.

"I don't know what to say. You guys do more for me than my family has ever done."

"What are you crying for? Why the tears?"

"These are tears of joy. I'm so overwhelmed with excitement. I'm honestly grateful for everything that all of you are doing for me."

"Brandi, we've been friends for a long time. Did you think we were going to let you deal with all of this shit alone? I know that Derick's working a lot and you've been tackling everything. It's okay, that's what we're here for. Learn to lean on your friends a little. Yeah, we all have a lot on our plates but we can still help when needed. I forgot to mention that the moving company will also unpack everything and put your stuff in the appropriate places. Kya and I will be there with you on moving day to assist. I'm not sure if Deion is going to be there. She has a meeting but she's trying to reschedule it."

"You girls are the best friends anyone could ever hope for," Brandi said.

"We're not only friends, sweetie, we're sisters and we're a family."

"Yes we are, and I love my big sisters!" Brandi shouted.

As Bailey got up from the sofa to refresh their cocktails Brandi said, "Nikko, can I ask you a question?"

"Oh shit this must be serious. You only call me Nikko for one of two reasons. When I've done something really bad and you're upset with me. Or you have something that's not pleasant to say," Bailey said.

"Well, you haven't done anything wrong. This time it's about me."

"Whew! Thank goodness it's not me this time. Yes, you can ask me anything."

"You've known me for a long time. You know that I'm not good with sharing how I feel or my thoughts. I often hold everything in but I need to know something."

"Okay, I need you to stop dancing around the question and just ask me."

"I'm also not as experienced with men as you, so forgive my ignorance."

"Sweetie, what is it?" Bailey asked.

"If your spouse is cheating are the signs normally visible?" Brandi asked.

"Sometimes the signs are visible and sometimes they aren't. Why?"

"It's probably nothing and I'm reading too much into it, but something's going on with my husband. He's been acting weird lately."

"What do you mean by weird?"

"He's always at work or at least that's what he says."

"First of all, working all the time is not weird. Look at me, Noah, Deion and Kya. We work all the damn time. Even when we're not in the actual office," Bailey said.

"The majority of the time I'm in the bed and asleep by the time he gets home. We haven't had sex in a month and he doesn't touch me at all! No kisses, no hugs, no form of affection, nothing whatsoever!" Brandi said.

"Now that's a problem."

"Whenever I want to talk to him about anything, he says he's too tired."

"Okay," Bailey said.

"He hasn't paid any bills with the exception of his car note in a whole year. He says that he's saving his money."

"Like hell he is! What the fuck is he saving his money for? Excuse my language."

"He said that he was saving for a new house. But I used my commission for the new house," Brandi said.

"So you have separate bank accounts?"

"No, but he keeps a tally of the money that he puts in and takes out. He told me not to touch any of his money."

"What the hell type of shit is that?"

"I stopped at his job today and he wasn't there. I was told that he called in sick. Not to mention I had just gotten off the phone with him and he said he was at work. I then went home and the bedroom was a mess. The bed was unmade and the pillows were all over the floor. I also kept calling him and I didn't get an answer. Then someone finally answered the phone."

"What the fuck do you mean, someone answered the phone? You don't know who it was and what the hell did they say?" Bailey asked.

"Some man answered the phone and said, 'Mr. Knight's office, how may I help you'."

"Get the fuck outta here. Some man answered the phone? You're joking, right? Are you trying to make me laugh or something?"

"No, I'm dead serious. Oh, and I forgot to mention the last couple of times that I spoke with him I could hear someone talking. He said he was going to lunch with some of his colleagues. I called him while you were in the kitchen and he was still acting like he was at work. I finally decided to call him out on his lies," Brandi said.

"And what the hell did he say?"

"He said he was at work and someone was lying about him."

Bailey chuckled and said, "Wow!"

"Are any of those signs of a cheating spouse?"

"Sweetie, I don't really want to tell you my opinion. I'm a little fucked up with all of that information you shared. But yes, those are some of the signs of a cheating spouse."

"Nikko, I love this man with all of my heart. He's the only man that I've been with. In the beginning of our relationship he was perfect and he treated me like a queen. Why would he cheat on me?"

"I can't answer that for you. But I can tell you that people cheat for different reasons. It doesn't have to be anything that you've said or done. The difference between men and women is when a man cheats he thinks with his dick. Chances are that's how they get caught up. But with a woman, we know how to keep our cool, handle our business, and take care of home all at the same time. For us cheating is not all about sex, there's more to it than that," Bailey said.

"Whether here or there, it's still not right."

"You're absolutely right."

"I'm a good woman and I know I am. What does he want that I'm not doing?" Brandi asked.

"Sweetie, he's the only one that can answer those questions."

"I don't understand why people lie. Don't they realize that once they tell a lie, they have to keep lying to cover it up? Eventually they'll forget the lie and then they get caught up in a web of deceit, when all they have to do from the beginning is be a man or woman and just tell the truth. It's that simple."

"I totally agree. Not that I'm trying to rationalize the behavior of a liar but I think sometimes people are afraid to hurt the ones they love. So they just lie. Not realizing that'll hurt much more in the end."

"I never have and I never will understand why people cheat," Brandi said.

"From what I know, cheating isn't always about sexual gratification. Sometimes it's about loneliness, companionship and attention."

"I disagree. I'm currently not getting what I need from my husband. Right now it feels like we're just roommates. But I haven't cheated on him. That thought never crossed my mind."

"Sweetie, everyone is not you. I suggest that you sit down with Derick and find out what's going on. There's only one way to find out—you have to ask. In a situation like this it's not always safe to make assumptions. I just hope that Derick isn't cheating because you're a damn good woman," Bailey said.

"Yeah. I hope so too."

"I know it's kind of hard to think differently, especially with what took place today. I will say this, depending on the people and the situation, your marriage can still work after someone is unfaithful. I think it depends on the people and the love they have for one another."

"That's so true. I know several people that made their marriage work after someone cheated. I also know people who have ended their marriage after someone cheated."

"When someone lies to you it's difficult to trust them. They literally have to work much harder to earn your trust. It's challenging but it's doable. Both parties have to be willing to try. You definitely can't keep throwing the infidelities in the other person's face."

"Anything is possible," Brandi said.

"When Noah had an affair in the past, I was crushed, I was devastated. But I forgave him. I never forgot about it but I forgave him. I'm not going to lie to you it was painful as hell and I didn't think I could do it, but I did. To me his reason for cheating wasn't sufficient. I love my husband and we worked at it and rebuilt our marriage. It took some time but we moved past it. Forgiveness is very powerful and it's not easy to do but we have to forgive one another," Bailey said.

"The Bible tells us that love is patient and love is kind. It also tells us that love endures all things."

"Sweetie, regardless of how much I care about you and love you, I can't tell you what to do. You know the source to go to and He will never lead you in the wrong direction."

"I know but I would have never imagined this happening to me. You always hear about the stuff that other people go through. You never think you would have to walk in their shoes."

"I know what you mean. There's a possibility that we're jumping to conclusions. Although I've never had the personality of a naïve woman, I hope and pray that our accusations are 150 percent wrong," Bailey said.

"Girl, I'm also hoping they're wrong. I don't think I'd be able to live through that hurt and pain."

"Don't talk like that. If Derick's cheating, you'll survive. You'll make it just like you've made it through every other trial, tribulation and storm that you've had to bear. Do you remember what you told me when Noah cheated on me?"

"Yes, I remember."

"What, what did you say to me that made a significant difference?" Bailey asked.

"I told you that not only would God carry you through the storm but he would place you on the other side."

"Okay then, practice what you preach, church lady. Don't get it twisted."

"Where's my goddaughter? I need one of her big hugs," Brandi said.

"She's with my mother-in-law but you'll see her this weekend."

"I guess I should be getting home, I have a lot to do."

"What are you going to that empty house to do? You don't have to pack because we've hired someone to do that for you, remember? Why do you want to go home?" Bailey asked.

"There's really nothing for me to go home to. I know Derick isn't there as usual."

"Okay then. It's 4:30 p.m., Noah should be home shortly and we'll go out to dinner."

"Where is Noah?"

"He went to play golf earlier. After that he was going to buy Ty's birthday gift."

"What are you guys getting her?" Brandi asked.

"I don't know. She's six years old and already has a lot of everything. I don't know what he's going to get her."

"I'll probably go out tomorrow and get her something else to add to his gift. Like you, I have no idea what to buy Ms. Diva-in-Training."

"Girl, who you telling? She wanted to have the slumber party and she wanted a dog. The slumber party is this weekend and I bought a dog the other night. I have no clue what else we could buy her."

"Does she need any dolls or toys?"

"Hell, no. Call her and ask her because I don't have a clue. I'm pretty sure she'll be calling here shortly. I'll let you speak to her then."

"Okay, Ms. Lady, those cocktails got my head spinning. I think I need to lay it down before I try to drive myself home," Brandi said.

"Girl, go ahead and do what you gotta do. You know where the guest room is. You're more than welcome to spend the night. Do you need to call your man and tell him where you are so he won't be worried and that you'll be here later than you anticipated?"

"I never got a chance to tell him that I was coming over here. I'll give him a call when I get upstairs. I doubt very seriously that he'll even notice I'm gone."

"Okay, go on upstairs and lie down. I'll let you know what we're doing for dinner. Do you need another cocktail for the road?"

"No way, I've had more than enough," Brandi said.

"Okay, just checking. Enjoy your nap. I'll be down here if you need anything."

Prior to lying down, Brandi called Derick to inform him she was at Bailey's house. Much to her surprise Derick answered the telephone sounding very pleasant. His disposition was totally different from the last time she spoke with him.

"Hey baby, where are you?" Derick asked.

"I'm about to lie down."

"Lie down. Where are you?"

"Why?"

"Because I'm in the house," Derick said.

"I'm at Bailey's house."

"When are you coming home?"

"Don't know."

"Why are you over there?" Derick asked.

"Why are you being so inquisitive all of a sudden? You never gave me a chance earlier to tell you where I was. I actually stopped by here to talk to Bailey about the foundation."

"You're still going ahead with your plans I see."

"Yes, it's a go. And at this point money is one of the things that I no longer have to worry about. Everything is covered. God is so good!" Brandi screeched.

"I thought we decided that getting money from your friends wasn't a good idea."

"No, sweetie, that's something *you* decided. I'm doing what I have to do."

"Okay, but when the shit hits the fan, don't come running to me. I won't be able to fix it for you."

"It's funny that you said that. That's exactly what I'm going to do from here on out," Brandi said.

"And what is that supposed to mean?"

"It means that I'm going to start doing me. I need to start focusing more on what's going to make me happy."

"Is there something that you want to tell me?" Derick asked.

"No, not really. All I know is today's a new day, and today is the first day of the rest of my life. I have some major changes that I need to make with self. Change is always good especially when it's for the better. Out with the old and in with the new."

"Sweetheart, you're confusing me a little. Are you about to make some major decisions that involve us?"

"Any change that I make with self of course will involve us. But don't you worry, it's all good. My darling, it's a new day."

"You already said that," Derick said.

"Yeah I know and I'm going to keep saying it. Life's too short to keep sitting back and watching it pass me by. As we all know, tomorrow isn't promised to anyone. I've always lived for others, to make them happy. I had a conversation with the pastor the other night. The more I think about that conversation the more I know I need to make some significant changes. He emphasized that it's all right to put your needs in front of others. It's okay to be selfish sometimes, take time out for self and to say no. He emphasized that you can't be everything to everybody. I now realize that I can't do everything for everybody."

"I hope you don't be telling him our business."

"Derick, don't start with that stupid stuff," Brandi said.

"You're right. Okay sweetheart, as long as you're happy. I just want you to be happy."

"That's peculiar, you haven't said that to me in over a year. I always looked to others to make me happy. But I've realized that people don't make you happy. People can only contribute to your happiness. It's about time I started making me happy."

"Love, you're a good woman and you deserve to be happy. When are you coming home?"

"Hmmm. I'm not sure about that. Bailey invited me to dinner with her and Noah. If it's not too late I'll be home after dinner."

"What do you mean if it's not too late? Do you plan on spending the night there?"

"That's something that you said. I didn't expect for you to be home because lately you've been coming home extremely late. That's why I accepted the dinner invitation."

"Do you want me to go to dinner with you guys?" Derick asked.

"No, you can go ahead with whatever plans you've already made." Brandi said.

"My plans were to come home, cook dinner, and make love to my wife."

"You don't say. I don't know the last time that you touched me, let alone made love to me. Oh yeah, about a month ago."

"I know. I've been so busy with work and all."

"Since you've been working so hard and all, why don't you get some rest? I'm sure you could use it. But I'm going to need you to do me a big favor," Brandi said.

"What's that, honey?" Derick asked.

"Make sure you change the sheets and get my pillows off the floor."

"What are you talking about?"

"I hate when you act as if you have no idea what I'm saying. As if I'm speaking a different language or something. I made the bed this morning and when I came home from work the covers were all disarrayed. The bedroom was nothing like I left it, it was a mess."

"Oh, yeah. I came home from work earlier to get my sinus medicine. But instead I did lay across the bed for a while," Derick said.

"Derick the way that bed looked you did more than lie across it."

"I jumped up and threw the covers off me when I realized I was late for a meeting. I might have tossed the pillows to the side but that's it."

"Yeah, okay, if you say so."

"And why would I need to change the sheets. Didn't you just change the sheets yesterday?"

"Yes I did change the sheets yesterday but that bed looked like someone did more than take a quick nap in it. Both you and I know that the sheets need to be changed. I'm going to leave it at that. As far as the other things that happened today, we'll discuss them later. Right now is not a good time to have this conversation. Will you be there when I get home later?" Brandi asked.

"Yes, I'll be here and waiting on you. Where else would I be?"

"The hell if I know," Brandi whispered.

"What did you say?"

"Nothing. It was nothing at all."

"What's going on with you today? You being all snippy and shit. Is it that time of the month?"

"Nope. Okay, well I guess we'll have our conversation later about the other stuff. I'll talk to you when I talk to you and see you when I see you."

"What does that mean?"

"It means what I said. Listen, Derick, it's been a long day, I'm tired and those cocktails got my head spinning."

"Oh, okay, that explains why you're acting all crappy."

"Whatever you say."

"Okay, go ahead and take your nap. I'll call and check on you later."

"Okay."

"Hey sweetheart, I love you."

Before Brandi hung up the phone, she chuckled and said, "I know. I love me too."

After hanging up, Brandi thought, *for all intents and purposes I'm impressed with me. I wasn't timid, I didn't bend, bow or back down and I said what I needed to say. For once in my life I didn't bite my tongue. And it felt damn good. I had no idea all of that was going to come out of my mouth. But I'm really glad it did. If he thinks I was different just now, wait until I get home tonight. He's not going to be able to handle the new me. The coy girl with the low self-confidence has left the building. I'm now sexy, sassy and confident! People can't keep pushing me around and using my kindness as weakness. It's a new bitch in town. All that feistiness has worn me out. Or maybe it was the cocktails. I need to take me a little nap to regroup myself.*

About forty five minutes into her sleep, Brandi jumped up. She looked around the room and realized she was at Bailey's house. She shook her head and said, "A dream. It was only a dream."

She got out of bed and went into the bathroom to splash water on her face. *When are these nightmares going to end?* As Brandi dried off her face she heard a knock at the door.

"Brandi, it's time for dinner." Bailey opened the door and asked, "Are you awake?

Brandi walked out of the bathroom and said, "Hey, girl, I'm awake."

"Okay, I was just checking on you. Did you enjoy your nap?"

"Kind of."

"Well, it's time for dinner. Are you hungry? When you get yourself together, come on down," Bailey said.

"I'll be down in a couple of seconds."

Brandi sat on the side of the bed and reached over to the nightstand to grab her phone. She noticed she had four missed calls from Derick. *What can he possibly want? I talked to him before I went to sleep.* Before Brandi had a chance to call him back he was calling again.

"Hello," she said irritably.

"Hey, where are you?" Derick asked.

"Where was I the last time that we spoke?"

"You said you were at Bailey's house."

"Okay, then that's where I am."

"I kept calling you because I was in the area and was going to stop by."

"Stop by for what? I thought I told you earlier there was no need for you to come here."

"Why don't you want me to stop by? What are you hiding?"

"Look, Derick, what do you want? If you don't have anything to say then I guess I'll see you when I get home."

"Oh, so you're coming home?"

"Why wouldn't I come home?"

"I thought you were staying all night."

"Why would you think that?"

"Because you've been drinking."

"I'm good. I can drive."

"What time are you coming home?"

"I don't know. Whenever I'm done doing whatever it is I'm doing. Is there something that you want? If not I'm about to go downstairs and have dinner with Noah and Bailey."

"Oh, Noah's there?" Derick asked.

"Ummm . . . why wouldn't he be? This is his house."

"I was just saying."

"Look, I'll see you later on," Brandi said.

"Why are you rushing me off the phone?"

"I don't think I need to justify that with a response, I just told you. I know you didn't blow up my phone for this crap."

"No, I was missing my baby, that's why I was blowing up your phone. Don't you miss me?"

"No, not really. Is there anything else?"

"No, that's all," Derick said.

"Okay. Don't forget that I need to talk to you about something when I get home."

"How could I forget? Okay. Well, I'll see you later."

"Okay, bye," Brandi said.

Brandi went downstairs for dinner. As she entered the dining room she noticed enough food on the table to feed a small village.

Brandi sat down next to Bailey and asked, "Oh my word, look at all of this food. Who cooked all this?"

"Girl, you know me. When I'm stressed I love to cook. I was indecisive about what to cook and I wanted to cook some of your favorites."

"Why did you do that?"

"Because you deserve that. Besides, it's kind of a celebration too."

"A celebration, did I miss something? Where's Noah?" Brandi asked.

"He's on a work call. We were sitting here waiting for you then he got a call about some work stuff. Then I was sitting here waiting for the both of you. This food is going to get cold."

"But why are we celebrating?"

"Stop asking so many questions. Just wait until later."

Noah entered the dining room and Bailey asked, "Is everything all right?"

"No," Noah said.

"Babe, what's wrong?" Bailey asked.

"All I'm going to say is that Maisha better start looking for another job."

"Oh shit! What now?" Bailey asked.

"Babe, I don't want to get into it right now. Let's enjoy this good food and Brandi's company. But I will say this, that bitch just cost us a lot of money."

"Huh? How much money?" Bailey asked.

"Babe, not now. If I keep thinking about that bullshit I'm going to lose my appetite," Noah said.

"Okay," Bailey said.

"So Brandi, Bailey and I have been discussing your foundation. We were trying to figure out how we can help and what we can do to get things going. We decided the best way was to make a small donation. In addition to a financial donation, we have a vacant building that you could have."

"What are you saying, Noah?" Brandi asked.

"I'm saying that if you want the building you can have it. We're not using it anyway and it's been vacant for about five years. The other space Bailey mentioned to you is entirely too small for your foundation."

"I'll take it!" Brandi shouted.

"Wait. You don't even know where it is," Bailey said.

"Girl, I don't care. I'll make it work. Besides, beggars can't be choosers."

"It might take a little work but we have a contractor that is more than willing to assist," Noah said.

"We can go look at the building whenever you have a free moment," Bailey said.

"Joe actually called me this afternoon and he's eager to get started," Noah said.

"Whatever you need done they're at your disposal. If the location needs new floors, additional offices, cabinets or whatever the case may be, he's going to take care of it," Bailey said.

"What? Wait, no, this has to be a joke. Stop it, are you serious? Am I still asleep, is this a dream?"

"Yes sweetie, we're very serious. Since your plans are somewhat premature, we've decided to donate $150,000 towards your foundation. While you were napping, I made a few calls to some of our business contacts. So far, I've spoken to six people and received financial commitments totaling $175,050. As soon as you get your paperwork done, business license and bank account organized, the checks will be put your hand. Oh, the $50.00 came from your goddaughter. She too wanted to help," Bailey said.

"Bless her heart, she's so sweet. I really don't know what to say but if this is a dream please don't wake me. You guys are awesome! You're the best! If it weren't for you I don't know what I would do. Thank you, thank you, thank you! Lord, thank you for these good people that you put in my life!" Brandi yelled.

"Brandi, you don't have to thank us. We're doing what we're supposed to. We want to help you because we believe in you. You have a great vision and it's a good cause. Also, I've known you for a long time and you have a big heart and you're the right person to help these girls," Noah said.

"I think I need me a celebratory drink," Brandi said.

"Oh shit, I forgot the champagne in the kitchen. Be right back," Noah said.

Brandi grabbed Bailey and hugged her tightly.

"Um, I can't breathe, are you trying to kill me?" Bailey gasped.

"Oh goodness, I'm sorry, but you and Noah have made me the happiest woman alive!"

"I also spoke to Kya and she is already planning your "Big" charity event gala. She seems to think having an open house once the location is completed would be perfect. She was already jotting down potential menu items, color schemes, the setup, and every damn thing."

"So everyone was working while I was napping?" Brandi asked.

"Yes, ma'am. Deion thinks it would be good if everyone receives a thank you gift for attending the gala/open house. She said she would pay for the gifts. She wants you to give her a call so you guys can talk about it."

"Wow, I'm at a total loss for words right now," Brandi said.

"Brandi, would you like some champagne or do you need something stronger?" Noah asked.

"Champagne would be lovely. I can't believe this. How can I ever repay you for everything that you've done for me?" Brandi asked.

"We already told you. Just help those young girls, that's how you can repay us," Noah said.

"You and your wife have been around each other too long. She said the exact same thing. You're definitely like-minded people."

"I have some materials that I downloaded for you. I was able to find some great information on the Internet for starting a not-for-profit foundation. I also printed a list of not-for-profit attorneys and a copy of all of my contacts with their addresses. Girl, get that money from those folks. Everybody loves to donate to a worthy cause," Bailey said.

"You did all of that in that short period of time? I wasn't asleep that long."

"Girl, you know I move quickly. There's no time to be playing around."

"I see. I guess I need to do what I need to do to get the ball rolling."

"Yes, you do," Bailey said. "Remember that I told you I was going to solicit the help of Eugene for your business and strategic plan? Well, not only is he going to do that but he'll also assist you with the beginning stages of paperwork. I spoke with Rachel and she'll assist you on a part-time basis. Unfortunately, she won't be able to assist until after she returns from her honeymoon in Barbados, of course," Bailey said.

"Of course."

"But we're all at your disposal, so use us, girlfriend," Bailey said.

"But I can't pay them right now. I can't pay anyone right now."

"Don't worry about that, no one asked you to pay them. They aren't expecting payment from you. They'll continue to work for us but they'll be helping you as well. We asked them and they're more than happy to help. Rachel also wants to volunteer there a couple of evenings a week."

"Stop. Just stop it. You guys are going to make me have a heart attack or something. I'm so excited that I don't know whether to cry, do my praise dance, or scream. But of course I can do all of that at one time."

"Girl, you're so crazy."

"I'm so happy right now and I feel like I'm on top of the world," Brandi said.

"Sweetie, you can do it all. Go on and get that praise dance in. Aww shucks, they better watch out for the church lady come Sunday. You're going to be shouting, running and dancing all over that church," Bailey said teasingly.

"Okay. I might have to wear some tennis shoes or something for comfort, no heels."

"Brandi, it looks like you have your work cut out for you. Are you ready?" Noah asked.

"Yes, I am, I've been waiting for this opportunity for a long time," Brandi said.

"Are you going to quit selling real estate?"

"I wasn't in the beginning. I thought that I would wait until the second year or so before I stop."

"After your charity drive you might secure enough funds to have a salary. Maybe you could sell real estate on a part-time basis. Focus on the foundation full-time and sell a couple of houses here and there."

"You know what, Noah? That sounds like a good idea. Considering I want my undivided attention to be on the foundation."

"But I'm sure you'll have to discuss everything with Derick first," Noah said.

"Noah, if I listen to Derick I wouldn't be starting the foundation nor doing anything else with my life. He keeps telling me to wait awhile. Now is not the time. We just got a house, you want a baby. Blah, blah and more blah."

"Is that right? I'm surprised he isn't on board with the foundation."

"I was surprised too. He definitely wasn't happy that I was going to ask you and Bailey for the money. He's been against everything. I started wondering if he was one of those men that were intimidated by women and power."

"Sometimes when people don't have the full story or know the full plan they're a little cynical. But when they want to do something, they want you to jump on the bandwagon. It's sad but some people just don't want to see you prosper, get ahead or be successful." Noah said.

"I don't know what his problem is. I would hate to think that my husband suffers from the crab in the barrel syndrome. He's hasn't been too supportive these days and I thought it was because of the things that are happening on his job. There's a possibility that the bank is undergoing some restructuring and layoffs."

"Maybe that's what's going on with him. The thought of losing his job and having no money to take care of home and provide for his wife is enough to stress a man out," Noah said.

"He's not taking care of home or his wife anyway," Brandi whispered.

"I didn't hear you," Noah said.

"Nothing. I didn't say anything. Anyhoo, today has been a great day and full of blessings. I'm forever indebted to you guys. I love you both so much."

"We love you too. Now finish eating your dinner because Noah bought your favorite dessert."

"No you didn't! You bought a German chocolate cake?"

"Yes I did. I went to the bakery by your job."

"You guys are too much. I don't think I'll be able to eat dessert after this spread the two of you laid out."

"If not you can take your cake home with you."

"I just might have to do that. By the time I get something else to eat and help clean up, I'm going to be ready to go to bed."

"Brandi, you don't have to help clean up anything. Girl, we got this," Bailey said.

"When Bailey says we got this, that means that Mrs. Jenkins will take care of it in the morning," Noah said.

"No it doesn't. It's not going to take that long to rinse off the dishes and fill the dishwasher. The only things we'll have to do is put the food into the Tupperware and wash the pots and pans. That will take all of twenty minutes. You know I don't leave any dishes in my sink. I don't get down like that."

"Yes I forgot, Anal Annie don't like untidiness," Noah said.

"You got that shit right."

"I probably won't get any sleep tonight," Brandi said.

"Why's that?"

"I'm too excited to sleep. Girl, I most definitely have to go to my closet and talk to God. The blessings that he showered on me today are unreal and I need to thank and praise Him."

"I know that's right. I know that God has a plan and purpose for us all, but you, sister, you deserve all the blessings. Trust and believe God has a whole lot more for you stored up," Bailey said.

"And I thank Him daily for the things that are to come. That's one thing about me, not only do I thank Him for what he did, but what He does and what's to come."

"We're all supposed to. Girl, I never forget to thank Him for my trials and tribulations. Folks forget that you're supposed to thank Him for everything. That includes the good and the bad. If it wasn't for Him, Noah and I wouldn't have any of the things that we have. Nor would we have been able to do anything."

"You were like that when we were younger. And I'm glad that those same values are still instilled in you," Brandi said.

"And she's bringing up the girls the same way. Sometimes I hear them tell her thank you for something she did or bought and she'll say, don't thank me thank God," Noah said.

"Brandi, I know that God has great things in store for you. You are truly a one-of-a-kind woman. You never ask for anything, the more you give of yourself the more people take. You deserve nothing but pure happiness."

"Thanks, Bailey. It's definitely a blessing to have a woman like you in my life. Your wisdom, encouragement and not to mention the way you push, push and push. There's no way in the world your friends can sit back and be idle. You definitely make sure that whatever goals we set, we see them through. Once we tell you about something, you don't want to hear any excuses or the word no."

"That's right. If there's something you want to do and you tell me about it, I'm going to make sure you do whatever you have to. To me there's no such thing as what you can't do," Bailey said.

"That's my wife. Even if you have a teeny tiny little idea, she's going to make sure you move forward with it," Noah said.

"She's a great friend to have in your corner. I think I'll keep her a little while longer," Brandi said jokingly.

"Sweetie, you are stuck with me for life."

"Babe, do you have any plans later on? Are you doing some work or were your plans to chillax?" Noah asked.

"Chillaxing sounds like a wonderful idea, why, what's up?" Bailey asked.

"I wanted to see if you'd like to go to the park or go for a ride or something."

"Maybe we can go to the movies. We haven't been to the movies in a while. Do you have something that you'd like to see?" Bailey asked.

"No not really, I was going to leave that up to you."

"I really don't know what's playing. The only thing that I've heard about is *"Think Like A Man Too."* Maybe we can go and see that?"

"I heard people say that movie was good." Brandi said.

"Don't tell me the ending."

"I haven't seen it yet. But I overheard one of the girls in my office talking about it," Brandi said.

"Would you like to go to the movies with us?" Noah asked.

"Oh, no. I've imposed enough for one day. You two deserve some alone time. But thanks for asking. After we clean up I'm going to be heading home. I can't wait to share my good news with Derick."

"First of all you're not helping do anything. All I need for you to do is go in the kitchen and get that damn cake. On your way out, grab the info that I printed out of my office."

"Okay, okay, don't beat me up. I won't help with the dishes. I probably should be getting home anyway, I do have a forty-five-minute drive ahead of me."

"Exactly! You're more than welcome to spend the night if you're not up for the drive. After the movies we'll be right home."

"I'll be fine. I'm not staying in this big ass house all alone."

"Ladies, if you'll excuse me, I'm going to start tackling the kitchen. Brandi, drive careful and I'll give the contractor your contact information. Don't forget to call us if you have questions or need some assistance."

"Thanks, Noah, for everything."

"You're more than welcome."

While Brandi and Bailey continued their conversation, Noah brought the cake to Brandi and said, "Enjoy."

"You're giving me the whole cake?"

"Yes, ma'am. We have our own German chocolate cake."

"Oh wow! I'm really going to have to start working out again."

"Don't start working out until you eat all of the cake," Bailey said.

"Well, let me get out of here. That husband of mine probably thinks I'm not coming home tonight."

As Bailey and Brandi walked down the hallway, Brandi remembered that she'd left her phone upstairs.

"Bailey, I have to run upstairs and get my phone. When you grab the paperwork can you get my purse too?" Brandi asked.

"No problem."

A couple of seconds later Brandi met Bailey at the front door. "It's surprisingly warm tonight. Tonight is a good night to stroll through the park," Bailey said.

"Yes. It's nice tonight. Very warm."

Bailey hugged Brandi and said, "Okay, momma, drive careful and call as soon as you get in the house. I'll have my phone on vibrate."

"Will do, and thank you for everything."

"No problem, I'm glad we could help. Get home safe and don't make any stops anywhere."

While driving home, Brandi thought about the things that needed to be done. *I have so much to do and I need to get started like yesterday. I no longer have to worry about the move, since my girls were gracious enough to hire a moving company. All I need to be doing is focusing on the foundation. If I go into the office tomorrow I'm going to change my hours. If I work part-time that's twenty hours a week. Maybe I'll go into the office twice a week and work a half-day from home. Better yet, maybe from now on I'll telecommute. I can call in to the staff meetings, set my appointments on designated days, and communicate via phone, Skype and email throughout the week. Now that's a plan. I know Derick is going to have a whole lot to say but I don't even care. I have things to do.*

Thirty five minutes later and Brandi was home. As she pulled into her driveway she saw Derick walking down the front steps. Brandi got the cake, paperwork and her other belongings out of the car.

As she walked up the steps she asked, "Where are you going?"

"Out. I'm going to meet a couple of the fellas for a drink," Derick said.

"I have some great news that I want to share with you," Brandi said.

"It's going to have to wait until later, I'm late."

"Okay, and?" Brandi asked.

"And I'm late. I waited home for you all day. Now you want to talk."

"Derick, you knew where I was so don't act like you didn't. I told you that I need to talk to you about something. Can't your friends wait?"

"Why should I make him, I mean them, wait on me? I have plans."

"I thought you said earlier that you didn't have anything to do."

"Things changed. I got tired of sitting around here waiting on you. Apparently being at Bailey's house was more important than being with your husband. Look, I'll talk to you later, I have to go."

"Do you? So, have a great time."

As Derick walked to his car, he looked at Brandi and said, "That's the plan."

Brandi went into the house, put the cake in the kitchen and got a glass of water. While she was leaving the kitchen she glimpsed at the calendar. *Heavens to Betsy, I have a gynecology appointment in the morning. If I wasn't trying to get pregnant I'd reschedule. Oh well, I guess I'll be going to bed after I take my shower.*

Brandi pulled out her phone and called Bailey.

"Hello," Bailey whispered.

"I'm home."

"Okay, that was fast."

"I actually got here in thirty five minutes, but I was talking to Derick."

"Shhh, you're too loud!" Noah said.

"Brandi, hold on one sec, let me go out into the hallway," Bailey said. Brandi listened as her friend ran up the aisle and out the doors. "Okay, so did you tell Derick your good news?"

"Nope," Brandi said.

"Why not?"

"Because he's not here, he went out. As I was walking up the steps he was walking down the steps."

"Emmm, oh, did he?"

"Yup, so I'll tell him my news some other time."

"Alrighty then. Well, relax and find something good on TV."

"Girl, I'm going to take a shower and go to bed. I have an early appointment tomorrow with Dr. Williams. I'll give you a call later on tomorrow," Brandi said.

"Okay, lady, goodnight."

"Goodnight." As Brandi walked up the stairs she looked into the bedroom. She noticed that Derick had changed the sheets and repositioned the pillows. Brandi undressed, grabbed her robe and went into the bathroom. For the next twenty five minutes Brandi showered and washed her hair, then she slipped on her nightgown and got into the bed. Shortly thereafter she drifted off to sleep.

Several hours later, Brandi was awakened by the sound of the telephone ringing. She reached over and grabbed the phone off the nightstand.

"Hello," Brandi whispered.

"Listen, it's late and I've been drinking so I'm not coming home," Derick said.

"Where are you and what do you mean you're not coming home?"

"I'm over at a buddy's house."

"Your buddy, who is it, Derick?"

"You don't know him."

"Well, I'll come and get you. Where are you?"

"Naw, that won't be necessary. Go back to sleep and I'll see you in the morning."

"Fine, whatever."

"Okay, sleep tight," Derick said as he hung up the phone. Brandi looked at the clock and noticed it was 2:22 a.m. For the next several minutes Brandi tossed and turned. Since she couldn't fall back to sleep, she turned on the television and surfed the channels. *I don't want to think that my husband's cheating on me but something is going on. Maybe he's just playing the tit for tat game. This could be his way of acting out since I spent the majority of the day and evening at Bailey's house. Whatever the case may be he's unquestionably acting a little strange.*

The next morning Brandi jumped up and looked at the clock. It was already 8:39 a.m., she should have been at the doctor's office at 7:30. Hoping they'd still be able to see her, Brandi picked up the phone and called the doctor's office.

"Dr. Williams' office, Rita speaking. How may I help you?"

"Good morning, this is Brandi Knight and I'm running late. Is it possible that I can still come in?"

"Yes, can you be here by 10 a.m.?"

"Yes, I can."

"Okay, we'll see you then."

Brandi got up and quickly showered and got dressed. By 9:45 she was walking into the doctor's office to be greeted by a pleasant woman sitting at the reception desk.

"Good morning," Brandi said.

"Good morning, Mrs. Knight."

Several seconds later the receptionist took Brandi to the examination room.

"Please get undressed, put on this gown, and sit on the table. The doctor will be with you shortly."

Brandi grabbed a magazine to read while waiting for the doctor. There was a knock and before she could say anything Dr. Williams was walking through the door.

"Hello," Dr. Williams said.

"Hi, Dr. Williams." Brandi said.

"So what are we doing today? I see it's time for your annual examination."

"Yes, and I'd also like to speak to you regarding infertility specialists. I'm ready to get pregnant. Apparently it's not happening the old fashioned way so I think I might need a little assistance."

"Okay. But I've reviewed the tests that you've taken to date and there's nothing wrong with you physically."

"Are you sure?"

"I'm positive. If you're trying to get pregnant we can also test your husband's sperm to make sure he doesn't have a low sperm count. It's not always the women that have problems getting pregnant, it's occasionally their mate. But don't worry, we'll figure it out."

"And if it isn't Derick?"

"Then you have what we call an unexplainable problem. Medically there's nothing wrong with you. It's probably your husband but the only way we can know for certain is to test him. I wouldn't worry, sometimes these things take a little while. Maybe right now isn't the time."

"Okay, I'll let him know," Brandi said.

"Within your examination today we will check for STDs, HPV and HIV and all that good stuff," Dr. Williams said.

"HIV . . . there's no need for a HIV test. I've only been with my husband," Brandi said.

"That's nice to know but you can't say there's no need. You never can be certain and it's better to be safe than sorry."

"What if I don't want the test?"

"I can't make you get tested. But I suggest to all my patients that they get checked for HIV. It doesn't matter how long you've been married or how long you've been in a relationship. It's best to get checked anyway. I've been married to my husband for eighteen years and I still get checked every six months," Dr. Williams said.

"All right, I'll get checked."

"After we're finished up here, I want you to schedule an appointment. I'll sit down and talk to you and your husband about the infertility tests, the specialists, and what to expect. This can be a very long and stressful process and I want to prepare you guys."

After Brandi's examination she got dressed and went into another room for her blood work. The nurse reiterated that the test results would be available between thirty-six to forty-eight hours. If Brandi was unreachable by phone, the results would be left via voice message and emailed. The nurse then asked Brandi to confirm her phone number and email address.

On her way home Brandi stopped at the shopping center to get something to eat, and to Staples to get some office supplies. Walking down the aisle, Brandi noticed Chase standing in the copy center.

She walked over to him and said, "I was just thinking about you."

Chase turned and said, "I hope they were good thoughts."

"Of course they were. How are you doing?"

"I'm good, I can't complain. How have you been? What are you doing here? Shouldn't you be finding me a house?" Chase asked teasingly.

"I'm on it. I have four houses to show you. I can guarantee that you will pick one out of the four."

"Okay, when can we go and see them?"

"Unfortunately I'm in the process of moving and that has taken up more of my time than anticipated. I'm also going to be cutting back my hours with the real estate. But, if you're available we can go out next weekend."

"Sounds good. I'm going to be in Los Angeles for a couple of days. I'll call you when I get back to town," Chase said.

"Okay. I'll also need that makeover sooner than June. There are some things going on right now and it's time for a new me, inside and out."

"Girl, I know that's right. Maybe we can see the houses in the morning and do your makeover that afternoon."

"I'll be there with bells on," Brandi said.

"Listen, I have to get going. I'm meeting my man for lunch and I'm running behind schedule. I'll give you a call next week. Smooches," Chase said.

"Okay, talk to you soon."

Brandi picked up few supplies then decided to head home. After she arrived and had relaxed some, she called the Salvation Army and scheduled a pick-up time. The only availability that the Salvation Army had was for the following morning. Once Brandi realized she had so little time for gathering the items she was donating, she decided to go through Derick's clothing and belongings. *I know that he told me not to worry about his stuff but the people will be here at 7 a.m., and once he gets home he isn't going to feel like doing it.* Brandi knew she'd need a little help to complete this project. Instead of working around the clock she called Kya.

After four rings Kya answered and said, "Hey, girl."

"Hey, Ms. Lady, are you in the office?" Brandi asked.

"No, not right now. Why, what's up?" Kya asked.

"The Salvation Army is coming to pick up all of this crap in the morning and girl, I need a little help."

"Okay, I can get there around 2:30. Do you have enough boxes?"

"Yes, I think I have enough of those."

"Okay, well I'll see you later on. Do you have something to make cocktails?" Kya asked.

"Girl, the little I did have is already packed up."

"I'll stop and get something. Did you call Bailey and Deion?"

"No, not yet, but I will after I get off the phone with you."

"Okay, well make your calls and I'll see you later on."

"See you later."

Following her call with Kya, Brandi called Bailey. Bailey's cellphone went straight to voicemail and Brandi left her a message. "Hi, it's me. I need a little help. The Salvation Army will be here bright and early to pick up the items I'm donating. Are you available to assist? I've already spoken to Kya and she'll be here around 2:30. I hate to bother you because I know you're busy. Please call me." Brandi also called Derick to find out if there were any items he wanted to keep.

"Hello," Derick said.

"Hey, what are you doing?" Brandi asked.

"If you're calling because you want to start an argument because I went out and didn't come home, now is not the time."

"Actually, I was calling because I need to finish packing up the stuff for the Salvation Army. They'll be here first thing in the morning so I need to get busy."

"So what is it that you want?"

"You know what, Derick, I only called you for one reason and one reason only. But I need to say this, you are a rude ass, self-absorbed son of a bitch. Yes, you're my husband and I love you but you need to get your attitude together."

"So where's all of this coming from?" Derick asked.

"I'm tired of you treating me like I'm a piece of crap or like I've done something wrong. I'm your wife and you act as though I'm your enemy or something. That's where all of this is coming from. You never know what you have until it's gone, remember that."

"So what's that supposed to mean?"

"It means you never miss your water until your well runs dry. Lately you've been doing what you want and when you want. You act like you don't give a darn about me one way or another. If there's something else that you want to do besides be my husband then by all means please go."

"What?" Derick asked.

"You heard me. I'm getting tired of this. Either you want me or you don't. I'm not going to try and hold on to or keep a man that doesn't want to be kept. I can't make you want me or make you stay. One way or another you need to let me know something."

"You are blowing this shit way out of proportion. I think you've been hanging around your friends too long. They must be pumping up your head or something."

"My friends have nothing to do with this. I'm just getting fed up with the way you're acting. I don't need anyone to pump me up or tell me what to say. This conversation is long overdue. I have other things to focus on and I have to take care of. I have to finish packing. Since you told me not to touch your stuff I was calling to see what it was that you wanted to keep. But I'm going to look at it like this, if you cared about moving then you'd have taken care of it. As usual, I will handle it."

"It's not that I don't care, I've just been busy."

"Oh yeah, that's right. You've been busy running the streets and doing God knows what."

"Whatever you say, Brandi."

"Yeah I know. Anyway, don't even worry about the packing and the moving. My girlfriends have taken care of everything. As a matter of fact, they're on their way to help me get everything prepared for the Salvation Army."

"Well, I'll go through my stuff when I get home," Derick said.

"Don't even worry about it. It will be taken care of by then. I'll talk to you later."

Before Brandi could get off the sofa the doorbell rang and she heard someone yelling through the door. "Girl, open the door, I gotta use the bathroom!"

As Brandi opened the door, Bailey ran past her and said, "Hey, be right back."

Brandi walked into the den and Bailey came back down the hallway towards her.

"Whew, I feel so much better. I would not have made it all the way home like that," Bailey said.

"What if I wasn't home?" Brandi asked.

"But you were, that's all that matters. Besides, I heard your message."

"Why didn't you call me back?"

"For what? You said you needed help so here I am."

"So you just happened to be riding around in Southeast looking for something to do?" Brandi asked.

"I had a meeting in Southwest. I heard your message when I was on the highway."

"You still driving and playing with that darn phone. You already drive crazy. I told you to stop playing with your phone while you're driving. You don't listen to me."

"Girl, I got it. I'm a great multi-tasker."

"Okay, a hard head makes a soft ass."

"Anyway, do you have something to eat? I'm a little famished," Bailey said.

"I stopped and picked up a salad from Subway on my way home from my doctor appointment. You're more than welcome to it. Or would you like to order something?"

"Yes. I'm in the mood for some Chinese food."

"Moo Shoo Shrimp or Chicken?"

"Neither. Shrimp with Broccoli and fried rice instead of white rice. Maybe we should order enough for Kya and Deion."

"Dang it. I forgot to call Deion. After I got off the phone with Derick I couldn't even think."

"I called Deion while I was driving here. She said she'd be here in about an hour," Bailey said.

"Isn't she at work?"

"No, she took her car to the shop. Someone busted her windows and flattened her tires. She was about to get a rental car."

"Get the heck out of here. That sounds like the work of an angry wife or girlfriend."

"Or an angry man. That's a little too much drama for me."

"Did she call the police?" Brandi asked.

"Yes she did. They came out and did a report. They also got the tapes from the parking garage."

"Hopefully they'll get whoever did this."

"She called me this morning and told me about it but she didn't even sound angry," Bailey said.

"I would still be crying. Maybe she feels like it was only the tires and the windows. It could have been much worse."

"It sure could have."

"I know Deion deals with a lot of different men, I just hope and pray that she doesn't get hurt."

"People don't always want to listen or hear what we have to say. Sometimes without saying it they really want us to mind our own business. But when it involves my family and friends, it's hard for me to turn my blinders on. Especially if someone is exhibiting self-destructive behavior."

"I feel like that too. On the other hand, I might not always like what's being said to me but I listen. More importantly, why would I involve people if I didn't want to hear what they have to say?"

"My point exactly."

"I just hope she gets it together. I always pray for her. I know the right man's out there for her. She just needs to stop with all this craziness."

"I agree. So, what's happening with the Knights? Why couldn't you think after your call with Derick?" Bailey asked.

"Child, Mr. Man is undeniably working my nerves and my patience. I really don't know what's going on with Derick these days. And I really don't have time to figure it out."

"Well, you said that a lot was happening at work and he had a lot on his mind."

"I'm starting to believe that's all bullshit!" Brandi yelled.

"Oh, my."

"No, seriously Derick has been acting so . . . so . . . strange for months. I don't even think strange is the appropriate word to describe his conduct and attitude."

"Sweetie, I don't know what to tell you. I hate to imply anything."

"For several weeks now I've been thinking long and hard about our marriage. Instead of us coming closer together we're growing apart. It no longer feels like we're a team. It feels like he just lives here. I'm sorry, I meant to say he occasionally drops by for a shower and to change his clothes," Brandi said.

"I'm sorry to hear that things aren't working out. I wish I knew what to say but surprisingly I don't."

"You're right, that's a first. You of all people have nothing to say—get the heck out of here."

As the ladies laughed Bailey said, "I must be sick or something, I always have something to say."

"Right! When you're quiet and have nothing to say I get scared," Brandi said jokingly.

"That is scary isn't it?"

"Yes. Very scary, but sometimes Derick acts as though I disgust him."

"Like you're irritating him or getting on his nerves, or is it more like you're nagging him?"

"No. He acts like I disgust him. For instance, it's no big secret that we haven't had sex in a while. The other night I tried to get something going. Girl, I started to think that my va-jj was drying up or something. I'm not going to lie, I was very horny and I wanted sex! I had the scented candles going, some soft music and I had on some very sexy lingerie."

"All of the right things to put him in the mood," Bailey said.

"Well, that's what I thought. I started kissing him, from head to toe. I left no spot untouched. When I got down to his dick he asked me, what are you doing? I said just lie back and relax,"

"And then you got down to business?"

"Nope, not really. I was kissing all over his dick and as soon as I put the tip of it in my mouth he jumped up."

"Get the fuck out of here. I haven't run across a man that doesn't enjoy some head."

"I actually thought all men enjoyed head. But then there's my husband," Brandi said.

"Wow, that's a first."

"Girlfriend, he jumped up so fast he almost gave me whiplash."

"What did he say?"

"Girl, he said that he wasn't in the mood because he'd had a rough day."

"Okay, I've never experienced anything like that. If Noah's sick, had a rough day or tired he still doesn't say no to sex. I guess everybody's different," Bailey said.

"After that he was pissed. You would have thought that I did something wrong. Since then I haven't bothered to touch him. I figured if and when he wants to have sex with me he'll let me know."

"I'm stunned," Bailey said.

"Imagine how I feel. Besides that and some other stuff I have to be completely honest with myself."

"About what?"

"Whether he's cheating, maybe he doesn't love me anymore or he doesn't want to be with me," Brandi said.

"Sweetie, the only person that can answer those questions is Derick. Have the two of you really sat down to talk?"

"I don't even get a chance to talk to him. I still haven't told him about the foundation and everything that happened yesterday. Whenever I try to talk to him either he's too tired, it's not the right time or he isn't here. The majority of the time he isn't here. I've been wondering if purchasing a new home is a good idea or a big mistake."

"I didn't know it was this bad. I know you've mentioned stuff here and there but I had no idea."

"Yup, it's bad. But I have too much to be thankful for. I can't worry about this right now."

"Are you all right?" Bailey asked.

"I'm great. If he doesn't want to be with me I just wish he'd say something. Instead, he does stupid stuff like stay out all night."

"Oh my goodness, not him too."

"Yes girl, he didn't come home last night. He called and said he was drunk and was staying at a friend's house. The last time that I saw Derick was yesterday."

"Is he at work?" Bailey asked.

"I have no idea. I called him on his phone before you got here but I didn't ask and he didn't volunteer any information. Who knows? Even when he tells me he's at work I don't know whether or not to believe him. The last time when I stopped by, he wasn't there and yet he argued me down that he was."

While Bailey shook her head she said, "Men. We can't live with them and we can't live without them."

As Bailey and Brandi got up to finish packing and sorting through clothes the doorbell rang.

"That must be Deion or the food. Get the money out of my purse for the food," Bailey said.

"You guys are over here helping me, so I will pay for the food," Brandi said.

As Bailey started walking towards the kitchen she asked, "Are there any paper plates in the kitchen?"

"No but I have a few plates and forks on the counter." As Brandi looked through the glass on the door Kya said, "Hey momma."

Brandi opened the door and said, "Hey girl. You're a little early."

"I know, I thought I wasn't going to get here until three-ish. I was meeting with a potential client but she had an emergency so here I is."

"And I see you got something to drink," Bailey said.

"You know I never go to anyone's house empty handed. Besides, you work better with a few cocktails."

"Do you ladies want to wait until after we eat before we start packing?" Brandi asked.

"That's fine," Bailey said.

"I don't have a problem with that. Brandi, can you grab some glasses?" Kya asked.

As the doorbell rang again, Brandi shouted, "Can someone get the door?" Bailey opened the door to the delivery man from the carry-out. She placed the food on the living room table then went into the kitchen to wash her hands. After returning to the living room Bailey started to unpack and check the food.

"Did you order me something?" Kya asked.

"Yes we did," Brandi said.

"What?"

"Crab Rangoon, orange chicken and egg rolls."

"Aw, shit, my girls hooked me up," Kya said.

"And you better eat all of it."

"Oh no, I'll save some for my midnight snack," Kya said jokingly.

"You and your damn midnight snacking. Your ass is going to be as big as a house," Bailey said.

"Whatever, that'll never happen."

As Kya kicked off her heels and sat on the floor she said, "So what did I miss and where is Ms. Deion?"

"I don't know, she should have been here by now. Let me text her ass," Bailey said.

"So, what are we discussing?"

Given that the topic was Brandi and Derick, Bailey waited for Brandi to inform Kya.

"Well, we were discussing my cheating ass husband," Brandi said.

"Oh Lord! Not another so-called good man gone bad!" Kya shouted.

"Yeah well, shit happens," Brandi said.

"Girl, when did you start all of this cursing, and what makes you think that Derick is cheating?" Kya asked.

"I don't know and yes, I've been cursing like a sailor lately," Brandi said.

"Your ass is starting to sound like me. Oh goodness, am I rubbing off on you?" Kya asked.

"No, girl, I think I'm just frustrated as hell. But anyway I think Derick is cheating because of his actions or the lack thereof."

"If you're having those feelings don't wait before asking him. Just get it out on the table," Kya said.

"I'm definitely going to speak with him. But he's always out, and I need him to be present to have this convo."

"Derick. Derick Knight. The church man? Is that who we're talking about?" Kya asked.

"Yes, ma'am," Brandi said.

"Lawd have mercy, what is the world coming to? I hope you're wrong," Kya said.

"I hope so too. If not then I guess I'll have to do what I gotta do," Brandi said.

"Ladies, throughout our lives we all deal with obstacles and storms. There's always going to be something. I strongly believe that whatever we're going through we can't give up. We have to keep doing what we do," Bailey said.

"I agree but sometimes it's hard to see the light of day. Some of the shit you go through makes you want to give up," Kya said.

"That's true but you can't. If my husband is cheating I refuse to get sad and depressed. I have other things to live for. God didn't create me specifically to be a wife. His plan and purpose for my life involves much more than wifely duties. I have too much to do. I don't have time to shut down."

"Right on, momma. I wish I'd felt like that back in the day when I was dealing with Jeff. Instead I did the opposite. I was a mess," Kya said.

"I remember. I thought I was going to have to kick your ass. It seemed like you didn't want to snap out of it. Figuratively speaking, you were a wreck," Bailey said.

"You were more than a wreck and I felt bad for you. But in time you got through it and you healed," Brandi said.

"Okay, okay, I got it," Kya said.

"Deion just texted me," Bailey said.

"Damn, it's about time. I forgot that you texted her," Kya said.

"She said she won't be able to come and help right now. Something has come up and she'll try to come over later. She sends her apologies." Bailey said.

"Bullshit! If you hadn't sent her a text then we'd have been sitting here waiting on her all damn day. She's so full of it," Kya said.

"Maybe something did come up. It could be pertaining to the vandalism of her car," Brandi said.

"If she stopped fucking other people's men then she wouldn't have to worry about all of that foolishness."

"Kya, it could have been a random attack," Bailey said.

"Yeah, sure, what the fuck ever. Someone's wife just randomly attacked her car because she's fucking her man. Anyhoo, Brandi, where should we start? We're at your disposal," Kya said.

"Upstairs. The bulk of what needs to be done is upstairs."

"Okay, ladies, we're a man down so let's get busy," Bailey said.

"We can start in the guest room. The majority of the items on the bed are going to the Salvation Army or Goodwill," Brandi said.

"That's a lot of stuff. From what I see it looks like you aren't taking much to the new house," Bailey said.

"The only things in this room that I'm keeping are the pictures on the wall and the knick-knacks. Everything else must go."

"Is this trunk going to the Salvation Army or what, because it isn't labeled?" Kya asked.

"Girl, that darn thing should be going in the garbage. I've had that trunk since I was in junior high school."

"It doesn't look like it's in bad shape. All you would have to do is paint it," Kya said.

"It's really not. Well, put a Salvation Army label on it. If they don't want it, I'm sure they'll get rid of it."

Kya opened the trunk and started unloading what appeared to be old clothing. She then asked, "What would you like to do with the clothes?"

"That old stuff can go too. I haven't worn anything in that trunk in over two years."

"Girl, you know everything comes back sooner or later. Don't get rid of your retro and art deco outfits," Bailey said jokingly.

"Girl, I'm not taking any of that crap with me. Besides, since I've been putting on weight I can't do a darn thing with those clothes."

"Okey-dokey smoky, I'm on it," Kya said.

After Kya finished clearing the clothes out of the trunk, she saw some magazines in the bottom of it.

"Um, Bran," Kya said.

"Yes, ma'am?" Brandi asked.

"Whose and all the hell magazines are these?"

"Girl, those magazines are probably just as old as the trunk, you can chuck them."

As Kya grabbed some of the magazines out of the trunk she said, "Don't think so. This one's dated November last year."

As Brandi walked over to the trunk she said, "What magazines?"

Kya handed Brandi a magazine with two men on the cover. One man was bent over and wearing nothing but goggles, flippers and a G-string, and holding a fishing net. The other man stood behind him wearing a fishing hat with a pole in his right hand and wearing fishnet stockings and rain boots.

"*Back Door Luvin'* for the outdoorsman, what the shit is this?" Brandi said. Kya handed Brandi another magazine with two men on the cover in leather motorcycle jackets, leather underwear and some black leather boots that came to their knees. *Studs Gone Wild!*

"What the what?" Brandi asked.

Bailey walked over to the trunk and said, "Oh my word."

"I don't know whose these are but there are at least thirty other magazines in here," Kya said. She pulled the magazines out one by one, and asked, "Is it safe to assume these aren't your magazines, Brandi?"

"Hell no, those aren't my magazines."

"Maybe they belong to Derick," Kya said.

As Brandi knelt down beside the trunk she asked, "Why would Derick need a bunch of girlie magazines?" Kya and Bailey looked at each other with a confused expression, shaking their heads.

Kya started flipping through the magazines. "Um, sweetie, clearly these are in no way, shape or form girlie magazines. Haven't you've noticed the titles and that it's only men on all of the covers and throughout them?"

Bailey opened another magazine and said, "*Good Lawd*! I didn't even know this position was possible for humans to do. Wow! It's a shame he's wasting all that dick on some man. What is this world coming to? And why would Derick need a bunch of boy magazines? That's the question you should be asking yourself."

"What? So you're saying that Derick is gay?" Brandi asked.

"At this point I don't know what to say. Maybe he's bi, but whatever he is, he's definitely not into pussy. If that was the case then we'd be holding copies of *Hustler*, *Playboy* or *Voluptuous* in our hands," Kya said.

"Kya, shut up. Why the hell are you being so insensitive?" Bailey said.

"Bailey, I'm not being insensitive, I'm keeping this shit real! Clearly there's something going on. Please tell me what straight man has in their possession magazines containing only men?" Kya asked.

"Sweetie, maybe the books belong to someone else," Bailey said.

"Bailey, come on, I'm not stupid and don't patronize me, don't do that. Why the fuck would my husband hold onto someone else's gay magazines? No matter how you try to dress it up I'm not buying it. That doesn't make sense to me nor does the shit sound right," Brandi said.

"I'm just trying to give him the benefit of the doubt," Bailey said.

"What the fuck for? It looks like Mr. Man has some explaining to do," Kya said.

"You're damn right! No wonder he didn't want me to touch his shit. No telling what else I might find around here!" Brandi shouted.

"Everything done in the dark comes out in the light sooner or later," Kya said. Brandi started throwing the clothes off the bed to find the phone. She dialed Derick's number. It went straight to voicemail. Brandi hung up the phone and called several more times. Still no answer and the phone kept going straight to voicemail. For the next couple of minutes Brandi kept calling and still couldn't reach Derick. Finally, she decided to leave a message.

"Derick I'm in the process of packing and I have found items that aren't mine and I don't think they are appropriate for the Salvation Army. As soon as you get this message you might want to call me!"

"Okay, I guess we now know why he's not fucking her and the reason he's never at home," Kya whispered.

"Girl, this is some crazy shit," Bailey whispered back.

"This crazy shit just got real. Derick got skeletons in the trunk," Kya whispered.

"As usual I guess he's too busy to answer the phone," Brandi said sarcastically.

"Sweetie, do you want us to leave?" Bailey asked.

"Leave for what?"

"When Derick comes home I know you don't want us here while you discuss this," Bailey said, stuttering for words.

"I might need you here so I won't go to jail."

"Momma, I hate to say this but I need for you to calm down," Kya said.

"Calm down, calm down, are you serious? Kya, I can't believe you said that dumb shit to me. It's one thing to think that your man is cheating. But it's another thing to find out he's cheating with another goddamn man. A fucking man! That is *not* a good feeling."

"Would you like a drink? Because I could damn sure use one right about now," Bailey asked.

Brandi looked at Bailey and said, "A drink might make matters worse. I need a clear head when I confront him. How could I not know? Am I that naïve and dim-witted that I didn't see what was right in front of my face? This is the reason why he's been acting distant and weird. I guess that's why he doesn't touch me or want to be around me. I have nothing that he wants. And all along I thought that it was me doing something to push him away. If I don't have anything that he wants then why the hell is he still here?"

"To keep up the charade because his big gay ass is afraid of what others would think of him," Kya said.

"Come on, Kya, it's the twenty-first century and no one cares who's gay. Stop acting small-minded," Bailey said.

"I'm just saying clearly there's a reason why it's called down-low. He wants the best of both worlds. Unfortunately, it's at the expense of others," Kya said.

"Sweetie, ignore her, you know she's ignant. You don't know if he has actually cheated," Bailey said.

"Give me a second, I'll be right back," Brandi said.

"Where are you going?" Kya asked.

"To get a glass of water and two painkillers, I have a slight headache. Do you need anything while I'm downstairs?"

"No, we're good," Kya said.

"Bailey, you need to keep this shit real with her and stop acting like Mr. Fudge Packer or Mr. Getting His Fudge Packed is innocent," Kya whispered.

"I'm just trying to spare her the hurt and agony."

"Either way you look at it she's going to be hurt," Kya said.

"I guess you got a point. I just hate that this is happening to her all of people, she's a good girl and doesn't deserve this bullshit."

"I know what you're saying but we can't control the actions of Fudge-a-licous."

"Maybe he hasn't done anything and maybe this isn't his stuff," Bailey said.

"You're starting to sound a little naïve. In other words, you're saying that Mr. Man is gay-curious and that's all? Even if he was gay-curious he's married to a woman."

Bailey looked at Kya and asked, "What would be the difference with his curiosity versus me being curious about sexing women?"

"Okay, bitch, I see where you're going with this. But that's different. It's a major difference between the two."

"Explain to me the difference."

"Because it's much different and you know that," Kya said.

"No, I don't. That's why I need your smart ass to explain it to me, but you can't. So stop being fucking judgmental about the shit. Just remember when you're judging Derick you're judging me too. "

"I don't care what you say or how you put it, he's a man and it's wrong!" Kya yelled.

"Right now your personal opinions really don't matter because you're being one-sided and petty. It's easy for you to see the wrong in him because you never liked him from the get go," Bailey said.

"Maybe that's because I knew something wasn't right with him. Besides, he's an arrogant asshole! That's why I can't fucking stand him!" Kya yelled.

"Shhh. Keep your voice down."

"Whatever. You can call me small-minded, judgmental or whatever else you like. I'm keeping it real and he's a fudge-packing, taking-it-up-the-butt asshole! There's no need to give that freak nasty bitch any benefit of the doubt."

"And it's not for you to decide either. Even if he is on the down-low, if she chooses to stay with him, there ain't shit that you and I can do about it."

"Shit! You're lying to me, there's a whole lot I can do," Kya said.

"Not one damn thing other than be her friend and be supportive of her decision."

"What the fuck ever. Whether here or there, this conversation isn't about you or me."

"Finally, you said something that makes sense. I'm sure whatever the situation is, it can't be easy for him either, mentally. This shit is probably tearing him up on the inside," Bailey said.

Brandi walked in the room and said, "You know what, I wonder if he was gay before we met or was this something that started after our marriage?"

"I don't know," Bailey said.

"Well I know, I told you when I first met him that something wasn't right with him, but noooooo you didn't want to hear it," Kya said.

"Maybe he didn't know how to tell you or he was afraid of your reaction. Or this could have been something that he's wrestled with," Bailey said.

"Bailey, what you're saying isn't making much sense to me. Why do you insist on being so goddamn naïve when all the signs are here?" Kya asked.

"There's three sides to every story, his, hers and the truth. Since Derick isn't here to defend himself it's not for us to decipher or try to figure out. Right now at this very moment our primary job is to be here for Brandi, not attempt to make up a story or add shit that we don't know to a story. The truth of the matter is we don't know shit, so we need to stop assuming," Bailey said.

"Well, I know how my husband has been acting and how he's been treating me. I believe he's more than curious. Finally all the pieces of the puzzle are falling in place. I had my suspicions that he was cheating but I never would have guessed that he was cheating with men. I wonder how long this has been going on. You don't just wake up one day and decide, hmmm I think today I'm gay. Those types of feelings don't evolve overnight. I just bought a fucking house! What am I supposed to do now?"

"You will continue to do what you have to. A failed marriage is not the be all and end all," Bailey said.

"That's true, but . . ." Kya said.

"But what? But what, Kya?" Brandi asked.

"Hell, I don't have a fucking clue what I'm trying to say. If this is overwhelming for me I can imagine how you feel."

"I thought this was the man that I was going to be with for the rest of my life. I thought that he loved me. My head is literally spinning right now. After all I've been through I didn't think that it could get much worse."

"Derick is your husband but he's not the beginning and end of your life. There's more to life. There's a whole lot that you haven't done yet. A lot that you haven't tapped into," Kya said.

"Girl, you're still young and there's a whole lot more of living for you to do," Bailey said.

"You know what, for the past couple of weeks Derick has been really adamant about me not packing his stuff. If he didn't have anything to hide then why would it be a problem? There has got to be something that he didn't want me to find."

As Brandi got up, Bailey asked, "What are you about to do? Where are you going?"

"I'm going in my bedroom, there's got to be more of this sick ass shit around here. Remember, Derick had this house long before we got married." Brandi said. The ladies followed Brandi to the bedroom and stood in the middle of the floor. Brandi immediately went to Derick's closet and started pulling down the totes that were stacked against the wall.

She turned to Bailey and Kya and asked, "Are you going to help me or are you just going to stand there looking crazy?"

"What is it that you'd like us to do?" Bailey asked.

"I'd like you to help me find what I'm looking for."

"And what's that? You don't even know what you're looking for," Kya said.

"Don't you know if you look for trouble, you find trouble?" Bailey asked.

"Yup, sure do. But apparently I didn't have to look for trouble, it found me. Grab a tote and get looking."

As Kya went through Derick's dresser drawers she said, "If Derick happens to walk in while we're throwing his shit all around he's going to be pissed."

"At this point I couldn't care less what Derick has to say. I think he'll have enough questions to answer. His shit all over the room should be the least of his worries," Brandi said.

"Bran, I know right now your mind is probably all over the place and you may not be thinking rationally but I really think that Kya and I should leave," Bailey said.

"Ewwwww, Brandi, can't you be more discreet with your play toys?" Kya said.

Brandi walked out of the closet and asked, "What the hell are you talking about? I don't have any play toys."

"Is this not your Magic Thunder ten-inch dildo?" Kya asked.

Bailey turned and said, "Magic Thunder . . . I hope that's a neck massager."

"Oh it's a massager alright but it's not used for massaging necks," Kya said teasingly.

"That's not mine. Where did you find that?"

"I got it in the back of your nightstand," Kya said.

"That's not my nightstand, that's Derick's."

As Bailey and Kya's jaws dropped, Kya looked at Bailey and said, "If this ain't a shitty damn mess!"

"Girlfriend, that's an understatement," Bailey said.

"What the fuck is really going on?" Brandi asked.

"Okay, now you're starting to sound like me and that's scary," Kya said.

Brandi sat on the bed with tears rolling down her face and said, "I'm so fucking stupid. I shouldn't have married the first man that told me he loved me. Because he told me what I wanted and needed to hear, I fell for it. He said he'd never hurt me. He promised me that we'd have a great marriage. He told me that he was different. What a fucking joke!"

"He's different all right," Kya whispered under her breath.

"I'm not going to sit here and listen to you bash yourself. The choices that he made have nothing to do with you. Nothing at all. He's a grown damn man and he needs to own his actions. So you need to cut it out," Bailey said.

"Sweetie, I agree with Bailey, this has absolutely nothing to do with you. Derick could have been gay from the jump. Maybe he just got caught up in the societal pressures of life. He did what society programs and tells us to do: get a job, get married, buy a house, have babies and live happily ever after. Unfortunately, that shit only happens in the movies. We black people got real life problems, okay," Kya said.

"I will bet you everything that I have, if he could turn back the hands of time and do things differently he would," Bailey said.

As Brandi began to sob, Kya said, "Unfortunately, it's a little too late for could have, would have, should have."

"Like any other bullshit that we endure, we'll get through this too. Whatever decisions you make we're here for you," Bailey said.

Brandi stood and said, "I can do this. The devil is a liar and I declare that I will get through this. Just when I make one step forward something always pulls me back."

Bailey hugged Brandi, and whispered, "It's time to tap into that inner strength of yours. You're a strong woman and yes, you will get through this."

As Brandi turned to pick up the Magic Thunder box, Derick walked in the room and said, "Hey ladies, what's going on?"

KYA

Tracey Dowtin

Chapter Three

"Why are you constantly making excuses for why the relationship isn't advancing to the next level?" Steve asked.

"What relationship are you referring to?" Kya said.

"The relationship between you and me."

"But Steve, we're not in a relationship."

"What are you so afraid of?"

"I'm not afraid of anything."

What Steve didn't know was that she wasn't afraid to give more, but she just couldn't. Kya knew she could not offer him what he wanted, nor did she try to. During the time they hooked up her attention was focused on someone else. She really cared about Steve but she was still recovering from a seven-year relationship with Jeff. From the beginning, Kya's expectation of Steve had been nothing more than sex. Not only that; she saw Steve as someone to chill with, have fun and converse with from time to time. Unfortunately Steve didn't know he'd only been needed for a brief period of time to fill a void in her life.

"I thought we had a rule, no strings attached, just fun. From my understanding we weren't going to pursue a relationship. It was you that said in view of your last relationship ending badly, it would be best if you stayed single and just date occasionally," Kya said.

"I must admit when our friendship revived I was only interested in a friendship with no strings attached, but that's all changed." Despite Kya's "ghetto fabulousity" Steve thought she was a good woman with a big heart. In the beginning, Steve had had no hope or intention of falling in love. Without warning, his feelings quickly developed. He often expressed how he felt and that made Kya uncomfortable as well as run in the opposite direction.

"Even with me having my guard up I managed to develop feelings for you," Steve said.

"I too have feelings for you but more on a friendship level," Kya said.

"Are we supposed to be friends with benefits or are we actually working towards a relationship? I know we're not dating because we never do anything other than fuck. You come over to my house sporadically and I think I've been to your home maybe three or four times."

"Not today, please. Can we have this convo some other time? I'm tired and I'm not in the mood for this right now. This topic is becoming redundant and I'm tired of hearing about it."

"I think we should discuss it now. I can't go another day without knowing what's actually happening with us. I know this conversation is redundant to you but I'm just a little confused and need more clarity. What are we doing?" Steve asked.

"Oh goodness, here we go with this shit again!"

"What shit? All I asked was a simple question that deserves an answer. Maybe if it had been established in the beginning I wouldn't keep asking."

"It was established in the beginning, just friends. Our initial conversation was centered on that very topic. Nothing more and nothing less and no damn strings attached. Why do I have to keep reiterating that?"

"Kya, on a daily basis our needs change and so do the things we want in life."

"The world does not revolve around Steve. Things don't always happen how and when you want."

"Apparently you're not trying to get to the next level. I guess we're supposed to keep going like this forever. I'm too old for the games and bullshit."

"Even though our friendship is a little different I like how things are with us. We help each other out from time to time, we talk and fuck. Therefore, I don't owe you anything, including explanations."

"I bet in your eyes that's the perfect recipe for a great relationship. Maybe that's why your ex wouldn't commit, you have no expectations of anyone."

"I damn sure don't expect anything of you or from you!" Kya yelled.

"Wow, so it's like that? The only thing I'm good for is my dick, giving you money and random conversations?"

"If that's what you want to say. But please know that I don't need your dick, money or conversations. I was doing great before you and will continue after you. Trust and believe that!"

"I can't believe you, you're not even trying to give me a chance. I'm good enough to do everything for you but not good enough for you to be with."

"I never once said that you're not good enough to be my man. I clearly stated that I'm not ready for a relationship. You keep pushing and pushing as if that's going to make me change my mind. It's not, you're only getting on my nerves with the bullshit. You can't make me be ready any faster."

"Man, you know what, you're full of shit," Steve said.

"I don't understand what it is that you want from me! You keep complaining about me not spending time with you. I don't pay you any attention and I treat you like shit! If that's the case, then why are you still hanging around? I don't need you for shit, so you can leave me the fuck alone! I'm getting a little tired of having this conversation with you over and over," Kya said.

"Kya, you don't have to speak to me like that. Am I hollering and cursing at you?" Steve asked.

"No, but this bullshit is starting to irritate the fuck out of me. It seems like this is all you have to talk about."

"I told you from the jump if we ever crossed paths again, this time I would do what I could to make it work. I thought we both wanted the same thing. That night that we spent at the hotel, that was one of the things we discussed."

"Yeah, but things change. I thought I wanted to be in a relationship with you but I don't."

"You've expressed to me that I'm a good man and I make you happy. Let me rephrase that, I contribute to your happiness. If you think I'm such a good man then why won't you be with me? Is there something else that you're holding on to?"

"You are a good man. Hell, you're a great man. There's no doubt about that. I'm just not ready."

"What is it that you have to get ready for?"

"Why do I have to keep justifying the reason or reasons why I don't want to be in a relationship with you?" Kya asked.

"Because I think you owe me that."

"I don't owe you a goddamn thing!"

"I guess if it's up to you, our friendship, relationship or whatever you're calling it will remain. We'll continue to be nothing more than fuck friends."

"I didn't say that."

"Then what are you saying?"

"Why can't we leave things the way that they are?"

"Because I want more," Steve said.

"Well, I can't give you more. Not right now, maybe in the future. Steve, we've been friends for a long time and you're the last person that I want to argue with. We've had maybe three disagreements throughout our entire friendship. But this bullshit is for the birds. Damn! You are really starting to get on my goddamn nerves. I'm just not ready, leave it at that! I need some time and some space. I have a lot on my plate right now and my mind's going two hundred miles a minute."

"Kya, what is all of this for? I only asked a simple question about us being in a relationship, that's all."

"You want something from me that I'm not ready to give you. It's like you're not listening to a word that I'm saying."

"Kya, I want you. I want all of you," Steve said.

"I'm just not ready! Why can't you accept that?"

"I'm not a stupid person or anything but I have no understanding why you're so angry with me. I have never done anything wrong to you. You're acting as if I did something to harm you. I've never disrespected you and all I've done is be there for you and express my love for you. I've only treated you with the utmost respect."

"Well, you're bringing this shit on yourself. Leave me alone about this relationship bullshit then we won't have an issue."

"From the day that I mentioned my feelings you've given me an ongoing list of reasons why being in a relationship is not good.

According to you we shouldn't even be discussing the topic. First you tell me we should get to know each other a little better. Then you say we should feel things out. You said we should just let it flow. Then you finally admitted that you haven't gotten over your last relationship and you needed some time to heal. The last reason that you gave I can understand, we all need time to heal. However, if you had mentioned this in the beginning then I wouldn't have asked and inquired. I would have backed off and given you ample space. So there's really no need to continue this conversation."

"I hear you, everything that you're saying," Kya said.

"But are you listening to what I'm saying?"

"Yes, I'm listening. If you feel it's imperative to have this conversation then we'll have it."

"I don't compare you with any of my other female friends nor do I put you in the same category with them. You're you . . . and that's what makes you different."

"It's nothing personal against you but there are some things that I need to iron out, things I can't talk about right now," Kya said.

"That doesn't even sound right or make sense. But I guess that goes on the list too."

"Steve, truly you are a good man. In fact, you're a great friend and every woman's dream. Right now I'm just not ready to commit myself to you fully. I still need a little more time."

"More time? You want more time? I just gave you a year and a half of nothing but time. Oh, but I guess we *have* managed to do some things in that time. We've discussed your problems, your issues with your friends and the craziness of your job. I can't forget the occasional fucks in between it all. Unless there's something that you're not telling me, then this all sounds like bullshit. Maybe you already have someone and you're just stringing me along. Or maybe you're just holding on to me until you find someone else deemed worthy to you. You could be recovering from the relationship that you say you needed to heal from. I don't know. I love you and I'm in love with you. But I'm just a little tired of what appears to be some game you're running. Therefore, I think it's time for me to get off this bus because I'm tired of the ride. It was nice to be a part of your life again. I thought I had a second chance to correct what we couldn't get right the first time around. I see now that it was a waste of time," Steve said.

"Yeah, well, you live and you learn."

I just don't understand you women. You say you want a good man but when you get one, you treat him like shit. I guess when you've dealt with men who act like little boys then you're satisfied. Maybe if I was the type to cheat, beat the shit out of you, and leave babies all over the place maybe that would turn you on. You would love me to death and want to be my wife."

"*FUCK YOU!*" Kya yelled.

"You know what, excuse my language but you're being a real bitch right now! I think it would be best if I leave."

"You're so right. You leaving right now is one of the best ideas you've had all evening."

"Kya, I hope and pray that you find whatever it is that you're looking for. Apparently I'm not the man for you. I wish you the best. Goodbye," Steve said.

"Goodbye? This is how you want to end our friendship?"

"If and when you think about me, always know that I genuinely love you."

"Can't you be a little more patient with me? I do need you. What am I going to do without my buddy?" Kya asked.

"My patience has run out. You don't need me, Kya. If you did, things would have been a lot different. I'm tired of going in circles with you." Without saying anything more, Steve got up from the dining room table, grabbed his jacket and headed to the front door.

"Are you sure this is what you really want to do?" Kya asked.

"No, this isn't what I really would like to do but you leave me no choice. I might be a man but I have feelings too. I'm tired of being hurt by you. Just know that I've patiently waited all of that time for you. I've waited for you to decide that I was good enough for you. If I didn't love you, then I would have been gone by now. I tried to stick it out and wait on you but you don't want to be bothered. Maybe you and I just weren't meant to be."

"Maybe not."

"I chose you, I wanted you." As Steve walked through the door, he looked at Kya and said, "Bye, have a nice life."

"I will, you do the same!" Kya shouted.

Shortly after Steve left, Kya tried to call Bailey but she was unavailable. She decided that she needed to relax and regroup her thoughts. She drew a hot tub of water with her favorite bubble bath, lit some aromatherapy candles, poured a glass of wine, turned on her favorite John Coltrane jazz instrumental, *In a Sentimental Mood*, and then sat in the tub. About thirty five minutes into her relaxing bath her phone rang.

"Hello," Kya said.

"Hey, are you asleep?" Jeff asked.

"Nope, why, what's up?"

"I have something that I need to take care of so I need to bring Lexi home."

"I believe you're shit out of luck."

"Seriously, Kya, I have something to do."

"Jeff, you are so full of it. You specifically asked to get Lexi tonight. You were very persistent about getting her tonight and for the next couple of days. I thought you were going to visit your mom in Jersey?"

"Something's come up and I need to take care of some business."

"Whatever came up must be much more important than spending time with your daughter. Oh well! I guess you don't want to include her in your plans."

"How about I get her next weekend instead?" Jeff asked.

"No. I have plans next weekend that include my daughter."

"Come on, Kya, I really have something to take care of."

"That's not my problem. But if you bring Alexis home tonight, then you don't have to worry about seeing her again. Apparently whatever or whomever you're doing comes before your daughter."

"You're a real bitch."

"Why, thank you for the compliment. Now would you like to tell me something that I don't already know?"

"I don't understand why we're going through all of this," Jeff said.

"Because whenever you pick up Lexi you always call with some lame ass excuse why you all of a sudden need to bring her home. It would be nice one day if you could act like a full-time father instead of a part-time dad."

"What is that supposed to mean? I am a full-time father."

"In whose eyes?"

"You're really blowing this shit up. It's not that serious."

"Oh, but no, it *is* that serious. Have you ever stopped to fucking think how she might feel? Have you ever thought to ask her? You need to make a decision—my daughter or those trifling ass bitches that you fuck with. You know what, just bring my child home. You can go to hell."

"Damn, it's like that?"

"Yeah, it's like that."

"You know what, I'll manage. I guess I'll have to get someone to watch her."

"Jeff, all I need for you to do is bring Lexi home. That's it, and you don't ever have to worry about us again."

"Never mind, Kya. You be tripping and shit. I don't say anything when you're hanging out in the clubs and shit."

"What can you possibly say? Nothing, not a damn thing! We're not together so I can do what I damn well please. Secondly, I don't go out all of the time. But when I do, Lexi isn't home."

"Whatever you say. I have something to take care of, I'll talk to you later on."

"Whatever, you do, you're great at doing that!" Kya said as she pressed the "end" button on her phone. Her relaxation was broken and she got out of the tub.

Because of the argument with Steve then the argument with Jeff, Kya couldn't fall asleep. For hours she tossed and turned. She knew it was much too late to call any of her girlfriends. It wasn't the argument with Jeff that had gotten to Kya, it was the argument with Steve that really worried her. Even though Steve was right, she didn't want to tell him and break his heart. *Either way you look at it, he's pissed off with me and his heart is broken too.* She knew Steve was in love with her and his feelings were authentic. Not only did he say it often but he showed it as well. She could also see it in his eyes. *I know in some situations the truth is often painful and hurts but I should have told Steve the truth. I know our friendship would have been different if he'd known about Jeff. Damn! I'm damned if I do and damned if I don't. Why can't I get it right?*

Kya glanced at the clock and realized it was almost 3 a.m. *I have got to get some sleep. I'm going to be tired as hell in the morning. What am I going to do about Steve? I really do care about him and would love to be with him. But I find it hard to really trust men after all that I've been through with Jeff. He's a good man but I'm just scared to tear down the brick wall I've built. Oh my God, this could be a test, a lesson, a learning experience or a blessing in disguise. And like always, I've failed yet another test by walking away from Steve.*

What if Steve was the man that God sent to me? What if he's the man I've been anxiously praying for? I turned my back on him because I wanted to be with someone else. Someone that ain't the shit on the bottom of a shoe. I let him go because of someone that doesn't love me or give a fuck about me, a man I have a toxic relationship with. Because I tried to make it work I've probably missed out on someone truly deserving of me. To make matters worse, the feelings I had for Jeff are long gone. I think I was just dealing with him to have something to do. Shit! What am I going to do now? I know it's too late to call him but I have to speak with him. He probably doesn't ever want to hear from me again but I'm going to damn sure try. I'll just send him a text, that way it won't wake him.

Kya sat up in the bed and grabbed her phone off the nightstand. She then typed: STEVE, PLEASE CALL ME. IT'S VERY IMPORTANT. I REALLY NEED TO TALK TO YOU!

For the next several hours Kya monitored her phones. Every so often she'd check to see if there were missed calls or texts. She checked to make sure the ringers on all of her phones were loud. She even called to check that the phones were working properly. *Okay, so Mr. Man is really in his feelings and not doing me. I can't blame him but damn, he could at least return a bitch's calls. Something could really be wrong and he's not being responsive. Oh well, I guess for now I'll give him some space. Maybe he's just sitting back and trying to make me sweat a little.*

*

Several days later and Kya still hadn't spoken to Steve. Kya called Bailey to share the series of events that had taken place.

"What's up, mama?" Bailey asked.

"Hey girl, how are you?" Kya asked.

"I'm good, I can't complain."

"How are things with Noah?"

"They're going but we'll chat about that later. What's up with you and why do you sound so down in the dumps?"

"I've really fucked up good this time," Kya said sadly.

"What else is new?"

"No, this time it's bad."

"What in the world did you do now?"

"I let Steve go."

"How could you let someone go that doesn't belong to you? Please explain that one to me. I have no understanding of that."

"We had an argument the other night."

"About what?"

"Because he wants to be in a relationship and I don't. I spoke to him horribly and I feel like some shit."

"Seriously, sweetie, what was the argument about?"

"I just told you. He's in love with me and wants to be with me."

"Is that right? I still don't see how that could make you end your friendship? But oh well, maybe it wasn't meant to be."

"I can't say it wasn't meant to be when I never tried to make it work."

"So what are you going to do now?"

"I don't know. I feel like I've lost my best friend and I don't know to get him back."

"Let me ask you a question. Have you ever thought about telling him the truth? That's something you should have done from the jump. Instead you chose to keep stringing this man along. You need to tell him about Jeff. You can't move forward with him when you still have the door of your heart open to your ex."

"I wasn't intentionally stringing him along. I had no idea it would go this far."

"Then what would you like to call it, leading him on?"

"No, that's not it either."

"Then what were you doing Kya? Please make me understand."

"I thought we were having fun."

"Did you ever think that while you were having fun, feelings wouldn't evolve?"

"No I didn't. Because we said fun only. No strings attached."

"Even though we sometimes build up a brick wall around our hearts, the right person can come along and tear it down, when you least expect it. If you didn't care about this man then you wouldn't be sounding like a sick puppy. You would have said, oh fucking well, and kept it moving. I think you need to own up to your feelings and be honest with yourself. Once you do that you'll be better off."

"Better off than what?"

"Kya, cut it out. Stop acting like you don't have a clue as to what I'm saying. Stop acting like you don't fucking get it."

"All I know is right now I'm hurting and I want the pain to stop. I miss Steve so much and I don't know what to do. I've been so distracted and I haven't been able to focus."

"Why's that?"

"Because all I've done is think about him. No matter what I'm doing, he's in my every thought. All throughout the evening, throughout the night and this morning. When I close my eyes, I see his face. He's in *all* of my thoughts."

"Then I suggest you get your shit together. Stop acting like a goddamn spoiled ass brat and get some act right."

"Damn bitch, where is all of that coming from? Is that supposed to be tough love? If so, I don't want it."

"Kya, don't act like you're so freakin' innocent. You know what I'm talking about. You know what you need to do. I don't know why you called me with this foolishness."

"I don't want to hear that right now."

"Apparently you called me for a reason."

"To talk! But if you're going to be bashing me and shit I don't need that right now. I know I was wrong."

"As long as you know, that's all that matters."

"You're a real smart ass. You know I don't feel well and you giving me all of this shit."

"What's wrong with you?" Bailey asked.

"My stomach feels weird. I can't explain it, I feel horrible. I don't have an appetite and the thought of food sickens me more."

"Girl, that's love. Love is a great thing but love can also hurt like shit."

"I'm not worried about that, I'm not in love anyway. I knew I should have ignored that friend request he sent me. Dammit."

"Girl, don't blame Facebook for your problems. You wanted to hang out on that website all day every day, like a dog in heat."

"Bitch. I was networking."

"Okay, networking. Well, how is that working for you?"

"It's all right," Kya said jokingly.

"Have you seen him on Facebook lately?"

"Nope. No comments. No status updates, no nothing."

"He probably blocked your crazy ass."

"Whatever."

"All I have to say is that love bug bit that ass, didn't it?"

"It's not funny."

"Maybe the next time you'll close one door before opening another."

"Yeah, I guess so. Life man, life is a bitch," Kya said.

"No my dear, life is bitter and it's up to you to make it sweet."

"Oh Lawd, here you go with the metaphors and shit."

"Seriously, people always complain about their life. In all actuality it's your responsibility to make *'your'* life the best life you possibly can. You only get one."

"I guess you got a point."

"At some point or another we all have to endure."

"And I do!" Kya yelled.

"Okay then, this is just another one of those obstacles that you'll go over and get through."

"I know that's right. Besides, it's really not that bad. I just need a chance to speak to Steve. Once I do I'll feel better."

"I agree but make sure you're saying the right stuff. You need to be honest with him about why you acted the way you did. The truth of the matter is he did nothing wrong. He absolutely, positively did all the right shit. It's was your simple ass that was throwing game. And it's your dumb ass that needs to fix it."

"Okay with the names, I got it."

"Riddle me this, you are referring to Steve right?" Bailey asked.

"Yes ma'am, who else did you think I was talking about all of this time?"

"I just wanted to make sure we're talking about the same man. The same Steve that did any- and everything he could for you? And all he wanted in return was for you to spend time with him. But you always brushed him off. The same Steve that's always at your beck and call, no matter what. The same man that just said to you last week to give him an opportunity to show you what a real man is all about? You even said how good a man he is and that every woman would love to have. We are talking about the same man right?"

"Yup, that's him."

"Is this the same Steve that you always talk about, but treat like a red-headed step child?"

"Yes and no. I don't think I treated him that bad. You make it seem as though I treated him bad for the hell of it."

"The hell you say. You did that man wrong. Just wrong for no reason. I thought he was crazy as shit for wanting to deal with you from the get go. But you always managed to make excuses. You know excuses only build bridges to nowhere, and look where they got you—no damn where. If you felt as though things were moving too fast and getting too heavy you could have bowed out gracefully. But *noooooo*, you just had to be an ass about the whole thing."

"I just thought that I'd try once again to salvage my relationship with Jeff that's all. There's no harm in trying."

"No there's not, but you've been trying for years to make it work with Jeff. You wanted the relationship not Jeff. Anything one-sided never works."

"Damn, Bailey, you don't have to keep rubbing the shit in!" Kya yelled.

"There's no need for an attitude. Why are you getting shitty with me? You're the one that ruined a good thing."

"I know but you don't have to keep throwing it in my face."

"You never know what you have until it's gone. Do you know yet?"

"Whatever."

"No matter how you acted or how much of an ass you were, he was still there through it all. Even when you had plans with him but you never showed up because you were with Jeff. He still forgave you no matter what you did. This man needs an award or something."

"What is the point to all of this?"

"The point is that this man genuinely loves and cares about your crazy ass. In spite of your imperfections, flaws, issues, faults, dishonesty, whatever, he still loves you anyway. All he asked of you was a chance to be with you. A chance to make you and your daughter happy. That itself speaks a lot about his character. "

"Damn, and he said all of that too. He said he loved me and he wanted to show me how a real man treats women."

"Is the well completely dry and missing the water?" Bailey asked.

"Yes, the well is definitely missing the water."

"I don't know why you're tripping, you didn't want him anyway, right? Now he can go and find a real woman that will treat him the way he deserves to be treated."

"Okay, damn! I realize that I made a big mistake. Probably the biggest mistake that I've ever made but what can I do?"

"I can't tell you what to do. I love you and I care about you but I can't tell you what to do or how to live your life. I can make suggestions but at the end of the day the choice is yours."

"Deep down inside I know what I want to do but I'm afraid. I'm afraid that I won't make the right choice."

"Babes, please don't let fear ruin your life. Life is about taking risks. You're not a psychic and you can't predict the future. You just have to jump out there—on faith. Whatever decision you make, God must be in the center of that decision. Instead of you trying to figure it out and work it out, just give it to Him."

"Maybe that's been my problem from the get go. I haven't included God in the bulk of my choices. And when I don't things always go bad," Kya said.

"Okay, so there you have it. Now you have your answer and know what to do. Give it to God and leave it there. Once you give it to him don't be meddling, just let him take care of it. Trust Him. Work some of that faith that you have."

"That sounds like a good idea," Kya said.

"Well listen, since you don't want Steve, I know a lot of women that would love to have him."

"I never said that I didn't want him and you're not making me feel any better."

"Good. You should feel like some shit."

"Now you're doing a good job of making me feel worse."

"I'm not trying to make you feel bad. Just look at it as tough love, my dear. Kya, you were with a man for seven whole years and he treated you like some dog shit. Then a man comes along and wants to be your knight in shining armor and you shoot him down. He wanted you as you are—broken, torn and with a whole lot of baggage. He wanted to rescue you from the bullshit that you've endured the majority of your adult life. But you just couldn't see past Jeff or leave him alone. Maybe you were okay with Jeff treating you badly. Maybe you love being with a no-good-ass nigga that only fucks you when it's convenient for him."

"Hell no! I'm not okay with that. I know I deserve better. Damn bitch, what the hell is going on with you, did I call at a bad time? You're being overly blunt today. What the hell has gotten your panties all in an uproar today?" Kya asked.

"Nothing's wrong with me. I'm just tired of you doing dumb shit and then wondering why things never work out for you. It's self-explanatory."

"I see you're not holding any punches back today."

"Do I ever? Did you really expect me to take your side? If you're wrong you're wrong. And you my dear, are very wrong the way you handled this Steve situation."

"I thought you'd be a little more empathetic or something."

"Sweetie, you know that I'm not the one that will lie, sugar-coat bullshit, pull wool over your eyes, or sell you a pipedream. I'm honest, candid and chances are I will not bite my tongue. So, if you want a friend that fabricates lies, makes the bullshit look good, and who lives in a world of illusions with you, then I suggest you find another friend. I'm me and will continue to be me. You have the option to love me or leave me the hell alone, it's totally your choice."

"I know all of that and I don't want you to sell me a pipedream or anything else. I know you have my best interests at heart. If I didn't want your opinion then I wouldn't have brought my drama to you. I'm in need of a drink right about now. A buttery nipple, diamond martini, or a blow job shooter is calling my name. I can't get this shit together to save my life."

"Oh really, you don't say," Bailey said. "I sympathize for you wholeheartedly, but if I was Steve I would leave your ass alone and never look back."

"Wow, I can't believe you said that."

"Believe it! Why should he think that you want to be with him after the way you treated him?"

"Because."

"Because what, Kya?"

"Because I will ask him to forgive me, and beg him to give me another chance."

"That's all?"

"I'm going to also tell him why I wasn't emotionally available. I'll be honest about what was actually holding me back."

"Now you're getting it. No matter how bad it might hurt, just make sure you don't leave anything out. Remember, you'll have to earn his trust back. But please be honest with him."

"If he ever accepts my calls or finds it in his heart to talk to me. I'll be completely honest with him and tell him everything."

"Good, I'm glad to hear that. If Steve is as great as you keep saying then he'll hear you. He'll look past all of your stupidity and forgive you. Then you and Steve can start all over. But the right way this time."

"Thanks for being so encouraging," Kya said sarcastically.

"Sure, anytime. Now I need for you to get yourself together. Get out of that funky mood that you're in. Get your ass up and dust yourself off."

"I will. I feel somewhat better. Even though you tore me a new asshole. I know what I must do."

"That's called tough love. We all need that sometimes."

"Well, I'm going to let you get back to work. Do you want to go out for drinks later?"

"I can't. I'm leaving here shortly to go to the boutique. Then I have a dinner meeting with Noah and some potential clients."

"Okay, maybe tomorrow. Thanks for listening, yelling and giving advice."

"No problem. I'll call you a little later on."

Because of Kya's lack of efficiency in the office she thought she'd be more productive if she worked from home. After her long conversation with Bailey she decided to try and do some work and began working on her monthly report. Her phone rang. Kya glimpsed at the caller ID and saw it was Bailey calling back.

"What's wrong?" Kya asked.

"You will never *believe* who I just ran into?"

"Who?"

"Steve," Bailey said.

"Shut up, are you serious?"

"Yes I am. I looked right at him and I didn't even recognize him."

"How could you not recognize him? He and I were at your house a couple of weeks ago."

"I was on the phone running my mouth and doing fifty other things at one time."

"Did he ask about me?"

"Nope, he didn't even mention you, even after I purposely brought you up. I shared with him that you and I spent the morning on the phone. He still didn't say anything about you."

"Is that right?"

"Yup. I thought it was weird that he said nothing about you. But then I remembered that you said he was an extremely private person."

"And that he is," Kya said.

"Child, he looked good as shit, Whew! There is something about a bearded man," Bailey said.

"Okay, thanks for rubbing it in," Kya said.

"Girl I can't believe that you let that fine looking specimen get away with his baldheaded ass self. And his skin, girl, that man is gorgeous. He looks like a chocolate Adonis."

"Bye, girl, I'm hanging up now. I have to get my reports done. Call me later on," Kya said.

"Okay, girl. Later."

Bailey's call had distracted Kya even more and she couldn't focus on her work. She decided to take a nap and complete her reports later on. Before drifting off to sleep she tried calling Steve once more. The faster her heart pounded, the more she wished he would answer the phone. Unfortunately he didn't.

Damn! I guess he really doesn't fuck with me anymore. Kya then left another message pleading for Steve to call her back.

When she couldn't fall asleep she lay in the bed pondering over the mistakes and decisions that she'd made throughout her life. She thought about the years she'd spent with Jeff. She even wondered whether she and Jeff might have had a good chance of their relationship actually working if he hadn't cheated. *I know we're all capable of change but why can't he see how his behavior ruined things? I've never done anything wrong to jeopardize our relationship. I don't understand why he treated me like that. Is our relationship worth salvaging yet again or should I just let go? There's no sense in me trying to take a nap. I'm just lying in the bed wasting precious time. I could be finishing up my work. Especially since the deadline is tomorrow. Furthermore, it's too early in the day for me to be sleeping, that's not even me.*

As Kya got up and went downstairs to get her laptop, her phone started ringing. *That could be Steve calling,* Kya thought. She quickly grabbed the cordless phone and looked at the number. *Shit, it's only Deion.*

"Hello," Kya said.

"Hey, Ky. What are you doing?" Deion asked.

"Shit, I'm about to do some work. Why what's up?"

"Nothing much. I was seeing if you wanted to hang out tonight."

"I wish I could but I have to finish these reports."

"Alrighty then, I thought you might be up for a little fun."

"Girl, if I didn't have this deadline I would love to hang out. I'm in need of a cocktail."

"Why, what's wrong?" Deion asked.

"Girl, baby daddy drama, and then some."

"Oh goodness! Are you sure I can't convince you to come with me?"

"No, not this time, I'll pass."

"Okay, well, I'm not going to hold you. Give me a call tomorrow," Deion said.

"Have fun and don't do anything I wouldn't."

"Darling, please, what would be the point in that?"

"Bye, girl."

Concluding the call with Deion, Kya immediately started working on her monthly reports. After an hour and a half she finished. *Whew! I can't believe I finished my reports so fast. I can still actually go out with Deion but I think I'll chill at home instead. Let me call Bailey and see what she's doing. She's probably still at the office knowing her.*

"Hola," Kya said.

"Hola," Bailey replied.

"I have something to tell you," Kya said.

"Uh oh, what's wrong now?"

"After we got off the phone earlier I was doing some thinking."

"Okay, and?"

"I've decided to give Jeff another chance."

"What? Get the fuck out of here! Have you lost your mind?"

"I thought about it and this is something I have to do."

"Are you doing this because Steve hasn't called you back and you feel like Jeff is your only chance?"

"No, those aren't my reasons."

"Didn't you tell me earlier today that your relationship with Jeff was over? Didn't you say you were tired of his bullshit? So when did everything change? Oh, he must have come over for an afternoon delight and fucked the shit out of you. Is that why you changed your mind?"

"No, I just thought I'd give him another chance."

"*O M freaking G*! Kya Renee Turner, are you high? Please tell me you're just joking! I know you're not going to settle with that shiftless Negro just to say you got a man. Kya you're better than that."

"I wouldn't say that."

"Then what the hell are you trying to say? There are too many women out here that settle because they think they have to. And they don't think they'll ever find a good man or Mr. Right."

"Please tell me the definition of a good man—Mr. Right."

"Girl, I really don't know what's going on with you. You say one thing but you do the total opposite. You need to get your shit together!" Bailey yelled.

"Whatever, Bailey, my shit is together."

"Clearly it's not if you're going to keep dealing with Jeff."

"See, that's why I didn't want to say anything to you about Jeff."

"Seriously, what the hell did you think I was going to say? Did you think I was going to say congratulations and I wish you the best? Hell fucking no!" Bailey shouted.

"I expected you of all people to be a little more supportive. But all this bullshit you're giving isn't necessary."

"You are absolutely right, my dear. Keep doing you. Do whatever it is that your heart desires and makes you happy. It's your life to live, not mine."

"Exactly. It's my life."

"I just hope that you aren't turning into one of those women that will deal with all the bullshit that a man throws their way because they feel like they need a goddamn man. I thought you were smarter than that."

"Right now a lecture is not what I really want to hear. You're supposed to be my friend – my sister."

"And I am, but that doesn't mean if you want to jump off a bridge I'm going with you to push you over the edge."

"I see you don't really understand so I don't think there is a need to keep having this conversation. It is what it is."

"True indeed."

"I mean damn, Jeff and I were together for seven years and I just think there still might be a chance that it could work, he'll change this time."

"Okay, whatever you say, girlfriend."

"So you don't think people are capable of change?"

"I sure as hell do. Anyone is capable of change. But riddle me this, Kya, if he hasn't changed in all of these years why would now be any different? Why would you continue being in a toxic relationship with this man?"

"I know that I can't change Jeff or his behavior and he has to change because he wants to. But everyone deserves a second chance."

"If I'm not mistaken you've given him chance after chance after chance. Apparently he doesn't want to change. So it's hopeless. How much more do you want to take from him? Girl, let that shit go and keep your ass moving."

"Anything worth having is worth fighting for, right?"

"I agree but . . ."

"But what?"

"But some shit just ain't worth fighting for. Especially when he's causing you too much pain."

"Well, we all have to go through shit. You know that better than anyone."

"What the fuck is really going on with you? Is there something you need to tell me?"

"No, I'm just saying."

"Saying what? What the hell are you saying? That you'd rather be in a mentally, emotionally abusive relationship than be with someone that treated you like a queen? That's what it sounds like you're saying to me."

"You just don't understand. You don't get it."

"You're right I don't! Just earlier today it was Steve this and Steve that. But now you've jumped back on Jeff's dick. Is it because Steve isn't putting up with the bullshit that you threw his way? Oh, you finally met your match and can't deal with it."

"Girl, please. This isn't about Steve."

"Then what is it about?"

"It would nice if you could be a little more supportive."

"Naw, I can't support this bullshit. That's crazy, Kya. Are you listening to what you're saying? You're contemplating going back to someone that treated you horribly. And you want support?"

"Yes, I do," Kya said.

"Jeff's dick must be dipped in gold and down to his knees. He's got you wide open," Bailey said.

"Think and say what you want. Like you said, the choice is mine and it's my life."

"You're so right. If you don't want my advice or comments then don't involve me in your bullshit. My plate is quite full these days, my sister. I have enough to worry about and I damn sure don't need anything else."

"I didn't call you for your advice or approval, I just wanted to share with you."

"I understand that your thoughts are going a hundred miles a minute. But you need to really think about what you're about to get into. Maybe you should just go away for a couple of days to regroup, clear your mind and relax. Would you like to do that?" Bailey asked.

"I can't go away at this very moment. Not this second. Besides, we have the spa trip coming up so I have to get my work finished."

"That's a part of the problem, you have too much going on and you're not thinking clearly. Honey, you need to slow down so you can get it together. You're doing too much and you're doing too much thinking. Give your mind a break. Why don't you drink a glass of wine and just chill the hell out?"

"I tried but that's not working. Bitch, I know you're not talking. Practice what the hell you preach."

"Girl this isn't about me, we're talking about you right now."

"Okay, I got it. I can handle it and don't need to run off to some island to figure it out. Well, at least not tonight anyway. Maybe I need to go somewhere and be like Stella and get my goddamn groove back."

"I know that's right."

"It's also a possibility that I may not be able to go on our spa trip."

"What the hell ever! Why, Kya?"

"I'm starting a new contract. But maybe afterwards I'll consider it. Anyhoo, are we done with this convo? I got shit to do."

"Ho, you called me at my place of business."

"Oh yeah, that's right."

"Well, let me say this and I'll let you go," Bailey said.

"Okay, what's up?" Kya asked.

"You know I'm your friend and I love you dearly. Ultimately, whatever decision you make, whether I like it or not, I'll still be your friend. And yes, as much as I hate heat, I will walk through the fire with your simple ass."

"Thanks girl, I really needed to hear that. Right now I just don't know what to do and I admit I'm all over the place."

"Sweetie, believe it or not this is the most tedious problem that I've heard all week. Trust me it's easy to figure it out. You know deep down in your heart what you should do. You know what's best for Kya. I also suggest that not only do you follow your heart but use your mind. Do you want to be miserable or happy?"

"Of course I want to be happy."

"Do you want a good man or a no-good-ass loser that can't keep his dick in his pants?"

"I want a good man, a real man and not a damn little boy."

"Okay, well I think you've just answered your own damn question. Go and get your man then."

"I'm trying. I wish it was that easy. I've been calling and texting Steve but he won't return any of my calls."

"It is that easy—trust and believe."

"What I do know is that every now and then our behavior or what we say can make a man pull away. When we're close to someone, we really know how to push their buttons. That doesn't mean that he doesn't want to talk to you or doesn't care about you. He just needs some time. Let him cool off first. Give him a little bit of space. Right now it's okay for him if he pulls away. After some time he'll be ready to talk. Don't think that he doesn't notice you blowing up his phone. He sees all of that and it's tearing him up not to respond. He wants to call you and talk, but he's angry and hurting. When he's ready to talk, he'll get in touch with you. Men and women are totally different and you know this. When we hurt we want to talk, talk, talk and talk some more. We want to let the world know what's going on. And men are totally opposite, they pull away. With them it's that whole autonomy versus intimacy issue."

"Thanks, Dr. Phil," Kya said jokingly.

"I'm glad to see you can incorporate some humor into all of this drama. But you know you fucked up, don't you? I just wanted to say that one more time."

"Please stop rubbing it in my face. I know I've fucked up royally."

"When real love is between two people there's nothing you can do to keep them apart. You'll always get another chance to get it right, but only if it's real. No matter what you do or say the couple always goes back together. Sweetie, your relationship with Jeff wasn't based on real love. It was based around convenience and lust. He was convenient for you and you were convenient for him."

"You think I'm in love with Steve?" Kya asked.

"I know you're in love with Steve. I've been waiting a long time for you to recognize that you're in love with Steve. You talk about him all of the damn time and when you do, you light up. No matter what we're discussing you manage to incorporate his name in the conversation. We could be talking about going to buy a pair of Manolo Blahniks and somehow you bring him up. You have this incredible glow all over your face if his name's mentioned."

"I care about him a lot."

"When you care about someone as a friend you don't light up like a damn Christmas tree. That's called love, Kya."

"And when I think about the things that he's done to me sexually, girl, I feel like I'm going to snap, crackle and pop!" Kya yelled.

"Okay, mama, that's too much information. Give Steve a couple of days to gather himself. He'll call you real soon."

"How can you be so certain?"

"Because I know. This is just a phase you guys are going through. The second phase of your life together will be much better."

"Um . . . you're being very optimistic."

"Hell, yeah! You better start claiming that good man."

"Okay, girl."

"Well, I've already claimed him on your behalf," Bailey said.

"Thanks. Are you still at the office?"

"No, I left the office a couple of minutes ago."

"Are you on your way home?"

"Heck no!"

"Where are you going?

"I'm in need of a little retail therapy, I'm going to get my shop on."

"Are you going to Macys or Niemans?"

"Neither, to my own boutique."

"Bailey, I was in your closet last weekend and there's nothing that you need."

"Well, I wasn't originally planning on shopping, I was just going stop by to handle some business. However, a new shipment of items was delivered today."

"Yeah, whatever. Don't forget, I've know you since we were in the playpen."

"Naw, babes, I'm not shopping tonight. I have to meet Chase to rectify his invoice and show him some new items."

"Who the hell is Chase?"

"You know, Chase—the fashion stylist."

"His name doesn't ring a bell."

"Kya, as much as you are in my boutique, I know you've met Chase."

"No, I don't recall ever meeting anyone named Chase. And you know I never forget a name or a face."

"When you see him, you'll remember."

"If you say so."

"Anyway, hold on one second, my husband's on the other line," Bailey said.

Kya waited.

"I'm back, girl. He has lost his damn mind," Bailey said.

"What?' Kya asked.

"He told me not to bring any bags in the house. And *not* to be late for a meeting that I have to attend in a couple of hours."

"I guess you heard that. But seriously, where are you really?"

"I'm not shopping. I told you, I'm at the boutique and waiting on Chase. But girl, we just got a delivery and got some bad shit up in here. *Haute!*"

"I'm on my way!" Kya shouted.

"Um, excuse me. You gets nothing, notta, zilch, my friend."

"What? What you talking?"

"You still haven't paid for the other shit you got."

"Uh huh, yes I did."

"Girl, whatever! I can't keep getting shit and giving you shit too."

"Yes you can, you're the HBIC—the head bitch in charge."

"Very true but still, somebody gotta pay for it. Besides, I already have four bags of stuff!"

"Ewwww, Noah's going to kick your ass."

"What the hell ever."

"I'm calling Noah. Didn't he say not to bring any bags in the house?"

"Yes, he sure did and what does that mean to me? I'm not going to take them in the house. Well at least not today anyway. I'll leave the bags in the back of my truck. Ha ha, how you like that?"

"You're a damn mess."

"And you know this. Don't be talking shit either, bitch, I did manage to grab some shit for your ass too. Even after I told you I was cutting you off."

"Aw shit, what did you get me?"

"I'm not telling you. You'll have to wait and see. Now, call and tell Noah that," Bailey said.

"Girl, I was just playing."

"I knew you'd change your tune. Anyway, let me get off this damn phone, I told him I was leaving shortly and I need to grab some shoes. So I have at least five more minutes to shop before Chase gets here."

"You know what?" Kya asked.

"What?"

"I temporarily lost my mind. I really need that spa trip. I was crazy to think I wasn't going. We're still going right?" Kya asked.

"Yes, ma'am, we sure the hell are. That's the plan."

"Good. I need to start working on a babysitter for Lexi."

"My girls will be with my mom, just take her over there."

"I just might do that."

"Girl, I need me a break bad."

"I agree. We all have been dealing with a lot of bullshit lately. I think we're in dire need of some rest, relaxation, rejuvenation, fun and plenty of cocktails," Kya said.

"Yes indeed. I believe this shit with Noah is really taking a hold of me."

"Have you confronted him yet?"

"No, not yet. I just walk around like everything is all good."

"What the hell are you waiting for?"

"I'm still thinking. I need to have a clear mind when I confront him about his infidelity."

"I don't know how you walk around like nothing's wrong."

"It's not the easiest thing to do, trust me. I'm almost sure he knows something's wrong. Especially since he ain't been getting the va-jj."

"Awww shit. This bitch is holding back the va-jj. That man is going to go crazy now."

"He'll manage, but he can always tell when I'm pissed about something. He also knows when something's brewing in my head. Trust and believe that. He acts like he has something to tell me but doesn't know how."

"I think you need to stop playing around and say something. Hell, just lay the shit out on the table. Besides, you need to get this bullshit off your chest. What's the worst that can happen at this point?"

"Girl, I'm good. I'm just not ready to have this conversation with him yet. It's not like he's breaking his neck and confessing."

"Whatever. I hope you know what you're doing."

"I do. So don't worry about me. I have it all under control. It's all good."

"That's what scares me," Kya said.

"Let me get off of this phone. I have places to be and people to see."

"Okay, later," Kya said.

Kya feverishly paced her bedroom floor. *I have got to find something to do with myself. I don't know if it's anxiety or a lot of nervous energy, but I have got to get it together. I can't manage to sleep, eat or concentrate. I've never felt like this before in my life. Even if I wasn't around Steve all of the time, we've always spoken throughout the day. Now I feel like I don't know what to do with myself. It feels like I lost my best friend. I'm so fucking bored. At this point I no longer feel like dealing with Jeff. If I call him I know his ass will be more than happy to come over and that's not what I want. It's time that I put some space between the two of us. With the exception of Lexi being his daughter, it's time he and I put our relationship behind us. Maybe I need to chillax and hang out with myself for once. Just do me for once. I don't always need a man hanging around me or all up in my face. Hell, I definitely need to heal from that nightmare of a relationship with Jeff. I definitely don't want to carry around all of the old ass baggage. It's not fair to make the new man suffer from the bullshit of another man, that's crazy.*

The next day, as Kya awoke, she thought, *I've wasted enough time with Jeff. I know he's never going to change. Why am I lying to myself and why am I trying to hang on to something that died a long time ago? If I can't be honest with myself, who can I be honest with? I'm no longer in love with Jeff. Fuck, I don't even like being around him at this point. How much more can I take? How long do I want to keep dealing with his foolishness? When is enough, enough? Right fucking now! I believe within my heart of hearts that I had a chance with a good man but I let him go. I let him slip through my fingers and why, for somebody that don't give a shit about me? Maybe it's not too late but it's not going to work if I don't close this chapter with Jeff. Oh goodness, the way things ended with Steve, he probably has nothing else to say to me. Why was I so stupid? I can't believe with the shortage of good men, I actually let one slip away. I was too stupid to see that I had a good man before me and he genuinely wanted me for me. He knew about all my issues and faults and wanted me anyway. He pushed me to pursue my dreams and to get more out of life. I know I've really messed up and I don't know what to do to fix this situation. I'll put it in God's hands. That's all I need to do. If it's His will that Steve and I are together then it will be.*

Kya sat on the side of the bed, glanced out the window and exhaled. As she walked over to her bedroom window and opened the blinds, she instantly felt as though a weight had been lifted off her shoulders. She realized she had a lot of errands to run but wanted to call Steve. She really didn't want another day to end without apologizing to him for the things that she said and how she behaved during the last time they saw each other.

Kya quickly went into the bathroom to wash her face and brush her teeth. As she walked downstairs she could hear her phone vibrating, then ringing. She assumed it was one of her girlfriends and ignored it. She walked into the kitchen to get a glass of orange juice and to fix herself breakfast. She wanted to call Bailey to see if she was available for lunch. But she knew once the two of them got on the phone, time would slip away and she wouldn't get anything accomplished.

When Kya finished cooking breakfast she went into the living room to grab her purse and phone. As she sat down, she saw one missed message and realized it was from Steve. Her heart immediately started pounding.

As eager as she was to see and hear what he had to say, Kya was hesitant. *Wow! This is weird, I got up this morning and my first thought was about him. I was going to call him when I got a chance. I must have willed him to get in touch with me.* She scrolled to the missed message and began reading:

GOOD MORNING, KYA, I HOPE THIS TEXT FINDS YOU WELL. I WAS WONDERING IF I CAN STOP BY LATER ON TODAY. I WASN'T THRILLED HOW OUR LAST CONVERSATION ENDED AND I HAVE SOMETHING THAT I NEED TO TELL YOU. GIVE ME A CALL WHEN YOU HAVE A FREE MOMENT.

Hmmm, I wonder what he needs to tell me and why does it have to be face to face? Oh shit, I hope everything's okay. I'm not going to respond right away because I'll look too press. I'm going to wait for a couple of hours then respond. I have got to call my girl Bailey, I need help to figure this shit out. After I shower and get dressed, I have to leave out but I'll stop by her office on my way home. Oh hell, I can't wait that long. I'll stop by her office before I run my errands. I better call Ms. Busy Body first. No telling what her work schedule is like.

As Kya got the jam out of the refrigerator she dialed Bailey.

After the third ring Bailey answered and said, "Good morning, love bug, what's up?"

"Hey girl, where are you?" Kya asked.

"Right now I'm on my way to work, just sitting in traffic."

"How's your schedule for the day? I wanted to see if you can do lunch. If not, I want to stop by for a quick chat before I run my errands."

"This morning my schedule is pretty much open, why, what's wrong?"

"Um, I just need to chat. I've been doing some thinking."

"Oh Lord. You know sometimes that's detrimental to your well-being."

"You are such a smart ass."

"I'm just playing."

"Steve sent me a text."

"Great, it's about time. What did he say?"

"I'll fill you in on that later. But I've finally figured out what I want to do and have made a decision."

"What have you decided?" Bailey asked.

"I have finally figured it out. I now know what I'm supposed to do and who I'm supposed to be with. I'll see you in about an hour."

"Alright, see you then."

Since time was of the essence, Kya grabbed her plate off the breakfast nook and went upstairs. She took a quick shower, put on some jeans, a white t-shirt with a silver "diva" logo and pulled on her boots. She then put her hair in a ponytail, applied a little Mac lip gloss and down the steps she went. On her way out of the door, she grabbed her purse from the kitchen, got her short leather jacket out of the hall closet, set the alarm, and left the house.

As Kya walked to her car, she knew that from the beginning of the conversation to the end, Bailey was going to have a lot of input. But that was Bailey and no one expected any less of her. Fortunately, Bailey was the one person that she could trust with her innermost secrets. No matter how much Kya got into or what she did, Bailey always had her back no matter what. Sometimes Kya wasn't in the mood to hear Bailey fussing and cursing. Nonetheless she appreciated her honesty and bluntness. She knew Bailey would never steer her in the wrong direction. *But first things first, I need to arrange a time to meet with Jeff. It's time to put this nightmare to an end. I'm really proud of myself for finally having the strength as well as nerve to end the relationship with Jeff. It's been long overdue and I'm ready to start the next chapter of my life. I'll call Jeff right now.*

"Hi Jeff, when are you bringing Lexi home?" Kya asked.

"Why, do you miss her?" Jeff asked.

"Of course I miss my little princess. Are you going to bring her home tomorrow afternoon or evening?"

"I need to go and buy some shoes and shit. I'll bring her home after dinner."

"Are you cooking dinner or are you going out?"

"Most likely we'll go out. If so, I'm almost sure she'll want to go to Ruby Tuesday's."

"Just make sure whatever she eats it's something healthy. Because of my schedule lately, I think I've been overdoing it with the carry-outs and fast food. So now, it's almost like Lexi expects that shit. But she's in for a big surprise. Starting tomorrow we won't be eating out all of the time nor will we be eating fast food. Make sure she enjoys Ruby Tuesday's because we won't be visiting them for a while."

"Will do," Jeff said.

"Well, when you bring her home do you think you'll have a couple of minutes to talk?"

"Of course, what do you want to talk about?"

"If I wanted to have the discussion over the phone I wouldn't have asked if we could talk when you stop by tomorrow. Don't you think?" Kya asked.

"Is everything okay?"

"Yeah, everything's A-Okay. Give Lexi a hug and a kiss for me and make sure you give her those vitamins. Tell her to call me later on."

"Okay."

After twenty five minutes of sitting in traffic, Kya finally arrived at Bailey's office. Kya inhaled then exhaled. *Let me take a deep breath and get my ass upstairs. The sooner this conversation is over, the better. It's almost like walking into the principal's office after you've done something wrong. I hope Bailey's in a good mood. If not I won't be able to get a word in edgewise. I hope no one's pissed her off beyond the level of pissedosity this morning. She sounded like she was in a great mood when I spoke to her earlier. Let me stop in the lobby and get her a pastry and a vanilla latte from Starbucks. Knowing her, she didn't have a chance to eat breakfast this morning.*

After leaving Starbucks and walking to the elevator, Kya noticed Noah heading in the same direction. Kya walked quickly so she could get to the elevators before Noah had a chance to get on and go up to the office.

"Are you running late this morning?" Kya asked.

Noah turned around and said, "Hey, what are you doing here? Are you playing hooky from work today?"

"Yes I am. I needed a day off. Why are you so late this morning? Your wife has been here for a while."

"Yeah, I'm running a little late. I stopped and got an oil change before I came in. If I listened to my wife, I'd be here at 7 a.m. with her, all seven days a week."

"I know, right."

"The four of you are definitely women that want the best out of life and don't have a problem working your asses off to get it. You talk about Bailey, the last time I checked you were working as hard as she was. How many jobs do you have these days?"

"You're funny. I only have two, thank you very much. I'm trying my best to only have one and that's my catering business. Until I get that where I want it, I'll continue working at the consulting firm."

"I will say this, at least you know when to take a break and you know the importance of taking time out for self."

As the elevator doors opened and Noah, Kya and four other people stepped inside, Kya said, "I wonder if I can get your wife to play hooky with me today."

"Ha ha ha. Good luck with that suggestion. She took this week off but came in after we realized Maisha almost cost the company *a lot* of money."

"Get the hell out of here."

"That's a whole other story. Maybe if you're convincing she just might leave the office. I'm sure she can use a day away from this place. Otherwise, if it's not an emergency and no one has died you can forget it."

As the elevator reached the eleventh floor, Kya and Noah stepped out and noticed Bailey standing at the receptionist desk, speaking with Eugene.

"Good morning," Kya said.

"Good morning, Kya. Diva, I love those boots," said Eugene.

"Cut it out, you know you got a pair just like these," Kya said.

Eugene chuckled and said, "Actually mine are silver and I wear a black t-shirt with the word diva on it."

"Eugene, I'm not messing with you today," Kya said.

"Okay, I don't think I want to hear all of this. I'm going to my office to see what I have planned for the day. Babe, did you bring us lunch today?" Noah asked.

"No, I didn't. I was going to order us something or go to the deli," Bailey said.

"If you go out could you let me know? I might need you to pick up something for me," Noah said.

"Okay," Bailey said.

"Well, let me get to my office before my boss fires my ass . . . again. Kya, it was nice to see you and girl, we got to hang out real soon," Eugene said. Both Bailey and Kya laughed.

"Damn, Eugene, how many times were you fired this month and who fired you?" Kya asked.

"I don't want to say anything but the person that fired me is standing next to you. She only fired me two and half times this month. That's much better than the previous months," Eugene said jokingly as he walked away.

Kya turned to Bailey with a confused look on her face and asked, "Did you really fire him two and a half times this month?"

"Hell no, I only fired his ass once. I bet that taught his ass a lesson. I'm a damn good boss and I'm very lenient but when you try that slick ass ghetto shit with me, there is no need for you to be here. After I fired him, I was in his office making sure he didn't take any of our shit with him. Girl, as I watched him packing he just broke down. The more he cried the slower he packed. I finally said, Eugene why is it taking you long to pack? All you have in here is a bunch of bullshit. This shit can fit in a grocery bag."

"Stop playing. You didn't have to talk about the man's flamingos," Kya said as she started to laugh.

"This all happened in a matter of ten minutes. I had to tell him if you don't hurry the fuck up, I'm throwing this shit in a bag my damn self."

"You're so mean. You'd have broken all the flamingos into pieces."

"I didn't give a shit. By the time he could pack those goddamn pink flamingos and little figurines everyone in the office knew. Within a matter of seconds it had spread through the office like wild fire. Noah came running down the hall and asked me to reconsider and give him another chance. I did but I made him sweat first. I made him sweat and cry," Bailey said.

"Ewwwww, bitch. No, you didn't. You never mentioned this. Girl what did he do?"

When the receptionist returned to her desk, Kya and Bailey moved to Bailey's office to continue their conversation. Bailey stopped by her assistant's desk to tell them to hold all her calls.

"Oh, by the way, before we get back to the Eugene story, this is your latte and cream cheese pastry," Kya said.

"Damn bitch, thanks for telling me. I thought it was yours the way you were holding onto it."

"My bad, I got caught up in this Eugene drama."

"Let me finish the story before Noah comes down here. He hates to hear me talking about it. He said I overreacted with the situation."

"Awwww, poor Eugene," Kya said.

"Poor Eugene my ass, he's lucky I didn't beat the shit out of him."

"So tell me what really happened?"

"A part of Eugene's position consists of him dealing with the contractors for the rental properties. He needs to make sure everything is running smoothly. He deals with the tenants, handles accounts receivable, payables, collects rent, and deposits the money into the bank. Girl, this one fine day I was in my office and the accounting manager came in and said there was some money missing regarding the rental properties. At first I didn't get excited, I thought because she was new she was misreading the financial statements.

But when I started looking at the statements it appeared as though there was a lot of money missing. I immediately hit the fan. Noah wasn't in the office or available because of a meeting so I couldn't tell him. I took my ass straight to Eugene and when I kept asking where was my money, all he kept saying was it was there. This lasted for about thirty minutes. I couldn't take it no more so I said get the fuck out of my office and don't come back. The shit just wasn't making sense. It turned out, his big smart-dumb ass put the money in the wrong account. Clearly this was not an account that he had any business touching nor did he have access to it. I don't know how he did it, but after I calmed down a bit Noah and I went to lunch. Noah kept trying to calm me down further but it wasn't working. After lunch Noah went to the bank and moved the money back to the appropriate accounts," Bailey said.

"And Ms. Bailey don't like nobody fucking with her money."

"You're damn right! All that day I kept trying to figure out how he got access to the other account. He kept telling me that it was an error on the bank's part. I had to tell his ass to man the fuck up. I said you did the dumb shit so take responsibility for your actions. I just recently started speaking to him, not to mention everything that he puts his hands on these days, I have to see first."

"I know that's right, girl."

"Girl, I was so pissed."

"And you had every right to be, you know how we can get when it comes to the funds."

"Exactly. I know you didn't come down here to hear about Eugene's drama. What did you want to talk to me about?"

"It can wait until later on. It's nothing important, I just wanted to share some stuff, that's all. But I'll wait. I know you have to get back to work."

"Kya, you get on my nerves with that. Clearly if it could have waited you wouldn't have called me so early. You didn't get that ass up and dressed to sit in traffic, come to my office, and listen about Eugene's bullshit. Now, what is it?"

"I'm going to make this short and sweet then we can go to lunch and shopping."

"Oh no, sister, I'm not leaving here till the end of my workday. But that was cute how you eased that in. Now stop trying to skip the subject and tell me."

"Okay, here it goes. I want to be with Steve."

"Bye, Kya!"

"No for real. I'm serious."

"No shit Sherlock. So what's new? We've already established that."

"Since the argument that night all I've done is thought about him. Throughout the months, his actions and the things that he has said to me really show me that he wants to be with me."

"Sweetie, nothing you're saying is new. We just had this conversation."

"I've been thinking really hard about the past seven years with dippy doo and the bullshit he's put me through. I'm not going to lie to you but after we had that conversation I was really going to give him another chance. I finally realized that he is not the man for me. I was just holding on to something that wasn't there. I purposely treated Steve like shit because I *thought* I wanted to be with Jeff."

"I don't know why people try so hard to hold on to someone that does not belong to them. If this person actually wants you and sees the value within you, you don't have to do anything extra. No tricks, backwards flips. All you have to do is just be yourself. You should never have to beg or try and convince someone of the reasons why they should be with you. If you know within your heart that you're a good person and they can't see what you bring to the table, let go and move the fuck on. It's that simple. I'm glad that you've finally come to your senses, *Halleluiah*!" Bailey shouted.

"Every time I lie down with Jeff it's like I'm playing Russian roulette with my life. I love him but he made me fall out of love with him a long time ago."

"Sometimes we repeatedly try to revive something that's dead. The life is gone and the love's gone. Now it's time to let go and move on."

"I'm definitely ready for a change and a new beginning—a better life. Not one that's filled with non-stop drama."

"Sweetie, I told you a long time ago when a man treats you like he doesn't give a shit that's because he genuinely doesn't give a shit about you. But you didn't want to listen. Sometimes you have to step back and let a person find out for themselves. You can't make choices for your friends. You can be there to support whatever choice they make. If they fall, you help them back up, you don't just leave them lying there."

"Throughout the years you've never left my side. I've had to go through a lot with Jeff and you've never left my side. You went through the bullshit with me. I can honestly say that you're a true friend."

"No. We've been there for each other. I've had my share of bullshit too."

"I guess after a while my family gave up on me and let me fend for myself. They told me that they didn't want to get involved."

"If you genuinely care about people it hurts to see them in pain. Whether it's physical or emotional, you don't want to watch your loved ones hurting. It hurt me seeing you like that and I wished I could make everything better. In the end the choice was yours. I always told you I'm going to be your friend no matter what decisions you make."

"We all make mistakes and fall short of God's glory. There's not a perfect person walking this earth. I always hoped and prayed I'd be strong enough to make the right decision."

"Whenever you guys broke up, for whatever the reason was, you always went back to him. That used to piss me off so bad that I literally wanted to beat the shit out of you. I was never trying to tell you what to do but throughout the years I have watched you hurt and suffer tremendously."

"I really thought he was going to make me happy. I don't know why I tried so hard to hold on to someone that doesn't belong to me. I feel like I've wasted seven years of my life. That's a lot of time to spend with someone who isn't deserving of me. I can't get that time back."

"Kya, people don't make you happy, they can only contribute to your happiness. Any happiness you get, you have to make for yourself. Don't look at it as wasted time. Look at it as a lesson, a valuable life lesson. Remember, we're supposed to learn from our mistakes. It's his loss not yours. Dust that ass off, shake off Jeff and his drama, and start all over. Be excited about the new beginning you're about to start. The next chapter of your life will be much better than the last one."

"I sure hope so. As long as I live, I don't ever want to go through that type of shit again."

"And you don't have to. Make sure you set your standards in the beginning of your next relationship. Don't be afraid to tell the next man what you want, what you expect, and what you won't deal with. I suggest before you jump into a new relationship that you take some you time. Don't rush into anything with Steve right now. You still have too much baggage with Jeff, so just take your time and heal. You and Jeff have a child together and will see each other often. It might be a little uncomfortable for you in the beginning but everything will work out. Have you told Jeff yet?" Bailey asked.

"No, not yet. I told him that I wanted to speak with him when he brings Lexi home Sunday."

"I think this calls for a celebration."

"It does, I know you'd love to have a Grey Goose honey deuce or a flirtini."

"That does sound good. We could do lunch and have a few cocktails couldn't we? I should leave and play hooky with you. I've spent the majority of the morning shooting the shit with you anyway. The only thing I've done today is checked my emails, voice messages, played with my new phone, and opened my mail."

"Other words, you ain't done much of nothing."

"That's correct."

All through the weekend, Kya thought about what she would say to Jeff. She pondered back and forth with her thoughts. She hoped not to leave out anything out. *I have to be strong, I can't back down and I have to stand my ground.* She knew this break-up was long overdue and the relationship had run its course. She wanted to have this discussion maturely and without being confrontational. Even though their relationship had not been the greatest, Kya believed they could still be friends because they had to raise Alexis together.

While Kya prepared the menu for an upcoming event, she watched the clock. She knew within a matter of minutes Jeff would be there and she'd have to break the news to him. It was Kya's preference not to have this conversation while Alexis was home but she didn't want to hold off any longer.

As Kya got up from her desk she could hear Jeff and Lexi at the front door. She went to the door to greet them.

Lexi ran to Kya and said, "Hi, Mommy."

Kya hugged Lexi and said, "Hello, sweetie, I've missed you."

"I missed you too, Mommy. I had a lot of fun. I hung out with my cousins. I talked to Grandmom and I saw my granddad."

"Is that right? Did you have a great time?"

"Yes, and my aunt said she wants me to come back over. She said I need to call her too."

"Okay. Can you do Mommy a favor?" Kya asked.

"Yes."

"I made your favorite snack."

"Peanut butter and chocolate rice krispie treats?" Lexi asked.

"Yes, ma'am. I've already prepared it for you. Can you take it upstairs and watch TV while I talk to your dad?"

"Okay. Can I go in your room?"

"Yes you can. I'll be up in a little while to get you prepared for bed."

Lexi walked over to Jeff, kissed him on the cheek, and said, "Bye, Daddy. Call me later on."

"I sure will," Jeff said.

After Lexi went upstairs Kya turned to Jeff and said, "Thanks for stopping by, I really needed to speak to you. This is without a doubt not a convo for the telephone."

"I had to bring Lexi home anyway," Jeff said.

"Would you like something to drink?" Kya asked.

"No, I'm good. What's so important that it couldn't wait until tomorrow?"

"I need to get some stuff off of my chest and rectify some issues."

"What's wrong, slim?"

"Have a seat. I'm not going to take up that much of your time."

"What's the problem, Kya?"

"I can't do this anymore."

"Do what, what are you talking about now?"

"I can't keep putting myself through this unnecessary bullshit. It's just not worth it."

"So this is about us?"

"Yes it is. I must admit I didn't want to let go of you. I wasn't ready to close the chapter completely on us. When, in fact, I should have let your trifling ass go a long time ago. You're not good for me."

"Hold up, don't come at me like that."

"I apologize but . . ."

"Whenever you don't get what you want, this is how you act."

"It's not about me getting what I want. It's about you treating me with the respect that I deserve and not like shit."

"Man, look, you can save all of this because today is really not a good day."

"Can you just listen? I just need for you to listen to what I have to say. After all of these years of bullshit, that's the least you can do. Can you do that?"

"Whatever, slim. Say what you got to say."

"First and foremost I love you because you're my daughter's father but I'm no longer in love with you. With all of the craziness and all of the other women, it's time that I moved on."

"Damn, slim, where's this coming from? You acted like you were happy the other night when I was fucking you."

"Can I finish please? It's taken me a very long time to get the nerve and strength to say this to you, please listen."

"Okay, go ahead. I'm listening."

"I kept hoping and praying that you'd realize the precious jewel that you had, but you didn't."

Jeff took a deep breath and said, "Is this conversation going to take all night? I have somewhere that I need to be."

"No, it's not going to take that long. As usual there's always something else that's much more important."

"I just need to know, I have someone waiting on me."

"Maybe if you stop interrupting, I can finish. Can I finish now, can you just sit there, listen and take all of this in?"

"Okay."

"Anyway. The more chances I gave you, the more you fucked me over. I did all I could for our relationship. We've been engaged off and on for seven years. What the fuck's all that about?"

"We weren't ready," Jeff said.

"No, *you* weren't ready. If you were truly in love with me like you kept saying then we'd have been married a long time ago. From day one you've cheated on me and I always found out. Or should I say, the more signs God kept revealing to me, the more I ignored them. Like a fool I still stayed with you anyway. That was my dumbness. It's like you didn't care and you wanted to get caught. You can't possibly say that you love and respect me."

"You know I love you."

"I don't know anything. I only know what you've showed me. Actions speak louder than words."

"You can say whatever you want, slim, I do love you."

"No, you love the thought of me. There's a difference."

"Whatever, man. Kya, I do love you. I'm not going to keep saying it."

"If you do, you have one hell of a way of showing it. I might be partly to blame. People only treat you how you let them. You treated me like the shit on the bottom of someone's shoe because I allowed it. I think you liked the fact I was always there no matter what. You took my love for granted, you took me for granted, and I'm tired of it. I'm fucking sick and tired of being sick and tired. Enough is enough."

"Enough is never enough. There's always more to come."

"Are you being sarcastic? Was that meant to be funny?" Kya asked.

"No, I'm just saying. Sometimes we want more so enough is not enough."

"Whatever, Jeff! I don't have time to decipher your fake ass metaphors."

"My bad, I can see you're being serious."

"That's a part of the problem, you take everything for a joke. There's a time and a place for all of that. At this very moment I'm trying to talk to you about us."

"You need to lighten up some. Maybe you're working too hard. It's not that serious."

"But it is. You think life is a game and it's not."

Jeff looked at his phone and said, "Kya, I won't play with you anymore. Just say what you need to."

"For a long time I asked myself what I was doing wrong. Why can't he be faithful and why do I keep dealing with it? I stayed with you because of love that I had for you. Then because of comfort and convenience, I kept hanging around. Now I understand what they mean when they say love is blind. In the back of my mind I'd always tell myself that love bears all things. But some things we shouldn't have to go through, especially if you give a person chance after chance after chance. I've come to the conclusion that it wasn't me and it never was. My first problem was I took everything that you threw my way. My second problem was that I settled. When in all actuality the problem lies within you."

"So now I have a problem. What's my problem, Kya?"

"You just can't seem to keep your dick in your pants."

"Okay, so why is that a problem, Kya?"

"You can't be serious?"

"I'm trying to figure out how is that a problem. Didn't I satisfy you?"

"You sure as hell did along with every woman in the DMV."

"Come on, Kya, I'm a man and that's what we do. We have to spread our seed around. Ask any man and he'll tell you that it's hard to stay with one woman."

"Jeff, that's not true. Unfortunately your dad raised you thinking that's how it's supposed to be."

"I thought you were okay with it. Hell, you stayed around for so long."

"You're an ignorant ass Negro. I can't believe that you're so ill-bred. I don't know if you're that stupid or just don't give a good goddamn. You really and truly have no understanding why it's a problem?"

"Nope, please enlighten me."

"Jeff, you *really* need me to tell you why it's a problem?"

"Yes I do. Explain to me why it's a problem."

"It's not a problem when you're in a monogamous relationship and fucking one person! But you, on other hand, manage to fuck any- and everybody and don't seem to care. It's sad but you don't seem to care where you put your little penis. You've fucked friends, sisters, cousins, aunts, whomever else and you didn't give a shit. As long as they got a pussy you were fucking them. For some reason you think you're God's gift to women. You're so narcissistic and focused on yourself that it's really scary."

"If that's what you want to say. I'm doing me. But, like I said, it couldn't have been a problem if you dealt with however I acted. Therefore, it must have been okay."

"But it wasn't. I've had bitches calling my house phone, mobile, work phone. The only ways they could have gotten my numbers is if they went through your phone or you gave them my numbers. Whenever I confronted you about it you would say stupid shit that didn't make any sense."

"Why would I give anyone your numbers? That don't even sound right."

"Jeff, the majority of the dumb shit you say doesn't sound right. Then I guess they got it from your phone."

"Well, I guess so. I have no control over what people do."

"I'm sitting here thinking about all of the shit you've put me through. I really and truly can't believe how naïve I was. The more I think about it the more I realize I probably wasn't in love with you. It was the dick. That's the reason why I stuck around."

"Why and how could you leave something this good? Aside from this good dick you know I treated you good."

"From the beginning we were never on the same level. From the jump you never wanted me. I must admit you played a good game."

"It was never a game, I actually had feelings for you."

"I mean you have put me through so much. Even today you sit here like you have no remorse for what you've done."

"Like you said, you allowed me to do it. Why would you expect for me to feel bad?"

"You are so heartless and unapologetic."

"I have feelings, I just don't trip off the dumb shit. Slim, life's too short for that. I care about you and I want to be with you, but you can't make me feel bad."

"Why would I want to spend the rest of my life with someone like you? It's meaningless."

"Why wouldn't you want to spend your life with me? We could work it out."

"I doubt that very seriously. You've hurt me way too much to give you another chance. I can't do that."

"You'll never find another man like me."

"And that's a good thing. I couldn't put myself through that abuse ever again."

"You're out of your mind. I've never abused you."

"Yeah you did. For seven long and painful years."

"I might have been with other women but I never abused you."

"Emotional mistreatment. That's a fucking form of abuse!" Kya yelled.

"Well, it is what it is."

"I can't believe how crass you're being right now. You can't be that insensitive. If I'd done half the stuff to you that you've done to me, you'd have kicked my ass."

"Naw, I wouldn't have put my hands on you. I would have left you alone."

"Whatever. You would have beat the shit out of me."

"The stuff that I did wasn't really that bad. You make it seem like I'm a bad person or something."

"Let's revisit some of your greatest accomplishments. Let's see, remember the time I found a used condom in my fucking car? What about the thong under the passenger seat of my car? You tried your damnedest to convince me it belonged to me. As if I don't know the type of fucking underwear I buy or wear," Kya said.

"I thought it was yours."

"No, it belonged to the bitch you fucked in my car. The one that you rode around with when your car was in the shop."

"Are you asking me or telling me?"

"I'm telling you. I guess because my dumb ass let you slide with that shit, you had to take it up a notch or two. Do you remember what you told me when I found the earrings on my bathroom sink?"

"No, not really," Jeff said.

"You said your mother was visiting for the weekend and stayed at my house."

"Okay, so my mom left her earrings at your house. What's the big deal?"

"You dumb motherfucker! How could you not remember that at the same time I was in the Bahamas with your mother? Besides that, she doesn't wear any goddamn bamboo earrings with the name Tinka Bell in them. Not to mention, she doesn't wear gold. She only wears silver or platinum."

"I didn't come over here for you to bash me about some bullshit."

"Oh, but no, sweetie, it's not bashing. It's all the truth. The truth hurts doesn't it?"

"If you want to use these as excuses then by all means go for it."

"Jeff, these aren't excuses. These are factual events that took place. None of the names or situations have been changed."

"Okay, so what's the point to all of this?"

"The point is everything that you've done hurt me," Kya said.

"Are you done?"

"Hell no! I'm just getting started. The icing on the cake was the bitch that showed up at my job with a baby in one hand and the DNA results in the other. Now that was priceless! Even after all of that, I still forgave you and took you back time and time again."

"Why wouldn't you? That's what love is all about."

"Sweetie, your definition of love is all wrong. Even being a good father and a great provider is not enough. Truthfully speaking, the dick is good but it ain't that damn good. It's not good enough for me to lose my mind or self-respect."

"Slim, you tripping like shit."

"So you're saying none of that stuff happened?"

"I'm not saying it didn't happen. Out of the blue you start bringing up this shit all over again. I thought we'd rectified all of that."

"We did. I forgave you, we moved past it and then you continued doing the same shit. You're still fucking other bitches and cheating."

"I'm not cheating on you because technically we're not together."

"We were trying to reconcile this fucked up thing that we called a relationship. You just told me the other day that you were ready to come back home. You said instead of a wedding let's go to the Justice of the Peace."

"True, I did because I thought that's what you wanted."

"I did. But you haven't changed one bit. If anything you've gotten much worse. Until you recognize that you have a problem you're going to continue to do the same stupid shit over and over. You need to make some changes with yourself. I know you've heard the saying, if you want different results then you can't keep doing the same thing. For me I need different results so I can't possibly keep doing the same thing over and over. I need a change and I have to be strong enough to walk away from this bullshit."

"Maybe if we go to counseling and talk to somebody. Everything will be fine, you'll see."

"Oh, hell no! Jeff you can't be serious. Counseling for what? You already said that you're going to keep doing you. When I suggested going to a relationship counselor months ago you refused. You kept saying that you weren't crazy, there's nothing wrong with you and you're not going, no matter what."

"Well, I've changed my mind."

"Since when?"

"A couple of minutes ago."

"No thank you. I'll pass. The only counseling I need is to help me get over you. But that's something that a little time and a lot of prayer will take care of. I suggest you seek counseling for yourself."

"Don't act like the majority of our relationship was bad."

"I'm not saying that. We had a few good times. But we've had more bad times than good times."

"Kya, what do you want from me?"

"I want you to be a good father and take care of Lexi."

"I'm going to do that regardless."

"I also think it will be best if you do get some counseling. Otherwise, when Lexi grow up she'll think she can screw anybody that she wants. At whatever cost."

"Naw, I'm not going for that."

"How can you correct her? According to your mindset your behaviors are justifiable."

"I'll break my foot off in Lexi's ass if she sleeps around like some whore," Jeff said.

"Then I suggest you get yourself together."

"So counseling is out?"

"Yes sir. Jeff, I can't be one of those women who settle just because. I can't, won't and will not settle for less than I deserve. I know my self-worth and it can't be compromised. If you and I continued our relationship then that's exactly what I'd be doing."

"So that's it. I don't have anything to say about the situation?"

"Nope. I think it's time that you grew up and learned how to keep that dick of yours in your pants. I hate to say it but your dick is going to be the death of you."

"You got to die from something."

"Okay, but you'll learn sooner or later. Besides that bum ass nigga you hang around, all of your other friends have settled down and gotten married. But not you, you think it's cute to keep adding all of these notches on your belt. You wanting to be a player is truly old and outdated. If you haven't noticed it's the players that are spreading AIDS around. You're going to catch something one day that you won't be able shake off. Do you ever read the newspaper or watch the news? Have you not noticed the rise of HIV/AIDS cases in the black community? I know if you didn't want to use condoms with me you're not using them with the other women. But with me you had no choice but to strap up when we fucked."

"Yeah, but it wasn't always like that."

"You're right it wasn't, until I started finding out about those whores."

"You can't feel the actual effects and wetness of a pussy with a condom on."

"Whatever, ignoramus, condoms save lives. You're just too ignorant to know that."

"I'm not going to keep sitting here letting you call me names and shit."

"I love you, but I love me more. No matter what you say there's no way possible that you can justify your behavior to me. So, our life together as we knew it is over. I don't know what the future holds but I hope you find what you're looking for. I don't have a crystal ball but I don't see any reconciliation in the forecast for us. The only thing that we need to discuss from this moment on is Alexis Monet Edwards. If it's not about her then don't call me. And you damn sure better not just be popping up on my doorstep unannounced like some lost puppy."

"Don't give up on me just like that, Kya. You owe me."

"I don't owe you anything. I owe myself and my daughter."

"Give me another chance then."

"Ha ha ha, you're so funny. But don't quit your day job. Stand-up comedy isn't you."

"I'm a good man," Jeff said.

"Stop it! You're hilarious! I think your definition of a good man is distorted."

"So you think I'm a joke now?"

"I now know and realize that there are still some good men out there."

Jeff sat on the sofa closer to Kya and said, "You're looking at a good man. Didn't I take care of my family and don't I take care of my responsibilities?"

"Stop it, you're killing me with the jokes."

"I take care of my family," Jeff reiterated.

"Those aren't the only things that represent a good man. It's more than taking care of your family financially and the babies that you make. A good man knows how to treat a woman and doesn't mistreat her."

"Slim, you need to think about this, if I were you I'd reconsider this shit. You'll want me back. One person's trash is another person's treasure."

"That's a true statement, but right now it's time for me to take my trash to the garbage."

Jeff looked at Kya and said, "If you're going to keep insulting me like this I'm leaving. I guess now you'll want me to pay child support and shit. That's fucked up, I take care of my daughter."

"Jeff, I haven't said anything about child support. Nor have I said you don't take care of Lexi. You're the one jumping the gun. I want and I expect you to continue taking care of your daughter. It's my belief that she'll get more without having the courts involved. Then again I could be wrong. Your club does make a lot of money."

"How much do you want?"

"It's not about the money. With or without you, Lexi will be taken care of. I was never with you for your money. Please don't get me mixed up with those ghetto ass bitches that you fuck with."

"I don't have a problem giving you money on a monthly basis. I just don't need to be blindsided by unnecessary shit. I'm already paying out a lot in child support."

"How is that my problem? See how your dick gets you caught up? I told you. But you haven't learned your lesson. I can say with all certainty, that there is a man out there that will treat me right and love me the way I deserve to be loved. I had one but I couldn't focus on him because I wanted you."

"So you've been cheating on me?" Jeff said.

"Man, go ahead with that bullshit and your funny ass. I have never cheated on you. Remember, according to you we weren't in a relationship anyway. That's what you said. There's no need to get into a long, drawn-out debate about what you think I've done. Like I said, I've never cheated on you. I happened to run across an old friend on Facebook. But because I was wrapped up in you, I couldn't focus on him. I didn't realize until it was too late that he was the man for me."

"You said I was the man for you. Slim, you don't know who you want to be with. You're confused."

"I'm far from being confused. I thought you were the man for me but I was sadly mistaken. I also thought you wouldn't hurt me either but you did. We all make mistakes."

"Here you go again with the insults."

"I'm not intentionally insulting you. I appreciate the valuable lessons that I've learned from you. Unfortunately, I treated him like shit then let him go. That was a mistake on my part. Hopefully he'll give me a second chance and take me back."

"How the fuck are you going to sit here and talk to me about some other nigga. What type of shit is this?"

"Jeff, it's over. We're friends right? I thought friends could talk about anything."

"I don't want to hear about some man you're fucking."

"We're no longer together."

"Whatever, man. I can't just let you go like this."

"Oh yes, but you can. I'm not your personal property and I don't belong to you. Besides, you let me go a long time ago. Just keep it moving, you're good with that."

"So you saying we can't work at it? I promise to change and go to therapy. All I'm asking is that you give me another chance. This time we'll get it right. We'll get married, have another baby and buy another house. We can start over. You mean so much to me."

"That all sounds good, but this is shit that I've heard for years. If I meant so much to you, then things would have been different. You had every chance to change. Now it's too little too late."

Kya got up from the sofa and added, "I'm going to get me a bottle of water, would you like something?"

"Yeah, I want you."

"That's not an option. Would you like something to drink?"

"No."

As Kya returned and sat on the love seat her phone rang. "Hello," she said.

"Hey, Ms. Lady," Deion said. "Are you busy?"

"Yeah, I'm sort of in the middle of something. Can I call you back?"

"Yeah, that's fine. Call me when you're done."

Jeff looked at her and said, "Damn, now you can't sit next to me."

"No it's not that, I just chose to sit here."

"Slim, is there anything I can do to change your mind about us?" Jeff asked.

Kya shook her head from side to side and said, "No, not at this point."

"I have to go but can we finish this conversation later?"

"Sweetie, I'm done. I have nothing left to discuss. I'm ready for my healing to begin. In order for me to heal, I need to let go of you, get you out of my mind and my system."

"I think there's more to discuss, you haven't given me a chance to say anything."

"Yes I did, you had a chance to say whatever you wanted to say. I'm just not open to conversations that consist of us reconciling. We've been there and done that and it didn't work. So now it's time to move on. I don't hate you and I'm not angry with you. We can't be together. Just leave it at that."

"I don't want to leave like this, I think we have more to talk about."

"No, the discussion is over. Unless we're talking about our daughter, there's nothing left to talk about. It's late and I want to go to bed."

"Can I spend the night?"

"Hell no! Why are you asking me questions when you already know the answer? My response has not and will not change. I don't want it! I've had a good day, please don't work my nerves. Don't you have someone waiting on you?"

"This is more important and I'd rather be here. Can I stay?"

"No, don't you have some bitch waiting on you? Go where you need to go, our conversation is over. The decision's made. I hate to ask you to leave but I need to go to bed."

"Is some nigga coming over?"

"Jeff, I don't think I need to dignify that question with a response. Time for you to go now."

"Okay, I see how the fuck you're being. I'll go but I'm not done with this conversation."

"Okay, Jeff, whatever you say, I hear ya. Enjoy the rest of your evening."

"Yeah, whatever," Jeff said as he slammed the door.

Kya sat on the sofa. *I feel like a weight's been lifted off my shoulders. I'm glad it's finally all over. Let me call Deion back before I go to bed.*

"Hey, D," Kya said.

"What's up, girl?" Deion asked.

213

"Girl, not a damn thing."

"Oh, okay. I haven't spoken to you in a couple of days. I was calling to see if you wanted to do lunch tomorrow. I have something I need to discuss with you."

"Oh yeah, what?"

"It can wait until tomorrow," Deion said.

"Oh, okay, around what time would you like to go? I have meetings all morning but I'm free after noon."

"Well, I'm free all day. I start my vacation tomorrow."

"What? It's about damn time you took a vacation. How long are you off?"

"Three long weeks!" Deion yelled.

"You go, girl. It's long overdue and much deserved. I hope you take it easy and get plenty of rest."

"I plan on it."

"Where did you want to go for lunch?"

"I don't know, I've been having a taste for Thai food lately. There's this place in Alexandria and their food is excellent.'

"I know the place you mean. Do you want to meet me at my house?"

"I can."

"Instead of driving from Georgetown to Clinton, why don't you meet me at my job?"

"Okay, that's even better. But one thing, how will I get home?"

"Girl, we'll figure that out tomorrow. Meet me at noon."

"Okay. I'll see you tomorrow."

"Okay, I'm about to take my ass to bed."

The next morning, as Kya prepared for her meeting, the receptionist called her and said, "There's a Stephen Jackson here to see you."

"Excuse me?" Kya asked.

"Stephen Jackson, do you want me to escort him to the conference room?"

"No, I'll be right out." Kya said. She quickly grabbed her purse and pulled out her makeup compact, checking her hair and makeup. *What the hell is he doing here?* Kya thought. She nervously went to her door, took a deep breath, and went to the reception area.

As she sashayed down the hall, Steve got up and said, "Good morning, Ms. Turner."

Kya smiled and said, "Good morning, Mr. Jackson. It's really nice to see you."

The receptionist cleared her throat and said, "Kya, your meeting will be starting imminently."

Kya turned and her voice had a sardonic tone as she said, "I know."

"I shouldn't have stopped by like this. I know you're busy," Steve said.

"It's fine. I'm glad that you did," Kya said.

"Can we go to your office? The receptionist hasn't stopped looking at us since we've been standing here."

"I can feel her eyes watching us."

Once Kya and Steve were in her office, she closed the door. As she walked to her desk he softly took hold of her arm and said, "I've really missed you."

"I missed you too," Kya said. Steve held Kya close, embraced her, then kissed her. "I have something that I need to discuss with you," Kya added.

Steve placed his forefinger on Kya's lips and asked, "Do you love me?"

"Yes, I do."

"Do you understand my feelings for you?"

"Yes."

"Have you put all of the bullshit behind you?"

"Yes."

"Are you emotionally available to me at this point?"

"Yes."

"Can I have all of you, mind, body and soul?"

"Yes."

"Will you let me spend the rest of my life doing whatever it takes to contribute to your happiness?"

"Hell, yeah!" Kya shouted.

"Okay. So where do we go from here?"

"We take baby steps, we take it slow."

"Sounds good to me."

"But, I need to tell you everything," Kya said.

"In due time. There's nothing that I don't know that would change how I feel about you. Whatever you feel like you need to tell me is a part of your past. We all have a past. It's done. That chapter is closed and you've moved on."

"That's one of the reasons why I love you."

Steve held Kya's hands and said, "I know you have a meeting so I'm not going to hold you. Can I see you tonight?"

"Yes, I'd love that."

"Around 8 p.m.?"

"All right." Steve gently kissed Kya on her lips and said, "Enjoy the rest of your day. I'll give you a call later on."

"I'll look forward to it."

As soon as Steve left Kya's office, she picked up the phone to call Bailey. Then the receptionist called Kya via the intercom and said, "The meeting—you're late. They're looking for you!"

Kya slammed down the phone and said, "Okay, okay. I'm headed to the conference room now."

Kya quickly walked to the conference room, sat down, and apologized for her tardiness. While the participants of the meeting got bagels, coffee or pastries Kya picked up her phone to text Bailey: *URGENT* CODE BLUE! THE PURPLE MONKEY HAS LANDED! I HAVE GOT SOMETHING MAJOR TO TELL YOU. MUST TALK! ASAP

Within a matter of seconds Bailey responded: WHAT? PLEASE TELL!

Before Kya could send another text, she was interrupted by the complaints of the CEO of her company. The more Kya tried to block out his grumbling, the louder he got. Kya's phone began vibrating and she saw that it was Bailey. She excused herself and went into the hallway.

"Girl, I can't talk now, I'm in a meeting. Do you want to go to lunch with Deion and me?" Kya whispered.

"I can't, meetings all damn day long," Bailey said.

"Steve stopped by my job."

"Get the hell out of here. Are you serious?"

"Girl, yes!"

"He just popped up?"

"YESSSSSS!" Kya yelled.

"What?" Bailey asked.

"Girl, they're looking for me, I'll call you later on."

"Okay, bye."

As Kya tried to get through the long and dreadful meeting, her attention was elsewhere. She was extremely happy and there was nothing that could hinder what she was feeling. *Oh my God, I can't believe he just showed up like that. One thing for sure and two things for certain, I know this man really cares about me. I have to do everything possible not to mess this shit up this time around. Geesh, how much longer is this meeting going to be? I got shit to do.*

As the meeting finally ended, Kya said her goodbyes and hurriedly went to her office. While she was preparing to leave, Deion walked in and said, "I'm here."

"Hey, girl, as soon as I finish getting my stuff we can bounce," Kya said.

"Um, Ms. Thing, you're wearing one hell of a glow this afternoon. What's going on with you?" Deion asked.

"Girlfriend, I'll tell you all about it. I don't like talking about my personal business in the office. The receptionist's got ears all over the place."

"I know how that can be. As least your receptionist's disposition, language and appearance is better than mine. Some days ours looks as if she got dressed in the Crayola factory."

As Kya laughed she said, "You are a trip."

"No, seriously she looks like she was in one of those machines and the colors exploded all over her. I don't know what the hell that girl is wearing to work. The last time I saw her I asked where she got her outfit from and she said she made it. Then when I said that the fabric was different she said she sewed together bits and pieces of old fabric that she was saving. What the fuck? Girl, I was laughing so hard I thought I was going to pass out. She said she makes all of her clothes."

"Yeah, I can see how that's possible. The last time I was at your office she asked me if I needed some new clothes. She then asked if I wanted her to make me some outfits. Of course, I wouldn't wear anything that looks like that crap she wears. I thought I would fuck with her so I inquired about how much she would charge and she said $250.00."

"Girl, that one there is truly a hot damn mess."

"Okay, I have all of my crapola, let's go."

Once Kya and Deion were in the car, Deion asked, "Okay, what's up?"

"Girl, all I know is I'm so happy right now and no one can steal my joy."

"Did you get a promotion?" Deion asked.

"Something like that. I realized that I was holding myself back. I was the one blocking and sabotaging my own blessings. I finally got the strength and courage to let go, just when I did, God sent me an astonishing blessing."

"What? Did you hit the lottery and didn't tell anyone?"

"Nope, it's better than money."

"What?"

"Love!"

"Child, please."

"Seriously, I let go of Jeff and God presented me with a wonderful man."

"Congratulations. If you're happy then I'm happy for you."

"Thank you and I'm ecstatic! Love is the greatest feeling in the world and it's completely free."

"That's what I hear. So, you've finally let go of that ex of yours?"

"Yes, ma'am. Girl, I'm so happy right now I don't know what to do."

"Well, I'm truly happy for you. You deserve to be happy and with a man that treats you right."

"Thank you, girl. This feeling is long overdue. I never, ever, ever, thought I'd find love like this, not in this lifetime."

"When did you break things off with the ex?"

"In all actuality we've been on the outs for a while. But last night I figured it was a good time to close the chapter once and for all, that's what I was in the process of doing when you called. It's finally over. Thank you, Lord. I feel like I should be celebrating."

"And you should. We'll have to have a couple of early afternoon cocktails."

"You got that right."

Because of the constant chatting back and forth, Kya and Deion arrived in Alexandria faster than anticipated. After being greeted by a pleasant hostess, the women sat down for an enjoyable lunch. As the waitress placed their silverware and napkins, poured their water and handed them menus, Kya said, "I already know what I'll be having."

Deion looked up and said, "But you haven't even read the menu yet."

"Girl, this is my spot and I always get the same damn thing. If I try anything different it's because it's on someone else's plate."

"What will you be having?" the waitress asked.

"I would like Shrimp Pad Thai with extra shrimp and two orders of Thai Coconut Custard. I'll have my dessert with the meal. Please put the dessert on the same plate. That's all for me," Kya said.

The waitress turned to Deion for her order.

"And I'd like to try the Pad See Ew with chicken and two spring rolls," Deion said.

"Could you also add a double order of chicken satay, please?" Kya asked.

"And your drinks?"

"I'd like a glass of sweet tea," Kya said.

"I thought you were going to have a cocktail?"

"I changed my mind. I'm going to need a clear head later on," Kya said.

"Oh, okay. I'd like a diet Pepsi with no ice."

Both women handed the waitress their menus and said, "Thank you."

"So, Kya, it looks as though everything's working out for you. You have a great man, career, your own business, and a beautiful little girl. Is there anything that you want that you don't have?" Deion asked.

"I haven't thought about that. Lately I've been thinking about quitting my job but there's no real need to do that. I've managed to work a full-time demanding job and run a successful business at the same time."

"Do you ever feel overwhelmed?" Deion asked.

"Sure I do. All the time. But when I have moments like that either I take a day off to regroup or go get a massage. It's also advantageous we take those random getaways. Those, too, kind of help me to recharge my batteries."

"I don't know how you do it. It seems like all you do is go, go, go. I have a hard time with one job let alone two."

"It's not that bad once you get used to it. Besides, where there's a will there's a way. I can't expect to have it all if I don't work for it."

"That's true. How does Lexi react to having a supermom?"

"She's fine. I try not to be away from her too much. Those weeks that I'm catering back-to-back events and working, she'll stay with Bailey or my sister. But I try to spend as much time with her as I possibly can. I don't ever want her to feel like I wasn't there for her. And I definitely don't want to miss any of her growing up. Even though I have issues with my sorry-ass ex, he tries to get Lexi as much as he can. Sometimes he says he's coming but ends up doing other shit."

"That's not good. Apparently his priorities are all screwed up."

"Girl, who you telling? I've been singing that same song for years."

"What could be more important than your child?" Deion asked.

"Leave it up to him, he's trying to build his businesses so it takes all of his time and energy. Then his other time is spent fucking bitches."

"What the hell ever. Family first."

"I tried to tell him that. It's okay to work hard but at the end of the day, you still have to spend time with family."

"Well, despite the ex, it seems like you have it all worked out. I'm really impressed, you're a super single mom and I commend you. I don't know if I could do all of that."

"Thank you. But trust me it's really not that bad. Especially when you have help."

"Is Lexi his only child?" Deion asked.

"Nope, the bastard has a twelve-year-old son and a couple of questionables."

"Oh, okay."

"Girl, my ex is a ho, with a capital H and O! I'm surprised he doesn't have more, his trifling ass fucks anything that's not nailed down. That's why we're not together now."

"I remember you saying something to that effect but I thought you were joking."

Kya hesitated, then said, "No, ma'am, sexual gallivanting is nothing to joke about. Look how I fuss you out about the dumb shit that you do and your sexual rendezvous. I'm afraid for you. But him, there's no talking to him. His philosophy is that the dick is supposed to save women. Like his dick has some type of magical powers. He's ignant as shit."

"Oh, wow."

"It's disturbing to me when a person is headed for self-destruction and they don't change their behavior."

Deion glanced out of the window and said, "Maybe we can't change."

"There's no such thing as what you can't do! For me that word doesn't exist and it's not in my vocabulary. It's really sad that the word 'can't' is a crutch for so many people. If people start saying what they can do and have a 'can do' attitude they'd be better off. Don't get it twisted, I have a lot of issues and flaws but I'm doing my best to get better at this thing called life."

"That's all we can do."

"It's very disheartening that some people don't change until something bad happens. Then they'll say I wish I would have, I should have. By all means I'm not trying to run anybody's life, I'm just trying to help."

"I hear you, girl."

"It's so funny how you never call him by his name," Deion said.

"I do call him by name. Whenever you hear me say that the sorry son of a bitch, trifling ass bastard, no-good-ass nigga, then you know who I'm referring to."

"But Kya, those aren't the names he was given at birth."

Kya laughed and said, "You're right, if I say Rosemary's baby, Satan's firstborn or the demon seed, then I'm talking about him."

"Girl, you need to stop, he can't be that bad, you were with him for seven years."

"That's true, D, but in all actuality, for the past three years we've been doing the on again, off again type of relationship. Even though we were fucking almost every other night and he paid my mortgage, we really weren't a couple."

"Well apparently the both of you were holding on to something. Otherwise, you'd have let go long before now."

"Like I told him, I think it was the dick that kept me with him for so long. I think I was hypnotized by it," Kya said jokingly.

"I know exactly how that can be."

"What, being hypnotized by some good dick?" Kya said.

Deion laughed and said, "That too, but I was referring to staying with someone for all of the wrong reasons."

"I don't know what's harder, staying in a bad situation or being afraid to leave a bad situation out of comfort and convenience. Either way you look at it, no one should stay in an unhealthy environment. Whether you're getting your ass kicked from Monday through Sunday or you're being verbally abused."

"You know fear has the tendency to paralyze and cripple you and sometimes you think there's no way out."

"I understand that, wholeheartedly, but come on now. There's always a way out. You don't have to just stand by and take the abuse and the other shit that goes along with it. Trust, I had to learn the hard way. Even though he wasn't putting his hands on me, the other shit he was doing was still abusive."

"I guess there's no way of us understanding what people go through until we walk a mile in their shoes. It took me years to get the nerve to get out of my marriage. Hell, some days I still walk around looking over my shoulder. That Negro was crazy and I'll always remember what he said he'd do if he saw me again."

"Girl, what the fuck ever! You're not his personal property and he can't do a damn thing to hurt you again. Fuck, he wasn't a real man anyway. Real men don't beat women nor do they treat them like some shit. A real man knows the value of a gem and knows how to take care of something precious."

"I agree," Deion said.

"Anyhoo, I don't want to spoil and ruin the mood by talking about my trifling ass baby daddy and his bullshit. Not today. I'm too excited about the new man in my life."

"Don't you think you're moving too fast?"

"No."

"But you just ended a seven-year relationship."

"Girlfriend, truth be told I got over that man while I was still with him. He made me fall out of love with him a very long time ago. It was my stupidity that kept me holding on to something that wasn't there. It was all an illusion. I wanted to see something that didn't really exist."

"What's your new man's name anyway?"

"Stephen."

"Stephen. So regal."

Yes, ma'am my new king."

"Girl, this next chapter of your life is going to be the greatest. I really wish you and your new man the best. It's long overdue for you."

"Thank you D, I'm so happy that I feel as if I'm dreaming or something. You might need to pinch a bitch to make sure this isn't a dream."

"No girl, it's no dream."

"Well, I can't wait until you meet your Mr. So And So."

"What the hell is a Mr. So And So?" Deion asked.

"Mr. Right!" Kya yelled.

"Girl, I'm in no rush. I'm enjoying my single life right now without being attached to anyone. Besides, I might have met my Mr. So And So."

"What? Are you shitting me? When, who, how?"

"Dang girl, slow down."

"Excuse me, Ms. Secretive. When did this happen?"

"I don't know what's going to come of it but I'm really feeling this guy that I've been seeing. I actually think that I've been hit by the love bug."

"For real? Get the fuck outta here. Not you?"

"Yes, ma'am, me."

"Oh, okay, maybe he's the one."

"Maybe, we'll have to wait and see. It's still a little early to know if a love connection will be made."

"Well, I do know that people come into our lives for a season, a reason, or a lifetime. At the time, we may not see the significance of this person in our lives. But it's for a reason or a purpose."

"Right. And they were put in your life for a specific reason, this I do know."

"Correct. Even if you're perplexed about them being there, it's for a reason."

"And sometimes we shouldn't question it."

"Exactly."

While Kya and Deion went back and forth, the waitress brought over their food. The waitress filled their water glasses and inquired if they needed anything else.

As Deion began eating, Kya asked, "What's your new friend's name, where did you meet, what does he do? Is he married, single, what's his story?"

"Dang, girl."

"What?" I'm just asking. Tell me all about this secret man you've been hiding."

"His name is Jay and he's a business man."

"Okay, what type of business is he in? A nine to five suit wearing business man, an entrepreneur or what"

"He's more of an entrepreneur and he sets his own hours."

"So, what's his hustle? Clothing, furniture, shoes, what?"

"He does a little everything."

"Oh, okay, whatever that means." Kya glanced at her watch and added, "Girlfriend, I'm enjoying this time with you but I's got to be on the move shortly."

"Why are you rushing? I thought we were hanging out this afternoon. Where are you going, do you have an event tonight?" Deion asked.

"Kinda, it's date night and I have to run some errands before Mr. Man picks me up. We're going to dinner and will probably finish our conversation about us."

"Excuse me, Ms. Thing, I know that's right. Bitch, you glowing all over the damn place, check you out. You even look different and shit."

"Girl, cut it out."

"I'm sorry, girl, I thought we were going to hang out but that was before the events this morning."

"I totally understand. We can hang out another time," Deion said.

As the ladies finished their meal, Deion picked the check up from the table and said, "Okay let's roll. I'm stuffed anyway, I had a big breakfast this morning."

"Yes, we'll have to do this again. I know all of our schedules are a little chaotic but damn," Kya said.

"We just have to make time. There's always time for the people and things that are important."

"I totally agree. I miss our weekly lunch and shopping excursions."

"We'll get it together and get back on schedule."

"Am I dropping you back off at my office? Where's your car?" Kya asked.

"Can you drop me off at Pentagon City?"

"Uh-oh, shopping time. Not a problem. But where's your car?" Kya asked.

"I parked at Pentagon City and took the train to your office. No, no shopping today I'm really not in the shopping mood. I'm going to get my nails done. After that, I'm going to do me and spend the rest of the day doing nothing."

"I know that's right. I wish I could join you but I got stuff to take care of."

Kya pulled in front of Pentagon City and Deion said, "Okay lady, I had fun. Give me a call a little later on."

"Will do. Are you okay?" Kya asked.

"Girl, yes, I'm good."

"Okay, I'll chat with you later on tonight."

When Kya pulled off she picked up her phone to call Steve. Steve answered and said, "Hello babe."

"Hey, honey, how's your day going thus far?" Kya asked.

"Great now that I'm talking to you," Steve said.

"Awww, you're so sweet."

"How's your day going?"

"Great!" Kya shouted.

"Good, I'm glad to hear that. Where are you?"

"I just dropped D off and I'm on my way to pick up Lexi's clothes for her recital."

"Okay, I'll be at your house around 7:30. Will you be ready by then?"

"Yes sir, with bells on."

"Okay, I have to run into a meeting but I'll see you later."

"Okay, I look forward to that."

Kya spent the next couple of hours running errands. After she finished she stopped at her catering company to make sure her staff were prepared for tonight's event. Much to her surprise she spent the next two hours there and needed to rush home and get prepared for her date with Steve. Kya quickly maneuvered through rush hour traffic and got home in forty five minutes. She grabbed a glass of wine, got her clothes out and showered. By the time she got out of the shower, she could her doorbell ringing. *Shit, I'm not even close to being ready*. Kya ran down the steps and opened the door.

Before Steve could say anything, Kya kissed him and said, "Babe, I'll be ready in fifteen minutes."

"Okay, babe," Steve said as he glanced at his watch. As Steve sat down and grabbed the remote, Kya ran back up the steps to finish getting dressed. For the next twenty minutes Steve watched the evening news and patiently waited as Kya got dressed. He knew that fifteen minutes actually meant thirty minutes in Kya's world. As Steve started surfing the channels, he could hear Kya walking down the steps.

"Okay, I'm done, babe, let's go," Kya said.

"Baby, I have something to ask you."

"What's wrong?" Kya asked.

"Nothing. I just want to know if you're ready."

"Yes, as soon as I put my shoes on I'll be ready to go."

"No, that's not what I meant."

"Then what do you mean?"

"Are you ready to receive all that I have to give you?"

"Ewww, that sounds a little freaky."

"No, I'm serious. Can you honestly say that you're ready?"

"Yes, my love. I'm ready."

"How can you be so certain that you actually love me?"

"I love you and I'm in love with you. I know this because my brain and my heart tell me. In addition to that, when I'm with you I feel like I'm on top of the world. When I'm not with you, I count down to the minutes that I'm going to see you. I've been in love before, but I've never felt love like this. Sometimes when you ring the doorbell, my heart feels like it just skipped a beat because it's beating so fast. When you touch me my body just quivers all over and it feels like I'm going to melt. When you hold me, let's just say I've never in my life been held the way you hold me. I feel like everything's going to be alright and that I'm safe. When you make love to me, not fuck but make love, my body responds in ways that I've never experienced. I know we're connected emotionally and that's truly a blessing. I trust, respect and believe what you say to me. My love for you grows more and more every day. Besides God and Lexi you're one of my first thoughts when I open my eyes in the morning, you're also my last thought when I close them to fall asleep. Not to mention I think about your ass all day every day. You actually fill me up and you make me a very happy woman. You're my lover, my best friend and you've been there through my good and bad times. You encourage me and uplift me when I need it. No matter what you're doing, you always have time for me and my daughter. You put us first and make us your priority. Because of those reasons and more, I wouldn't trade you in for the world. To top it off, no man has ever made me feel the way you do, period. Is that enough or do you want to hear more?"

"That's enough for now, you can save some for later."

"Okay, are we ready to go?" Kya asked.

"In a minute, I have something to say. You know that I'm in love with you and I want to spend the rest of my life with you," Steve said.

"Yes, we've had those conversations often."

"I just wanted to double-check and make sure I'm not the rebound guy."

"Cut it out, silly, why are you talking crazy? You're not my rebound guy, you're my restoration man. I know with all certainty that God put you in my life to restore and build me back up. You're that man that I've been waiting for my whole life."

"Is that right? I wanted to check before I asked the next question."

"Yes, sweetie, that's right. What's the next question? Look, man, you're going to make us late, we had reservations for 7:30. Can we play twenty questions on our way to the restaurant?"

Steve grabbed Kya's left hand and asked, "What's that?"

Kya looked down at her hand and asked, "What's what? There's nothing there, what are you talking about?"

"My point exactly, there's nothing there and it should be."

"Something like what, Steve? What are you talking about? What should be there besides my fingers? And why in the hell are you acting so crazy tonight?"

Steve let go of Kya's hand and knelt before her. He then pulled out a four carat emerald-cut yellow diamond ring. Before he could ask Kya anything, the tears started falling from her eyes. Steve looked up at Kya and asked, "Why are you crying?"

"Because," Kya said.

"Because what?"

"Because I'm finally happy, and it's almost like a dream, please pinch me if I'm sleeping!"

Steve then said, "Kya."

Kya jumped up and started screaming, "Yes, Yes, Yes, I'll marry you!"

Steve looked at Kya and asked, "What are you talking about? I haven't asked anything yet!"

"Oh, okay, my bad. Whew! I got a little ahead of myself," Kya said as she sat on the sofa and anxiously waited for what Steve had to ask. She could feel her heart pounding fifty miles a minute.

"Kya, are you ready?" Steve asked.

"Yes, I'm ready."

"Will you marry me?" Steve asked.

"Hellllll to the yeah!" Kya shouted.

DEION

Chapter Four

"Hey, girlie, are we still on for tonight?" Kya asked.

"Girl, I'm just walking through the door. Do I have time for a quick power nap and a shower? I was hoping we could go out around 9:30 or 10," Deion said.

"That sounds good. My babysitter's in class right now. She can't get here until around 9:45 anyway. I should be at your house around 10:30."

"Okay, do you need me to pick you up or would you like to meet at the club?"

"D, why pick me up when the club that we're going to is so close to your house? I'll pick you up and I'll give you a call when I'm on my way."

"Okay, sounds like a plan, I'll talk to you later on."

"Will do, enjoy your nap. Do you also need a wake-up call?"

"No, I'm good, I just need to relax for a little while. Even if I don't fall asleep I just need to chill. I need to unwind from the day that I had."

"Okey-dokey, chat with you later, my dear," Kya said before hanging up the phone.

Before Deion laid down for her nap, she thought it would be better if she got her outfit together. *Hmmm, I'm really not in the mood for dressing up. I'm not certain of the dress code for this club that we're going to. Maybe I'll put on something sassy and sexy. I've been eager to wear my new Valentine ruffled leather jacket that I bought from Saks. Even though it's the beginning of spring it's still a little nippy at night. So I can get away with wearing that jacket. I can also wear a pair of black leggings or blue boot-cut jeans with a white V-neck t-shirt. Either or would be perfect with that jacket and I could also wear my Valentine rosette peep-toe pumps. Perfect! Now I can lay my big ass down, I've had a long and exasperating day and could really use a nap.*

About twenty minutes into Deion's nap, the doorbell rang. She sat up in the middle of her bed and looked at the clock. At first she thought she was dreaming but the doorbell kept ringing. *What the fuck, I know that's not Kya. It's way too early to go to the club. Besides, I just got off the phone with her. I thought she was going to call when she was on her way. That damn girl is so ready to go out. Shit!*

Deion grabbed her robe and put it on as she walked downstairs to the door. The closer she got to the door she realized it couldn't be Kya. *Kya's never on time for anything. If Kya says she'll be here at 10:30, that actually means 11 p.m. And it's only 7:45. If it's not Kya it must be that damn girl in 2A that's looking for a job.*

Deion quietly tiptoed to the door and looked out of the peephole. *What's Jay doing here and how the hell did he get into my building?*

Deion opened the door and before Jay had a chance to say anything Deion immediately started yelling.

"How did you get into my building? Why didn't you call first and what are you doing here?"

"Damn! What happened to hello, it's nice to see you and how are you?" Jay asked.

"Why didn't you call first? You can't just be showing up unannounced and without calling. What if I had company or something?"

"What company? Call for what? When did we get there?"

"Because that's common fucking etiquette. Traditionally when you pop up at someone's house all willy-nilly you don't get in."

"Maybe that other nigga won't get in but did you forget who I am?"

"The next time you decide to show up on my doorstep unannounced, you won't get in. Just remember that. It's that simple. Look, what do you want, Jay? I'm tired, I had a rough day and I'd like to get some rest before I go out."

"Go out?" Jay asked.

"Yes, go out."

"Where do you think you're going?"

"What part of O-U-T don't you understand?"

"Oh, you keeping secrets now?"

"Look, Jay, I don't have time for this right now. I'm going back to bed. This conversation has taken longer than I wanted it to. You can keep sitting here on joke time all by your damn self.

"Okay, let me stop playing. I wanted to stop by and see you, I miss you."

"What the hell ever."

"Let's go upstairs and take a nap."

"I don't need you to take a nap with me. I can take care of that on my own."

"I got something you can take care of," Jay said.

Deion sat on the arm of the sofa and placed her head in her hands. As much as she loved Jay's company he could sometimes be a little annoying. She looked up at Jay and said, "Not tonight, I'm tired as hell. I already told you that."

"Okay, let's go take a nap. I could use a quick nap before I go to the club anyway."

"Okay, but that's all we're going to do because I'm really fucking tired. We're going to get in the bed and take a nap. That's it!"

"Okay, I gotcha."

"I'm serious, Jay."

"Damn, D, you don't act like you're happy to see me. You haven't even given me a hug, a kiss, a handshake or anything." They both got up and started up the steps. As Deion walked slowly upstairs, she turned back, looked at Jay, and rolled her eyes. At the top of the steps she turned around and gave Jay a hug.

"There's your damn hug," Deion said. She then backed away and headed down the hallway to her bedroom.

"Damn, that's it?" Jay asked.

"What else did you expect?"

"Something more than a hug."

"I'm going to finish my nap, you can do whatever. I told you today was one of those days. I'm in need of some quiet time and some relaxation, not this bullshit."

"Would you like me to help you relax?" Jay asked.

"Ummmm, no! I just want to get some rest!" Deion started to undo the knot of her robe.

Before she could finish Jay asked, "What do you have on under that robe?"

"Why does it matter? I have on an outfit."

"It doesn't look like you have on any clothes."

Deion removed her robe and said, "Because it's my birthday suit."

"Ha ha, you're so funny."

Deion took off her robe and walked towards her bed,

Jay said, "You can't possibly expect me to relax now."

Deion crawled into her bed, looked at Jay and asked, "Why not?"

"You just took off your robe and you don't have shit on. How am I supposed to take a nap now?"

Deion pulled the blanket up over her body and said, "Easy, get your ass in the bed, close your eyes and go to sleep."

Jay quickly started taking off his clothes then got into Deion's king-sized bed. Deion was lying on her side and Jay moved closer to her.

"What are you doing?" Deion asked.

"What are you talking about? I'm only trying to put my arm over you. I want to hold you. What, I can't touch you now? You're really acting brand new. You act like you don't want to be bothered with me. You never act like this."

"Because I'm tired, Jay, how many more times do I need to say that?"

"Did your other boo just leave here or something? Why are you so tired?"

"What? What other boo? I don't have a fucking boo. Why don't you just shut the hell up and go to sleep? You're seriously starting to work my damn nerves. We're going through all of this because I want to get some rest. You've got to be fucking kidding me."

Jay adjusted his pillow and got closer to Deion. Deion could feel his dick as he moved closer to her ass. Without saying a word Deion knew she wasn't going to get any rest. As much as she loved having sex with Jay, right now the only thing on her mind was sleeping. Since she'd never resisted before, she knew she wouldn't be able to resist now. Deion slightly adjusted her body and moved Jay's dick from behind her.

"I can't help it, he's happy to see you too," Jay said.

"You need to tell him to take his ass to sleep as well."

Jay softly kissed Deion on the neck and asked, "Are you sure you want to take a nap?"

Deion thought, *Lord have mercy! I'm going to try to hold out as long as I can. Maybe if I keep playing hard to get he'll think I'm not interested and leave me alone.*

"Oh, I see what you're doing. You want me to beg for the pussy."

"No, I don't want you to beg for anything."

"That's how you're acting. You know your pussy's good and I have to have it."

"Whatever, Jay, tell me anything." *Hell, I might as well give in because he's not going to leave me alone. Besides, I am a little horny anyway.*

Jay slowly kissed Deion on the back of her neck again. He began rubbing her back. Then he moved his hands to her breasts and gently fondled and caressed them.

Deion moaned softly as Jay rolled her over on her back and he kissed her lips. He looked at Deion and said, "You know you want this dick so stop faking."

Jay repositioned himself on top of Deion. He kissed her neck very gently, then worked his way down to her breasts. He slowly circled her nipples with his tongue, showing equal care and attention to both. Deion moaned as Jay moved his hand and slowly played with her clit, then he inserted two of his fingers inside her. After a while, Jay grabbed his dick and gently rubbed it over Deion's clit, then her pussy.

As Deion moaned louder, Jay asked, "How bad do you want this dick? Tell me how bad you want this dick."

"I want this dick, I want it so bad," Deion said.

"I don't think you want this dick bad enough."

"Jay, come on, stop teasing me and fuck the shit out of me."

"I thought you were so tired and wanted to rest?"

"Stop playing with me."

She grabbed Jay's dick and moved it inside her, opening her legs wider and wrapping them around Jay's back. Jay slowly moved back and forth; it was like his body moved to the soft moans that Deion let out.

"Jay, I love how you fuck me," Deion whispered.

"I'm enjoying every part of this pussy. It's so good." He rose up, lifted Deion's legs, and placed them over his shoulders. He grabbed her ass and began fucking her faster.

"Is this what you want?" Jay asked.

"Yes."

"I don't think you want it bad enough."

"I do and you know I do."

Jay changed position again, turned Deion over and placed her on her knees, holding her hips in his tight grasp.

"That's it, that's the spot. Oh Jay, fuck this pussy," Deion whimpered. As Deion moaned louder and louder, all she could think was this dick was too good.

"Is this my pussy?" Jay asked.

"No," Deion murmured.

"Tell me it's my pussy."

"No."

As Jay began fucking Deion harder he whispered, "It's not . . . it's not my pussy. Tell me it's my pussy."

"It's your pussy, baby, it's your pussy."

Jay turned Deion over on her back, held her leg up over his shoulder and continued to fuck her from the side. He then placed her other leg over his shoulder and began fucking her harder but then suddenly stopped.

Deion grabbed hold of Jay's dick and asked, "Why are you stopping? Give me this dick."

"Your pussy is so good . . . it's so wet and you're going to make me come. I'm not ready yet, I want to enjoy every part of this pussy."

Deion sat up and closed her mouth around Jay's dick.

"Suck it . . . I knew that's what you wanted," Jay said.

Deion played with his tip with her tongue. Up, down, and then placed his dick back in her mouth. After a while, Deion got up, Jay sat on the edge of the bed and she mounted him. After a couple of minutes of riding him as if she was an experienced cowgirl, and after her second orgasm, Jay finally came.

"Oh my goodness, D, your pussy is the best."

They both lay back down and, as Deion placed her head on Jay's chest, he said, "Now you should be relaxed and can take your nap."

As Deion looked up at the clock, she mumbled, "I'll try. At this point I have about forty five minutes before I start getting ready."

Shortly after Deion and Jay's fuckfest, she drifted off into a deep sleep. She could feel Jay tapping her and saying something about the phone.

"What?" Deion whispered.

"The damn phone keeps ringing, answer it."

Without opening her eyes, Deion reached over and picked up the phone off the nightstand.

"Yeah," Deion whispered.

"Yeah, bitch, what the hell are you doing? I was about to leave your ass. I've been calling you for the past twenty minutes. I started to think that you changed your mind and was ducking me," Kya stated.

"Girl, I overslept. Okay, I'm up. I'm about to jump in the shower. Let me buzz you in."

"Are you sure you're up to going out? We can postpone and go another night."

"Didn't I say, come hell or high water, I was going out tonight? I need to get out, have a few drinks and shake a little ass."

"Okay, bitch, light a fire under that ass and let's get to getting!" Kya yelled.

"Ten minutes, I'll be down in ten minutes."

"Hurry the hell up, we gotta go."

"Okay!" Deion shouted.

"I'm in need of a drink bad and you're holding me up."

"Okay, well come upstairs and make a damn drink then."

"Hell, no. I don't feel like coming up there. You just hurry up."

"Bye, girl, I'll be downstairs in a few."

"Make sure you put something sexy on too. Tonight could be your lucky night."

"For what?" Deion asked.

"You might meet your future ex-husband tonight."

"Girl, please, I'm not even tripping off of that. I'm going out to have fun. Let me get off this damn phone so I can get it together. Are you sure you don't want to come on up?"

"No, I'll wait down here. I have a few calls to make anyway. Just hurry the hell up."

Deion got up to get in the shower and realized Jay had already put his clothes on.

"Call me later on," Jay said.

"Okay," Deion said.

Jay kissed Deion on the forehead and said, "Have fun."

"That's the plan."

"Just don't do anything I wouldn't."

"Whatever that means."

"Call me when you get in."

"For what? Don't be clocking me."

"I might come back over," Jay said.

"We'll see. Okay, I'll talk to you later. I have to get ready."

"Okay, be good."

"I most certainly will not."

As Jay walked out of the bedroom, he grunted then said, "You better."

While Kya sat in her car waiting for Deion, she decided to check her emails. As she reached into her tote bag to grab her iPad, she noticed Jeff coming out of Deion's building. She blew her horn but Jeff didn't notice her.

She then rolled down her car window and yelled, "Jeff, Jeff, over here!" Jeff looked around and saw Kya waving her arm in the air like a crazy woman.

He walked over to her car and asked, "What are you doing here? I know you're not following me again."

"No, I'm not following you this time. You're no longer my man. So I don't give a shit where you are, what you're doing and who you fuck."

"Are you following your new man then?"

"Hell, no! I don't have to follow him. I trust him. What are you doing around here?"

"What are you doing sitting in the car like a stalker?"

"One of my girlfriends lives in that building. I'm waiting for her. You never answered my question."

"What question?"

"What are you doing coming out of that building? Is this where your ho lives or are you creeping?"

"I don't have any reason to creep. I'm a single man and I don't owe you or anyone else any explanations."

"Ewwww, feisty are we?"

"One of my buddies just moved here. I was stopping by on my way to the club."

"Yeah, yeah, whatever you say."

"You're looking good, girl."

"I know."

"Your ass is so conceited."

"Thank you, I'm wearing this new thing."

"What's that?"

"My dear, it's called happiness. Aren't I wearing it well?"

"Slim, you full of shit."

"That I'm not. You're just mad because we aren't together. It's okay, you'll find another fool to deal with all of your bullshit."

"Anyway, why aren't you at home with our daughter?"

"Because I'm going out, don't question me."

"If you stop hanging out in the streets long enough then you probably have a chance at being a good woman."

"Negro, please, I am a good woman. A damn good woman. Don't get me mixed up with those bitches you fuck with," Kya said angrily.

"Man, go ahead with that."

"You just couldn't keep your dick in your pants."

"Ha ha, slim, you funny as shit."

"You know I'm telling the truth. That's the reason we're not together now."

"We're not together now but we'll be back together before you know it. You know you miss this dick."

"Ha ha ha, that was funny. Sorry, sweetie, that chapter of my life is closed. I got a man, a good man."

"You got jokes. You're in the wrong line of work, you should be a comedian."

Kya waved her left hand out of the car window and said, "Oh, you must have not heard."

"Heard what, Kya, what are you talking about?"

"Sweetie, I'm engaged!" Kya yelled.

"Get the hell out of here. Engaged to who?"

"To a wonderful man that loves me and treats me the way a woman should be treated."

"Stop playing, Kya. You probably bought that damn ring and you're walking around saying you're engaged."

"I will be Mrs.—well that's none of your damn business. I'll be married in a couple of months. Don't worry, you're not getting an invitation to our wedding."

"Anyway, I'll believe it when I see it. So, do you want me to come over later?"

"Hell, no. Did you not hear me? I have a man, a fiancé, a husband-to-be."

"I don't believe you."

"I'm surprised your mom or Lexi didn't tell you."

"My mom, what does she have to do with this?" Jeff asked.

"Because she got an invitation. Hell, she's even met him. I'm surprised she didn't tell you."

"And she's going too?"

"Yes my dear, she's going to help my mom look after Lexi."

"Oh, so you're really serious about this shit? How long have you known this dude?"

"Why are you trying to be all up in my business? Don't worry about what's going on over here."

"I am going to worry about some dude around my daughter."

"Child, please! Get over it. Did you think my life was going to stop because our so-called relationship did?"

"It's all good, not a problem."

"I know. Go and swing that dick somewhere else."

"Slim, I'll see you tomorrow. Daddy might give you a little bit if you act right."

"No, thank you. My man takes good care of me and my needs."

"Yeah, I bet. You still want me."

"Actually, I don't. Make sure you call first before you pick up Lexi tomorrow."

"Man, whatever, you better not have that dude all up in my house and around my daughter."

"Negro, please, you don't run shit over there."

"Oh, I'm running shit. Especially since you still ask for money to pay the mortgage."

"It's better to pay my mortgage than pay child support don't you agree? Bye, boy, oh and call your mother."

Jeff turned and said, "Call my mother, for what?"

"I don't have a clue. She told me earlier that you're not returning her calls."

"Yeah, all right, I'll give her a call. I'll holla at you later on."

"Yup," Kya replied.

She looked at the clock and decided to call Deion again. Deion picked up the phone and said, "I'm on my way down."

"Girl, I'm about to leave your ass."

"I'm grabbing my keys and purse now. I'll be down in three seconds."

"Come on, mama, let's get a move on. We got things to do and people to see."

While Kya was waiting for Deion to come downstairs, she got a text from Jeff. Kya immediately thought, *What the hell does he want now?*

She opened the text and it read: YOU KNOW YOU STILL WANT THIS. THAT DUDE IS JUST TEMPORARY. IT'S NOT GOING TO LAST. YOU'RE HOOKED ON BIG DADDY.

As Deion got in the car, she noticed Kya holding her phone and laughing.

"Seriously, what the hell is so funny?" Deion asked.

"Girl, my crazy-ass baby daddy. I was just talking to him then he sent me a crazy-ass text," Kya said.

"Oh, okay, what, you hung up on him?" Deion asked.

"No, he was here."

"Here, where?" Deion asked.

"Here. He was coming out of your building."

"For real? Why was he here? Does he live in my building?"

"Hell, no. Girl, his broke, lying ass wishes he could afford to live in a place like this. He claims that one of his buddies lives in your building."

"Oh wow, okay. Small world."

"Yes, too damn small. I told him I was getting married and he wasn't happy about that."

"Maybe if he acted right you'd be marrying him. From the stories you told me about him he couldn't get his shit together."

"And it's still not together. But that's not for me to worry about."

A couple of minutes later, the ladies arrived at the club. Since Kya knew the owner of the club they didn't have to worry about standing in the long line that stretched around the corner. Once they arrived at the front door, Kya informed the bouncer that Chanel was waiting for them. Moments later, a tall, thin woman approached Kya.

"Hey, girl, it's about time you got here. I was starting to think you weren't going to show," Chanel said.

Kya introduced Chanel and Deion, and then Chanel escorted the ladies into the club. For a brief period of time they stood and glanced over the five-floor, lavishly decorated club.

"Wow, this is so nice," Kya said.

"Thank goodness there aren't a lot of youngsters in here," Deion replied.

"It's definitely a mature crowd. You don't have to worry about the young bucks being in here," Chanel said.

"I didn't think you guys were going to open this soon. The last time I was here the contractors were having some issues or something," Kya said.

"Girl, Kevin fired their asses and got a whole new crew. They worked day and night so we could open on time," Chanel said.

"Where is your husband anyway?" Kya asked.

"He's somewhere around here running his damn mouth," Chanel said.

"I'm curious to know how you came up with the name Club Sphinx?" Deion asked.

"That's a long story and I'll tell you all about it a little later. I have a private table reserved for you in the VIP section. I figured you'd want to be on the first floor so you can see everything," Chanel said jokingly.

"And you know that's right," Kya said.

"Let me take you to your table. Then I need to find my husband."

"Okay, we're right behind you."

As the ladies walked through the club, Kya noticed a number of people surrounding the bar making small talk, laughing and drinking.

"That's a first," Kya said.

"What?" Chanel asked.

"The bar isn't crowded."

"That's because we have two bars on each floor," Chanel said.

"Get the hell out of here," Kya said.

"This is really a nice club. How long have you been open?"

"Huh, what did you say? I can't hear you," Chanel said.

Deion moved a little closer to Chanel and said, "I said this is a really nice club. How long have you been in business?"

"We just opened last week."

"Some of my co-workers told me this is definitely a nice spot. I didn't tell them that we were related," Kya said.

Once they arrived at their table Chanel informed them that the waitress would be over to get their drink orders. She also explained what was on each level if they wanted to check it out.

Before Chanel walked away, she said, "By the time you place your dinner order Kevin I and will be back. We're having dinner together."

"Okay, we'll be here," Kya said.

"Okay, I'll see you ladies in a couple of minutes, once I locate my hubby."

"Sounds good."

After Chanel walked away, Deion tapped Kya's hand and said, "I didn't know you were related to them."

"Yes, ma'am."

"How?"

"Kevin's my first cousin."

"Why didn't you tell me?"

"There was nothing to tell. I would have mentioned it sooner or later."

"I can't believe you."

"What? I was going to tell you. There's no way we would have sat here all night and you wouldn't have known. A couple of my co-workers mentioned how nice it was, but I wanted to check it out for myself. I knew it was going to be off the hook. My cousin doesn't do half-ass projects. He do the whole damn thing."

"Yeah I see. Is he the same Kevin that owns The Lighthouse and The Blueroom?"

"Yup, that's him."

"Stop playing. All of this time I had no idea that y'all are related."

"I know you've had to hear me mention him a thousand times."

"No, I haven't."

"Maybe because I don't call him by his name, I refer to him as JB."

"Okay, I've heard that name a lot but I didn't put two and two together."

"Well, now you know."

As Deion scanned the room, the waitress approached the table and said, "Hey ladies, my name is Tia and I'll be your waitress for the evening. How are you tonight?"

"We're great," Kya responded.

"Do you ladies know what you would like to drink or do you need more time?"

"We're ready, we'd like two blow job martinis," Kya said.

"Okay, I'll bring them right out. I was also told to bring you an appetizer sampler."

"Okay, sounds good," Deion said.

"Let me put your drink orders in and I'll be right back."

As they waited for their drinks, Kya grabbed her phone out of her purse and placed it on the table.

"Are you expecting an important call?" Deion asked. Kya looked at her phone and noticed she had six text messages and three missed calls.

"No not really, but I do have a child and at any given moment anything can happen."

"True. Where is Lexi anyway?"

"She's at Bailey's house."

"Oh, okay. I thought your sister was going to watch her."

"She was but she needed to study for finals or something. I didn't want Lexi to be a distraction so Bailey picked her up before I left."

"Okay. Y'all really watch out for each other. And definitely have no problem watching or caring for each other's babies."

"That's the way it's supposed to be. We're not just good friends we're a family. And family look out for one another."

"My blood family doesn't even have the type of bond you two have. I wish I was close to my family. But oh well, it is what it is."

"It's never too late to get things right."

"I just don't feel like all of the drama with them."

"But at the end of the day family is really all you have."

"That's what I hear."

Before Kya could respond the waitress appeared with their drinks as well as appetizers.

"Wow, that was quick," Kya said.

"Is there anything else I can get you ladies? I know you won't be putting your dinner order in until a little later on."

"No, I think we're good for now. But you might need to keep the drinks coming," Kya said.

"I was told to make sure your glasses aren't empty the remainder of the night," Tia said.

"Oh really?" Deion asked.

"Yes. I'll let you get started on your appetizers. I'll check back on you in a couple of minutes."

"Okay, thank you," Kya said.

"Girl, this is excellent service. I don't think I've ever been in a place like this," Deion said.

"Girl, where have you been hanging at?"

"Apparently not at the right places."

"So where were we? Oh, talking about your family."

"Girl, I don't want to discuss anything sad or depressing. I'm here to have fun and I don't want to talk about them folks."

"Oh, okay. Well then, how are things with this mystery man in your life?"

"Which one?" Deion asked.

"Damn, how many do you have?"

"I have several friends. Remember, I'm single and unattached."

"Okay, well I'm referring to the guy that you deal with the most."

"Jay?" Deion asked.

"I guess. I never pay too much attention to their names. They change quite often."

"Things are good, if we can stay away from the bedroom. Girl, it's like my pussy talks to him. I have never been with a man that makes my body feel the way that he does."

"Too much information."

"I'm just saying. When we have sex my body actually shakes all over."

"Still too much information."

"And when I come, it's like, woo-hoo, I just explode!" Deion yelled.

"Thanks for sharing, the mental picture and graphics are just what I needed," Kya said jokingly.

"Just keeping it real. I know you're not talking, you're the most open person that I know. I share everything and don't hold any of the details back."

"Some things I do keep to myself."

"When?"

"I don't tell everything. Your right hand don't always need to know what the left hand is doing."

"Whatever you say, you tell it all. Not only that, you tell how you feel, what you feel . . . everything."

"I disagree."

"Well, whatever. I know because I listen to all of your stories."

"Anyway, moving on. Do the two of you do anything besides have sex? Do you go out like on a real date?" Kya asked.

"Once in a while we go to dinner or hang out. We're both so busy that we really don't get a chance to hang out as much as I'd like."

Kya sipped her drink, and said, "That's a first."

"What?" Deion asked.

"Since I've know you, your motto has always been no strings attached. Fuck 'em and leave 'em alone."

"Sometimes things change."

"I see. He must have some dick. So I take it he's not just a friend with benefits. It's more than that?"

"He's a friend but I don't think either of us expects anything else right now. We're still baby stepping until we get to that point."

"Just don't lose your mind over some dick, girlfriend."

"Never that! I mean he's a good guy but I don't know if he's the one for me."

"Why would you say that?"

"Because I'm not sure if I'm ready to settle down, I like doing me."

"That doesn't mean that he's not the one for you just because you're not ready to settle down."

"Besides, I still have a brick wall with a chain and lock protecting my heart. I'm too afraid of getting hurt."

"Eventually you'll have to tear that shit down that you've built. Open your heart to love and be loved. Not all men are bad. Besides, living in fear is paralyzing, crippling and detrimental to our progress."

"I know this but I'm too afraid to give any man my all."

"You shouldn't be afraid. I understand what you've been through and how you feel. Trust me. You can't hold all men accountable for what one man has done to you."

"That's the thing, it wasn't just my ex that hurt me. It seems like every man that I tried to be serious about has hurt me in some form or fashion."

"Again, all men aren't bad. Granted you had a few that were rough around the edges. Life doesn't stop there. Try again."

"Maybe you're right but at this stage in my life, I'd rather just do me until I can figure things out."

"You better not be wasting valuable time. And why haven't we met this mystery man anyway? Is he married?" Kya asked.

"No, he's not married."

"The only thing that you've told us about him is his name and how good the dick is."

"That's not true. I share stuff about him."

"Like what? We don't know shit about him. Do you even know anything about him?"

"Of course I do. Look how much time we spend together. He just has a lot going on, he's a busy man. I'm not trying to be tied down. More importantly, I still have plenty of male friends. He's my number one boo."

"Whatever the hell that means. You still haven't answered the question."

"What question?"

"When do we get to meet the Mr. Mystery?"

"In due time y'all will meet him so stop tripping. Right now I'm still feeling him out and getting to know him."

"Yeah, I bet you're feeling him out. I'm just shocked that you even mention this guy. You never talk about any man. Uh-oh, you must be really feeling this guy. I told you before he might be the one.

"I didn't say all of that. I'm a little afraid and want to be careful. I'm just not ready to put my heart into it yet. You know I'm afraid of being hurt."

"We can't live our lives in fear."

"True but I want to take my time. I don't think I'm ready for a relationship as of yet."

"Okay, then take baby steps and see where this could go."

"Trust me, I am. I'm still doing me. Maybe I'll bring him to your dinner party on Saturday."

"That'll be nice. At least we could finally meet him."

"It depends on his schedule because he works a lot."

"Okay and your point being what? We all have jobs. Hell, some of us got more than one and a few side hustles."

"His time is limited."

"But he makes time to fuck."

"That's different. He owns a couple of businesses and they keep him pretty damn busy."

"What kind of businesses does he own?"

"He owns a car detailing shop, a landscaping business, two night clubs and a barber shop."

"Oh wow! How nice you got yourself an entreprenegro. Ain't nothing wrong with that. I was unsure of what type of job he had. You mentioned the other day he was a business man. But you weren't clear on his profession."

"Yeah, he's an entreprenegro. It's alright. I don't see him as often as I like because he's always working."

"That's how it is when you're the boss. Working for yourself isn't as glamorous like people make it seem. You definitely gotta put in a lot of time, effort and energy."

"Yeah, I guess."

"Look, how many hours you work and you work for someone else. Just imagine how it would be if you were your own boss. Trying to build and make your business successful."

"I guess you got a point."

"I don't care if he has twenty businesses. He doesn't work seven days a week and three hundred and sixty five days a year. If you mean anything to him then he'll make time for you, no matter what."

"But we aren't on that level yet. Maybe he feels the same way I do—no strings attached."

"That's bullshit."

"Because he's so busy, I'm appreciative that he can fit me into his schedule."

"It sounds like you're settling for what you can get," Kya said.

"No, not really. We're friends."

"Right, friends with benefucks."

"Don't you mean friends with benefits?"

"Hell, no. I mean what I said, benefucks. That's all y'all do."

"We're content with how things are."

"The two of you should talk and figure out what it is y'all are doing."

"I guess you got a point. But we don't have those type of conversations."

"So, besides the occasional fuck, do you really do anything else? Don't lie."

"We go out to eat every once in a while."

"So you don't talk about having a relationship or the future?"

"Yeah we talk, but just not about relationship stuff."

"Hmmmm, that's different."

"What's different about it? Not everybody wants to be in a relationship. Some of us are content just doing us."

"My dear, you're definitely not getting any younger and you should want more for yourself. Casual sex isn't a commitment."

"I understand what you're saying and I agree, but it also depends on the people. Everything isn't for everybody."

"True but relationships aren't like buying clothing."

"If we determined in the beginning the nature of our friendship, then that's what it'll be."

"Very true but you said the two of you haven't had that convo. If a possible relationship was discussed in the beginning things might be different."

"Different how?"

"Instead of being an option you'd be his priority."

"But I'm good with our arrangement."

"It sounds like you're a business deal or something. At least if you were in a relationship you'd have more of a commitment, duty-bound. You'd do more than get together to fuck. Whatever your status is determines the amount of time y'all spend together."

"What's that supposed to mean?"

"Do I really have to explain this to you? I know you already know."

"Kya, I really don't have a clue what you're trying to say."

"What I'm saying is if he's really feeling you and your wifey status, you'll see him all of the damn time. The two of you would be together every day or every other day. You'd see his ass a whole hell of a lot. Trust and believe you would be a priority in his life. If you're only friends with benefits, then you'll see him when *he* wants to fuck. And if you're just some bitch he fucks with, then you'll only be seen when the other bitches aren't available. It's that simple."

"Girl, where do you get this shit from?" Deion asked.

"It's called reality. Been there and done that."

"Haven't we all?"

"It's okay to have friends but you don't have to fuck 'em all. No one ever said that having friends was a bad thing. There are plenty of men and women that are friends and don't have sex."

"So you think that's all I do?"

"I'm just going by what you tell us. On a weekly basis there are at least two men that you've fucked. The majority of the time it's never the same man. That's all I'm saying. If it's a lie then you told it."

"Why is it hard to understand that I'm trying to stay away from commitments?"

"That's unnatural."

"No, it's not. I'm not looking for a monogamous relationship."

"So you're like a stop and shop—just fuck and roll."

"Whatever."

"Why is being committed to a man any different than anything else in your life?"

"Because it's a big difference, that's why."

"There are a lot of things that you're committed to."

"Like what?"

"Your career, your crazy-ass family, our friendship. Do you need me to go on?"

"Of course, but those things are different."

"Why are they different?"

"After my horrible marriage I just don't want to commit to a man. I find it extremely difficult to trust any man."

"That is such bullshit! Then commit to a fucking woman!" Kya yelled.

"You know I don't get down like that."

"D, you're full of shit. And you need to stop using your marriage as an excuse. You're not the first nor will you be the last to have a fucked-up relationship. Get the hell over it and move on."

"I guess you don't understand."

"Then make me understand."

"For whatever reason I find it easier to deal with attached men versus unattached men."

"The last time I checked, my IQ was over 140. That shit doesn't make any sense to me whatsoever."

"It's like I'd rather deal with them only when I need to and I don't have to commit to them. I don't owe them anything, I don't have to see them often only when it's convenient for me."

"In other words it's okay for you to ruin other relationships and happy homes?"

"Pretty much."

"You're just a cold-hearted bitch!" Kya screeched.

"Call it whatever you want. I don't care what you say or think about me. But trust and believe all men have more than one woman. So I don't understand what the big deal is with me having more than one man."

"Girl, you're hopeless. I don't know what island your common sense flew to. But you need to get your shit together. Trust and believe. All men don't have more than one woman. There are a whole lot of monogamous men out there."

"Where?"

"Why don't you stop looking, keep your legs closed and let him find you."

"One day I will, but not today."

"Ugh! I really don't know what to say about you."

"I don't understand what the big issue is."

"The big issue is you change sex partners more than I change my damn panties."

"Excuse me. I have male friends but I wouldn't say I have a whole hell of a lot of them."

"The hell you say. Bitch, you got a lot of male friends. Let me rephrase that. You have a lot of fuck partners."

"What's wrong with having friends?" Deion inquired.

"Nothing, but you fuck 'em all."

"I have needs too."

"So do I, but I'm not running around all loosey-goosey either. I just hope one day you'll wake up from la la land and get your shit together. I hope and pray if this guy is the man for you, that you're handling this friendship differently."

"What's that supposed to mean?"

"If he is in fact a good guy like you said, just don't scare this one off with your BS."

"And what's that supposed to mean?" Deion asked.

"You can be a little controlling at times. You want what you want, when you want, and how you want. If a person isn't at your beck and call or bowing down because you said so, then all hell breaks loose."

"I'm not that bad."

"Shit, ask that simple-ass assistant of yours."

"Kya, seriously, I'm really not that bad."

"Okay, if you think you're not then maybe the rest of us are tripping. But you're definitely a control freak."

"I can't believe you said that. I know that I can be demanding but that's totally different from controlling something or someone."

"How is it different? Demanding and controlling go hand and hand." The waitress walked over with two more blow job martinis.

"Thank you," Deion said.

"You're welcome. How's the appetizer sampler?" Tia asked.

"We've barely had anything. We've been busy running our mouths," Kya said.

"Okay, try it out and I'll be back shortly to check on you."

"Thanks," Deion said.

"D, do you remember that guy named Charles that you were dating?" Kya asked.

"Yes."

"Now that was a nice guy. That poor fella did everything that you said. Whenever you snapped your fingers he went running. If you said jump he asked how high and would continue jumping until you said to stop," Kya said jokingly.

Deion laughed and said, "You don't ever lie. He was a nice little man."

"My point exactly, but he was more like your puppet. You controlled everything in that relationship, friendship or whatever you want to call it. I can't even say that was a relationship. He was more like your son, your personal assistant, your chef—everything."

Deion laughed and said, "He had some freedom, it's not like he was my personal slave."

"What the fuck ever! You told him when he could go, if he could go. You also needed to know who he was with. He couldn't wipe his ass unless you gave him permission. What type of shit is that?"

"Yes that's true but he enjoyed it."

"No, the hell he didn't. He just wasn't man enough to stand up to your ass. I can't even say he was a real man. I'm still questioning whether he had balls or not. A real man would not let you control him like that."

"He had balls."

"All I know is he wasn't a real damn man. I know he had low self-esteem and some other issues but damn."

"You make it seem like he was crazy."

"He was crazy as shit to deal with that foolishness. He'd have been better off in jail. At least he'd have had some freedom."

Deion laughed and said, "Cut it out. He was happy."

"Ha ha, you really got jokes. Charles took your foolishness as long as he could. Then he grew some balls and got his ass to getting. And has never looked back. He got tired of your crazy bullshit."

"I kinda miss him sometimes. I hated that he took that job in San Francisco."

"Girl, he took that damn job to get away from your sick ass. He was tired of being abused and fed up with your bullshit."

"He asked me to go with him but I couldn't at the time."

"Now you know he really didn't want you to go. He asked because he knew that you couldn't leave the DMV. Especially since you'd just got that promotion, he knew you weren't going anywhere. That poor man didn't know which way was up unless you told him. Nor did he know his ass from his head."

"We talked for a while but then we lost touch. I guess the new job was keeping him busy."

"Poor fella, you had that little man so stressed out that he started to go bald."

"He was okay."

"I bet your ass any amount of money he's in therapy right now because of what you put him through. You mentally abused that man. He ain't ever going to be right."

"Oh cut it out, I wasn't that bad."

"You keep saying that like you're so innocent. You probably used to beat the shit out of him too. Wow, he was a battered man."

As Deion chuckled she said, "Stop it. You're going to make me piss myself."

"I'm glad you think it's funny. I still pray for that man. I hope he's manned up by now and isn't being battered by another sicko."

"I really don't think I was that bad."

"Because you weren't the victim, Charles was. Girlfriend, it's not a relationship when you control someone's every step, every move or their life, period. That makes you a tyrant. Who the hell in their right mind would want to be in a relationship like that? If they do, then they got some self-esteem issues or something."

"I'm not a tyrant and I don't think I'm that bad."

"Ask Charles' therapist, I bet he or she will tell you different."

"Yeah, whatever."

As Deion and Kya finished their second drink, Chanel approached the table.

"Sorry, ladies, I thought I was going to get a chance to hang out and have dinner with you. Unfortunately, Kevin had to go The Blueroom so I've been working and schmoozing with people."

"Is everything alright?" Kya asked.

"The manager got sick and he had to go to the emergency room."

"Oh, wow, I hope he'll be okay."

"I hope so. Kevin and I were looking forward to having dinner with you," Chanel said.

"It's okay, no worries. I understand he had to do what he had to do. We can have dinner some other time," Kya said.

"You can go ahead and place your dinner orders. I have to finish schmoozing and making sure everything's good with the staff. Some of them just aren't the brightest."

"I know what you mean," Deion said.

"I'm good. I've been nibbling on this sampler. This is actually enough for me, I'm kind of full," Kya said.

"Me too. The sampler's great. It's enough to feed a small village," Deion said.

"I'm glad you're enjoying it. If you decide to order dinner just let Tia know and she'll take care of you. I have to get back to work, a woman's job is never done," Chanel said.

"Girl, you have never lied!" Kya yelled.

"It seems that the chef was having some issues in the kitchen. I need to go and check on him. I'll try to come back in a little while. God knows I need to give my feet a break," Chanel said.

"It's not easy walking around in those stilettos all night, is it?" Kya asked.

"Heck no and I'm tired as hell on top of that. I've been here since 8 a.m. Girl, when I get in the bed I'm going to be out cold," Chanel said.

"I know that's right. You better take a break."

"I will as soon as I get a chance. Don't sit here all night. Explore the club and check things out. Let me know what you think."

"I will in a few minutes," Kya said.

"Go dance and have some fun," Chanel said.

"Oh I will," Kya said.

"See you a little later," Chanel said.

"She's really nice. How long have she and Kevin been together?" Deion asked.

"About ten years but they've only been married for five," Kya said.

"Oh, okay."

"She is definitely a good woman."

"Why you say that?" Deion inquired.

"She stuck by him when he was a hot mess. He was on drugs really bad and he wasn't trying to get it together."

"Oh really?"

"Yes, despite all that he put her through, she never left his side."

"He doesn't even look like someone that didn't have his shit together."

"Child, looks can be deceiving."

"True. So where did he get the money to start all of these clubs?" Deion asked.

"He's always had good jobs and he's always been a firm believer in investing money. I guess that's how he was able to start his businesses. I really don't know, I never asked. But Ms. Girl gotta pretty large bank account too."

"Really?" Deion asked.

"Yes! When her grandfather passed he made sure she'd be taken care of the rest of her life. She doesn't have to want or need shit. Her grandfather was some type of real estate guru and left her everything."

"I bet her family was pissed."

"I don't think so. Besides her and her mom, no one else in the family dealt with him. I guess they didn't expect to get anything. I can tell you one thing, she gave her mom a nice size check and big momma doesn't want for shit either."

"Wow."

"One thing that I know is that she and Kevin are really happy. My aunt loves her to death."

"Do they have any children?"

"No, she can't have children."

"Awww, that's unfortunate."

"They're in the process of adopting a baby girl."

"That's good. I bet they'll be great parents."

"I know they will."

"How long has Kevin been clean?"

"Ummm, I think it's been about four years."

"That's good."

"Yes, it is. We're all proud of him."

"I guess for some people love really does endure all things."

"Yes it does," Kya said.

"Unfortunately, I haven't experienced that type of love as of yet."

"Not yet but it can and will happen, one day. You just need to let your guard down."

"I don't know if I'm ready for that type of commitment yet. I'm damn sure not going to hold my breath."

"Girl, I don't know what I'm going to do with you."

"I'm being honest. Me plus love equals a major disaster."

"Okay, you're going to see. Mark my words, one day when you least expect love to show up that's when it'll happen. Trust me, I know."

"We'll see."

"First you need to stop with your risqué behavior. Then you need to unlock that chain you have around your heart. More importantly, you need to change your thinking. You need to speak good things over your life. Once you begin speaking good things over your life, things will start to happen."

"Oh goodness, here we go with this again. Can we change the subject? I'm tired of talking about me and my lifestyle."

"If you just look at your behavior for the past year then you'll understand what I'm saying."

"Look at what, that I love to fuck? Why do I have to justify to you that I love to fuck?"

"You really don't. I just want you to understand that your behavior is a bit unsafe."

"Because I love sex?"

"It's not unsafe because you love sex. Who doesn't love sex? It's unsafe because of how you go about it. That's what makes it so unsafe."

"I disagree."

"I don't know if you're going through a phase or what. Maybe you're just a nymphomaniac," Kya said jokingly.

"Get the hell out of here."

"In all honesty I don't know what the hell is up with you. All I know is whenever you meet a guy you're dropping your breeches before you learn his last name. Then you start buying them shit and giving them money."

"That's not true."

"Seriously, D? It's like you're compensating them for fucking you."

"That is not true. I get to know them first."

"What, for an hour? No you don't, D. When is the last time that you were in a serious, monogamous and committed relationship that lasted at least six months?"

"I don't recall but it's definitely been a while."

"Because it hasn't happened."

"That's not what I'm looking for right now anyway. I just want to have friends and a little fun."

"The only relationship that I remember you being in is with your psycho crazy-ass ex-husband."

"Let's not bring him up please. That was a different chapter of my life and I want to keep it closed."

"But our past is a pertinent part of our present."

"That might be true but that chapter is closed and not up for discussion."

"Okay, I'll leave it alone. As your friend, all I want is for you to be happy. I want you to be with a man that will treat you the way you deserve to be treated, like a queen not like some street poontang."

"I appreciate that but I'm good."

"We've all been through bullshit and drama at some point in our life."

"Yeah, that's true."

"I'm keeping my fingers crossed and praying that Mr. Mystery is the man for you. Hopefully, he'll start spending more time with you. Perhaps your benefuck will blossom into a real relationship."

"Just because he's busy and don't have time for me doesn't mean that he's not feeling me."

"Okay, whatever you say. Girlfriend, it's no fun digging some man that doesn't give a fuck about you. Especially when he only deals with you when it's convenient for him."

"That's definitely not the case. Have you ever stopped to think that this is convenient for me?"

"Okay, we shall see. I'm just saying if you don't stand for something, you'll fall for anything. But time will tell."

"Girl, you're tripping. I'm starting to think you have a personal vendetta against men or you're jealous."

"Jealous of what?"

"Of me. Maybe you want to live vicariously through me, although you won't admit it."

"Girl, I love you to death but you got me fucked up. You should never put my name in the same sentence with the words jealous or vicariously."

"I just don't understand why you're so obsessed with my life."

"Because I love you and I care about you."

"Okay, if you say so."

"D, the difference between you and me is I know my value and self-worth. I myself have wasted time with an undeserving man for years. However, I learned from my mistakes. I now know to handle things differently. Life's too short to keep playing games and wasting time. Besides, I'm wifey material not just some bitch you fuck with here and there or whenever it's convenient."

"I agree wholeheartedly, but not all of us want to be wifey. I look at it like this, what is it that a man can do for me that I can't do for myself?"

"I feel for you and I know a lot of women feel just like you. But it would be nice to have a mate to share your life with."

"Yes, that would be nice but I haven't come across that man as of yet. I'm not saying that I won't but right now I'm content doing me."

"Which really means, that you want your cake and eat it too? You want to keep fucking all of these men and having casual sex like it's okay."

"Pretty much."

"What about love?"

"What about it?"

"Don't you want love?"

"Girl, I've given up on the love thing. The only thing that love has done for me is beat the shit out of me. All of the men that I've been with have only hurt me in some way or another."

"Except Charles," Kya said jokingly.

"Yeah, except Charles. I got tired of waiting and hoping for 'Mr. Right' to come along and rescue me."

"I understand how you feel, we've all been there but heartache come and goes. Broken hearts do mend and there are still a few good ones out there, somewhere."

"Life is very precious and I just want you to be careful out here. The casual sex thing went out of style at the same time as MC Hammer's pants. You can't be fucking people all willy-nilly."

"Well, there's nothing wrong with me having sex here and there. I don't know what our future holds or if there's a future for myself and Jay. I have fun with him and enjoy his company."

"Uh huh, but you don't see him that much?"

"I see him enough."

"In your book what does enough mean?"

"Maybe once a week, or once every other week, it depends on his schedule."

"Girl, wake up. You're just another piece of pussy to him. No more and no less. You're just a quick fuck every once in a while. Maybe you're the one that does the special tricks that the others don't."

"Whatever, Kya."

"Are you serious? What planet are you living on? Girl, what about AIDS and shit?"

"What about it? I'm careful."

"Yeah, right."

"What am I supposed to do? If you haven't noticed, I'm single. Am I supposed to be celibate until I meet Mr. Right?"

"I'm not saying you have to be celibate, just very careful."

"I know your ass ain't talking."

"I'm not saying I'm a saint and I do have sex. But I have a man and I'm not fucking everyone in the DMV."

"Now that was a low blow, Kya. You didn't have to go there."

"If he's a good guy why don't you at least take the time to really get to know him?"

"I don't know. I really and truly don't want a relationship. I often get the short end of the stick in a relationship. I'm tired of being hurt. I've been emotionally and physically abused more than I care to admit. So right now, it's on my terms. I don't want their money or anything else."

"But you'll take the dick."

"That about sums it up. That's the only thing that I want from them—their dick."

"That's sad."

"All a man can do for me is fuck the shit out of me and that's it. If I don't feel like being bothered, I can pull out the magic bullet or the bunny. I can take care of business my damn self."

"That's way too much information."

"What?"

"Bitch, I don't need to know nothing about your self-gratification."

"I was just sharing."

"Thanks for sharing but I don't need to know all of that."

"Oh, okay."

"What about companionship? You're still young. Is this what you want to do the rest of your life? Don't you want to share your life with someone?"

"Why do you keep asking me that? Again, I'm content with how my life is and what I'm doing. I've tried that before and it didn't work. So what else am I supposed to do?"

"For one you can put a chain and lock around your knees. Stop passing your pussy out like it's free cheese. Don't get me wrong, I haven't always had the best relationships either. I've been through some shit. But I didn't give up on men. There are a whole lot of good men out there. But we're so wrapped up in the losers that we miss out."

"Kya, thanks for your advice, but a long time ago I built a brick wall around my heart. I don't really feel like tearing the wall down just yet, I'm protecting my heart. I don't like the feeling of heartbreak and disappointment. So I'm doing me. I haven't asked you for any advice so why are you in my business?"

"You're right, you didn't ask me for my advice but I'm telling you anyway. What you're doing isn't right. Hell, I'm scared for you. What if you pick up the wrong guy and he's a psychotic maniac? Then your ass will be dead and gone. And for what? Some dick."

"I learned a long time ago that there's always going to be someone who doesn't approve of you. They talk about your lifestyle, appearance, religion, significant other or whatever. They always have something to say and I couldn't care less what people think or say about me. I don't live for everyone else, I live for me."

"You're missing the whole point and I can't talk to you. Why are you always so defensive?"

"Because you're always in my damn business."

"I'm just trying to help you."

"I don't need your damn help, I'm good."

"If you say so."

"I may not be tall, statuesque or look like you. I may not look like a supermodel and I might be a big girl, but I got men lining up for me. I'm smart, attractive and have a nice size bank account."

"If you're so damn smart then why do you insist on giving your va-jj to every Tom, Dick and Harry? If a man says hello to you than bam, your panties hit the floor or even the pavement."

"I don't want to hear this bullshit."

"It's not like they're actually interested in you and what you bring to the table. They're lining up for free pussy and the bank card. After they get what they want from you they're done. You don't mean a damn thing to them."

"So you really think I'm paying for the dick?"

"Bingo, you got it!" Kya yelled.

"That's fine because they don't mean a damn thing to me either. Kya, we didn't come to the club for you to lecture me about my life. Girl, I'm just living life the best way I can, being me and having fun. I fuck who I want, when I want, and there's nothing wrong with that. So stop tripping, it's all good. This conversation is redundant and I hate redundancy."

"D, I just want you to know it's not okay. Not only are you very loose but you also don't care if they got a wife, girlfriend or anything."

"Why is that for me to worry about? That's their problem not mine. Kya, I'm done with the conversation about me and my life. Either you find another conversational piece or I'm going home."

"Okay, one last thing and then I'm done."

"What now?"

"It's just a little test."

"What kind of test?"

"Stop having sex with him and you'll see if he's really into you."

"Huh, what? Why the hell would I do that? What is that going to prove?"

"It'll show you if he actually cares about you."

"I can't do that."

"Why can't you?"

"Girl, you know I can't go without dick, my pussy's not used to withdrawal, she'll go into shock."

"Maybe it's time you give your pussy a break. She's been very busy lately."

"The hell you say. I'm not doing that. What's the purpose of that?"

"To see if Mr. Mystery is really feeling you. Tell him that you've decided to be celibate."

As Deion laughed, she said, "He'd never believe that bullshit. Hell, I wouldn't be able to tell that lie and believe it."

"If he's really digging you then he'll wait. Let him know that you're no longer giving out community service hours to men. You desire, want and deserve a commitment. Tell him you've decided to be celibate until you get married. If you're just another piece of ass then he's gonna roll and you'll have your answer."

"Okay. I'm going to have to prove you wrong."

"We'll see," Kya said.

"How about you and your new boo?" Deion asked.

"See, you're doing it again. Whenever we start asking you questions about Mr. Mystery you always try to change the subject and elude the questions."

"I'm not eluding anything. I'm just tired of discussing my sexual habits and my life. Therefore, I'm switching topics. Let's talk about you, you're great at that."

"Whatever, it's not about me and my man, we're discussing you right now. We don't know if this man is a serial killer or what. We can't keep calling him the Mystery Man. Does he really exist or is this man just an illusion?"

"Oh, he really exists and he most definitely isn't an illusion. I already told you his name and the businesses that he own. You can call him by his name, you chose to call him the Mystery Man."

"Jay? Is that short for something or is that his real name?"

"That's his real name."

"What's his last name?"

"Girl, I'm not getting into all of that with you. You'll meet him soon enough."

"Yeah, okay, whatever you say."

"Now who's avoiding questions?" Deion asked.

"I'm not avoiding any questions."

"Again, how's your man?"

"My man's great! I love him, he loves me, we're in love and very happy. Pow! It doesn't get any better than that."

"In love . . . seriously?"

"Yes, ma'am," Kya said.

"Isn't that a little too quick?"

"You can't put a time frame on when you fall in love. The unexpected happens when you least expect it. Didn't I tell you that earlier?"

"Damn that was quick."

"It's not like I just met him last month. I've known this man for years."

"Is this the same man that you met on Facebook?" Deion asked.

"I didn't meet him on Facebook, we got reconnected on Facebook. There's a difference between the two."

"If you're happy then I'm happy for you."

"I'm very happy! I had to get rid of that unnecessary baggage that I was carrying around. Once I did, I opened my heart to love and to being loved, then boom! It happened."

"Wow, I can't believe that."

"You and me both. Sometimes I have to pinch myself to make sure I'm not dreaming. He's everything that I've always wanted in a man and more. This is the man that I've been praying for my entire life."

"You think so?"

"I know so. I thought after my baby daddy that I didn't want to deal with anyone. At least for a while. I wanted to focus on self. I wasn't even thinking about men or getting into a new relationship. D, girl, I'm so happy."

"And I'm happy for you but everyone don't have a happy ending like you."

"I have never felt this way in my life for any man. I wouldn't trade him in for anything in the world. I thank God for sending this man to me."

"I guess it was meant to be. As long as you're happy that's all that matters."

"Thanks, girl. So, aside from the mystery man in your life what else has been going on with you? Did you enjoy the rest of your vacation?"

"I really didn't do anything exciting. I did manage to decorate the condo at last and I still worked from home a couple of days."

"Then that wasn't a real vacation. I'm glad you finally finished decorating, it's about damn time. You still had shit all over the place and boxes were everywhere."

"I know, right."

"Why didn't you tell us? We'd have helped you."

"I enjoyed it, it's not like I had a lot of stuff to unpack anyway. Besides a few personal effects, everything else was brand new."

"I forgot you donated everything to Goodwill. What's going on with the house?"

"It was finally sold and I'm glad about that. I was getting tired of paying that mortgage for an empty damn house."

"It's about time. You've been trying to sell that house for over a year."

"I decided to decrease my asking price. When I did that, it sold within a week."

"What are you going to do with all of that money?"

"All of what money? It's not like I got a whole hell of a lot for it. Most likely save it unless I decide to treat myself to something nice."

"Girl, you treat yourself often."

"You damn right, and so do you."

"I sure as hell do."

"Okay then. Am I supposed to sit around and wait for someone to take care of me and my wants? Hell no, I take care of me."

"I guess you got a point."

"Most likely I'll save the money. You never know if and when I'll decide to stop working. I want to retire early. I just might start my own marketing firm or invest it. I really haven't thought too much about it."

"I hear that. There's nothing like living a debt-free life. I'm still paying for financial mishaps from my younger days."

"It was that bad?"

"Yes. Unfortunately, I'm paying for the mistakes of someone else."

"I hate that."

"I bet I'll never co-sign for another man as long as I have breath in my body. But you live and you learn."

"I know that's right. Don't say anything to Brandi but I've decided to make a significant donation to her foundation. I haven't mentioned it to her as of yet so please don't say anything."

"My lips are sealed. She's going to be thrilled."

"Hopefully everything will work out for her. She's extremely passionate about this foundation. That's pretty much all she talks about."

"I know. She's excited about getting it started and helping these young girls."

"Girl, I have to go to the bathroom. If the waitress comes by, order me another blow job martini. I'll be right back," Deion said. "Then I have to hit the dance floor. I didn't come to the club to sit here and talk to you all night long about nothing. We could have stayed home for that. There are too many men in here for me to be sitting up in your face. I might run into some new dick on the way to the bathroom. If so I might be a while. Other than that, after I go to the restroom I'm going to shake some ass. Shit, I have things to do. I hope you're not going to be posted at the table all night. Go dance, mingle or something."

"After I finish my drink, you'll probably see me mingling. I saw a couple of people that I know. I want to go and say hello."

"Okay, you know where to find me."

"Uh huh, I sure as hell do," Kya said.

About two hours later, Deion decided that she needed a break from all the dancing. While walking through the club she ran into Kya at the bar talking to a couple of guys. Deion walked up to Kya and stood next to her.

Kya introduced the guys to Deion then said, "I'll call you tomorrow so we can set something up." Afterwards the guys walked away.

"Damn! Who the hell were they?" Deion asked.

"I work with them," Kya said.

"Have you fucked them yet?"

"Are you crazy? Hell, no! I think it would be a little problematic to fuck your co-workers. You're the only person that does that."

"Shit, what the hell ever. Those are the best ones to fuck. If you need a little bit during the day then bam, a quickie in the copy room or on your desk," Deion said.

"No bitch, I don't get down like that."

"Well, I do."

"Yeah, I know you do, that's your problem now. Are you ready to go?"

"Yes I'm ready, I'm having company tonight. I have to go home and get prepared."

"A late night visitor? Oh, the mystery man. I'm sorry, Jay."

"Hell, no!" Deion yelled.

"Then who? And don't you have to work tomorrow?"

"Yes, and what does that mean? I got this."

"Who's coming over?" Kya asked.

"That guy that I was dancing with for the past hour. Girl, I could feel his dick through his pants and child, I gotta have a little bit of that tonight!" Deion emphasized.

"I'm not saying a word and I'm going to mind my own business."

"Wow, that's a first."

"Well, I'm ready because I have to get up super early tomorrow," Kya said.

"Okay, let's go. I need to get ready for Sean anyway. Maybe we can come back Friday night, I really like this place."

"I don't know about all of that. I do have a child and a man. I'm not single and can't be hanging out in clubs all week."

"Excuse me, I'll come back Friday night by my damn self."

As the ladies walked to the car Deion said, "You know I got the DJ's telephone number too and he also wanted to come over tonight."

Kya looked at Deion and asked, "I thought the other guy's coming over?"

"Yeah, he is. I told Mr. DJ that he'll have to come over tomorrow because I already have plans for tonight. Maybe Mr. DJ will play some songs for me," Deion said as she danced to the car.

Kya shook her head from side to side, then said, "You know what, I don't have shit to say. Not one damn word. I'm actually speechless and don't know what to say to your freak nasty ass."

"I love you too, mwah!"

"You are out of control and that's all I'm going to say."

"Girl, there's nothing to say. Like I told you earlier, I'm enjoying my life and having fun. You only have one life to live and I'm going to enjoy mine while I can."

"If you say so, D, but I suggest you be cautious."

"No doubt. I keep a supply of condoms in my nightstand. All shapes, sizes, colors and flavors."

"Ummmm. I don't want to hear this shit. Your ass is too much."

"I'll be sure to tell you all about my rendezvous tomorrow."

"No thank you, ma'am, I don't even want to hear about it."

"Okay, though it might be good."

"Again, no thank you, I don't need hear the explicit details of your sexventures."

As Kya drove to Deion's condo, it appeared that every other word that came out of Deion's mouth pertained to sex. This man, that man, and various locations. Within a matter of minutes they'd reached Deion's house and Kya was happy that she was finally there. Her head had begun pounding and it felt like it was going to explode.

Deion looked at Kya and said, "Thanks girl, I had a great time tonight. I might have had too much to drink but I had a ball!"

"Okay, Ms. Lady, you be careful and I'll chat with you in the morning."

Deion grinned and said, "Most definitely. There'll be a lot to talk about I'm sure."

"I don't want to hear it, I said."

"Whatever, you get home safe and call me when you get in."

"I'll just text you, you might be a little tied up."

Deion chuckled and said, "And swinging from the ceiling fan too!"

"Yeah, I know," Kya said.

*

About an hour after Kya dropped Deion off at home, Deion's doorbell rang. She grabbed her robe and picked up the phone to buzz Sean in. Deion then ran downstairs to wait for Sean and open the front door. Shortly thereafter, Sean walked through the threshold, and immediately extended his arms and gave Deion a hug.

Deion hugged Sean and said, "Come on in."

As Sean walked towards the sofa, Deion asked, "Would you like something to drink?"

"Sure, what do you have?"

"I have whatever you want," Deion responded flirtatiously.

"Well, in that case I'd like you and some Henny."

"Oh really? Let me get your Henny, you can have me later. Do you want one shot, a glass or should I just bring the bottle?"

"Bring the bottle."

"Would you like some ice, and do you need a chaser?"

"Nah," Sean replied.

"Are you hungry too? Would you like something to eat?"

"Yeah, I am a little hungry but I'll take care of that a little later."

"Are you sure? I can whip something up for you."

"Oh no, don't worry. Trust me I'll take care of that later on."

Thirty minutes later and Sean and Deion were laughing and talking as if they were old friends, not people who had met only a few hours earlier.

"Whew, I better stop, I have to get up early tomorrow. I can't keep sitting here drinking. I definitely have to be in the office in a couple of hours," Deion said.

"So do I," Sean said.

"I'm feeling really good right about now. I had a fucked-up day but I had a great evening."

"Then what's up?"

"I hate to be rude but I think this Henny is getting the best of me. I think I need to lie it down before I say or do something wrong."

"Would you like me to lie down with you?" Sean asked.

"I don't know about all of that."

"Would you like for me to leave?" Sean asked.

"Hell, no." Deion stood up, grabbed Sean's hand and led him up the stairs. After they reached Deion's bedroom, she laid across the bed as Sean stood in the middle of the floor.

"Are you going to stand there all night or are you coming over here to lie beside me?"

"Hell yeah. I'm coming over there with you, Ms. Lady." He took off his shoes then proceeded to lay down.

As he approached the bed, Deion said, "I'm sorry but you can't get in my bed with those jeans on."

"Not a problem, I get you."

When Sean lay next to Deion on the bed, she grabbed his hand and placed it over her waist.

"So you just want to spoon?" Sean asked.

"For now. When my head stops spinning then I might find something else for us to do."

"Oh yeah, is that right?"

"Yes, sir."

"Then what'll happen next?"

"Then I'm going to fuck the shit out of you."

"Well, ummmm, can we get right to it then?" Sean asked.

"Be patient. Good things come to those who wait. I just need a few minutes to get my head together. It's spinning a little right now."

"Okay, well, I'm ready when you are."

After a while both Sean and Deion dozed off, exhausted from the night of partying and drinking. Deion was awakened by the sound of her cellphone. She grabbed it from the nightstand and noticed she had four missed calls from Jay. Deion turned off her cellphone then placed it back on the nightstand. She looked at the clock and realized it was 2:46 a.m. *Damn*, she thought, then looked over at Sean and lightly shook him. Sean didn't respond but he let out a loud snore. *Okay, I guess he's tired but this is not what I had in mind. I'm going to have to wake his ass up one way or another.* Deion took off her robe and knelt beside Sean. She reached for Sean's dick through the opening of his boxers. She slowly massaged him, placed him in her mouth and then licked the head. After a couple of seconds, Sean woke.

Deion looked up and asked, "Should I stop?"

"No, ma'am, keep going." Sean placed his hand on Deion's head and guided it up and down. After ten minutes of sucking Sean's dick and gently massaging his balls with her tongue, Deion finally sat up. As she wiped her mouth, Sean got up and placed Deion on her knees. He then started eating her pussy from the back. As Deion softly moaned and grabbed the comforter in her hands, Sean inserted his tongue, moving it back and forth. He then sucked her clit with his fingers inside her.

"Nice and wet," Sean whispered. As Deion moaned, Sean got up and pushed his dick inside her.

After a while, Sean asked, "Can I put this dick in your ass?"

"No."

"Why not?"

"Because I said so."

"Turn over and lie on your back," Sean said.

Deion did as he said and he continued to fuck her. He then placed her legs over his shoulders and, as Deion grabbed Sean's thighs, he let out a long moan and laid his head on Deion's chest. Sean breathed heavily for the next couple of seconds.

He got up and said, "Whew, that was good. Where's your bathroom?" Deion looked at him as if he had lost his mind.

"Where's the bathroom? Are you done?" Deion asked.

"Yes, I came."

"Is that it?" Deion asked.

"Yes, I gotta go."

"What do you mean you gotta go? I want more."

"Sorry, babes, if I don't get home soon my wife is going to be tripping and shit."

"Your wife?"

"Yes, my wife."

"You never said that you were married."

"And you never asked either."

Deion sat up and looked between her legs then felt the bed.

"What are you looking for?" Sean asked.

"Your come."

"It's inside of you."

"What do you mean it's inside of me?"

"I mean it's inside of you. Look I gotta go, where's the bathroom so I can wash my dick off?"

"It's down the hall next to my closet." Deion put on her robe. *This is some bullshit. That quick fuck was nothing. Maybe I should have let the DJ or Jay come over. Damn!*

After about five minutes, Sean came out of the bathroom and started putting on his clothes.

"When can I see you again?" Sean asked.

"I don't know. Give me your number and I'll call you."

"I can't do that."

"Why not?" Deion asked.

"Because me and my wife are on the same plan and she checks my phone records."

"Then I guess we won't hook up again."

"There's other ways."

"Like?"

"I can just stop by from time to time."

"Negro, are you crazy? I don't know you like that for you to be dropping by my house whenever you want."

"But you think you knew me well enough to come to your house and fuck you?"

At that very moment, all Deion could hear was Kya's voice in her head. She looked up at Sean and said, "I think you should leave."

"Don't worry, as soon as I get my shoes on I'm out."

Deion stood by her bedroom door with her arms folded and waited for Sean to put his shoes on. He grabbed his jacket, walked towards her and gave her a kiss on her forehead.

"Thanks for a good time," Sean said.

"Yeah, sure." Deion stood as if she was frozen and at that very moment she began to think that maybe Kya was right.

As Deion followed Sean to the front door, Sean said, "Maybe I'll see you again soon."

"Yeah, maybe."

"Okay, I'll holla at you some other time. Have a good night."

"Yeah, you too."

After Deion locked her door, she poured herself another drink and went upstairs to her bedroom. As Deion drank her glass of Henny she pondered about the conversation she'd had with Kya. After Sean left she couldn't help but feel as though she was nothing more than street poontang.

For the next couple of minutes she felt numb and like she had just made the biggest mistake of her life. She glimpsed the clock and realized she only had a couple of hours before she had to get up. Shortly after she finished her drink, she got into the bed and closed her eyes.

As tired and drunk as she was, Deion couldn't fall asleep. She lay there for the next hour, tossing and turning and thinking about her actions. After a night of hanging out with Kya and her late-night guest, Deion finally fell asleep around 4:35 and it seemed as if she'd only just drifted off to sleep when the alarm clock went off. She rolled over and grasped the fact that it was now 6:30. She dreaded getting out of bed and going to work.

After hitting the snooze button three times, Deion finally sat up in the middle of the bed. *Oh my goodness, I just went to bed. I'm not feeling this work thing today. I've only had about two hours of sleep and I'm a hot mess today.* With her face placed inside of her hands she thought today would be a good day to call out. However, she had pertinent meetings and needed to be in the office. *If I didn't have to be in the office I'd keep my ass in the bed all damn day. I wonder if it's too late to reschedule them. My fucking head is pounding and I'm not in the mood for any bullshit today. Ughhhh! I'm so not feeling this today. Note to self, don't party too much or have late-night rendezvous when I have to go to the office earlier than usual.*

Deion finally got out of the bed, slowly walked downstairs and brewed a cup of coffee in her Keurig machine. *I'm going to need to start my day off with some dark magic.*

After making the coffee she moved slowly up the steps and got into a cold shower. She knew if she took a hot one it would only make her fatigue worse. Then she went into her large walk-in closet and pondered about what she wanted to wear. After grabbing a black Calvin Klein dress and a pair of red Valentino heels she felt like she was beginning to make some progress.

Deion glanced at the clock and realized that she should have been in the office by now. After putting on her clothes she went into the bathroom to put on her latest collection of MAC makeup. *Thank goodness for short hair, all I have to do is tease, spray and go.* Prior to leaving the house, Deion made another cup of coffee in her to-go mug, grabbed her briefcase and headed out of the door.

As Deion walked to the metro station she stopped at the corner deli and got a pack of extra-strong headache pills. *I really don't feel like going into the office. Dammit, if I didn't have to meet with these clients today I could have taken a mental health day. God knows I'm in desperate need of one. I can't remember the last time I had a hangover. I'm almost certain the most tedious thing today is going to irritate the shit out of me and set me off. I'm not in the mood for foolishness or bullshit.*

Even though Deion lived less than two blocks from the metro, it felt as though she'd been walking for ten miles and she wondered whether she should just jump in a cab. By the time Deion reached the corner of her block, she'd flagged down a taxi and was heading to the office. On her ride to work, she grabbed her phone out of her purse to call Kya.

Since Kya didn't answer the telephone Deion left her a message and said, "Hey, girlie. I really enjoyed myself last night. I haven't danced like that in years. Anyhoo, I wanted to tell you that I had a nice time and I'm looking forward to going again. Call me when you get a chance. Oh and by the way, I'm not pissed with you about the shit that you said to me. Don't forget to call me. I also want to tell you all about my sexventure."

As the cab driver pulled in front of Deion's office, she saw a guy walking on the other side of the street that resembled her ex-husband. *My eyes must be playing tricks on me. I know that couldn't have been Brian that I saw. I know he's not playing stupid and ignoring the restraining order. He knows he isn't supposed to be anywhere near me. Wait a minute, I'm really tripping . . . his ass is still in jail.*

Once Deion got out of the cab, she looked up and down the street, then walked into her office building. Waiting for the elevator, she knew that Karema would be the first to get on her nerves. The elevator reached the twelfth floor and she walked down the hallway and through the double glass doors.

As soon as she got into the office, Karema greeted her with, "Good morning, how are you?"

"Good morning, Karema, I'm fine, and yourself?" Deion asked.

"I'm okay."

Deion let out a grunt, "Ughhhhhh!"

"Oh okay, I know that feeling. I've been there before. Are you feeling okay? You look horrible."

"Thanks, Karema, for your insight. I'm fine. I just have a really bad headache."

As Deion walked towards her office, Karema yelled down the hallway, "K is looking for you. He wants you to call him once you get here."

Deion turned around, walked back towards Karema and asked, "Who's K?"

"K. You know K."

"Sorry, I don't know anyone by that name."

"Kenneth, but I call him K for short. That's a little nickname that I gave him. I have a nickname for everybody," Karema said.

"I'll give him a call as soon as I get settled. Are the people from Staunton and Associates in the conference room?"

"No not yet."

"No?" They should have been here thirty minutes ago, that's not like them to be late. Did they call to say they're delayed?"

"One of their assistants called and said they were running late."

"Okay, this'll give me a chance to get some things together. Thanks. Can you let me know as soon as they get here?"

"Will do."

Deion entered her office and noticed it was filled with Casablanca and Stargazer lilies. Four vases on her desk, three on her coffee table, four on the window ledge and five sitting on the file cabinets. *What the hell's going on?* Deion thought. She placed her purse in the chair and walked over to her desk.

Karema walked into Deion's office and said, "I don't know what's going on but you must be doing something right. My man has never given me flowers before. Not even the fake ones that are in the dollar tree."

Deion looked at Karema with disgust and asked, "Wasn't my door closed?"

"Yeah, but I figured you weren't busy because you just got here. So I thought it was okay for me to come in."

"The appropriate thing to do when someone has their door closed is to knock."

"It's not like you were naked or something. Besides, I listened at your door before I walked in. You weren't talking or anything so I figured the coast was clear."

"Next time, please knock. You always knock when you see a closed door. I shouldn't have to tell you that. What is it that you need, Karema?"

"My bad, I was coming to see who the flowers were from."

"I don't think that's any of your business," Deion said politely.

"Well, I can see you're in a shitty ass mood."

"Excuse me?"

"I was just saying. I can see you don't feel like being bothered or being social. So I'll just bounce."

"Yes, please do that and close the door behind you."

As Karema walked out of Deion's office and closed the door, Deion thought, *We have got to stop hiring ignorant bitches. She is dumber than a box of rocks. My four-year-old niece has more common sense than this grown-ass woman.*

Deion walked over to her desk and pulled the card out of the flowers on her desk. As she opened the card she couldn't help wondering who had sent the flowers.

She picked up the card and it read: *I still love you and I want you back. You know our paths will cross again one day. It's not over until I say it's over. Call me at 301-555-6234. When I told you I love you to death, I really meant it! There is no one or nothing that will ever keep us apart.*

Deion assumed she had gotten someone else's delivery by mistake. *I don't know who sent these flowers or what this card means. I guess I won't find out because I'm not calling this number. It's obvious these flowers aren't for me and this is some sort of mistake.* Deion tore up the card and threw it in the waste basket.

Deion picked up the phone and called Karema's extension. When Karema finally answered the phone Deion said, "Karema."

"Yup, how can I help you?"

"Can you come here, please?"

Instead of just walking in, this time Karema banged on Deion's office door as if she was the police.

"Come in, Karema," Deion said.

"The door was closed, are you sure you want me to come in?"

"Yes Karema, I just called and asked you to come in here. Where did these flowers come from? Who delivered them? Are you sure they were delivered for me?"

"Yes, ma'am, boss lady."

"Did a delivery receipt or any other paperwork come with the flowers?"

"Yes, ma'am."

After a couple of seconds of silence, Deion asked, "Okay, so where's the paperwork?"

"I shredded it."

"Why?"

"It had your name on it."

With a puzzled look on her face, Deion asked, "Why?"

"Because you said to avoid identity theft, shred anything with your name on it."

Surprise, surprise, the bitch finally listened to what I told her. She actually got something right and it's about damn time. I'm going to have to give her a gold star for that one. Maybe she does have a chance of holding onto a real job for the first time in her life.

"Before you shredded the delivery receipt did you read who the flowers were sent from?"

"Yes."

"Who?" Deion asked.

"I don't know."

"You don't know? Are you 100 percent certain that they were addressed to me?"

"I did know but I forgot. It might come back to me later on. And yes, they were addressed to you. I can read."

Ewwwww, I'm going to hurt this bitch, Deion thought. "Okay, that's all. You can go back to your desk and finish doing whatever you were doing. But the next time I get flowers or any type of delivery, save the delivery receipt so I can see it first. Then you can shred it. I would like to know who the sender is before the paperwork is destroyed."

"Look, you're confusing me and I don't like to be confused. I can't focus once I'm confused. That will mess up my whole damn day. I've already gotten disciplined once today. I don't need to be stressed out like this. Y'all are really working my patience and my nerves today. You need to make up your mind, you keep changing stuff. Fine, I'll save the paper the next time."

"'Whoa, whoa, wait! You can't possibly be speaking to me in that tone!"

"I am speaking to you and my tone is fine. I'm just saying."

"What are you saying?"

"I'm saying that y'all be up in here tripping. Karema do this, Karema do that. I try to write everything down so I won't get confused."

"Karema, it's not that hard to remember."

"It's hard for me to remember. I got a lot of stuff going on in my head. Y'all keep adding more to my plate."

"Okay, Karema. But if you can't remember those little things maybe you should find a more suitable profession."

"I can't help that I get confused fast. I didn't take my stress pills today because Day Day took my pills and sold them."

"What? Wait, that is too much information and I don't even need to know all of that.

"Let me get myself together, give me a sec. Wousa. Wousa."

Deion sat in her chair and rubbed her temples.

Karema stood in the middle of her office repeating, "Wousa. Wousa. Wousa," and followed this with several deep breaths and counting to ten. "Whew, I'm okay now. What was I saying?"

"You said that you got disciplined this morning. What are you talking about?"

"Okay, what happened was that I was on the phone talking to Moniqua's school and the lady in human resources was just standing at my desk staring at me. So I asked her, is there something you need? She said something about me being on a personal call for over an hour. Then she said people were complaining because I was loud, fussing and using vulgar language. I don't even know who Vulgar is, how can I use something of his? I asked her did Vulgar say I stole something from him? Because I don't fucking steal. I might borrow shit but I don't steal. I return everything I borrow."

"Okay," Deion said. The more Deion tried to hold back her laughter, the funnier Karema's story became. But she was only laughing hysterically on the inside. In the back of her mind she was also hoping and praying this would be Karema's last day.

"I mean this woman was really working my last nerves. So I told her to roll out," Karema said.

"Roll out?"

"Yes. Roll the fuck out."

"Karema, isn't she in a wheelchair because of a recent car accident?"

"Yes and so what? That meant it should be easier for her to roll the hell out."

"Why would you tell someone in a wheelchair to roll out?"

"Because. I couldn't tell her to turn around and walk away. Let me finish the story because I have to call Moniqua's school back."

"By all means, please finish your story."

"So anyway, when I get to her office, she said I had a double discipline on my record. One for too many personal calls and the other one was for being discrima— discrima— something."

"Discriminatory?" Deion asked.

"Yup. That's it."

As Deion shook her head, she said, "Okay, Karema. Do me a favor and cancel and reschedule all of my afternoon meetings."

"Until when?"

"Another day this week, depending on the availability of the clients and staff."

"Okay, I'll try."

"Thanks, Karema. You can go back to your desk."

Karema looked at Deion with a look that could kill, then turned around and strutted back to her desk.

You try to give people a chance and look how they act, fucking stupid. I think I might have to send her to some etiquette and professionalism in the workplace classes or something.

Once Karema had left, Deion put her head on her desk. *Lord, why me? Not today please, I don't think I can take any more of Karema and all of her antics or drama today. My head's killing me and she's definitely making it worse.*

She finally gathered herself and started getting prepared for her meeting. As she quickly re-read the proposal for Staunton and Associates, Karema knocked on her door.

"Yes?" Deion asked.

Karema opened the door and said, "You had a call from the people."

"What people, Karema?"

"The people that you were having the meeting with."

"Staunton and Associates?"

"Yes, them."

"Okay and what did they say, are they on their way?"

"No, they called because something happened and they want to reschedule."

"Okay fine, I'll get in touch with them. Thanks."

"Would you like me to reschedule that meeting too?"

"No, thank you. I'll take care of it."

Deion decided that, since her all of her meetings for the day were cancelled, she would go home. Instead of sitting in the office with a miserable headache and dealing with Karema, she would much rather be at home in bed. Despite deadlines, meetings and the calls that she needed to make, today she just couldn't get it together. Deion sent several of her co-workers an email informing them that she wasn't feeling well and would be going home for the day. After she finished gathering everything she needed, she got her purse and briefcase to leave.

On her way out she stopped at Karema's desk and said, "Since I'm not feeling well, I'm going home. I have my laptop and will have my phone on. I'll be checking my emails periodically. Also, can you have these flowers discarded?"

"You want me to throw them out?"

"Yes, ma'am."

"Can I have them?"

"You sure can. As long as they're gone before I return in the morning."

"Okay, that's fine. Thanks. Damn!"

"Excuse me?" Deion asked.

"Day Day got my car. I don't know if I can carry all of those flowers on the bus."

"I'm confident you'll figure it out."

"I knew something was wrong with you. I could tell by the way you looked and how you were acting. I hope you feel better. I'll pray for you."

"Thanks, Karema."

"Are you sure I can have the flowers? They're so pretty and I know they were a lot of money."

"Yes, if you can't take them then throw them in the garbage."

"Oh hell, no. I'll find a way to get those bad boys home."

"Fine. I'll see you in the morning."

"Okay, see you tomorrow. Call me if you need anything."

Karema nodded.

As Deion left the office her phone rang.

"Hey, D. I just called your office and some girl said you were sick. Is that your new assistant?" Bailey asked.

"Unfortunately yes, but she's only a temp and thank goodness for that! Please don't get me started on her crazy ass. Clearly something is wrong with that damn girl. I know for sure her elevator isn't reaching the top floor," Deion said.

"Damn, she's that bad?"

"Yes! Don't get me wrong, I understand that the system is designed to get these girls jobs. I get that, but they need to send them to some classes or train them for the workplace before placing them in a position."

"I think that's what they do. She can't be that bad."

"You just don't know what I go through with her. But anyway, what's up?"

"I was calling to see if you wanted to go to lunch."

"Girl, I'm on my way home to get in the bed."

"Are you okay, what's wrong?"

"Yeah, I'm fine. I just got a hangover and my head's pounding. I'm going to go and get in my bed, take some pills, and call it a day."

"I know that's right. So I guess you're not in a mood to hang out, huh?"

"Sorry, sweetie, not today."

"Where are you now?"

"In front of my office, about to get a cab."

"Oh okay. Well, I'm right around the corner, would you like a ride? I'm going by your house anyway so I can drop you off."

"Sure."

"Okay, I'll be there in less than two seconds."

As Deion hung up her phone, Bailey pulled up. Deion got into the car and asked, "Are you playing hooky today?"

"No, ma'am, just taking an early lunch. I need to go up Georgetown, would you like a ride?"

"Sure. So, why are you going to Georgetown? Isn't it a little early for retail therapy?"

"Girl, are you crazy? It's never too early for retail therapy. You better ask somebody."

"Yeah, I forgot who I was talking to, the Queen of Retail."

"I'm actually going to Friendship Heights."

"For what? What are you buying now?"

"I'm not going to buy anything. I have a doctor appointment."

"What's wrong with you? Are you sick?"

"I haven't been feeling too hot lately. I've been having some issues with my stomach."

"Really? Are we expecting?"

"Expecting what?"

"A little Noah."

"Hell, no."

"Something might be going around. My stomach's been bothering me lately too. I think I might have food poisoning or something."

"That could be it, what did you eat?"

"I went to this Mexican restaurant for lunch the other day and my stomach has been hurting ever since. The smell of food makes me sick to my stomach."

"Are we expecting?" Bailey teased.

"Um, no, I better not be."

"So you're not for certain?"

"Anything's possible but I know I'm not pregnant."

"Okay, if you say so."

"As for you, Ms. Busy Bee, maybe your body is trying to tell you something. Learn to chill the hell out and stop ripping and running so much."

"Girl, I have stuff to do and I can't sit around the house doing nothing."

"Maybe your body's just tired and you need a break. Learn how to be still for second. You don't have to do everything in one day."

"What the hell ever. I have never seen anyone like you. I'm starting to wonder if you even sleep. You're like the damn energizer bunny, you just keep going and going and going."

"I do rest."

"When?"

"I get my rest."

"I think your body is trying to tell you something. But you're ignoring all the signs. Clearly your battery is running low."

"Girl, please. I got to keep it moving. I'll get rest when I die."

"Whatever you say. But I think you need to slow down some."

"Thanks for being concerned, but I'm good."

"I hope you are pregnant, that'll slow that ass down."

"D, I hate to disappoint you but I'm definitely not pregnant."

"How do you know? How can you be so sure?"

"If I'm pregnant then we'll all be millionaires."

"If I'm not mistaken you're pretty damn close to that level already. But why would you say that?"

"Girl, I got sterilized last year. No more babies coming out of me."

"I didn't know that."

"Yes, ma'am. Last summer."

"Ohhhh, you never said anything."

"There was nothing to say or discuss. I really didn't have an option in the matter."

"Okay, now I understand. I'm sorry, I didn't know."

"Don't be sorry, it's okay. I've finally accepted that I won't be able to have any more children."

"I expect that was tough for you and Noah."

"Yes, it was. He actually took it worse than I did."

"You can always adopt. It's a lot of babies that need parents."

"That's true, but for now we're good. We discussed adoption but for now we're going to wait."

"Hell, you can get one of my nieces. My sister damn sure doesn't know how to be a good parent. Her kids could use parents like you and Noah. Girl, she's a damn mess. Can't hold a job to save her life."

"Are you serious?"

"Yes! She's so wrapped up in this man that she doesn't even pay attention to those damn kids. It amazes me how people that shouldn't have kids do, and the ones that really want to be parents can't."

"I know what you mean. Maybe one day she'll get it together."

"When?"

"Girlfriend, I don't know but hopefully sooner rather than later."

"That bitch is a mess. But my mom sees no wrong in her. She thinks the sun rises and sets on my sister's ass."

Bailey laughed and said, "That's why your mom is always cleaning up her shit. She created that monster."

"You're damn right. I try my best to avoid them but the kids are always calling for something they need. They even asked if they could live with me."

"And what was your response?"

"I haven't said anything yet. I'm still thinking about it. I'm not ready for all of that stuff yet."

"All of what stuff? Being a responsible adult?"

"I am a responsible adult. I'm not ready to play mommy just yet."

"Girl, you need to get it together too. Apparently those babies need you. Stop being selfish."

"Whatever, I like my life just the way it is. Single, unattached and doing me. I only have to worry about self."

"Like I said, selfish!" Bailey yelled.

"Call it what you want, I'm good. Anyhoo, what are you doing after you leave your doctor appointment?"

"I'm going back to the office. Why, what's up?"

"Nothing. I just thought since you're not feeling well you'd go home and relax.

"You know that's not going to happen. I have some things that I need to finish up."

"Of course you do. I forgot who I was talking to."

As Bailey pulled in front of Deion's condo, she asked, "What are you doing the rest of the day?"

"Not a damn thing. I'm getting my big ass in the bed and calling it a day. This hangover is kicking my ass."

"Yeah, Kya told me y'all had a good time last night."

"I think I had too much fun. I'm damn sure paying for it today."

"Yeah, I see."

"Are you coming upstairs for a little bit? You still have a lot of time before your appointment."

Bailey parked the car and they proceeded into the building. While waiting for the elevator, Bailey looked at Deion and said, "So, tell me about your new assistant, she seems like she's a handful."

"Girl, please, a handful is an understatement."

"That bad, huh?"

"You just don't know what I have to go through with that damn girl."

"Have you spoken to her about what she's doing wrong?"

"Not exactly."

"What do you mean not exactly?"

"Let's just say she's not that easy to talk to."

"Then you got a problem."

"Tell me about it. I hate to be judgmental but I really think something's wrong with her."

"Maybe this is her first job and she's not accustomed to an office environment."

"I don't know what her problem is. I just know I can't keep dealing with her foolishness. She is driving me fucking crazy."

"How is her work ethic? Is she at least productive?"

As the ladies entered Deion's condo, Deion stopped, turned to Bailey and said, "I really don't know how to answer that."

"Okay, that's different."

"I mean she works but you have to micro-manage everything with her. Let me rephrase that, she does the majority of her work. But when she's having a bad day, which is about four times a week, she's not productive whatsoever."

"Wow!"

"It's like she doesn't get it and really doesn't care."

"Fire her."

"I don't have to because she's taking care of that on her own."

"How long has she been there?"

"About three weeks."

"Oh goodness, well, maybe your organization isn't the place for her,"

"How about this, you hire her and take her off of my hands. You like to help people out."

"No, thank you. I have enough going on with the idiots that work for me. I definitely don't need to add another one to the bunch."

Deion laughed and said, "I know that's right."

"So, Ms. Lady, what else is going on in your world?" Bailey asked.

"Nothing much, just the same ole shit on a different day."

"I know the feeling."

"I really don't have anything to complain about. Life is what it is."

"I wouldn't exactly say that. Life is what you make of it. If you don't want anything out of life then you just live day by day doing the same ole shit."

"I'm not saying I don't want anything out of life. I just view it differently now than I did in the past. I don't stress nor do I worry about anything. I live in the moment."

"I kind of understand that. Granted, I live each day like it was my last. However, I still do what I need to for the future of my children. I have to make sure they'll be set and okay. Everything I do is for them."

"I get that but I don't have any children. So I can live my life whatever way I desire."

"I guess that's why you do the things that you do."

"Meaning?"

"The way you are with men."

"OMG! Between you and Kya, y'all are really working my nerves with this bullshit."

"I haven't said anything yet."

"I know, but I'm almost positive where this is going."

"So I heard you had a late-night visitor."

"Yup."

"D, why would you bring some man home that you just met?"

"I didn't bring him home, he came over after I got home."

"That's the same damn thing."

"Okay, so I won't tell you."

"Why in the hell would you invite some stranger to your house? That is not smart or safe."

"Girl, it's all good. Am I supposed to go to his house or some hotel instead?"

"I think you could have gone to a hotel. Wait a minute, what the hell am I saying? You shouldn't be fucking someone you just met in the club any damn way!"

"Why not?"

"D, fuck what you heard, casual sex these days just ain't the way to go!"

"The best sex. Fuck and roll."

Bailey sighed, and said, "Girl, don't make me knock the shit out of you."

"For what? What did I do? Because I like to have fun?"

"You classify fucking strangers as a way to have fun? Seriously? You are on some different shit."

"What did I do wrong?"

"You really don't get it, do you? I can see if it was the same guy that you're fucking but it's not. I thought you were dealing with someone?"

"I am . . . kind of, sort of. But I'm still single."

"So you and homeboy aren't exclusive? You're not working towards a relationship?"

"I'm not really sure. Don't get me wrong, I'm feeling him and everything but I like doing me and not to have to answer to anyone."

"I know I'm not the smartest person but let me see if I understand. You deal with someone on a regular basis but the two of you aren't in a relationship. It's more a friend with benefits situation. Y'all both fuck other people as well as each other. Did I get it right?"

"Yup, you got it."

"Have y'all even discussed being in a relationship?"

"I swear you sound just like Kya. No not really. We haven't had that convo. I'm not even sure that's something we want to do."

"You'll never know if you don't discuss it."

"When I see him next I might bring it up."

"Is he married or do you even know?"

"No, he's not married."

"Have you asked?"

"No, for what?"

"Don't you care?"

"Yeah, I care."

"Do you know anything about this man other than the size of his dick?"

"I know a little bit about him."

"A little is not enough."

"If he doesn't volunteer any information then I don't ask."

"Girl, you are definitely a different breed. I suggest learning more about the people that you invite into your bedroom."

"If I'm content with how things are I don't understand why it bothers y'all so much."

"It's how you go about things that concerns us. We understand that it's your life but we don't have to agree with the stupid-ass choices you make."

"Even if we have a convo, we might just decide to be fuck buddies, so what's wrong with that?"

"There's nothing wrong with that if you're using rubbers and not fucking all of the other men. Maybe this man actually wants a relationship. If you stop throwing your pussy in his face you just might find out. Or better yet, try talking to him and finding out his intentions."

"I'm almost positive we want the same thing. But I will have a convo with him. I do like him a lot so I guess it wouldn't hurt to find out what his intentions are."

"Good! I'd think at some point you'd get tired of being fuck buddies. We're too old for that shit."

"I'm not going to lie, I think about being in a relationship. I have fears that I still hold on to from my past. I want to make sure the man I'm with is the right person before jumping in there."

"So you're going to continue to keep fucking all of these men until you decide if this guy is the right one?"

"Yup."

"That doesn't work for me."

"That's the thing, it doesn't have to work for you. It's not about you. I think it's about me and my life. I don't get you and Kya. Am I supposed to live the way y'all think I should? Hell, no! This is my life, my decision and my body. The last time I checked I don't owe anyone any explanations. I'm a grown woman."

"You are so right, it is your life, but when we see you making foolish decisions, of course we're going to say something. If we didn't care we wouldn't say shit."

"Well, I'm doing me."

"There's nothing wrong with doing you. You just need to be wiser about the choices that you're making, that's all I'm saying."

"I know I'm far from being perfect. I have imperfections and flaws. However, I am working on me and trying to do better."

"I understand and none of us are perfect. As long as we have breath in our bodies, we'll always be a work in progress. All we can do is try to do better."

"Bailey, you know I love you to death but right now isn't a good time for this convo."

"If not now, then when?"

"Not today, that's for damn sure. I'm sleep-deprived, I have a headache, and I'm hungry."

"Oh, I see this isn't the topic of choice for you. Okay, then we'll have this convo some other time."

"If you say so."

"What's that supposed to mean?"

"I don't understand how and why my sex life is detrimental to everyone else's life."

"Because we love you, we want the best for you, and we care about your well-being. That's why."

"Well, I don't want to keep having this discussion with you and Kya. Y'all are tripping."

"D, you just don't get it."

"Maybe I don't. But I'm getting tired of this topic. Find something else to talk about."

"Okay, if you say so."

"Thank you."

"No problem, but I will say this, be careful out there. The times have changed and so have the people."

"Thanks for the advice but I got it."

"At the end of the day, ask yourself this question. Am I happy and satisfied with my life?"

"What's that going to prove?" Deion asked.

"If you're completely honest with yourself then you'll make some changes."

"So what are you now, my life coach?"

"No, bitch. I'm your friend and I care about you."

"Okay. Whatever."

"So what's going on with you?"

"The same ole shit. Work, business, dealing with family and friends and other issues."

"Girl, you don't have any issues or problems."

"Why don't I? I got problems like everyone else. I just don't see the need to keep talking about them and complaining. There's no need to whine about it."

"True. That doesn't resolve the problem."

"Right. I'm going to do my best to fix it. But I don't see the need to keep bitching and complaining about anything."

"You got a point."

"We all got problems, but I do the best I can to rectify mine. I don't always do what I want to do, but I do what I got to do."

"I hear you. How is business these days, have you been listed by *Time Magazine* as one of the wealthiest women yet?"

Bailey chuckled and said, "No not yet. My businesses are all doing well, though."

"Good, I'm glad to hear that. You'll get on that list one day."

"That's my goal and I'm trying very hard to accomplish it."

"The way that you work and all that you've acquired, you'll get there real soon."

"That's the thing, it isn't just me, Noah's a part of it too."

"But you already had a lot before Noah even came into the picture. Before your dad passed away he made sure you were set for life."

"True, but Noah had money and businesses too. We just combined what we both had."

"The power couple with it all."

Bailey looked at her watch and said, "Something like that. Girlfriend, I got to go. I'm sitting here shooting the shit like I don't have somewhere to be."

"Your doctor's office is only around the corner."

"I know but I wanted to try to get in early so I can get out of there."

"Before you go, let me tell you what happened earlier."

"What's up?"

"I got an unusual surprise at work today."

"Really? Did you get another promotion?"

"No, but when I got to work my office was filled with flowers."

"Awwww, that's nice, your boo sent you flowers."

"No, it wasn't him."

"Then who? Someone else's boo sent you flowers?"

"I don't know who sent them."

"Didn't a card come with the flowers?"

"Yes, but they didn't say who they were from."

"That's strange. What did the card read?"

"Something about I still love you and it's not over until I say it's over. The person also left a telephone number for me to call."

"Did you call the number?"

"Hell, no! If they really wanted me to know who sent them, they'd have left their name on the card. I don't have time to play Sherlock Holmes. I told Karema that she could have the damn flowers."

"That was nice of you."

"But that's not the kicker."

"Oh goodness, what did you do now?"

"I didn't do anything but on my way to work, I thought I saw Brian."

"Brian? Brian who?"

"Brian Thomas."

"Your ex-husband Brian? No, it couldn't have been him."

"That's what I said. I must be tripping or something."

"Yes, you're tripping. That man isn't getting out of jail anytime soon. Furthermore he doesn't know where you live or work."

"I know but I saw a guy walking down the street that looked just like him."

"Girl, your eyes are playing tricks on you. Don't worry, it wasn't him."

"Okay. Well I'm not going to stress about it."

"I don't think you have anything to stress about. But I would have called the number to see who sent the flowers."

"I wasn't that interested. I couldn't care less."

Bailey got up from the sofa and grabbed her purse. She stretched and said, "Let me get to this damn doctor's office."

Deion walked Bailey to the door and said, "Call me later on if you're not too busy."

"Will do," Bailey said.

Shortly after Bailey left, Deion texted Jay and told him she needed to talk to him. After waiting an hour for his response she decided to call him. Deion called Jay consistently for fifteen minutes and he neither answered the phone nor returned her call. She also texted the DJ she'd met at the club and cancelled the get-together they had planned for that evening, but the DJ didn't respond to her message.

I hope he reads my text, I just don't feel like being bothered right now. I'll have to hook up with him some other time. I'm going to fix me a sandwich then get back into my bed. I'm done for the day. Once Deion had eaten, she lay down to relax and, after couple of minutes of watching *Madea's Big Happy Family,* she drifted off to sleep.

Several hours later, she heard someone banging on her door and she jumped up, ran downstairs, and looked through the peephole. She couldn't see anyone, so headed back upstairs when her doorbell rang. Deion went back to the door and looked through the peephole again. This time she saw Jay standing outside.

Deion opened the door and he said, "I know you heard the damn door. I've been banging on this fucking door for twenty minutes. What, you got company?"

"You should have called first. I was asleep."

"Can I come in the fucking house or do I have to talk to you from the hallway?"

"Please don't start with the bullshit, I am not in the mood for that." She stepped back and Jeff walked into the house and sat on the arm of the sofa. Still tired and drowsy, Deion sat on the chaise across from him.

"So what do you want to talk about?" Jay asked.

"What?"

"You texted me earlier and said you wanted to talk. What's up?"

"I realized that I really don't know a whole lot about you. We've been dealing with each other for a while now and there are a whole lot of unanswered questions."

"What is it that you think you need to know?"

"For one, what are your intentions?"

"Intentions for what? What are you talking about?"

"What are you intentions with me?"

"I intend to do what we're doing. We're chilling."

"No we're not, Jay. All we do is fuck, that's it."

"What else are we supposed to do? I thought that's all you wanted. In the beginning we said no attachments."

"What if I want more from you, what if I want a relationship? I might want more than the occasional fuck. I might want more of a commitment from you."

"I am committed to you. I'm committed to occasionally fucking you. That's it. No more, no less. Why do you want to mess up what we have? We got a good thing going on. We're chilling and having fun."

Deion shook her head and said, "You're full of shit."

"Damn. That's how you feel?"

"I want to know, how long are we going to keep this up?"

"What are you talking about? Are you on your period? Because you act a little strange when you're on the rag."

"Can you answer the question?"

"Which one? You keep asking a lot of questions."

"What are we doing, Jay?"

"See, there you go again."

"Because you're not answering any of my damn questions. What are you hiding?"

"Not a motherfucking thing. I told you from the get go that I wasn't ready for a relationship. So I don't know why all of a sudden you're pressing me for one."

"Wow."

"When I'm ready for one I'll let you know. I don't have time for this bullshit."

"Oh, okay, I get it. It's okay for me to fuck and suck you. It's also okay when I pay your bills, buy you shit and give you money. But when I want to take our relationship to the next level it's a problem."

"Look man, we are not in a relationship. We're just cool-ass friends that do shit for one another. I'm good with how things are."

"Of course you are because you're the one that's reaping all of the benefits."

"Look, D, I just want to do me without any attachments. At the end of the day I don't feel like dealing with all the shit you go through in a relationship. The fussing and a bitch trying to keep tabs on me and shit. I go through enough bullshit with my baby mothers."

"Okay, it's all good. I guess I have the answer to my question."

"What's that supposed to mean?"

"It means that I'm tired of being your fuck mate. I'm trying to be about you but that's not something you want. So, I guess we can end this now."

"Is that what you really want? You know you can't live without this good dick."

"Whatever, Jay. I want more and you're not willing to give so I have to move on."

"So we're not fucking anymore?"

"Um, probably not."

"That's it. Our friendship is over?"

"Oh, we're good. We just won't be fucking anymore and I know how to deal with you . . . with a long-handled spoon."

"I can still come over from time to time and give you this dick right?"

"Nah, I'm good."

"Girl, you know you can't get rid of me that easy."

"Yeah, I can. I don't hate or dislike you and we can remain friends but I'm definitely moving on. I'm tired of being your go-to woman for money, sex and all the other shit."

"You make it seem like I'm using you."

"Pretty much. All you want from me is what I give you and I'm tired of being used."

"D, I'm not using you but if that's how you feel, cool. So can we kick it from time to time?"

"It depends on what that means."

"Can we go out and chill sometimes?"

"Sure, whatever."

"Can we fuck before I leave?"

"Nah, I'm good."

"So you really don't fuck with me anymore?"

Deion looked at Jay and said, "When you figure out what you want, let me know."

Jay stood up, stretched and said, "Oh right. Well, I have somewhere I have to be. I'll give you a call later on."

Before Deion could get to the front door, her doorbell rang. "Sure, Jay. Whatever you say." Jay turned to Deion and asked, "Who the hell is that? Are you expecting company?"

"How the hell do I know who it is when I'm standing here with you? It's probably that damn girl from next door."

Oh shit, I hope it's not the DJ.

As Deion and Jay went back and forth, the doorbell continued to ring. "D, you not going to see who it is?" Jay asked.

"You're more concerned about who's at my damn door than what's going on in here."

As Jay walked to the door and opened it, he noticed a man walking away. "Yo, what's up? Were you just ringing my doorbell like that?"

"My bad, I must have the wrong address."

Wait, that voice sounds familiar. Deion stood in silence as Jay continued to question the guy at the door.

"I mean you must think you have the right address, you keep ringing my damn door bell," Jay said.

"I apologize. I was looking for someone.'

"Who?" Jay asked.

As the guy walked away, he looked back and said, "It's all good. Sorry to disturb you."

Deion continued to stand as still as a rock. She knew with all certainty that, the person ringing the doorbell wasn't at the wrong address.

With the door still ajar, Jay looked at Deion and said, "Make sure you lock up, there's some real weirdoes walking around in your building. Okay, so I'm out. I'll call you later." Jay turned, kissed Deion on the cheek and said, "Keep that pussy tight and wet for me."

Deion shook her head, and said, "Goodbye Jay."

Tracey Dowtin

Revelation . . . The Uncovered Truth

Tracey Dowtin

Chapter Five

Brandi opened the front door of her new home and greeted Kya, Bailey and Deion.

"Good morning, ladies. Welcome to my new house, come on in!" Brandi exclaimed.

"Good morning, lady! I love your new place, it's gorgeous," Kya said.

"I'm so proud of you. You go, girl!" Bailey shouted.

"Let me know if you need roommates. I can have mine and Lexi's shit packed and moved in by tomorrow afternoon," Kya said.

"This place is really beautiful, Brandi. Congratulations lady, you've done well and I'm so proud of you," Bailey said.

"There's still a lot to be done, but I'll get it together soon."

"Like what? Everything looks good to me," Bailey said.

"I still have to finish unpacking and get some of the rooms upstairs in order. The moving company that you ladies hired was wonderful. Thanks again for that."

"I'm glad we could help. Moving can be so stressful and time consuming," Deion said.

"Feel free to look around while I finish cooking brunch."

"I'll wait until you can give us the grand tour," Kya said.

"Me too," Bailey said.

"Shall we go to the kitchen? Would anyone like a drink, a mimosa perhaps?" Brandi asked.

"I sure as hell would, and make mine strong. I actually would prefer more champagne than orange juice," Kya said.

"Isn't it a little too early for a drink?" Deion asked.

"The hell you say. It's never too early for a cocktail. Besides, we're celebrating," Kya said.

"Aha, Kya turn down a drink, I don't think so." Deion chuckled.

"The hell with you. You act like I'm a lush or something," Kya said.

"Oh stop it. Kya, you know Deion didn't mean anything by that. She's just joking around, you're so sensitive this morning," Bailey said.

As the women walked down the hallway to the kitchen, Brandi continued preparing brunch. Kya stood at the French doors of the kitchen and stared into the large backyard and asked, "Where's your husband, will he be joining us?"

"No, he won't be joining us, he went out of town this morning. He's attending a conference in Atlanta. I guess he'll give me a call once his plane lands or he gets settled," Brandi said.

"Sure he will," Kya whispered.

"Well, he should be calling you soon, it only takes two hours to fly to Hotlanta," Deion said.

"I can't believe you let him move in anyway. After we found that entire collection of freak nasty shit, I thought you'd be done with him," Kya said.

"Kya, don't start," Bailey said.

"Start what? What am I doing? I'm just keeping it real." Kya sat at the table across from Bailey then asked, "What? Why are you looking at me like I'm the scoundrel? You make it seem like I'm doing something wrong by asking questions."

"That's not why I'm looking at you like that. Just leave the shit alone. Can we at least eat first before we start with the drama and bullshit?" Bailey asked.

"Kya, he said all of that stuff didn't belong to him. Why shouldn't I believe him? How can I prove that it was his and he's cheating on me and with a man at that?" Brandi asked.

"Ummm, is there something that I missed?" Deion asked. Bailey looked at Deion and shook her head. "Then what's Kya talking about?" Deion asked.

"Let's just say when you hear about it you'll need more than a mimosa," Kya said.

"Oh goodness," Bailey said.

"I'm just saying there are ways that you can find out if your man is packing fudge or he's a fudge packer," Kya said.

"What was I supposed to do, Kya? He said the stuff didn't belong to him."

"And you believed him?" Kya asked.

"Why wouldn't I believe my husband, Kya?"

"Seriously? I can't really believe you're being that damn naïve. I remember there was a time when I trusted and believed everything my Lexi's dad would tell me. And you see where that got me," Kya said.

"But all men aren't the same," Brandi said.

"That's very true, my dear. But you haven't been with enough men to know their games and bullshit," Kya said.

"Maybe I haven't but I trust and believe my husband,"

"Okay, well I hope and pray that he isn't doing anything and that he won't hurt you. If you love him then I guess I'll like him, just a little. He's still suspect and I got my good eye watching his ass," Kya said.

"Girl, shut the hell up, you are crazy as shit," Bailey said.

"I might be crazy but y'all know I'm right," Kya said.

"Lord, please help her," Bailey said.

"But I will say this, before you disregard his potential gayness you should have tested him," Kya said.

"Tested him, how the hell was she going to do that? The last time I checked they don't sell gay kits in the stores," Deion said.

"No they don't but there are other ways," Kya said.

"What ways?"

"One way would have been an ass test," Kya said.

"*Excuse me?*" Deion yelled.

"I hate to ask but, Kya, what the heck is an ass test? Brandi asked.

"If you want to know if he's a fudge packer there's a test that you can give him," Kya said.

"And how would she know, because of the way he fucks her?" Bailey asked.

"That's another way you can tell, I'm glad you mentioned that. Some down-low men won't fuck their woman and some only like it one way," Kya said.

"So what makes you a sexpert on down-low men?" Deion asked.

"Girl, research of course," Kya said.

"And how did you conduct this so-called research?" Bailey asked.

"You know I have plenty of gay friends and cousins and they don't keep shit to themselves. They are open books and tell it all," Kya said.

"Okay, tell me about the ass test," Brandi said.

"The ass test is when you and your man are making love, fucking or whatever you want to call it," Kya said.

"Is this a test that you buy at CVS or something?" Brandi asked.

Kya looked at Brandi and said, "Hell, no! Sometimes I really wonder about you, Brandi. We just said it's not a test that you buy," Kya said.

"So how do you administer an ass test without him knowing?" Bailey asked.

"When you're getting your fuck on, you ease your hands down to his ass and slip your finger in that little outlet," Kya said.

"*WHAT?*" Brandi yelled.

"Oh hell no, girl, Noah would beat the shit out of me if I did some shit like that," Bailey said.

"And that would be the reaction of a heterosexual man. If he jumps or says stop playing before your hand approaches his ass, then he's straight and you have nothing to worry about. He's all man and definitely likes the va-jj. But if he lets your hands go anywhere close to or in his ass, then Houston we have a problem. Clearly he likes to be poked in the butt-butt."

"Where the hell do you get this stuff?" Deion asked.

"Ladies, trust me, he might be a little pissed but it's worth the effort," Kya said.

"I don't know about all of that," Bailey said.

"Me neither. Sounds like you're setting yourself up for an ass whooping," Deion said.

"Maybe, but at least you don't have to wonder if your man likes the same thing you do," Kya said.

"Well, I did what I was supposed to, I asked Derick if those books, dildos and other stuff belonged to him and he said no," Brandi said.

"But did you ask him if he was fucking someone else . . . perhaps another man?" Kya questioned.

"No I didn't."

"Okay, there you have it. You still don't know. For whatever reason, you're afraid to know the truth. I kind of understand that but I don't want you living in denial land, my dear," Kya said.

"It's not that, I know that my man isn't doing anything crazy like that. He wouldn't be foolish enough to jeopardize our marriage or my life like that."

"I'm glad that you have so much faith and confidence in him," Kya said.

"Hey, Inspector Gadget, leave the shit alone. We're here to have a great time," Bailey said.

"I just don't understand why Brandi is ignoring all of the signs. All of the answers to the questions that you've asked yourself have been revealed. And you still choose to ignore the pink elephant in the room," Kya said.

"Kya, have you ever thought that maybe Derick is telling the truth?" Deion asked.

"Now you're starting to sound like Brandi," Kya said.

"I'm just saying. Not all men are bad."

"You're right, not all men are bad but all men aren't good either," Kya said.

"If that's the case it goes both ways. Not all women are saints either," Bailey said.

"You're right," Kya said.

"I remember several years ago I was watching this special about men on the down-low. They said they have these clubs and one of the conditions of the membership required the man to be married and in a heterosexual relationship. I couldn't believe that shit," Deion said.

"Now that's some bullshit," Bailey said.

"Girl, they even have down-low dating services," Deion said.

"Get the hell out of here. That's like condoning these guys to infect their women with HIV," Kya said.

"Well, I would at least hope that they have enough common sense to wrap it up," Bailey said.

"I don't know, we've all been in a situation where the heat of passion made us forget to use protection," Kya said.

"That's very true, but if you have a woman at home and you're fucking men, how the hell could you forget to wrap it up?" Bailey asked.

"Some people just don't give a fuck. That's just ignant as shit," Kya said.

"How could you ask your wife or girlfriend that you've been in a relationship with for years, all of sudden to use a condom? Her antennae would go up immediately," Bailey said.

"But the shits aren't doing that. They fuck these men and then take shit back home. It's always the bitch that ends up with AIDS after he's gallivanted all around town. That's really sad and they can't possibly have a conscience," Kya said.

"I don't have anything to worry about. My man wouldn't dare do anything like that," Brandi said.

"Yeah, okay," Kya said.

"I was really feeling this guy one time but I later found out that we both liked dicks," Kya said.

"So I guess your gaydar didn't go off?" Bailey asked.

"Hell, no! Everything about him said he was a straight man. He acted like a 100 percent heterosexual man. Girl, I was all prepared to give him some of these cookies. I later found out that I didn't have anything he wanted," Kya said.

"How did you find out?" Deion asked.

"I told him that I was attracted to him and asked him out. We went out a couple of times and I was all prepared to fuck him. Actually that's all I wanted. After one of our dates we went back to his house and I just knew we were going to get busy. I started to get undressed and he asked me what I was doing. I was like, huh? He said thank you, and I'm flattered but I don't swing that way. Girl, I was so embarrassed and took my ass home," Kya said.

"Okay, but that doesn't mean he was gay," Bailey said.

"What man doesn't want pussy, especially if you're putting it all up in his face? A gay man," Kya said.

As Bailey laughed, she looked at Kya and said, "Maybe he just didn't want you."

"What the hell ever, who doesn't want me?" Kya asked.

"Oh goodness, and the self-centeredness begins," Deion said.

"It actually never stops. But anyway, I later met his partner at my company's Christmas party," Kya said.

"Can we talk about something else?" Brandi asked.

"Yeah, I agree, let's discuss something else," Bailey said.

"Okay, I'll leave it alone right now, but I'll bring it back up later on. But riddle me this. If you found dildos and shit in Noah's closet how would you feel?" Kya asked.

"I think you know me well enough to know how I would react to something like that. Next topic," Bailey said.

"Kya, I agree with Bailey, there's a whole lot that we can discuss. Let's change the topic. This conversation isn't the most pleasant. It's too early in the morning to be mad or pissed off," Deion said.

"Why, does the truth hurt?" Kya asked.

"That's a good question and I don't have the answer," Bailey said.

"Of course you do, we all have the answer to that question," Kya said.

"In my opinion, the truth hurts even if it's not deliberate because we don't want to face reality," Bailey said.

"I don't quite understand that," Brandi said.

"When people lie that's a false hope, it's like selling you a pipe dream. A lie is something that is kept in the dark and hidden but once revealed it tears you down, hurts and can ruin you," Bailey said.

"It's definitely a difference between telling the truth versus a lie. No matter how bad the truth hurts I'd rather know the truth," Kya said.

"I just don't understand why people lie," Brandi said.

"Girl, it would take us the rest of our lives to answer that question," Kya said.

"Ladies, we're here to have fun and celebrate, not be in a somber type of mood. Brandi's cooked all of this food and it's sitting and getting cold," Bailey said. "Let's eat, drink and have a wonderful day. Brandi, where are the dishes that we're going to use? I can start setting the table," Bailey said.

"Thanks, sweetie, everything's in the cabinet next to the refrigerator," Brandi said.

"What would you like me to do?" Kya asked.

"I would like for you to sit there, drink that mimosa and not say anything," Brandi said.

"I can sit here and drink but I can't promise to be quiet. Maybe I won't say anything for the next couple of seconds."

"I was always taught that if you don't have anything good to say then don't say anything," Deion said.

"Is that why you're always so quiet?" Kya asked.

"Perhaps, or maybe I just don't have anything to say," Deion said.

"Well, I was taught not to bite my tongue. Therefore, I say what I have to say," Kya said.

"But you don't consider the other persons feelings. You just blurt shit out without thinking. You need to think twice before you speak once," Bailey said.

"Ain't that some shit, don't you got a nerve," Kya said.

"I always think before I speak," Bailey said.

"Sometimes I think my tongue is just quicker than my brain. I don't intentionally try to hurt anyone or their feelings, I just don't see the point in holding back what needs to be said," Kya stated.

"It's not what you say Kya, it's how you say it that makes a difference. Of course none of us wants anything to be sugarcoated, just be a little more sensitive as to how and what you say," Bailey said.

"I'll try but you too should practice what you preach," Kya said.

Bailey smiled and said, "We'll both do better."

"So, Brandi, when are you having the housewarming party?" Kya asked.

"I was hoping to have it the next time we were scheduled to go to the spa. Before you ladies say anything, hear me out," Brandi said.

"This better be good because you know we enjoyed ourselves so much last time that we've been looking forward to our next visit," Kya said.

Brandi sat down at the table and said, "I think we should reschedule the trip until the end of the summer. We're planning all of these trips but I didn't consider the financial part of it. I don't have it like that to go on a trip every other weekend."

"Okay, and your point is what?" Deion asked.

"I just got this new house and I have renovations and repairs to make to the other house."

"And you also have a husband who is supposed to help share expenses. But I forgot he's saving his money for other stuff," Kya said.

"Yeah, but . . ." Brandi said.

"Yeah but my ass. When you got married your incomes were combined. It became a two income house. I still don't understand why you are paying for everything?" Kya asked.

"That's not what I'm saying. I'm not paying for everything, I just have a lot of financial obligations right now," Brandi said.

"That's bullshit, Brandi. You pay for everything inside of the house. You buy food. You cover entertainment and other shit. He only pays his damn car note. If that's not paying for everything then I don't know what the hell is. You're talking to us, your girls, remember? So what's the real issue? What's really going on? You've been just as excited about the spa getaway as we have," Bailey said.

"I just didn't take a lot into consideration, that's all. I don't have it like that," Brandi said.

"I'm still waiting for you to make a solid point," Deion said.

"I also have a lot of furniture and other whatnots to buy for this house. In addition, as luck would have it, my transmission went out. Before I buy a new transmission I'll get a new car first. So I'm asking that we cancel the next spa trip, for now."

"Sweetie, I hear you but we're not cancelling the trip. We all have been looking forward to this trip after last time. Hell, we all need a getaway," Kya said.

"I guess your housewarming party will take place the weekend after we return from the spa," Bailey said.

"Sounds like a plan to me," Kya said.

"And me, too," Deion said.

"I can't go, not now," Brandi said.

"Can't is a word used by weak people. You can and you will go. Even if that means I have to pack your ass in my suitcase, you're going," Kya said.

"You don't need any money for the trip anyway. The trip was all inclusive and we've already paid for it," Kya said.

"Exactly, so what do you need money for? Everything's taken care of. It sounds to me like you're making excuses," Bailey said.

"I'm not making excuses, I just can't afford the trip right now."

"Well, my dear, you are shit outta luck because the package is non-refundable. So if you don't go it's just going to be a waste of money anyway," Kya said.

"Okay, I guess I'll be going to the spa," Brandi said.

"Brandi, the whole time you were referring to I. I have to do this, I have to do that. I'm like Kya, the last time I checked you're married. I'm not trying to get in your business but what is your husband doing?" Bailey asked.

"Apparently not a fucking thing," Kya said.

"It doesn't really matter to me when we go. I need a break too but I don't think we're being fair to Brandi. We really haven't taken her finances into consideration. We know she's trying to start a foundation and do everything else. I have a suggestion," Deion said.

"What, D?" Bailey asked.

"Brandi, if we cover your spa expenses will you go?" Deion asked.

"Okay, maybe everybody is storing shit in their short-term memory bank. Let me reiterate. Everything is already paid for, and no refunds!" Bailey yelled.

"That's right," Deion said.

"That's a part of the problem," Brandi said.

"What do you mean?" Kya asked.

"Because you keep covering a lot of my expenses as is. I feel bad that I do have a husband that doesn't help me do shit financially. It's not your place to keep covering everything for me," Brandi said.

"Hmmmm. I knew the truth would come out sooner or later. They always say everything in the dark comes to light," Kya said.

"What do you mean Derick doesn't help you financially?" Bailey asked.

"Nothing," Brandi said.

"Oh it's something, it just came out of your mouth," Kya said.

"What the hell is he doing with his money?" Deion asked.

"D, I really don't know. He keeps telling me he's saving his money and his money is tied up."

"Tied up? What the hell does that mean?" Kya asked.

"I don't know."

"Brandi, I'm having a hard time grasping this one. What do you mean you don't know? Haven't you asked?" Bailey asked.

"I tried to talk to him about it but he kept telling me that the situation is being rectified," Brandi said.

"What the hell is that supposed to mean?" Deion asked.

"I don't know," Brandi said.

"You can't keep saying you don't know. That doesn't even sound right. Don't you guys have a joint bank account?" Bailey asked.

"Yes. But he made it clear when we got married, not to touch his money. He keeps a tally of what he puts into the account."

"And you agreed to that?" Kya asked.

"What choice did I have?"

As the room became quiet, Bailey, Kya and Deion looked at one another in shock. For the next couple of minutes the ladies didn't say a word.

Kya got up and said, "I think I need a real drink." She turned to Brandi and asked, "Is there any other alcohol in here besides champagne?"

"Yes, there's some other stuff in the den. It's in a box beside the patio door," Brandi said.

"Okay. Does anyone else want a drink?" Kya asked.

"Yes please," Bailey said.

"No thanks, I'm still nursing this mimosa," Deion said.

"No thanks, I'm good," Brandi said.

"I'm at a loss for words but for me to sit here and not say anything is killing me," Bailey said.

"I know you ladies have a lot to say and think I'm crazy," Brandi said.

"I really don't know what to say about the situation. I mean it does put a lot into perspective," Bailey said.

"Your finances, how you run your marriage and household aren't really our business. Your well-being is," Deion said.

Kya entered the room and said, "I disagree."

"In a way of speaking, if you want to be technical it's not our business," Bailey said.

"I still disagree."

"It's not our business. Brandi is a grown-ass woman and how she handles her business isn't ours," Deion said.

"And I still disagree," Kya said.

"Why do you disagree?" Bailey asked.

"When people put you in their business and they ask your opinion they then make it yours. They opened the door for you to come and make your comments. When you care about someone and their well-being of course you'll be pissed and concerned if their shit is a mess. I'm not going to sit here and act like I agree to what's going on in Brandi's house, because I don't," Kya said.

"I get what you all are saying, however, everything is not for everybody," Bailey said.

"Some people aren't strong enough to handle shit on their own and need guidance," Kya said.

"Ladies, we all know that I'm nothing like the three of you. I'm not an expert about life, men or anything. I think I'm a good person and just try to live my life the best way I can. I try my best to be good to others, treat them with respect and do what's right. For whatever reason, someway and somehow, things go bad for me," Brandi said.

"Don't say that. You are without a doubt a good person, a good woman. You have a huge heart and you're good to everyone. Don't look at it as bad things happen to you. Think of it as bad things happen for a good reason," Kya said.

"We all know in the midst of a bad situation something good always happens," Bailey said.

"Very true, and stumbling blocks are always turned into stepping stones," Bailey said.

"That's true but I just don't understand why things are hard for me," Brandi said.

"Be careful what you say. The last time I checked, God was showering you with blessings. Things might seem a little bad right now but everything will work out. It's all a test, my dear. Just a test," Bailey said.

"I hope like heck I pass this test because it's been rough," Brandi said.

"Another part of your problem is that you hold everything in. We all have issues and problems but you act like you don't want to bother us with your stuff," Deion said.

"Like you said, we all have issues and problems, and no I don't want to burden you with my drama," Brandi said.

"But we can't help you if you don't say anything," Kya said.

"We're family and we're here to help you in any way that we can," Deion said.

"Sweetie, maybe you should learn to put self first. Sometimes we focus so much on making others happy that we lose focus on our own happiness. It's okay to put self first occasionally. If you're not happy it's impossible to make someone else happy," Bailey said.

"Brandi, out of the four of us, it's your disposition that I admire the most. When you're having a bad day no one can tell and you always have something positive to say. Right now I'm not feeling your pessimistic attitude," Kya said.

"Kya, we all have bad days. I think right now I'm just tired, have a lot on my mind, and have more on my plate than I can handle," Brandi said.

"Always remember if you think positive, then positive things will happen. There's no room for negativity. You are what you think. Think big and great things will happen. It's happening now, my dear, aren't those dreams of yours coming to pass?" Bailey asked.

"Somewhat."

"Just look around. This new house, you're starting a foundation, and you need to trust and believe God has more in store for you than you realize. So stop stealing your own joy and do what you have to in order to get where you need to be," Bailey said.

"You better stop playing and work that faith of yours," Kya said.

"Like anything else you want or need, pray about it, give it to God and leave it there. Your marriage, your new home and business, just pray, pray, pray. All you have to do is keep pressing forward, sweetie," Bailey said.

"I will. Thank you, ladies, and I appreciate your words of encouragement. My keywords for the day are faith, love, hope, strength, forgiveness, patience, confidence and peace. I refuse to give in to the stress fairy," Brandi said.

"Good! Life is too damn short for the foolishness!" Deion yelled.

"So, what are we going to do about the spa trip?" Bailey asked.

"We're going, that's what we're going to do," Brandi said.

"We sure as hell are," Kya stated.

"Okay, I was going to suggest rescheduling the trip to a later date but I guess there's no need for that," Bailey said.

"Are we still going to Vegas for D's birthday?" Kya asked.

"That's the plan. Why, you don't want to go?" Bailey asked.

"Hell yeah, I still want to go, I was just asking,"

"Maybe after our week in Charleston we hold off on trips for a while."

"Uhhhh, hell no! You know I have to have my getaways. I can't function nor am I productive if I don't have my getaways," Kya said.

"I'm just trying to come up with some suggestions, we still need to be considerate of Brandi's request," Deion said.

"You ladies can still go, but I won't be able to go on all of the trips," Brandi said.

"You need to cut that shit out. You know damn well we're not going if you can't go," Deion said.

"Brandi, I understand the point that you've made. We'll worry about that bridge when we have to cross it. As of now, we're still going on our trips," Bailey said.

"I don't see the financial part being an issue anyway," Kya said.

"It's not and I'm not going to have another long, drawn-out conversation about our upcoming trips. We just went through that," Bailey said.

"Ladies, no matter how you want to put it, I can't accept any more money or gifts from you. You've done enough for me financially. You have families that you have to worry about," Brandi said.

"I don't think you've ever heard any of us complain about what we do for you. We're not those types of friends and you know it. We don't talk about what we do for each other. Everything that we do for one another comes from the heart," Bailey said.

"You're damn right! We don't do shit and then talk about it. There are no ulterior motives with us. We don't do anything expecting a pat on the back or recognition from other people.

Whatever we do is because we're best friends, we care about one other, and we're sisters," Kya said.

"We're going to ignore this shit that Brandi's talking about and move forward with our trips as planned," Bailey said.

As Brandi started waving her hands in the air, she said, "Um, hello ladies, I'm sitting right here. You guys are chit-chatting about me like I'm not in the room."

"That's because we're not paying you any attention. We're trying to get things in order right now," Deion said.

"Anyhoo ladies, I have a great idea for a housewarming gift. Kya, if you could cater the food that would be great. I'll come over the night before and help you cook. I'll also pay for the food," Bailey said.

"Okay, I can do that. The way the weather has been lately it might be hot. Hopefully we will be able to cook on the grill as well. I'm sure Derick can handle that task," Kya said.

"I'll get the beverages, alcohol, ice, chips and other snacks. I can also get the paper goods, decorations and gifts for the guests," Deion said.

"Excuse me, don't I have a say in any of this?" Brandi asked.

"No you don't. All you have to do is be here," Kya said.

"D, don't worry about the paper goods or decorations, I can take care of that. Besides I have plenty in stock, I do events remember?" Kya said.

"Okay. Then let me give you money since you're using your staff and materials," Deion said.

"Girl, I'm not tripping off of that," Kya said.

"If for any reason Derick is working or out of town, Noah can cook on the grill," Bailey said.

"I would hope that he'll be here. It's an event for the both of us, not just me," Brandi said.

"We'll see," Kya said.

"Well, what's my role in this? What am I supposed to do? Apparently you guys have everything figured out," Brandi said.

"As of now, all we need for you to do is show up and be blissful, social and happy. Be your normal self. Oh, can you draft the guest list with their addresses and email it to me? I'll have Nina mail out the invitations this week. You'll need to register for your gifts. I'm going to have Nina write on the invitations that gift cards are appreciated," Bailey said.

"Yes, I can do that," Brandi said.

"Now that we have all of that figured out can we eat? I'm hungry and this food looks and smells good," Deion said.

"Unfortunately, some of it needs to be reheated," Brandi said.

"No it doesn't, I put all of the hot food in the buffet servers on the island and turned them on low," Kya said.

"When?" Bailey asked.

"A couple of minutes ago when I refreshed my drink," Kya said.

"I was wondering what you were doing," Bailey said.

"Damn you, nosey," Kya said.

"Well ladies, I hope you enjoy," Brandi said.

As the ladies began preparing the plates, Kya took another sip of her mimosa and said, "I have some shit for y'all."

"Can it wait until after we eat? I'd like to eat in peace. I definitely don't want to hear anything that will make me lose my appetite," Bailey said.

"Um, no," Kya said.

"I'm like Bailey, I hope it's nothing that will make me lose my appetite," Deion said.

"No, it's nothing like that, it's actually a little funny," Kya said.

"Yeah I bet," Deion said.

"Okay, so let me get Brandi up to speed about the breakup with me and Jeff. I finally gained some wisdom and was strong enough to break things off with him," Kya said.

"Who's Jeff? Is he someone new?" Deion asked.

"Hell no, Jeff is the fiancé that I had for seven years."

"I always thought his name was Jay, but that's because in addition to a few other choice names, that's what Kya called him," Brandi said.

With a puzzled look on her face, Deion said, "Oh okay, now I get it."

"Anyhoo, a couple of days later I called and told him to come and get the rest of his shit from my house. I told him if he didn't I was going to drop it off at the thrift store. I'm not going to lie, when he got there he looked so goddamn good. He looked good enough to eat. Those were actually my intentions but I had to get it together," Kya said.

"So you fucked him?" Bailey asked.

"Girl, I felt like it was my civic duty to fuck him one last time. Girl, he must have just come from the barber shop. You know it's something about a bald-headed man with hair on their face. I don't know if it was his appearance or his cologne but I was ready. That shit drives me crazy!" Kya yelled.

"I knew it, you fucked him," Bailey said.

"You sound like you were running around like a dog in heat," Brandi said.

"I think I was," Kya said jokingly.

"Kya, you are too much for me," Brandi said.

"I'm too much for myself most days. Anyway, I thought that I'd give him a mercy fuck for the road. Besides, I was horny as hell."

"You didn't. Haven't you given him enough mercy fucks throughout the years?" Bailey said.

"Yes, but girl I was so horny that I couldn't walk straight."

"Kya, you are crazy as shit," Bailey said.

"We were about to do a little something and he started to get undressed. I had just gotten out of the shower so mama was all fresh, clean and smelling good. I lit a couple of candles and had the soft music playing. I was trying to set the mood for a perfect exit fuck."

"Is an exit fuck the same as an exit interview?" Deion asked.

"Almost. Except I don't know anyone that gets fucked at the conclusion of an exit interview," Kya said.

"I hope not," Brandi said.

"Y'all know an exit fuck is normally the best fuck that you've ever had with a person. They might not know but you have no intentions of fucking them again. So, you go all out. This is the final finale . . . buffet style and anything goes,"

"Lord have mercy . . . I don't know what we're going to do with this girl," Brandi said.

"After we got into the bed, we started kissing and he started fondling the boobies. Then he started kissing me on my neck and . . ." Kya paused.

"Before you finish, please save the graphic details," Bailey said.

"Okay, I won't go into explicit details. Let's just say the foreplay lasted for a couple of minutes. He ate the coochie better than he's eaten it in seven years. Ladies, after that I was definitely in the mood to get busy and go all out. I was about to give him a little head . . ."

"Kya, seriously!" Bailey yelled.

"What?"

"I just asked you to save the overt detailed shit. We don't want to hear all of that."

"Sorry, I haven't learned to bite my tongue yet."

"Well, you need to try harder."

"Okay! I then started kissing him all over his neck, then chest. I was working my way down to . . . King Kong."

"Should we assume King Kong is his dick?" Bailey asked.

"Bingo, you got it. So anyway, I got on my knees and positioned myself between his legs. I'm kissing his stomach, meanwhile I playing with his balls and dick at the same time. Child, I was about to put his dick in my mouth, then I noticed these little pieces of white shit all over his dick."

"Huh? What the hell was it?" Bailey asked.

"I'm getting to that part. I said Jeff, what the hell is this shit all over your dick? He acted like he didn't know what the hell I was talking about. I sat up, turned on the light and pointed it out. The closer I got the more I realized it was a rubber. It was a broken fucking rubber!"

"Are you serious?" Brandi asked.

"Yes, a goddamn rubber. This nigga thought he was about to get some head and fuck the shit out of me. Apparently he'd just finished fucking someone else. I said you nasty motherfucker! Then I asked him, why the fuck are you walking around with remnants of a popped condom on your dick? Of course, he just stood there looking simple and shit. You just got finished fucking somebody? Apparently the rubber popped and your trifling ass didn't even wash your dick. But you walk around smelling like a bottle of cologne. How nasty can you be? I'm about to suck and fuck you and you got booty juice and condom pieces all over your dick from some other bitch. I jumped up and said, get your shit and get the fuck out of my house."

"He's a nasty ass Negro. Even when you talk about him my stomach just turns," Bailey said.

"But Kya, he was a ho when you were with him. Why would you think he'd be any different now?" Brandi asked.

"Bitch, more importantly, how are you going to sit here and act as if that story was supposed to be hilarious? You were honestly about to give this man some head, without using a condom. Not to mention you were going to fuck him. What the hell is wrong with you? Aren't you engaged? Where was Steve when all of this was going on?" Bailey asked.

"I don't know. I think he was playing golf with your husband. I just couldn't help it. I was a little weak. The dick is good as hell. I just wanted a little for the road," Kya said.

"No, you were being a dumb ass. Keep fucking with Jeff and your ass is going to be walking around with something you'll never get rid of," Bailey exclaimed.

"Okay, we all make mistakes, I'm not a saint but damn," Kya said.

"All I can say is wow. That crazy-ass story in its entirety was just a damn mess. Not to mention you almost fucked up a good thing over Jeff. *Again*! I can't believe you Kya. His nasty ass walking around smelling like Col-ba-dussy," Bailey said.

"What the hell is that?" Deion asked.

"Cologne, balls, dick and pussy. And Ms. Dog-on-Heat over there had her face all up in it. Just nasty," Bailey said.

"Whatever, bitch!" Kya said.

"Not to mention he still got the broken condom all over his dick. He nasty ass shit!" Kya yelled.

"You're nasty too! You can't believe him, but you're not innocent in all of this. Just nasty. Ewwww," Bailey said.

"Nothing he does surprises me," Kya said.

"Well, you sure as hell surprised me, Ms. Nasty," Bailey said.

"Now that's nasty," Deion said.

"I don't even know what to say about that, I'm just going to have to pray for that poor brother," Brandi said.

"Somebody needs to pray for his sick McNasty ass," Kya said.

As Bailey laughed, she said, "Sweetie, you always have a funny ass story to tell. Don't get me wrong, I'm almost for certain you didn't think it was funny at the time. After listening to it, I don't think it's funny. But because you're so animated when you're telling these stories, that's what make them funny. Girl, thank goodness you left his ass alone."

"The sad part is I really wasn't tripping that he'd fucked someone else. I'm used to that. He fucked other women throughout our entire relationship. I think I was more pissed off because I didn't get to fuck at all. I was all prepared, then nothing happened."

"Girl, he's a shitty damn mess and so are you. You better get your shit together before you lose Steve. Whatever nasty ass urges you got, you need to repress that shit. Don't even think about it. Bury it in the back of your simple mind," Bailey said.

"Why are we still talking about it? Can't we let the past be left in the past?" Kya asked.

"Hell, no! You definitely are losing all of your cool points on this one, my dear," Bailey said.

"Jeff would be a good man if he could if he could just keep his dick in his pants," Kya said.

"He'll get it together one day. But that's no longer your problem to worry about. You have a good man now. So let Jeff and his foolishness go. I'm serious, Kya," Brandi said.

"Hopefully," Bailey said.

"Like you said, Brandi, that's no longer my problem or concern to worry about," Kya said.

"It should be."

"Why's that? I won't be fucking him so why should I care?" Kya asked.

"You should care because that's Lexi's father," Bailey said.

"Yeah, well, whatever."

"But on a serious note, its men like him that are passing out diseases and leaving babies all over the place. I hope you've been tested," Bailey said.

"Tested . . . for?" Kya asked.

"Diseases, pregnancy. What else could I be talking about?"

"Of course I have, do you think I was that stupid not to take care of self? I had an appointment last week. I was tested on everything from HPV to chlamydia. Any and everything she could test me for, I got the tests. I also took my AIDS test a month ago. Don't worry, I'm good. I'm in perfect health and I definitely take care of my temple."

"I hope so. But you almost gave up your temple without thinking," Brandi said.

"I can't be having any issues with my va-jj," Kya said.

"Okay, I was just checking. You can never be too careful. I'm married and have been married for ten years. However, I still get checked for diseases as well as AIDS on a regular basis. I love my husband but I love me more," Bailey said.

"The first time I was tested was recently. My doctor was insistent about me taking it. I asked her why, when I've been married for four years," Brandi said.

"What? Why not? It doesn't matter that you're married. Get tested anyway," Bailey asked.

"Because I've only been with two people in my whole life."

"I don't care, you still should get checked. At this point you definitely need to get checked," Kya said.

"What does that mean?" Brandi asked.

"Like Bailey said you can never be too careful. It's a whole lot of people that lost their life over someone they trusted," Deion said.

"I just never had a reason to take the test," Brandi said.

"Girlfriend, in this day and age you have a whole lot of reasons to be tested," Bailey said.

"All I know is this bitch was pissed off," Kya said.

"Why, because he's no longer your boo?" Brandi asked.

"Hell no, because I was horny as shit and I needed to get mine off," Kya said. As the ladies laughed, Kya added, "That shit isn't funny. I felt like I could explode at any moment."

"Then why didn't you call and get your man off the golf course?" Bailey asked.

"I think I secretly wanted to fuck Jeff one last time. I now know that it wasn't meant to happen. If I did, I'd have lost a king and got a joker because I tried to reshuffle the deck for a damn quickie. Damn!

I couldn't do anything else but go to sleep pissed off and horny," Kya said.

"Kya, you are truly a trip. But the only person you could have been pissed with is yourself," Brandi said.

As Bailey laughed she said, "If you couldn't wait until your man got there then that's a problem. Either you should have pulled that little bunny out of the closet or took your ass to bed."

"That shit is not funny."

As Deion sat and listened to Kya's story she thought it was a coincidence that she and Kya were dealing with a guy with the same name, the same looks and the same characteristics. She wanted to ask more questions about Jeff but she didn't want the ladies to be suspicious of her inquisitiveness. Not to mention she recalled the last time she and Jeff had sex. In fact, she remembered it was a couple of weeks ago. Towards the end of what she liked to call their sexathon, the condom popped. Right after they finished having sex, Jay had jumped up and started to get dressed. She remembered asking him why he wasn't taking a shower and he said he didn't have time. She also recalled Jay saying that he had somewhere to be. She also thought about how immoral it would be if her man was also Kya's former fiancé. That would be totally strange. She also realized if they were in fact the same person then that could only mean one thing. That they both were sleeping with the same man at the very same time. *Oh no, that can't be the case. Why am I tripping? Out of all the men in the DC area, what are the chances that Jay's the same guy?*

"D! D!" Brandi shouted. "What's going on with you? You sitting over there all quiet and stuff, what's wrong?"

"I'm good, just a little tired and my stomach feels a little weird," Deion said. *Maybe I should ask some generic questions to see.*

"Deion, are you sure you're all right? You've been a little quiet today," Bailey asked.

"I'm fine, I was just listening to you ladies talk," Deion said.

"Oh, okay. Would you like something else to eat or drink?" Brandi asked.

"I'm fine, I'll grab something else to eat in a little bit."

Skeletons

For the next several minutes Deion sat there in a trance. As the other ladies continued laughing and talking, Deion didn't say a word.

"D, D . . . Deion, girl, what the hell is up with you?" Kya asked.

"I'm actually not feeling well. I think I should go," Deion said.

"Why don't you go upstairs and lie down for a while? You're more than welcome to," Brandi said.

"No, I really should go."

"Um, Deion, don't you remember that we all rode together? Your car's at my house," Bailey said.

"Oh shit, I did forget. Well, I can just catch a cab."

"You want to catch a cab from Fort Washington all the way to Upper Marlboro. Bitch, is you crazy?" Kya asked.

"I just think I need to leave. I don't want to put a damper on the festivities."

"Deion, if you're not feeling well just go upstairs and lie down for a while," Brandi said.

"I don't want you out and about if you're not feeling well. I can take you to your car," Bailey said.

"No, I don't want you ladies leaving on my account. Maybe if I just lie down for a minute I'll be fine."

"I know my food didn't get you sick. Do you think it's something else you ate?" Brandi asked.

"No, I just feel really sick. My stomach's turning and it just doesn't feel right."

"Brandi, do you have some ginger ale or a coke that'll settle her stomach?" Bailey asked.

"Yes, let me get her a glass of ginger ale and some crackers," Brandi said.

"Oh my goodness. I've seen that look before. You're either pregnant, stressed out, or upset about something," Kya said.

"Girl, it's none of the above. I haven't been sleeping well lately. Maybe it's the insomnia or working those long hours."

"Oh no, mama, clearly something's wrong. It's written all over your face. I had a dream about fishes last night. All types of those funny-looking bastards. Somebody's pregnant. I damn sure know it's not me," Kya said.

"Don't look at me," Brandi said.

"Yeah, mama, it's not you. You definitely got to fuck in order to make a baby," Kya said. "I know it's not Bailey." Kya pointed her finger at Deion, she said, "It's gotta be D. Watch what I say. Y'all don't have to believe me right now. In a couple of weeks we'll have the answer," Kya said.

"Hey, crazy girl . . . crazy girl," Bailey said.

"Who, me?" Kya asked.

"Yes you! Zip it. Shhhhh. Don't say another damn word. I'm putting you in time out."

"Okay, I'll be quiet for a couple of seconds but when I start talking again it's on," Kya said.

"You're a sick person. We should have taken you for treatment a long time ago," Brandi said.

"Brandi, I think I will lie down for a bit," Deion said.

"Okay, sweetie, let me take you upstairs. I'll also get a cold rag for your forehead. Maybe you just need to rest for a while."

"Thanks, Babes. Ladies, save some of the juicy gossip until I get up."

"Okay, I'll try," Kya said.

When Brandi returned to the kitchen she said, "Well, my story isn't as funny as Kya's but I have started therapy."

"Good, I'm glad to hear that. How's it working out?" Kya asked.

"Some days it's difficult to relive the past and the abuse that I endured. I cry a lot but I'm finally happy to be getting the help that I need."

"Whether you know it or not, you're a very strong and courageous woman. We are proud of you. It will take some time but don't ever forget that we're here for you," Bailey said.

"I wish you'd told us early on, but I understand why you didn't," Kya said.

"I'm just glad that I finally shared with you guys and you weren't angry with me," Brandi said.

"Come on, Brandi, why would we be angry with you? You did nothing wrong. You were a child and you were the victim. Your father sexually abused you and you had nothing to do with that. Stop blaming yourself because it wasn't your fault. I know first-hand how it is to hold onto something and not share. Sometimes we worry about how people are going to take the information and how they're going to react. But holding secrets and trying to keep them hidden is a horrible feeling. Sometimes that can almost be like a full-time job," Bailey said.

"I concur," said Kya.

"How can holding on to secrets be like a full-time job? You lost me with that one," Brandi said.

"You work extremely hard at hiding information. Chances are this information is detrimental to you or other people if someone found out about it. Therefore, you do what you have to do in order for the secret to be hidden," Bailey said.

Bailey and Kya started to clean the kitchen and the doorbell rang.

"Brandi, are you expecting anyone?" Bailey asked.

"Maybe it's a delivery or something," Brandi said.

"Well, I guess there's only one way to find out. Go and answer the damn door," Kya said.

"Shut your sick ass up. I'll go and get it," Bailey said. As she walked to the door, she saw a silhouette of a man through the glass panels, then realized it was Noah. She opened the door and asked, "Hey, what are you doing here? Is everything all right with the girls?"

"Hey, babe, everything's fine with the girls. Mrs. Jenkins is at the house with them. I was just running some errands and thought I'd stop by."

"Okay, come on in."

"No. I'm not staying. What time are you going to be home?" Noah asked.

"Probably around 7 p.m. What's wrong, Noah?"

"We never got a chance to talk the other night."

"Yes, I know. But you drove all the way out here to remind me that we need to talk?"

"Naw. I was in the area and just drove by."

"Why are you acting so strange? If you like we can talk now. Whatever it is that you need to talk about, must be important," Bailey said.

"Babe, it can wait. I'm headed back to the house. I told Mrs. Jenkins that I wasn't going to be out very long. Tell the ladies I said hello."

"Okay, I will," Bailey said and Noah turned to give her a kiss. "Babe, are you sure everything's all right? If you want I can go home with you."

"Everything's fine. I didn't mean to interrupt your day with your girls. We can talk when you get home,"

"Okay, sweetie, let me get back in here and finish cleaning."

When Bailey went back into the house, Brandi was walking down the hall and asked, "Who was that fine black man that you were talking to?"

"That was my boo," Bailey said.

"Does your boo know that you're married?" Brandi teased.

"Of course he does. We're all one big happy family," Bailey said jokingly.

"Girl, let me stop playing. Why didn't Noah come in and get something to eat?" Brandi asked.

"He was on his way home. He was out running errands or something."

"That was Noah at the door? That's so cute, he was checking on his wifey. He could have come in to say hello," Kya said.

"He wanted to get back to the girls," Bailey said.

"Oh, okay," Kya said. "I hope you and Noah will be okay."

"One way or another I'm going to be fine."

"I know you will but I'm hoping that everything will work out," Kya said.

"Girl, don't worry about us. If it's meant for us to be together then it will work out. If not, then I'll just have to keep it moving."

"What's going on with you and Noah?" Brandi asked.

"Nothing much, just something we need to work out."

"You know I'm here if you need to talk," Brandi said.

"I know but it's all good. Anyway, I think someone should check on Deion. She was asleep before I left the room so I just put a blanket over her. I don't know what's going on with her but she didn't look too good," Bailey said.

"Maybe she's overworked, over-sexed and overly pregnant," Kya said.

"Kya, you just don't quit," Bailey said.

"Seriously, she's been acting really weird for a couple of weeks now. I don't know if it's work-related or if it's because of her new boo. You know how it is sometimes when a new man comes into your life," Kya said.

"No, I don't know how it is. Please explain," Bailey said.

"Sometimes a new man wants you all to himself. The people or things that you used to do then become a faded memory, a thing of the past."

"Kya, that's not true," Brandi said.

"Yes it is, particularly if you're dealing with an insecure, jealous and crazy-ass man. If that's the case then you can kiss your girls goodbye," Kya said.

"In some cases that's true. But Deion isn't going to let some man dictate to her what she can or can't do. That phase of her life is over. After she got out of that hellish nightmare I don't think she'll ever go back to it," Bailey said.

"I'm glad you have so much faith and confidence in her. In the beginning no one can never tell if their partner is crazy. It takes a little time before you see a person's true colors. I just hope her weirdness don't have to do with some man. I damn sure hope she's not pregnant," Kya said.

"Maybe that's what she needs, a baby," Brandi said.

"She doesn't need a damn baby, not the way she's living," Kya said.

"Maybe a baby will change her life, for the better. I'm sure she wouldn't be doing the same shit with a baby," Bailey said.

"It's a whole lot of ho's out there and they have children. And what? They still find the time to ho and fuck around," Kya said.

"Okay, that's a valid point. All I'm saying is I hope the girl is okay. Whether it's a new man or a baby, she's our friend and I want her to be happy and healthy," Bailey said.

"She has been acting a little funny lately. I was wondering what was going on with her," Brandi said.

"If there's something wrong she'll let us know," Bailey said.

"Bailey, how's Noah doing?" Brandi asked.

"Noah's doing well. However, right now he's sweating bullets."

"What did you do?" Brandi asked.

"Not a damn thing. Don't you mean what the hell did he do?" Bailey asked.

"Noah doesn't do anything but work hard and take care of his family," Brandi said.

"That's not all he does," Kya said sarcastically.

"Yes, he does work hard. He doesn't take care of our family, *we* take care of our family, together," Bailey said.

"Okay, did I miss something?" Brandi asked.

"Noah has been a little busier than usual."

"I know you guys are working on major deals and new projects," Brandi said.

"Our company isn't the only thing that's keeping Noah busy. He has a new hobby."

"Oh, okay. Well, isn't that a good thing? The both of you have always been extremely busy," Brandi said.

"It appears that Noah's extracurricular activities entail him fucking another woman."

"Bailey, are you being serious or are you just joking around?" Brandi asked.

"Sweetie, that's nothing to joke about, I'm being very serious. Noah's cheating on me."

"Oh my goodness! Why didn't you tell me?" Brandi asked.

"You have enough to worry about. I didn't want to burden you with my problems."

"I don't care what I'm dealing with, you should have said something. How come you're so calm?"

"I have cried about it but at this point my tears have dried up. I refuse to waste any more tears crying over some man."

"He's not some man, he's your husband," Kya said.

"Yeah, well, whatever. Like I said, some man."

"You're so calm that you're actually scaring me," Kya said.

"Am I supposed to be running around the house screaming and crying all over the place? Am I supposed to be confined to a dark bedroom starving myself or over-eating? Or would it be better for you if I was on the phone calling everyone I know? Sharing the ins and outs of my husband and his infidelities. Kya, how is it that you think you know I'm supposed to act?" Bailey asked.

"Okay, I get it. Point well taken. You're just so calm that it seems surreal."

"I'm older and I'm definitely wiser. I also have two beautiful daughters that I have to take care of. Noah is the one that messed up, not me. Maybe that's the reason he's walking around looking like a sad-ass puppy. Good for that ass. Whatever he's dealing with is because he did it to himself. He cheated. That was his choice, for the second time. My life will go on with or without him."

"I can't believe this. You and Noah are a great couple and a great team. I often wish that my marriage could be like yours," Brandi said.

"Brandi, I have expressed the same sentiments. You two were made for each other. I believe that you were destined to be together and you are soul mates. Despite what's going on, I still hope and pray that my marriage to Steve will be as great as yours," Kya said.

"Don't get me wrong, Noah's a good man, he really is. Maybe he's just not the man for me. Maybe our marriage has run its course."

"No, Nikko, don't say that. Pray and let God handle the situation. Before you make any decisions like leaving Noah, please give it to God. Whatever is God's will should happen, not yours and not Noah's. But God's will," Brandi said.

"Oh goodness, you called me Nikko so I know you're being sincere. Ladies, thank you for your heartfelt concerns. You both know me better than anybody and you know I'll be fine. I'm not going to make any drastic choices without thinking first. I have a lot to consider and a lot to think about."

"Bailey, if you and those girls left Noah that would crush his entire world. Noah can't make it without you and those babies," Brandi said.

"Well, if that's the case then Noah should have considered his entire world before he fucked Joi!" Bailey shouted.

"Joi . . . Noah's cheating with Joi again? No, no, I don't believe that. How do you know it's Joi?" Kya asked.

"She's the person that's been calling my house."

"Just because she's calling your house doesn't mean that she's sleeping with your husband. So I take it you received the call trace information. How long have you known?" Kya asked.

"Yes, ma'am. I have all the information I need. I've known about the affair for the past few weeks."

"Why didn't you say anything to us about this shit?" Kya asked.

"I don't know why I haven't told you. One of the reasons is that I've been pondering over my choices. Often, we have to grasp the situation before running and telling everyone."

"So Noah is aware that you know?" Brandi asked.

"I haven't mentioned anything to him about it whatsoever."

"Why not?" Kya asked.

"I wanted to wait."

"Wait for what?" Brandi asked.

"I wanted to wait and see how long it would take for him to say something to me."

"Sweetie, are you really okay? Is there something I can do?" Kya asked.

"I'm great. I've never felt better. The only thing you can do for me is take the girls tonight."

"Okay, what's going on?" Kya, asked.

"I don't want them in the house when we have this conversation."

"I can do that. After I pick up Lexi, me and the little ladies will go out to dinner."

"Thanks, sweetie."

"I'm impressed. Ms. Lady, you darn sure wear stress well," Brandi said.

Bailey winked at Brandi and said, "Of course I do. You never let 'em see you sweat. Girl, I looked in the mirror the other day and I was glowing. I had to say to myself, 'Damn, I look good'."

"I know that's right," Brandi said.

"When I'm stressed I always look good. I guess because you have to keep pressing. Despite what you feel on the inside it doesn't have to show on the outside. You can't be walking around looking a hot mess," Kya said.

"Don't get me wrong, when I first found out I was angry. I was hurt, upset, bitter and I wanted to get my babies and leave his ass.

Once I got my thoughts together, I said, hell, no! I'm not leaving my house. If anyone leaves it will be him. I was a little shocked because this is the same person that he cheated with before. That bitch pussy must be dipped and draped in gold."

"You know I love Noah and I look at him as my big brother. I'm not trying to take his side but maybe it wasn't his fault," Kya said.

"It wasn't his fault? Then whose fault was it? Get the fuck out of my face with that bullshit. So, are you saying that the bitch just slipped and fell on his dick? Kya, don't do it, you know I'm not the one for it. If you don't know what to say or you don't have anything just don't say shit. Keep those stupid-ass comments to yourself," Bailey said.

"How has his behavior been?" Brandi asked.

"For the past couple of weeks you could tell that he was uneasy and had something on his mind. Because of my disposition he didn't know how to take me. It appeared as though he wanted to say something but didn't know how to. His ass is scared as shit. All of a sudden he's finding me on the other side of town and making it a point to stop just by to say hello. Get the fuck out of here."

"Girl, this shit is really tearing him up," Kya said.

"Yes it is. Didn't I say earlier what holding on to secrets could do to you? Holding shit in will tear you up. If he doesn't tell me soon he'll probably go berserk."

"So, I guess tonight the shit will hit the fan," Kya said.

"I guess so."

"I feel really bad," Brandi said.

"Why? Did you tell him to fuck someone else?" Bailey asked.

"No," Brandi said.

"Then why do you feel bad?" Bailey asked.

"Because he could lose everything that he loves. He could lose everything that you and he built together."

"I gave him more than enough time to own up to it. I've asked him numerous times and he's denied it each and every time. He probably knows that he has to tell me eventually. Especially after I told him those calls were being traced. Even after that, he still didn't say anything. But he really started looking simple when I put the va-jj on lock."

"Oh goodness, the va-jj is still on lockdown?" Kya asked.

"It sure as hell is and he's not used to this. We normally fuck like rabbits. He hasn't got any in over three weeks."

"Damn!" Kya yelled.

"Poor fella," Brandi said.

"Before you got the call trace results, did you really know that he cheated?" Kya asked.

"No, not really. But when I first got the phone calls I started to feel the way I did a couple of years ago. From that moment my stomach was aching and wouldn't stop. I knew I wasn't sick or anything. It was my intuition. I could feel that something wasn't right."

"When did you get the results from the trace?" Kya asked.

"I had them that same night. Remember that night we stayed at my mother's house? Shortly after I got off the phone with Noah, I called Verizon. They gave me the information I needed. Then I got on the Internet and pulled additional information. It was Joi that was calling my house. Not only that but I also pulled our phone records. Do you recall those calls that I was getting all day and night? Whoever it was would hang up after I said hello. Yup, that was Joi too."

"Go ahead, Inspector Gadget. Maybe you're in the wrong profession," Kya said.

"I just don't understand men. Why do they cheat with a hood rat when they have a real woman at home?" Brandi asked.

"Because they let that tool between their legs do all of the thinking for them," Kya said.

"Right! Men get caught up because they don't think with their brain, they think with their dick," Bailey said.

"You can say that shit again. It's always those quick fucks and one-night stands that bring them down every time," Kya said.

"Sometimes they do get caught up with someone, but for them it's not that serious. It's all about the sex. Yeah they might be feeling the hoochie and all but you won't find too many men that are going to leave wifey and the fam over some pussy," Bailey said.

"Well, what the hell was wrong with Jeff?" Kya asked.

"Jeff loves pussy and wanted to have his cake and eat it too. Jeff isn't ready for monogamy, he thinks the more pussy the better. And another thing, Jeff is too afraid of commitment. Yeah, he might talk that talk but actions speak louder than words," Bailey said.

"And we've all seen what his actions are capable of. Jeff got to learn to love Jeff before he can think about loving someone else. He's not ready for marriage or commitment," Kya said.

"Whew, this is too much for me, I think I need to refresh my cocktail. Anyone want another drink?" Brandi asked.

"I think I'm going to need something stronger. How about Bailey making us some Grey Goose honey deuces?" Kya said.

"Sounds good to me. Let me gather the ingredients," Brandi said.

"Kya, do you think I'm a bartender?" Bailey asked.

"Nope. Your drinks taste better than ours," Kya said.

"Maybe because you don't know what you're doing. You add stuff that isn't supposed to be in the drink," Bailey said.

"Whatever."

"Kya, since you aren't doing anything, why don't you go and check on D?" Bailey said.

"And we'll relocate to the den," Brandi said.

"Fine, I'll be right back. I'm going to wake her ass up," Kya said.

When Kya got back downstairs, she joined the ladies in the den. "Deion is knocked out and knocked up. Say what you will, she's not tired she's fucking pregnant. Oh Lord, I wonder who the daddy is?"

"Kya, stop assuming, you know what they say about people that make assumptions," Bailey said.

"Well, call me an ass then, I've been called worse things than that. Anyhoo, I tried waking her up but she didn't budge."

"Stop saying that damn girl is pregnant. It just might be you," Bailey said.

"The hell you say, I'm celibate," Kya said.

As Bailey laughed hysterically, she looked at Kya and asked, "Since when, this morning?"

"Yeah, Kya, those fishes you dreamt about could be about you," Brandi said.

"Y'all got jokes I see. I know for a fact I'm not pregnant," Kya said.

As Bailey handed Kya her cocktail she said, "Drink this very, very slow. It could be detrimental to your well-being."

"Oh shit, you must have added a lot of Grey Goose," Kya said.

"Yes, I did. It might be best if you sip that drink. If your ass passes out you'll be spending the night in Fort Washington," Bailey said.

"How can you be so certain about the pregnant thing?" Brandi asked.

"I know the art of practicing safe sex," Kya said.

"Girl, whatever. When you say you're practicing safe sex that means you're not getting any. Or you're not doing stunts, tricks or using special effects!" Bailey yelled.

"Whatever. I don't have any problems getting the ding-ding," Kya said.

"So what are you guys going to do? Is the wedding still on or have you driven him completely crazy?" Brandi asked.

"Yes, the wedding is still on," Kya said.

"So when did this happen? I never got the full story," Brandi asked.

"My bad. At least I told you I was getting married. So, he stopped by my office one day, we kinda reconciled. This was the first time that we actually saw each since I acted out. We were going to dinner to talk things over, Steve came to my house and when I came downstairs, he popped the question. That's it."

"Dang, Ky, when did we get there? We should have celebrated," Brandi asked.

"I was going to tell you the full story of the reconciliation today. We've been talking about so much other shit that I haven't had a chance to," Kya said.

"Well, congrats and I'm happy for you," Brandi said.

"Ditto, sis. I'm glad you got your shit together and realized this is the man for you, it's about damn time," Bailey said.

"Yeah, I must admit I was being an asshole but it took for me to almost lose him for me to realize what I actually had right in front of me. He's not just a good man, he's a great man!"

"Yup, most people don't realize what they have until it's gone. When it's too late. Wow. Kya Mae is getting married," Brandi said.

Kya smiled from ear to ear, while waving her left hand, to show her four carat emerald-cut yellow diamond ring.

"Yes I am."

"But you almost ruined it again. Please don't do anything foolish with Jeff or any other man. So when's the big day?" Bailey asked.

"Ummmm, he wants to get married this year. He mentioned in the summer, maybe August," Kya said.

"That's only a couple of months away, are you serious?" Brandi asked.

"Yup."

"Why so soon? Don't you want to wait at least a year?" Bailey asked.

"For what?"

"To get to know each other a little better. Hell, live with each other for a little while and feel each other out. Test the water before you dive in head first. Do you think you know all that you need to about this man?" Bailey asked.

"Yup. But each day I'm sure I'll learn a little more. I've known people my whole life and still don't know everything about them. No matter how well you think you know someone they have a way of shocking the hell out of you."

"I concur," Brandi said.

"I thought I knew Jeff until he flipped the script on me," Kya said.

"That's what I'm saying. Get to know him more before you jump the broom," Bailey said.

"I know that this man genuinely loves me and is in love with me. I know that he isn't faking the funk and really wants all I have to offer him. I know that this is real. I know that I want to spend the rest of my life contributing to his happiness. That's all I need to know," Kya said.

"Okay, well, do you, my sista?" Bailey said.

"I thought you of all people would be happy for me."

"I am happy for you. I just want to make sure you're not jumping into things," Bailey said.

"The one thing I know about Ms. Kya is that she's not one of those women that deals with a man just to say she has one. That's not her way," Brandi said.

"True, very true. Well, if you're happy, my dear, then I'm happy for you. Your happiness is all I care about. I know that Steve is a great man. I ran into him that day and we had a conversation. I know he's not just playing with your heart and bullshitting you like Jeff did," Bailey said.

"I thought you said y'all didn't talk, it was just hi and bye," Kya said.

"The left hand doesn't always need to know what the right hand is doing. Besides, the convo was about you and him. There was no need for me to run to you and tell you a damn thing. I could tell the way he spoke about you that he was going to ask you to marry him," Bailey said.

"I see . . . with your secretive ass," Kya said jokingly.

"Anyhoo, it's great news and I definitely wish you two the best," Brandi said.

"Thank you and I look forward to spending the rest of my life with this man."

"I hope he knows what he's getting himself into," Bailey said.

"Excuse me, what does that mean?"

"You crazy as shit."

"Oh yes, he knows. I thought you were going to say that I wasn't good enough for him or something."

"Girl please, you are all that and a bag of chips."

"Oh goodness, please don't make her head any bigger than it already is," Brandi said.

"Never that," Kya said.

"We have a short period of time to plan this shindig for the diva," Bailey said.

"Yes, ma'am," Kya said.

"A couple of months is enough time to plan this wedding. We need to get started as soon as possible," Brandi said.

"Yeah, but we have a lot to do," Bailey said.

"Excuse me, ladies, hold your horses. We want a small, intimate wedding, very small. Only close relatives and friends."

"So that means at least two hundred people?" Brandi asked.

"Hell, no, less than a hundred. We don't want a big wedding. Something small and elegant."

"Why? Not you," Bailey said.

"Yes me. Besides, I don't need my wedding to be a show, that's not what that day is all about. In all actuality, no one will remember the details of that day but him and me. More importantly, no one really needs to be there but the two of us."

"Aww, my little sis has grown up overnight. Bitch, you really have changed," Bailey said.

"If you want different results you have to do things differently. And it all starts with your thinking. Isn't that what you told me?" Kya asked.

"Yes, ma'am, you got it."

"I'm glad God has put this man in your life and from what I know, he truly loves you," Brandi said.

"All I know is that we have to start planning . . . now! I can put a great event together but I normally have a little more time to work with," Bailey said.

"No worries, that's already taken care of," Kya said.

"Huh? You just got engaged and everything's done?" Bailey asked.

"We're having a destination wedding and the resort handles everything."

"Oh really, going somewhere tropical?"

"Nope. Vegas baby!"

"Kya, you're not going to have a traditional church ceremony? Your mom is going to be pissed with you," Brandi said.

"No, ma'am. When have you known me to do anything traditional? There is nothing traditional about me."

"How does your mom feel about this?" Brandi asked.

"I haven't asked her. Besides, this doesn't have anything to do with my mom. It's our wedding day and we're doing what we want. It's not about what everyone else wants. I don't get down like that. And you definitely know that I don't do stuff because of what other people want."

"I guess you have a point but I just thought you'd want a traditional day," Brandi said.

"Nope."

"What resort in Vegas are you talking about?" Bailey asked.

"The Wynn or the Venetian, I'm leaning towards the Wynn. I stayed there recently and love it."

"Nice. Nice and very expensive," Bailey said.

"Girl, yes, so that's why we're having a small ceremony and reception. We realize that some people that we want to attend may not be able to because of finances. Therefore, we'll assist them financially."

"You shouldn't have to do that. If they really want to be a part of your big day then they'll do what they got to," Brandi said.

"No, but times are hard and everyone don't have money out the ass."

"True," Bailey said.

"Well, what do you need for us to do?" Brandi asked.

"We have to go dress and accessory shopping and that's it. Everything else is taken care of."

"Wow, seems like easy planning to me," Bailey said.

"It is, and I'm glad that I won't have a whole lot to do."

"Girl, I'm so happy for you," Bailey said.

"Thank you. It feels like I'm dreaming or something. I've been waiting for a long time for this to happen."

"See, all you had to do was clear the clutter out of your life," Bailey said.

"Ain't that the damn truth," Kya said.

"When Jeff finds out he's going to shit bricks," Bailey said.

"He already know. I told him. I don't know why, he couldn't recognize what he had. Oh well, his loss."

"Well, I hope you'll at least let us give you an engagement party," Brandi said.

"I sure will."

"Everything's falling in place for you," Bailey said.

"Yes it is, but I have a little bad news."

"Oh goodness, you just had to ruin the moment. What's the problem?" Bailey asked.

"We might be moving."

"Okay, so what's bad about that?" Brandi asked.

"Unfortunately, he told me that he might be getting a promotion."

"Please tell me why that's a bad thing," Bailey said.

"If he gets this promotion then we'd be moving to New York. That's why it's a bad thing. I'll have to leave my girls."

"Sweetie, that's not so bad. The last time I checked, US Airways and Amtrak were still in business. We'll just have to fly back and forth to see one another or take the train. I'm sure we'll talk on the phone a whole hell of a lot," Bailey said.

"I guess but I'm not used to not seeing y'all. That might be hard for me to grasp."

"Sweetie, it'll be fine. New York isn't that far away. You make it seem like you'd have to move to the other side of the world," Brandi said.

"We'll make it work," Bailey said.

"I guess we'll all accumulate a lot of frequent flyer miles," Brandi said.

"You might be right," Kya said.

"When will Steve know if he got the job?" Bailey asked.

"Within the next couple of weeks. They're still in the interview process."

"Okay, we'll cross that bridge when we come to it. It's nothing to be stressed or worked up about. It's a good thing," Bailey said.

"Yeah it is, but New York, it's high as hell there."

"Yeah I know, but you'll be fine."

"What are you going to do about your business?" Brandi asked.

"I'll open another location in New York and come back to DC periodically. I just have to make sure that I hire the right person to oversee everything."

"Right. You don't want just anybody running the show. Not everyone is capable of running a business. It will also have to be someone that you trust."

"I know."

"All jokes aside, I'm really happy that you and Steve are back together and you're getting married. Maybe this time you won't screw it up. Even though you almost did," Bailey said.

"You don't have to worry about that. I'm not going to lose him again."

"You never know what you have until it's gone."

"That's definitely a true statement. Steve is going to be my husband. I like the way that sounds."

"I know that's right, claim that man. As long as you know how to act this time," Brandi said.

"Don't keep making it seem like I'm a bad person."

"We never said that you were a bad person. You're just a little crazy that's all," Bailey said jokingly.

"Are you bringing him to the housewarming party?" Brandi asked.

"If y'all act right I'll think about it."

"You know you're pressed to bring your man and show him off," Bailey said.

"I sure as hell am. I's got me a good man, girl, I don't know how to act."

"Just act like you got some damn sense this time and don't do anything stupid," Brandi said.

"Girlfriend, you don't have to worry about me. I've gotten myself together and made significant changes to self."

"I've noticed. I really thought maybe you were sick or something because you've been different lately. That smart-ass mouth of yours has toned down tremendously," Bailey said.

"I'm trying to do better."

"Keep up the good work."

"Brandi, you make it sound like I'm a student or something." Kya chuckled. "You don't tell a grown-ass woman to keep up the good work. What the hell?"

"Well, what am I supposed to say? I'm trying to encourage you to keep doing whatever you're doing," Brandi said.

"Then you say exactly what you just said. That would suffice."

Brandi stood and said, "You're right, I did sound like a teacher. My bad. How's this? Keep doing what you're doing, girl. Whatever changes you're making are definitely working in your favor."

"I like, I like," Kya said.

"Okay, I'm convinced both of y'all are crazy as bedbugs," Bailey said.

"Uh, should someone go and check on D again? She's been asleep for a while," Brandi asked.

"She's okay, probably just tired that's all," Bailey said.

"I bet she is."

"Uh-oh, the old Kya returns," Bailey said.

"What? I'm just saying I bet she is tired. It's not easy to have fuckfests all the time without getting proper rest. That's all."

"Girl, cut it out. She's dealing with a lot of BS at work these days," Bailey said.

"That's what happens when you screw all the men in the office," Kya said.

"No, that's not it. They're trying to fire her but don't really have grounds to do so."

"Whatever. She could have avoided the unnecessary drama if she'd kept her legs closed," Kya said.

"So, Brandi, I'm not talking to Kya until she gets herself together. She's on a time out," Bailey said.

"Whatever," Kya said.

"Anyway, a new firm took over her company and of course they brought their own staff. They're trying to put one of their staff in D's position," Bailey said.

"So that means they're going to promote her, right?" Brandi asked.

"Actually, it would be more like a demotion," Bailey said.

"Get the hell outta here. They can't do that," Kya said.

"You're right but it doesn't stop them from trying," Bailey said.

"That's just wrong," Brandi said.

"Yeah, I know. D's trying to hold on and fight for her position."

"She could always go to another firm. Despite how I act, I do care about the damn girl. She shouldn't have to put up with that bullshit. I'd say the hell with them, get a nice severance package, and keep it moving," Kya said.

"But she worked really hard to get to where she is," Brandi said.

"When I spoke to her the other day, it sounded like she was going to leave. I think she's currently researching and weighing the pros and cons of starting her own firm," Bailey said.

"I've been telling her that for a while. I think that would be a great decision. Probably the best one that she's ever made," Kya said.

"Who knows what she's going to do? The choice is totally up to her," Bailey said.

Brandi got up and said, "I'm going to go and check on her. Do you ladies need anything while I'm up?"

"No, I'm good," Bailey said.

"More Tostitos and a bottle of water. Thank you, ma'am," Kya said.

As Brandi approached the threshold of the living room, Deion entered.

"What did I miss?" Deion asked.

"Well, well, well, if it isn't the black Sleeping Beauty. It's about time you got the hell up. We were going to leave your ass right here," Kya said.

"You missed a whole hell of a lot. Too much to backtrack," Bailey said.

"Y'all couldn't save all the juicy stuff until I got up? I was only taking a cat nap."

"Girl please, that was longer than a cat nap. Are you well rested and do you feel better?" Kya asked.

"Yes, ma'am. It felt like my body was glued to that damn bed. I don't even sleep like that at home."

"You need to get more rest," Bailey said.

"I know."

"Let me give you a quick recap. My husband is cheating on me. Kya believes you're pregnant. Kya and Steve are getting married in Vegas this summer. That's all," Bailey said.

"Well damn! That's a lot. Wait, did you say Noah's cheating?" Deion asked.

"Yup, but the story's too long to get into."

"Oh my goodness, I'm sorry to hear that," Deion said.

"Would you like a cocktail?" Brandi asked.

"Yes I would. Whatever we're drinking, make mine a double."

"Bailey made Grey Goose honey deuces," Brandi said.

"Okay, let me sit down and gather myself. I think what you said went over my head."

"Okay, I'll repeat it for you but slow this time. Kya and Steve are getting married. You got that part?" Bailey asked.

"Yes, I already knew that. Congratulations, Kya."

"Thanks."

"Noah is cheating on me."

"Stop playing," Deion said.

"I'm not playing."

"Why the hell are you so fucking calm?" Deion asked.

"Ummmm, D, how would you like for me to act?"

"I don't know but you're too calm."

"That's the same thing I said," Brandi replied.

"Am I supposed to be running around crying, screaming and hollering?" Bailey asked.

"No, that's not what I'm saying. You just appear to be calmer than most people in this situation, that's all I was saying," Deion said.

"Because you're so calm, I wonder what you're thinking," Kya said.

"The only thing I'm thinking about is my next move."

"What's that supposed to mean?" Brandi asked.

"If I leave or stay."

"Wow, I can't believe this," Deion said.

"Well, believe it. If Bailey has her mind set, there's nothing the three of us can do to persuade her. Hopefully you'll give Noah another chance," Kya said.

"I don't know what I'm going to do yet. But I'm sure I'll figure it out soon," Bailey said.

"Please don't make any illogical decisions," Deion said.

"Don't just think about the bad stuff either, think of the good as well," Kya said.

"Most definitely. Girl, I got this and will be fine," Bailey said.

"No matter what, you never let them see you sweat do you?" Deion asked.

"Of course not. Girl, no stress and no worries, I'm good."

"Are you sure?" Kya asked.

"Yes, ma'am. Y'all better be worried about Noah and not me."

"Okay, just checking," Kya said.

"Kya, I found Mr. Right a long time ago. He provides all of my needs, comforts me, protects me, heals me, loves me unconditionally, He's my companion and my counselor. I can talk to Him about everything and He's always there when I need Him. His name is Jesus. I'm grateful, blessed and I thank Him for all that he's done, all he's doing and everything he has in store for me," Bailey said.

"Preach, sister," Brandi said.

"I'm just saying, every time something bad happens that's not an excuse to throw in the towel. Get up, dust your ass off and keep it moving. Life goes on, my dear," Bailey said.

"I know, but still. Sometimes things are hard to deal with," Deion said.

"I agree. As long as we have breath in our bodies we will always go through something. We all will face different trials throughout our lives and we all are faced with making decisions. What I have learned is no matter how big or tedious the trial or decision is, you have to include God in it all. There is no way humanly possible that we can or will make it without Him, so there's no need to try," Bailey said.

"So, so true!" Brandi shouted.

"All we have to do is put Him first and watch the mountains being removed, stumbling blocks turned into stepping stones and doors and opportunities you didn't know were there being opened," Kya said.

"If you noticed, I don't react to the BS and drama like I used to, I put it all in His hands and leave it there. I know I'm going to be okay. I might hurt for a while but I'll get over it. Noah has more to lose than I do."

"You're right but I'm hoping by the grace of God that everything will work out between the two of you," Brandi said.

"If not, life goes on," Kya said.

"When a person walks out of your life, the best thing you can do is to let them go. That means your season together is over and they didn't value you anyway. Meanwhile, you have to press forward and move on. Embrace being single, your womanhood and make yourself happy. Do you, and enjoy life because it will go on," Bailey said.

"One person's trash is another person's treasure," Kya said.

"My current mood is that I'm happy, feeling fabulous, I'm too blessed to be stressed, and too anointed to be disappointed," Bailey said.

Brandi reached over and gave Bailey a high-five, then said, "Girl, you're going to make me start shouting up in here."

"And you look good too. You look like there's nothing wrong and everything's all good," Deion said.

"Everything *is* all good," Bailey said.

"Just because you're with someone that doesn't mean they're the person that you're supposed to be with. There's a season for everything," Kya said.

"Don't get me wrong, I love my husband with all my heart but if he doesn't realize what he risks losing, then that's his problem not mine," Bailey said.

"It's never too late to realize what's important in your life and fight for it," Deion said.

"I agree wholeheartedly but I'm going to put this in God's hands," Bailey said.

"That's the best thing you can do," Brandi said.

"Okay, so I'm definitely awake now, what was the third thing that you said?" Deion asked.

"Oh, Kya thinks you're pregnant," Bailey said.

"Oh goodness! Here we go with this bullshit again. Kya, please stop saying I'm pregnant. You better hope like hell that I'm not pregnant," Deion said.

"Why would your potential pregnancy affect me? It's not mine," Kya said.

"Because if I'm pregnant I'm dropping the baby off at your house," Deion said.

"No thanks, I already have my baby. One baby is enough for now, I'm not trying to have another one no time soon."

"I really can't believe that Noah of all people is cheating on you," Deion said.

"Well, believe it. Now, moving on to the next topic. I really don't want to spend the next couple of hours listening to why y'all think I should stay," Bailey said.

For several seconds the room became uncomfortably quiet and no one uttered a single word.

As Kya got up to fix another drink she looked at Deion and asked, "Hey D, can I ask you a question?"

"I don't know, it depends, Kya, I'm not really in the mood for your BS today," Deion said.

"I guess that means yes," Kya said.

"If it's going to be something that pisses me off then please don't go there," Deion said.

"Now D, come on. How am I supposed to know if a simple question will piss you off or not? There's only one way for me to know and that's to ask."

"What, Kya, what's the question?"

"Do you ever feel bad when you fuck married men? Do you feel remorseful and have regrets?"

"What?" Deion asked.

"Do you ever feel bad when you fuck a married man?" Kya repeated.

"Kya, please don't go there," Bailey said.

"Go where? It's a simple question," Kya said.

"Why are you putting me in this shit? What does Noah's cheating have to do with me? What are you getting at?" Deion asked.

"How else would I know the answer to a question if I don't ask? Or do you have a 'don't ask and don't tell' policy going on?" Kya asked.

"I'm not going to justify that with a response. This isn't about me," Deion said.

"I could make the assumption that you don't care. To you it doesn't matter if he's married, unattached, or whatever. The only thing you require from any man is that he has a dick," Kya said.

"I think that comment was totally unnecessary," Brandi said.

"All of what she just said was totally unnecessary," Bailey said.

"Let's just keep it real. Our girl's marriage will possibly end because her man cheated. You're so concerned about her and have all this empathy for their marriage," Kya said.

"So, what's your point, Kya?" Deion asked.

"My point is I don't understand how you can be so empathetic with them when in reality you ruin marriages or relationships. Isn't that really being a hypocrite?" Kya asked.

Deion looked at Kya and shook her head.

"You really don't have to answer or respond to that, D. No one in here is trying to make you feel bad or put you on the spot," Bailey said.

"No, I'm going to respond," Deion said.

"Okay, I'm waiting. I really think you're being a hypocrite," Kya said.

"When I meet men it's not like I set out to meet married men only. If they don't value and respect what they have at home then why should I?" Deion asked.

"In other words, you don't care. That makes you as guilty as they are," Kya said.

"That's not what I'm saying."

"Then what are you saying?" Kya asked.

"Don't penalize me for the choice that somebody else has made," Deion said.

"That doesn't even sound right. Again, you're just as guilty as they are. You, too, are making irresponsible choices, it's not just the man, it's you too, my dear. I don't get what part of that you don't understand."

"Then I guess it's not for you to understand," Deion said.

"Maybe it's not. But I understand that you need help."

"Help? What the hell do I need help for? Because I love sex?" Deion asked.

"I think you're a nymphomaniac," Kya said.

"What the hell?" Deion asked.

"Or you could possibly have a high sex drive. Are you taking that Viagra for women?" Kya asked.

"Kya, go to hell," Deion said.

"Seriously Kya, that's enough," Bailey said.

"We talk about any and everything but when I mention her sex problem nobody wants to touch that topic," Kya said.

"You're right, we do. But maybe this isn't a topic Deion would like to discuss. Just leave it alone," Bailey said.

"The hell you say! That's the problem, we just sit back and don't say shit. And that's not okay."

"Kya, I'd appreciate it if you mind your own business. And you always have *a lot* to say about my life. My sex life doesn't have shit to do with you. Nor does it affect your life," Deion said.

"But that's where you're wrong because it does affect us. If I didn't give a shit about you then I wouldn't say a word. I don't know what type of friends you've had in the past but we're not them," Kya said.

"Deion, in Kya's defense I understand where she's coming from. However, I believe her candor is a little off-track. She means well, and I understand you being defensive, but just hear us out," Bailey said.

"So I guess you feel the same way?" Deion asked.

"Yeah, I do," Bailey responded.

Deion turned to Brandi and asked, "So you're in this too?"

Brandi softly replied, "Yes."

"Ain't this some shit. The whole time I thought we were here to visit Brandi in her new house and all along y'all trying to run some intervention bullshit on me?" Deion asked.

"In all actuality we did come here to visit Brandi and have brunch. As much as you want to believe it, we didn't set this up on your account," Bailey said.

"Because you're being so defensive you really don't hear anything that we say. Your guard is up and I get that. But, sweetie, you need to take heed of what we're saying. We would never tell you anything to hurt you," Kya said.

"Kya, first of all look at how you come at me about this bullshit. I don't feel like I need to justify my sexual appetite to you or anyone else," Deion said.

"No you don't, but when your sexual behavior turns to self-destructive behavior then it's definitely a problem," Bailey said.

"We've watched your self-destructive behavior for months now. I think it's time for you to take control of the situation and get some help. I'd hate for you to decide to get help after you find out you have a disease or something. Then it's going to be too late," Kya said.

"Kya, like I told you before, I don't need help because I like to fuck. What type of shit is that?"

"I appreciate that you're not going to get help until you realize you have a problem," Kya said.

"I don't need help. What black person you know goes to a therapist because they like to fuck? Where do they do that?" Deion asked.

"They go when they have a sexual addiction, that's when," Kya said.

"That's them but I don't need to talk or see a damn psychologist because I like sex."

"There's nothing wrong with liking sex or having sex, that's not an issue. What bothers and concerns me is that you engage in risqué sexual behavior with numerous partners. That's my issue."

"Who died and made you an expert on sexual addictions? I love dick! So what?"

"I'm not an expert but I've been doing some research on sexual addictions in women. You have all of the symptoms, my dear," Kya said.

"Whatever you say, Kya. I'm really trying not to hear this BS right now."

"D, if you're not willing to listen to what we have to say at the very least, then it's useless. There's no need for us to have this conversation," Bailey said.

"I don't want to have this conversation and I'm done talking about it," Deion said.

"Are you serious, D, you can't listen to what we have to say?" Kya asked.

"Let me reiterate just in case you missed something. I don't want to talk about this crap anymore. And I'm not willing to listen to anything that you have to say to me."

Kya got up from the sofa and walked over to Deion, stood in front of her and asked, "Is that how you really feel?"

"Yes, that's how I really feel so leave the shit alone."

"Kya, it's Deion's life, just leave it alone and I guess we should mind our business," Brandi said.

"It's hard to mind your business when someone constantly involves you in their business," Kya said.

"I understand that but leave it alone. If she doesn't want to discuss it just let it be. Damn!" Bailey said.

"When you care about your friends you want the best for them. What type of friend would I be if I saw a friend in need and stood on the sideline and did nothing?" Kya asked.

"I understand where you're coming from but what can we do?" Bailey asked.

"Leave it alone and mind our business like she asked. That's what we can do," Brandi said.

"Y'all do what you want but I won't leave it alone. I can't because I care," Kya said.

"You don't have anything else to do but worry about who I'm fucking?" Deion asked.

"Excuse me?" Kya asked.

"Why the hell are you so worried about what the hell I do?" Deion asked.

"Because I'm your friend that's why."

"Whatever, you're full of shit. You walk around as if you're holier than thou and don't have skeletons in your closet," Deion said.

"Oh no, my dear, you got it all wrong. I have issues and problems just like everyone else. I never act as if I'm holier than thou because I know I'm far from being perfect. For the record, I'm nothing like I used to be. I've made significant changes in my life. And guess what, sweetie, I got a shitload of skeletons just like everyone else—we all have a past. I don't hide a damn thing and I'm very open with my shit," Kya said.

"I'm single, having fun, and doing me," Deion said.

"It's okay to do you. However, it's the way that you're going about things, that's what scares the hell out of me. I dread getting a phone call informing me that something's happened to you. You invite these people into your home and don't know anything about them. Not only is that scary but it's dangerous too," Kya said.

"I'm doing what makes me happy."

"You can honestly say that you're happy?" Bailey asked.

"Yes, I'm happy. Why is that so hard to believe?"

"It's not," Bailey said.

"So, y'all can stop lecturing me and stressing over nothing. I'm good."

"That's easier said than done. I worry about the people I care about. That's what I do and you know this," Kya said.

"Why don't you stick to one man and let the others go?" Brandi asked.

"When I think I've found the right one then I'll leave the others alone."

"There are some nice guys that go to my church," Brandi said.

"Hell, no. Those are the worst ones," Deion said.

"That's not true, they aren't the worst ones."

"Brandi, no harm intended but you haven't dated or dealt with enough men to know how they actually are," Deion said.

"I could hook you up with someone really nice. He's never been married, no children, great job and handsome," Brandi said.

"No, thank you."

"Why not?"

"Because I don't like blind dates. I'd rather meet guys on my own terms."

"That doesn't make a lot of sense to me but okay. I just thought I'd help," Brandi said.

"Thanks but no thanks, I'm good," Deion said.

"When's the last time you had a real date and not just a meet and fuck?" Kya asked.

"Why is that your business?" Deion asked.

"Why are you so goddamn secretive?" Kya asked.

"If you must know, I went on a date the other night."

"No, bitch, a real date?"

"Yes, a real date."

"I find that hard to believe. Do tell."

"But why do you need to know every single detail of my life?"

"Why do you find it necessary to evade every question I ask?"

"Because it's not your business," Deion said.

"Can you tell us about your date, please?" Kya asked.

"Sure, no problem. What is it that you have to know?" Deion asked.

"I just want to know about your date."

"On my way home from work the other night I met this guy on the train. We chatted for a while and exchanged telephone numbers. He then asked me what my plans were for the night. He asked me if I wanted to go to dinner but I declined."

"You declined. Really?" Kya asked.

"Yes. Can I finish?"

"Sure go ahead."

"So we chatted and texted throughout the week. Because the both of us are extremely busy with work we had major schedule conflicts. Within the second week of all of the texting and chatting we finally set up a time to meet."

"Okay and then what?"

"The day before we were going to hook up I ran into him on the train. We talked and he asked if I wanted to go get a drink. I told him I'd had a long day and just wanted to go home and relax. He then asked if I wanted to go with him to pick up his car and he could take me home."

"So he wanted you to ride the train with him, pick up his car and then take you home? Wouldn't you get home quicker if you just took the train all the way?" Kya asked.

"I think he wanted to spend some time with me and get to know more about me. So I let him take me home."

"Bad move, but okay, finish."

"Before we got to my house he begged me if we could stop and have at least one drink. So I said okay."

"Okay, it sounds like you had a real date indeed."

"We stopped, had a couple of drinks, talked and then he took me home."

"So, when are you going to see him again, is this man single, unattached, or what? What's this guy's story?" Kya asked.

"He said that he wasn't married and was single."

"Overall, how would you rate your date? Did things end on a good note?" Bailey asked.

"I'd say that the date went fairly well. We talked about everything and we even agreed that we'd still go out to dinner the following day."

"Okay, sounds good. What's his name?" Brandi asked.

"Mike.

"Does Mike have a last name?" Kya asked.

"I didn't get that," Deion said.

"How could you go out to dinner with someone and not even get his last name? What did you discuss for hours?" Kya asked.

"Life, work, stuff like that."

"Uh huh, I see," Kya said.

"What?"

"Oh nothing."

"Spare the sarcasm."

"I'm not being sarcastic. One day you'll realize that I had to show you all of this tough love. It's for your own benefit," Kya said jokingly.

"Sure, Kya. Whatever you say."

"How did your second date go? What was the chemistry like and is this someone that you can see yourself being with?" Brandi asked.

"Brandi, it was only drinks. There was no love connection. We were just kicking it," Deion said.

"Sometimes you know right away if someone's worth your time or not," Brandi said.

"Wait, just drinks, I thought you went out to dinner the following night?" Bailey asked.

"It never happened," Deion said.

"It never happened, why not?" Kya asked.

"I don't know, I tried calling him and texting him earlier that day but he didn't reply. I even sent him a message on Facebook and he still hasn't responded."

"He's married," Kya said.

"No, he's not."

"Did the two of you talk a lot or did you do more texting?" Kya asked.

"Because we both were so busy we did more texting."

"Yup, he's married."

"I'm just going by what he said. I don't know what happened. Maybe he wasn't interested after all."

"That night that you had drinks that was it?" Kya asked.

"What are you getting at now?" Bailey asked.

"Can you let Deion answer?" Kya asked. "Y'all were chitchatting and texting, had drinks then the communication stopped. Naw, something isn't right with that picture."

"We had drinks, talked and he took me home. That's it."

"Oh, okay, well as long as you had a great time that's all that matters," Bailey said.

"Yeah, I did," Deion said.

"What does he do?" Bailey asked.

"He's a lawyer."

"That's good. Maybe he's just overloaded with work and hasn't had a chance to call you," Brandi said.

"Brandi, it takes a split second to send a text or make a phone call. He could have acknowledged your calls and texts at the very least," Kya said.

"I don't know. It's not like I was looking for a relationship with him, it was just something to do."

"From the sounds of things neither is he. Who paid for the drinks?" Kya asked.

"I did. Why does that matter?"

"He asked you out so he should have paid, that's common etiquette."

"He said he left his wallet at the office."

"And he didn't realize that until the check came? How did he pay for the metro?" Brandi asked.

"I guess he had his smart trip card. I don't know, I didn't ask."

"So you took the train to his car, went out for drinks and he took you home. Since then no form of communication whatsoever, that's different," Bailey said.

"I'm really interested in knowing what you talked about. Do you think you said something that turned him off?" Bailey asked.

"We'd been talking for a little over a week. I don't think I said anything to turn him off. Really, it's not that serious."

"Did you say something to him that first night on the train or did he say something to you?" Kya asked.

"He gave me a compliment and I said thank you. From there we just had a generic conversation. Oh, I see what you guys are doing. You're picking me to see if I fucked him. You've been bluntly asking whatever you want, why is now so different? If you're trying to find out if I fucked him the answer is yes. I fucked him and I also gave him a little head too and it was great."

"Oh, my. Were you drunk?" Brandi asked.

"Why do people insist on using alcohol as a justification to do and say whatever you want? That's bullshit," Kya said.

"No I wasn't drunk, I did it because I wanted to."

"You know what, I'm not saying anything else. For the first time in my life I'm not saying another damn word. I'm going to close my mouth the same way you should close your legs," Kya said.

"Kya, that wasn't nice. That was a low blow," Bailey said.

"What the fuck ever. Maybe that's a part of the problem. Everybody keeps tip-toeing around Deion and her bullshit. It's as clear as the night is long, she has a problem."

"Anyway, as I was saying. I wasn't drunk but I was a little tipsy and I was feeling good. He was taking me home and while he was driving he put his hand on my leg. The next thing I know he was playing with my va-jj. At first I was shocked but I started enjoying every minute of it. He must have had magic fingers or that magic touch."

"Why do you say that?" Brandi said.

"Because shortly after he started playing with me and fingering the va-jj, I came."

"After that he pulled over and y'all had sex on the side of the road?" Bailey asked.

"Nope. After he finished with the va-jj, I then leaned over and unbuttoned his pants. Then I started giving him some head as he drove. After we got to my house I invited him up but he said he couldn't stay."

"Of course he couldn't, you'd already sucked him off. Why would there be a need to stay?" Kya asked.

"We got to my house, pulled into the garage, he opened my door and after I got out of the car. I kissed him on the cheek and told him I had a great time and said goodnight."

"Uh huh, then what?" Kya asked.

"We started kissing and I honestly had no idea what was going to happen next, or at least I didn't plan on it."

"Plan on what? What did you do, what happened?" Bailey asked.

"After I said goodnight he grabbed my hand, put it on his dick and said it doesn't have to end now. I was a little confused because he just told me that he couldn't stay. He started kissing me again. I said let's go upstairs but he kept saying he couldn't. The next thing I know he bent me over the hood of the car, moved my thong to the side and started fucking me."

"That's rape!" Brandi yelled.

"No it wasn't. It was definitely consensual," Deion said.

"How is that not rape?" Bailey asked.

"Because I wanted it, I wanted all of what he gave me. I didn't say no, stop or don't do that. I wanted it and I enjoyed it."

"Wow! That's a bit much. I hate to ask this question. Did you?" Bailey asked.

"Did I what? Did I use a condom? No, we didn't use a condom before you ask. I didn't know what was going to happen and it's not like I carry a travel pack of rubbers around."

"You just ought to," Kya said.

"Deion, it's obvious that you need to keep condoms in your purse, car, briefcase, *and* in your office," Bailey said.

"Lord, please help this girl. Forgive her because she knows not what she does," Brandi said.

"You don't need to pray for me, Brandi, I know exactly what I'm doing. I wanted to fuck him and that's what I did. I don't understand why y'all act like there's something wrong with what I do."

"I don't even know what to say to you anymore. Clearly, you don't hear shit that we have to say to you. You definitely don't understand what we're getting at so keep doing what you do. I don't have shit else to say about the situation," Kya said.

"Oh my, you don't have anything to say? Really, that's nice to know," Deion said.

"Come on, D, you need to raise your morals, values and self-respect for yourself. You're going to keep attracting the same type of man if you don't," Bailey said.

"That's not true," Deion said.

"Why isn't it?" Brandi asked.

"You deserve better than this. You can't keep having casual sex as if it's okay. I can see if you were fucking the same man but you're out there spreading your joy juice around like it's nothing. It's the twenty-first century and AIDS is taking all prisoners," Bailey said.

"You're just nasty!" Kya shouted. "It's hoes like you that give us good ones a bad rap."

"Hoes like me? The last time I checked, your backyard wasn't completely clean. Your shit stinks too. Ho!" Deion shouted.

"D, I've never done any nasty shit like that. You're fucking around and abusing your body like it's nothing. Your body is your temple and you need to take better care of it. Stop giving your pussy to every man that says hello or gives you a compliment," Kya said.

"There are still some good men out there but you need to give them a chance, my dear," Bailey said.

"You really want me to believe that a good man is going to come along and snatch me up? Get the fuck out of here with that. The last one that I thought was good beat my ass from sun up to sun down. Yeah, in the beginning I thought he was a good man and look what happened," Deion said.

"Because you were in a bad marriage don't make all men the bad guy. Don't penalize them for one man's behavior. They're not all your ex-husband. And you need to stop carrying that baggage around. Let that shit go, girl, that's the only way you're going to be able to move on," Bailey said.

"It doesn't take a rocket scientist to figure out why Mr. So and So isn't calling you back," Kya said.

"D, he blocked your number after he got what he wanted," Brandi said.

"Who does that? Why would he?" Deion asked.

"Ummmm, maybe because he got all he wanted from you that night and he doesn't want to be bothered with you anymore," Kya said.

"I don't think that's it," Deion said.

"D, stop being so goddamn gullible. Damn, you piss me off with that dumb shit!" Bailey yelled.

"Excuse me?" Deion asked.

"Let's just be real about this whole situation. You didn't even know this man. No wonder he's not calling you back. You paid for d and d," Bailey said.

"What's d and d?" Deion asked.

"Drinks and dick," Bailey said.

"What the fuck is wrong with you? Are you suicidal? Are you trying to kill yourself? Do you have a death wish or something? What's the problem, Deion?" Kya asked.

"D, you just sat here and told us that story as if we should be praising you or something. It's almost as if you expect us to be happy about what you just told us. Aside from what Kya's saying, sweetie you really do need help. If you won't talk to us then you need to talk to someone professional," Bailey said. "Every day the shit that you do becomes more and more lewd."

"I don't get it and I don't understand," Brandi said.

"It's not for you to understand. I don't need any of you in my business. Whatever I do with my life and my body is my choice. I'm a grown-ass woman and I don't need y'all for shit. If you have a problem with my lifestyle you have two options. Mind your own business or stay the hell out of my life and in your own lane," Deion said.

"You know what, you're right. It's your life and you do whatever you want with it. If you want to be a freak nasty bitch, that's your choice," Kya said.

"Fuck you, Kya," Deion yelled.

"But you keep putting us all up in your damn business so it's hard to stay out of it. I've expressed my concerns with your behavior several times. You chose to ignore all the signs that you need help. If you want us to stop and out of your life, the choice is yours. It's like you're asking us to watch you commit suicide. I can't condone that and I'm not going to sit back and watch it either," Bailey said.

"You really want us to sit around and keep watching you slowly kill yourself? Because that's what you're doing. She's not listening and she's acting like we're the ones hurting her. She's not going to realize she needs help until something bad happens. She's going to run across the wrong psycho crazy man or she's going to get something she can't get rid of. Then it just might be too late to seek help," Kya said.

"I think y'all being a little dramatic and overreacting. It's really not that serious," Deion said.

"I don't understand how you can say it's not that serious. It is serious but you just don't get it," Bailey said.

"Please leave me alone about this bullshit," Deion said.

"Do as you wish. You want us to mind our business then that's what I'm going to do," Kya said.

"Wait a minute. I think we need to discuss this further. We're friends, we're family and we can't turn our back on her now. So what if she's not listening to what we have to say, she still needs us," Brandi said.

"Sweetie, there's nothing to discuss. Deion made it perfectly clear that she wants us out of her business or her life. I guess whichever one we decide, she's okay with it one way or another," Bailey said.

"Maybe we all need to calm down and tackle this differently. No yelling, cursing or screaming. Let's just talk this out," Brandi said.

"I don't have shit else to say," Deion said.

"We were supposed to have a good time and I don't want anyone leaving angry or with ill feelings," Brandi said.

"I'm not, I'm good," Deion said.

"Deion, you get one life to live so do whatever makes you happy. I'm going to stay out of your business and mind mine," Kya said.

As Bailey shook her head, she looked at Kya and said, "Wow, that'll be a first."

"Listen ladies, I couldn't have asked for a better group of friends. When you hurt, I hurt. I love y'all and I care about y'all. I just want you to have the happiness you all deserve," Bailey said.

"Ditto," Kya said.

"And whatever choices you make, I'm still going to be your friend regardless. At the end of the day, it's not for me to be judgmental about what you do," Bailey said.

"That all sounds good but I don't appreciate the shit y'all say," Deion said.

"Because we care about your well-being," Brandi said.

"What I have learned is that there is always going to be someone who does not approve, those are the people that always have something negative to say, the pessimists. It could be about your appearance, lifestyle, friends, spouse or significant other. It seems like no matter what you do, they never shut up," Deion said.

"Friendships are no different from relationships, you have to work at them. We all have our own opinions and will have disagreements. It's my expectation that none of us will ever turn our backs on one another," Brandi said.

"The definition of a friend, according to *Webster's Dictionary,* is one attached to another by affection or esteem, one that is not hostile but a favored companion. My definition of a friend is all of that and then some. This person also knows all about you, your issues and flaws, the good and the bad, and is still your friend regardless," Bailey said.

"True," Kya said.

"I'd love to sit here and have this conversation, but I have to go," Bailey said.

"I know, but before we go, can we do one thing?" Kya asked.

"What's that?" Deion asked.

"We're all approaching new chapters in our lives as well as new beginnings. Let's leave these issues, baggage and drama behind. Let's leave all the bullshit and start anew," Kya said.

"After all that's been said today, do you really think none of this will come back up?" Bailey asked.

"It probably will but we can tackle it differently. I love y'all and I don't want any bad feelings among us," Kya said.

"Okay, done. I can do that," Bailey said.

"Me too," Brandi said.

"Fine, whatever," Deion said.

"Let's leave the past behind us and look forward to the future with a fresh start. We all have a lot on our plates and things to do. There's no need to be tied down with unnecessary crap," Kya said.

"Before someone says anything else that they might regret or gets too pissed, I really have to go," Bailey said.

"I thought you were going to take care of that situation tonight?" Kya asked.

"No, I asked him to be home by 4 p.m. I knew we'd be here all day. But I really need to go and handle this situation with Noah."

"Are you up for it?" Brandi asked.

"Of course I am. There's no need to put it off any longer."

"I just want to make sure you're okay."

"I'm good," Bailey said.

"Are you sure?" Kya asked.

"Yes ma'am, trust me I'm good. If I wasn't, you'd know. Let me say this, I know sometimes I'm frank and I very rarely bite my tongue. I can be like a mother hen and a little overbearing but that's because I care," Bailey said.

"Don't you mean you're frank, overbearing and a mother hen *all* of the damn time?" Kya said.

"You always have something to say," Bailey said.

"I appreciate the way you are, don't ever change. I darn sure don't need a friend that's not frank and honest. I appreciate those qualities about you," Brandi said.

"You girls are like my little sisters, that's why I'm over-protective and try to watch out for you," Bailey said.

"Then I guess I would have to be your little, big sister. Considering I'm older than you," Deion said jokingly.

Bailey chuckled and said, "Right."

"I thought we were going to be here until later but it's okay. I can go and pick up the girls and do an early dinner and a movie. I also have to go to Macy's and get some stuff for Lexi. Brandi and Deion, you're more than welcome to spend the evening with me and the little divas-in-training," Kya said.

"I think I just might do that. I'm not doing anything else but sitting here looking crazy," Brandi said.

"I'm going home to relax," Deion said.

"I really hate our day ending like this," Brandi said.

"My day isn't ending, I'm just switching gears. I have other things that I need to focus on and take care of. And I'm not leaving here pissed or angry. It is what it is. We talked everything out. Even if some things aren't rectified, it's all good," Bailey said.

As Kya grabbed her purse from the table, she turned to Deion and said, "You know we're not trying to hurt you. I need for you to understand that. We wouldn't tell you anything that would be damaging to you."

"Yeah, D, we love and care about you and want to help," Brandi said.

"I understand that but I'm me and will always be me. It's not your job to try and change me. My character, demeanor, status or personality won't change because you think it should. When judgment day comes I don't have to answer to any of you," Deion said.

"Deion it's not a coincidence that you have the symptoms. Nor are we making any of this up. We can only go by what you tell us," Bailey said.

"I'd hate to think you make this stuff up just to have something to say," Kya said.

"You do exhibit the signs of someone with a sex addiction. The risky behaviors and all of your thoughts are consumed by sex. But I'm not going to say you have a sexual addiction," Bailey said.

"That's not true. Despite what you think I do have other stuff on my mind," Deion said.

"Every day it seems like all you focus on is your next fuck. Not to mention your behavior has literally turned your world upside down. I have never seen anything like this in my life. I just want you to ponder over that," Bailey said.

"Just think about the last encounter you had with metro man. You met him on a train, chatted for a brief period, had drinks and then he fucked you in a parking garage. He consistently said to you that he didn't have time to go upstairs. But he had sufficient time to fuck you in a garage. I don't know who was treated more like a whore, you or him. He got free drinks and some free pussy," Kya said.

"In all seriousness, sexual addiction is like any other addiction. The compulsive, continued behavior despite negative consequences, and the obsessive thoughts in planning and obtaining sex. Sweetie, they have a twelve-step program for sex addicts," Brandi said.

"Oh my goodness, can you see me walking into a room filled with people and saying, my name is Deion and I'm a sex addict? Then everyone will turn to me and say, hello, Deion. Hell no! I can't do that."

"Sweetie, then how else are you supposed to get help? You have to start somewhere. I don't think this is something that you'll be able to tackle on your own," Brandi said.

"More importantly, she has to recognize that there's a problem," Kya said.

As Deion sat and listened to her friends talking she couldn't help but wonder if she really had a problem. *What am I doing? What happened to me? I thought I was smarter than this. I didn't start acting like this until after my divorce from Brian.*

"I know Brian was an abusive asshole and he treated you like shit. Maybe sex was your way of self-medicating or filling a void of some sort. Maybe it was, for what happened within that nightmare of a relationship," Bailey said.

"After Brian and I got a divorce I started seeing a therapist. I don't know if sex addiction is something that he can handle but I'll give him a call just to talk, one visit. I can't promise that I'll be sitting up in his office all of the time discussing my sex life," Deion said.

"Well at least that's a start," Bailey said.

"That's all we're asking, just get some help," Kya said.

"What I do know about addictions is that first you have to admit you have a problem. That's the first step in any recovery. Until you admit that then you'll continue with the self-destructive behavior," Bailey said.

"So I guess I can say you have a problem too," Deion said.

"What problem?' Kya asked.

"Umm, you're a compulsive shopper, a shopaholic or whatever the hell you want to call it," Deion said.

"Oh no sister, I just like to shop," Kya said.

"And I like to have sex, so what's the problem?" Deion asked.

"Because I'm not hurting myself, that's the difference," Kya said.

"Anyway, it's still an addiction. Therefore, your ass needs help too," Deion said.

"Look now, we're not going to get into that today, we'll save that for another time," Kya said.

"Just hear me out, do this for me. And you know I never ask you to do anything," Bailey said.

"That's true, what is it?" Deion asked.

"I want you to go home, get a glass of wine, turn on some relaxing music and take a long, hot bubble bath. I want you to think long and hard about the things you've done since your marriage ended. Then think about all that was said here today. I don't know if you believe what we've told you or not. I believe subconsciously you know there's a problem but for some reason you're afraid. That is without a doubt understandable and I do sympathize with you wholeheartedly," Bailey said.

"I'm sure once you have one or two sessions with any therapist they'll be able to point it out," Kya said.

"Kya, I never said I didn't believe what you were saying to me. I would rather a professional confirm that there's something wrong with me. None of us have a degree in psychology. Therefore, how can we give my behavior a label?" Deion asked.

"When I did my research I completed a survey and the results read, Go and get help immediately!" Kya shouted.

As the ladies laughed at Kya's comment, Deion said, "Okay, Kya, I hear you."

"So when are you going to call the therapist?" Bailey asked.

"First thing Monday morning," Deion said.

"If you need someone to go with you for a little moral support, I'm more than happy to go," Bailey said.

"I appreciate that, Bailey, but I know you have enough on your plate right now," Deion said.

"It's not a problem. I'll go with you to the therapist and I'll also go with you to the meetings," Bailey said.

"Yeah, and if Bailey's not available just let me know and I'll go with you," Kya said.

"Me too. Let's make it a group outing," Brandi said jokingly.

"I think we should be heading out so I can get on this highway. It's nice out today and everybody and their momma's on the beltway," Bailey said.

"Yes, because the longer we sit here the more I'm going to want another Grey Goose honey deuce," Kya said.

"And you have to drive with my babies and goddaughter in the car. Unless Brandi's going to drive, having another drink isn't an option. And don't forget you're going to have my babies the whole weekend," Bailey said.

"Damn, I did forget," Kya said.

"You won't be able to go home, get in the bed, and sleep it off, not tonight," Bailey said.

"Shit! I almost forgot. Then I think we should be hitting the highway," Kya said.

"Let me go grab my shoes and purse. Do you think I need a jacket?" Brandi asked.

"Right now it's 76 degrees. You'll probably need a jacket later tonight, I'd grab a light one just in case," Kya said.

"Okay. Ladies, I know it might be hard to believe but I really enjoyed our day. It was like group therapy with food and drinks," Brandi said.

"Okay my dears, we gotta go," Bailey said.

"Okay, let's roll," Kya said.

As Bailey drove home the mood was different from how it had been throughout the day. Everyone appeared to be much happier, less argumentative, and focused on what they needed to do. Even though they'd had major discussions on a range of different issues, their friendship was a tight bond and kept them together. From the current mood in the car you wouldn't think that anything serious had occurred that day and there was plenty of laughing and joking. They discussed their upcoming trips, Kya's wedding plans, Brandi's housewarming party and Brandi's new organization. The closer Bailey got to her house the more she thought about the impending conversation she needed to have with her husband. Because of the nature of the conversation she knew the outcome had the potential to be dreadful. The more she tried to get it out of her mind the more she knew she had to be realistic about the situation.

As the ladies drove, Kirk Franklin's song, *I Smile* on the radio. Kya immediately turned up the volume and started bopping her head back and forth.

"I love this song and the words hit right home. You look so much better when you uh oh," Kya sang.

"I normally listen to this song a couple of times a day," Brandi said. "Even though it hurts, I smile!"

"That's what you're supposed to do," Kya said.

"Everything will be fine, you'll see," Brandi said.

"I'm not stressed or worried about it. Let me rephrase that because that makes it seem like I don't care. I'm concerned about the situation and how it might affect my family. However, I'm not stressing about it," Bailey said.

"That's nice to know," Kya said. After the song ended Kya turned the volume back down and started playing with her phone.

"It's unfortunate, but actions have consequences," Bailey said.

"Where did that come from?" Kya asked.

"Just thinking. Kya, could you hand me my phone please?"

"Who are you calling? You need to pay attention to the road."

"Girl stop playing, I can multitask. I need to call Noah," Bailey said.

"I thought your phone was programmed into the car?" Kya asked.

"It is but I think I broke something. I can't get it to work right and I haven't had the time to take it to the dealership."

Kya dialed Bailey's house number and handed her the cell. Noah answered the phone with a hint of melancholy in his voice.

"Hey. Kya's going to take the girls for the night. Can you get their bags and make sure they're ready? I'm about ten minutes from the house," Bailey said.

"Why is she taking the girls?" Noah asked.

"Because they're spending the weekend with her and Lexi. Why does that matter?" Bailey asked.

"I was just asking. Okay, I'll get them together," Noah said.

"Besides, we need to talk about some things and I don't want them around when we have this convo."

"Okay," Noah responded.

"You did say that you need to talk to me about something. I assume whatever it is will require my undivided attention," Bailey said.

"Yes, I do need to talk to you but the girls can stay home," Noah said.

"Nah. They wanted to hang out with their godmom and Lexi this weekend anyway. I think it's best if they're not there."

"But you don't even know what I want to discuss."

"You're right, I don't. The way you looked earlier, it has to be damn important."

"Okay, babe, I'll get their bags together."

"Thank you, I'll see you in a few."

Bailey ended the call, sighed and said, "Goodness gracious! I'd give anything not to have this convo. Lord, please give me strength, guide my tongue, and order my steps."

"Girl, you got this, everything will be good," Kya said.

"I'm glad you're so optimistic. But I don't think he'll walk away with a slap on the wrist this time. Maybe if I'd handled the situation differently in the past I wouldn't be going through this shit again. You let someone get away with something once and then they test you to see if they can get away with it again," Bailey said.

"Yeah, don't I know," Kya said.

"Ladies, I'm telling you now so you won't be shocked. There's a strong possibility that I'm going to leave Noah."

"Oh shit! I knew it," Kya said.

"Think about this and don't do anything extreme and impetuous," Brandi said.

"Brandi, I've been thinking about this for the past couple of weeks."

"I know there's nothing that we can say that would change your mind or your thinking. But don't end your marriage over some bitch. It's not worth it," Deion said.

"If I end my marriage it will be because he didn't respect me or value me enough to be faithful."

"I just hope that you can find it in your heart to give him another chance," Kya said.

"He's already had another chance. He's the one that dipped out, not me," Bailey said.

Kya looked at Bailey and said, "If you say so."

"What's that supposed to mean?" Brandi asked.

"Nothing. I'm going to leave that alone," Kya said.

"Kya, what the heck are you talking about now?" Brandi asked.

"Nothing. Just forget it," Kya said.

"Okay, ladies," Deion said, as the car pulled into Bailey's garage. "I have a lot to think about. I heard everything that y'all said to me today. Whether I agree with it or not. While I'm relaxing, I'm going to think long and hard about my actions, my behavior, and my life in general."

"That's what I like to hear. Well alright now!" Brandi yelled.

"Are you sure you don't want to hang out with us?" Kya asked.

"Nah, I'm going to go home and relax," Deion said.

"Okay, call when you get home. You are going straight home, right?" Bailey asked.

"Yes, mother, I'm going straight home."

"Bailey, we're not coming in, send the girls out," Kya said.

"Okay, sweetie. Thanks for keeping the girls. I'll give you a call first thing in the morning," Bailey said.

"Not a problem. Call me later on if you need to talk, vent, yell or anything," Kya said.

"Thanks, Brandi, for having us over. It was a different type of brunch but I still enjoyed the day with you ladies," Bailey said.

"You're welcome. Please call me later on," Brandi said.

"I will, sweetie. Have fun tonight and don't let Kya drink too much," Bailey said.

"I won't," Brandi said.

"I'm going to send the girls right out," Bailey said.

As Bailey went into the foyer, she was greeted by Noah, Tyanna and TyShae.

"Hello, babies. Did your daddy tell you that you're going with Aunt Kya?" Bailey asked.

"Yes, Mommy, but I want to stay home with Daddy," Tyanna said.

"I thought you wanted to hang out with Lexi and Aunt Kya this weekend? I'll come and get you tomorrow if you still want to come home," Bailey said.

"Is Lexi in the car?" TyShae asked.

"No, sweetie, Aunt Kya has to go and pick her up. Then you're going to dinner, the movies and shopping. Aunt Brandi is going too. You're going to have fun," Bailey said.

"Alright. I'll text you later on," TyShae said.

Bailey chuckled and said, "Okay, love. Come and give me a hug and a kiss. Make sure you watch your sister."

"Okay, Mommy."

As Bailey hugged her daughters she said, "I love you girls and be good girls, okay?"

"I love you too," TyShae said.

"Me too, Mommy," Tyanna said.

"Aunt Kya is outside waiting for you," Bailey said.

"I'll walk them to the car," Noah said.

Bailey stood at the front door as Noah walked their daughters to Kya's car. She then went into the kitchen for a bottle of water. On her way out of the kitchen, Noah was coming back into the house.

Bailey started walking up the steps and said, "I'm going upstairs to change my clothes. Are you coming up so we can talk?"

"Yes, let me make me a drink first. Would you like one?" Noah asked.

"No, thank you, I'm good," Bailey replied.

"I'll be up in a few minutes."

After fixing a drink, Noah proceeded to the bedroom. "Have you had anything to eat?"

"I ate earlier today," Bailey said.

"Are you hungry, would you like to go to dinner?" Noah asked.

"Nah. I'll fix something later on."

"How was your day with your girls?" Noah asked.

"We had a nice day. Well, at least after we resolved some underlying issues. Brandi's house is really nice. I'm so proud of her."

"Was Derick there?" Noah asked.

"No, he's out of town."

"So Brandi did the move herself?"

"No, the ladies and I hired a moving company to take care of everything. Derick was home the morning of the move but apparently he left at some point that night."

"Why would he fly out so late? He could have just waited until the next morning and taken an early flight."

"My dear, you're asking the wrong one, I don't have a clue. I guess he needed to be wherever he was going that night. I don't know and I really don't care," Bailey replied with a sarcastic tone.

"Why are you getting smart?"

"Actually, I'm not. I'm just saying that I don't care about Derick's travel itinerary. That isn't my primary concern. It's other shit that I'm concerned about, seeing as it affects Brandi."

"What's that supposed to mean? What's going on?"

"It doesn't matter right now. That's a topic for another day."

"Is she okay?"

"She's good, just busy with the move and trying to start this foundation." Knowing what it was that Noah had to tell her, Bailey tried to wait until he approached the subject but she thought, *Enough with the goddamn small talk. We need to get this shit out of the way. Besides, it's taken long enough for him to man up and tell me. Enough with the freakin' procrastination.*

As Bailey undressed and put on her robe, she walked towards Noah and asked, "What is it that you want to discuss?"

"Why, are you going back out?" Noah asked.

"No, I'm in for the night, I'm not going anywhere."

"Can't we chill for a minute before we talk?"

"Let's just get the convo out of the way, please. I'm tired and it's been a long day. Just say it. Just spit it out."

Noah sat on the edge of the bed with a weary look on his face. "What, Noah?" Bailey asked.

"Babe, several months ago I started feeling like I was losing you. We weren't communicating like we used to and it felt like you were becoming distant. Not to mention you were working all of the time."

"Noah, we both work a lot. How else could we live the lifestyle we live if we didn't work so much?"

"I know that, but you were becoming different. It was almost like you didn't want to be here or around me."

"For real, Noah, we're together all of the time. Did you forget that? Do we not live together and run a very successful businesses together? Which means we're pretty much together the majority of the day and night!" Bailey yelled.

"No, I didn't forget, but it was like you were becoming a little standoffish and didn't want to be bothered."

"That's bullshit. If I didn't want to be bothered I wouldn't be here."

"Whenever I'd try to talk to you, you never had the time. When you got home you worked more. And when you weren't working you were with your girls."

"Are you serious? We both hang out with our friends. Now you're penalizing me for hanging out with the girls. Get the hell outta here with that bullshit."

"I couldn't figure out why you were becoming so distant. I started feeling like you were dealing with someone else. I actually thought you were cheating on me."

"If you felt like that why didn't you confront me?" Bailey asked.

"Because it seemed like it never was the right time. I also didn't want to jump out there and look stupid for accusing you of cheating."

"Why would you think that I'd cheat on you?"

"It was your overall behavior. Even when you were here you weren't really here. It was like your mind was preoccupied with other stuff and not me."

"If that's the case then you should have said something. There's always an opportunity to talk. Especially if you think there's a problem somewhere. When I need to talk to you whether it's pertaining to our household, our daughters, you and I, or our businesses, I do. So that's shit that you're talking, save it for someone else."

"Babe, you're not always available and there were plenty of times that I tried to talk to you," Noah said.

"Noah, unless I'm travelling we sleep together every night. So no, I don't agree with what you're saying to me."

"I tried. I was going through stuff and needed you."

"Noah, where are you going with this?" Bailey asked.

"You just didn't have time for me anymore."

"We both work full-time, demanding jobs. If I'm not mistaken, normally after dinner and the girls are in the bed, we both work more, whether it's reading a report, checking or sending emails, or whatever. You're just as guilty of that as I am. Fortunately, or unfortunately, we have to invest a lot of time into our company. Would you prefer someone else ran our businesses? If so, that can be arranged and we can be together all day every damn day!" Bailey yelled.

"No, that's not what I'm saying."

"Then what are you saying? What is it that you're really trying to say? Get to the fucking point!" Bailey repositioned herself and sat next to Noah on the bed.

"I started talking back to Joi," Noah said softly.

"What? What did you just say? Look at me, Noah! What did you say?" Bailey yelled.

"I've been talking to Joi," Noah repeated.

"You've been talking to Joi. Is that what you said?"

"Yes."

Bailey snickered and said, "So, in other words what you're telling me is you and Joi have been occasionally chatting? That's it?"

"Kind of."

"What the hell does that mean? Stop dancing around the damn question and just answer."

"In the beginning we just conversed and would occasionally meet for drinks. We never even talked about sex. We just had normal conversations here and there. She was just someone to talk to."

"You felt that you had to turn to someone that you used to cheat on me with, for comfort?" Bailey asked.

"I couldn't talk to you. I felt like with your friends, the businesses, your many projects, and the kids you became distant." Noah said.

"All the shit that we've been through and you felt like you couldn't talk to me. You're full of shit. Get the hell out of my face with that bullshit. What you're saying right now isn't making any sense."

Noah looked at Bailey with a gloomy look on his face. "I'm sorry, babe," he said.

"There is no justification for you cheating. I don't give a shit if I moved to the moon. You should not have cheated . . . again! There is one thing you're right about. You are one sorry-ass son of a bitch."

"I don't know why I did it. It just happened."

"Don't expect me to be sympathetic because you look like a sick-ass puppy. So if you only conversed and had drinks then why the hell are you acting as if there's more to the story?" Bailey said.

"Because there is."

"Then I advise you to tell me what you have to, and stop procrastinating with what you have to say."

"I would see her at the club whenever I went. But one day instead of having drinks at the club we met at her house. My intention was only to go to her house and talk. However, we ended up having sex. Babe, if I could turn back the hands of time I wouldn't have done that. She was just a friend that I could talk to."

"If you had something that you needed to discuss then you should have come to me. I'm your wife, your friend, and your goddamn lover. You had no reason whatsoever to go to another woman for anything. No one made you do anything. You did it because you wanted to. You made that choice. But you know what? I hope it was worth it."

"Babe, I'm sorry and I regret what I've done."

"You're right about that. You're a sorry-ass son of a bitch! You aren't any different than those other motherfuckers out there walking around!" Bailey shouted.

"I am different. Don't compare me to everyone else," Noah said.

"Negro, please! You're just another man that lets his dick do the thinking for him. Why the fuck did you lie to me? I kept asking you if you were cheating but you kept denying it. Why lie, Noah? Didn't you know that I would find out sooner or later? If there was something else that you wanted then you could have left me the fuck alone. If I wasn't giving you what you needed or desired then you should have talked to me."

"I didn't know how to tell you. I didn't want to hurt you, nor did I want you to take my daughters and leave. I know what I want, and it's you," Noah said.

"Oh no, my dear, clearly it's not me that you want."

"Can we just work this out?"

"Work this out, you've got to be tripping. This is the second time and you want me to keep taking this shit. Hell, fucking no. This I don't deserve! When you fucked Joi you made the decision for me. I won't keep dealing with this. I can't," Bailey said.

"Can we just try to fix it?" Noah asked.

"What the hell for? So you can do it again? I can't let that happen. I love me too much to allow you to keep hurting me. What reason do I have to stay?" Bailey asked.

"Love is the reason that you need to stay."

"Love didn't keep you from fucking someone else. Love didn't keep you from lying to me. If you loved me so much then we wouldn't be having this conversation right now. And guess what, my dear? Sometimes love isn't enough."

"She doesn't mean anything to me. Babe, it was a mistake and I hope you find it in your heart to forgive me."

"A mistake, Noah? This is the same bitch that you cheated with before. But you want me to forgive you and think it was a mistake?" Bailey asked.

"Yes."

"You have lost your mind. I don't even trust you at this point."

"I promise it won't happen again."

"Déjà fucking vu! That's the same shit you said before," Bailey shouted.

"I promise, babe, I can't live without you."

"If that were true then you would have made wiser choices. Let me ask you a question, are you in love with her?" Bailey asked.

"Why would you ask me that?"

"Why wouldn't I ask you that question? You've cheated twice over a two-year period with the same bitch. So I'm just wondering why you keep going back."

"No, I don't love her."

"And no, I don't believe anything that you have to say at this point."

"I need you to listen to what I'm saying. Let me explain."

"I've been listening to what you said. However, save your explanations. I don't want to hear them. Right now, I just need to gather myself and figure out the next step," Bailey said.

"We're going to fix this. I'm not losing my family over this," Noah said.

"You're funny as hell."

"I'm serious, Bailey, I want us to fix it."

"What you want no longer matters to me. I have to worry about my daughters, not you. You're their father and I will never keep them from you but you and I are a done deal, it's a wrap."

"That's not what I want. Bailey, please just think about it and let's work it out."

Bailey sat on the bed shaking her head from side to side.

"I don't know if I want to ask this question or make an assumption, but at this point it's not even safe for me to make any assumptions. But I'll try my hand. Who else have you been fucking?" Bailey asked.

"No one."

"Maybe you've never stopped fucking the tramp from the get go. So that also means that you knew she worked at Jeff's club all along," Bailey said.

"Yes, I knew."

"And you lied about that too. What the fuck else have you lied to me about, Noah?"

"Nothing, that's it," Noah said.

"I don't know what to believe anymore. If you tell me that the goddamn sun is shining I better go outside and see for my damn self. I can't even trust you anymore, Noah. We can't have a marriage if the trust isn't there."

"Babe, you know that I love you. I didn't mean to hurt you."

"I suggest you save that bullshit for someone who might believe you because I sure as hell don't. Love is not supposed to hurt nor does love keep hurting you over and over and over. But like the song says, 'love don't love no fucking body'. You don't know shit about love. If I and our daughters are that much of a hindrance to you, then you should have left a long time ago. You have two daughters, you'd be mad as hell if someone did this to them. So when you do your shit, think about how someone could possibly treat your daughters."

"I won't let that happen."

"You can't control your own dick. What makes you think you can control someone else's?" Bailey asked.

"I'm not going to let my daughters be treated like shit."

"But it's okay for you to treat their mother like shit?" Bailey asked.

"No, that's not what I'm saying."

"Riddle me this, how long have you been fucking her?" Bailey asked.

"I don't know, it only happened a couple of times."

"Don't tell me you don't know. How long have you been fucking this bitch? Bailey asked.

"For about six months."

"Wow. Seriously, Noah, I really don't believe this shit. This is what I'm going to do for you. I'm going to go in my closet and grab some clothes. I'm then going to go into my daughters' bedrooms and pack some clothes for them as well. After that I'm out of your hair and you don't ever have to worry about me. We'll stay in the other house until we rectify and finalize everything."

"I'm not letting that happen."

"You really don't have a choice in the matter. The next time you see me will be in court. You can see your daughters whenever you want."

"I'm not letting you go."

"You don't have a choice. You can't make me stay and I don't want to stay. I told you the last time that you cheated I wasn't going to deal with this bullshit. Because I don't have to put up with this. But I guess you thought I was just talking. I'll come back at a later date or hire someone to get the rest of our shit. It's officially a wrap, sweetie! I'm fucking done!" Bailey yelled.

"Wait, babe, that's not what I want."

"Who the fuck are you? Who gives a fuck about what you want? It's not about you anymore. You have forfeited your right for me to give a fuck about you and your feelings. I have to do what I have to, for me and my daughters. You don't give a fuck about us."

"I know you're upset. You just need some time to cool off," Noah said.

"Noah, apparently you don't have a clue as to what my needs are. But I really hope Joi was worth it. I hope she was the fuck of the century. Guess what? She can have you. You're now a free man."

"Bailey, let's talk about this."

"There's nothing left to talk about. I've given you twelve years of my life. No more! I'm so fucking done with you! Just remember that you had a good woman and you didn't know how to treat her. Your loss will be someone else's gain."

"Can you just listen to me?" Noah asked.

"What the fuck do you want? Listen to what? I've listened to all I need to listen to. I'm not going to keep listening to you tell me that I'm the cause of your infidelities."

"I didn't say that you're the cause."

"Noah, in the beginning of this conversation, you clearly pointed out what I didn't do for you. I worked a lot, I was distant, I wasn't communicating. That shit came out of your mouth."

"Babe, I don't want to be with anyone else. You're my life, you're my world, and I'm nothing without you. I made a mistake and I'm sorry for that. I'm human and I'm not perfect. Please don't turn your back on me. Don't walk away from us. Please don't tear our family apart," Noah pleaded.

"Noah, you tore our family apart when you put your dick in that bitch. So, I'm going to let you be with her. I'm stepping aside and getting the fuck out of your way. What I don't need is you playing Russian roulette with my life. There's too much shit out there and I'm not prepared to catch something because of you. I thought we had a good life. Hell, in fact I thought we had a great life. But I guess I was wrong, I wasn't woman enough for you, huh? You just had to go out there gallivanting with some whore." Bailey got up from the bed and starting grabbing some clothes. Then she dragged her suitcase out of her closet.

"Bailey, don't leave. Please stay tonight, and let's talk about this. We can figure it out."

"What is it that I need to figure out? I haven't done anything wrong."

Bailey went into the bathroom to get her toiletries but her phone rang and she re-entered the bedroom to answer the call.

"Hey, girl. We were worried about you and wanted to check on you. Is everything okay?" Kya asked.

"Kya, can I call you back? I'm in the middle of packing right now. I'm going to come and get the girls in the morning. I'll call you when I'm on my way," Bailey said.

"What? What the fuck is going on over there?"

"My husband has cheated on me yet again and I'm leaving. I'll call you back later on."

"Wait a minute. Bailey, are you sure this is what you want to do? I know you're upset but give him a chance to explain," Kya said.

"I can't do that. I'm done. I don't have time for this bullshit. Look, let me go. I have to finish packing. Kiss the girls for me."

"Wait, I need for you to listen to me. Noah's a good man and he made a mistake. Bailey, please think about this," Kya said.

"Why are you advocating for him? You know what, let him explain to you why he can't be faithful," Bailey said.

"Come on, Bailey, you know just like I do that he loves you and you love him too. Bailey, the love that you and Noah have is real. Please just stay. Just sleep on it. Please, do that for me," Kya said.

"I hear you. I gotta go," Bailey said.

After Bailey hung up the phone, Noah walked up to her and asked, "Can we finish this conversation?"

"No, I'm done, but please feel free to continue it with Joi."

Bailey then went back to the bathroom. She turned on the faucet and stood in front of the sink. *Lord, I don't know what to do. I hope I didn't make the wrong decision.* Bailey splashed some water on her face then put her hair into a ponytail. She looked in the mirror as tears formed in her eyes. *I just can't stay with him.*

Noah walked into the bathroom and stood in front of Bailey.

"Can I get you anything?" he asked.

"Please. Please, just leave me alone," Bailey said.

Noah stood in the threshold, looked at Bailey and said, "I love you. I hope you find it in your heart to forgive me."

"Ha, ha, ha, that's a joke."

"I really think it's too late for you to go and get the girls. You should wait until the morning," Noah said.

"You're right, it is too late to pick them up. Besides, they'll want to know why we're spending the night at the other house."

"I also think that you shouldn't go to the house tonight, that's a long drive. I know you don't want to be around me right now. I'll sleep in another room."

"Okay, Noah. Can you please leave the bathroom? I need some time to myself and want to be alone right now."

Noah left and Bailey sat on the side of the tub with her head in her hands. She lifted her head and sighed as her tears started to flow. *Why am I crying? I'm supposed to have thick skin and I'm supposed to be the strong one. I hate feeling weak and vulnerable. I guess we're all entitled to a pity party.* She undressed and got into the shower. For the next several minutes she held her head back and let the water hit her face. After crying and reminiscing over her life she began to feel like her life was over. *I don't know if our marriage can be fixed or if it's even worth fixing. How I can be with someone that I don't trust? Noah and I have always had great communication, trust, respect and love for one another. Someway, somehow things went bad.* Bailey let the hot water ease her mind and soothe her soul.

Noah came in the bathroom and asked, "Babe, are you up for going out tonight?"

"Go out with you, hell no. You've got to be kidding me. No, I'm not in a going out kind of mood."

"I was wondering if you wanted to go and get something to eat and have a few drinks."

"No, thank you. I have something I need to do."

"What do you have to do or is it you just don't want to be around me?"

"Noah, if that was the case then I wouldn't have a problem telling you that. I really want you to leave me alone right now. I need some space and time to think."

As Bailey stepped out of the shower, Noah handed her a towel. "You know that we can get through this," Noah said.

"Can we really?"

"Yes, we can."

"How can you be so certain? I can't be with you if I don't trust you."

"Because of the love that we have for one another, we can get through this."

"Right now, love isn't enough for me, Noah. This is the second time that we've been down this road."

"I know, but I'm positive that we can work through it. No matter what our issues were, we've always overcome whatever obstacles that we faced."

"I agree but this time it's different."

"How is it different?"

"How many different ways can I say I don't trust you?"

"Do you want a divorce?" Noah asked.

"At this very moment, I don't know what I want. I just don't want to be around you. I always thought for us divorce was never an option. But I guess I was wrong about that too."

"Let me fix it."

"Noah, I don't want to spend the rest of my life thinking that you're being faithful and you're not!" Bailey shouted.

"I'll do whatever it takes to earn your trust back. Maybe we can see a marriage counselor."

"I don't know. I just need some time to think about it and sort things through."

"I understand how you feel but I don't want our marriage to end. If it's space and time that you need, I'm okay with that. I just don't want you and my daughters to leave."

Bailey walked to her closet and grabbed some jeans and a shirt. She then walked over to her dresser and got some underwear and a bra.

"Are you going somewhere?" Noah asked.

"Why do you keep asking that question when you know the answer? I'm going to the other house."

"I thought you didn't feel like going anywhere?"

"I don't feel like nor do I want to go anywhere with you. If you must know, I want to go to the office to pick up some things. Why?"

"I was just asking. Do you want me to go with you?"

"No. Because I'm going to the other house when I leave the office."

"Babe, I can't tell you what to do. I can stand here all night long begging and pleading with you. I love you with all of my heart and I want to make things right between us."

"Noah, I would love to believe that. It's just . . . you've expressed those exact sentiments before. It's not that I want our marriage to end, I just don't want to keep going through the same unnecessary bullshit the rest of my life."

"Then give me another chance. You'll never have any reason to doubt or mistrust me, I promise you that."

"All I'm asking you is for a little time to think about it. I hear everything that you've said. I comprehend very well. However, I need to make the best decision for my well-being as well as my daughters."

"Okay, take all the time that you need."

"Please don't suffocate me, just give me my space."

"In the meantime, would you like me to contact a marriage counselor?" Noah asked.

"Do what you want to do. We all make mistakes but we're supposed to learn from them, not keep making the same ones over and over. I vowed to be with you for better or worse and I promised that I would never turn my back on you. You're a good man, a good father, and I know that. But I asked you not to take my love for granted," Bailey said.

Noah knelt in front of Bailey, held her hands and said, "I will never take your love for granted. We *will* get through it."

"Right now I can't promise that I'll give you another chance to get it right. I forgive you for what you've done but I'll never forget. I also need to heal from your actions and this situation."

"I'm sure we can get things back to normal," Noah said.

"Normal, I don't even know what that is anymore."

Noah walked up to Bailey, put his arms around her and held her. He then kissed her and said, "I love you. I love you with all my heart."

"I hear ya."

"You can't say you love me back?" Noah asked.

"I'm not even feeling that right now," Bailey said.

Noah got up and asked, "Would you like something to eat or maybe a drink?"

"No. I'm going to sit here for a minute and get my thoughts together before I head out. I'm a little exasperated and tired right now."

"Why don't you wait until the morning? I'll feel more comfortable with that. I don't want you driving around all night."

"You still don't get it, I don't even want to be in the same house with you right now."

"I get that but why don't you lie down awhile? Like you said, it's been a long day."

"I just need a couple of minutes of some me time, I'll go in the office and relax for a bit, since you find it hard to leave the room as I've asked."

"Okay, I'll leave you alone. Get some rest, babe."

"I just need to recharge my battery. My mind's going one thousand miles a minute. I need to get my head together," Bailey said.

"Okay. I'll be in the family room watching the play-offs."

"Who's playing tonight?"

"Boston and Orlando."

"That's going to be one hell of a game. You know Orlando is going to win."

"We'll see."

"Can you wake me up in an hour or so?" Bailey asked.

"Yes, I can do that."

As Noah walked out of the bedroom, he turned and said, "By the way, I almost forget to tell you that Maisha called a couple of times while you were out."

"What did she say?" Bailey asked.

"She said it's imperative that you call her."

"Okay, I'll give her a call later on or tomorrow."

"I hope she has a doctor's note. She's been out of the office for a long time now," Noah said.

"I don't know. I haven't spoken to her in a couple of days."

"I know she's not sick and she wasn't on vacation. If she wanted a vacation then that's all she had to say. Instead of being sly about the whole situation," Noah said.

"I can't worry about her BS right now either. It is what it is," Bailey said.

"Can you let me know what's up with her after you speak to her?"

"Yup," Bailey replied. "Right now Maisha and her drama is not on my list of things to worry about."

"Okay. Get some rest. I'll check on you in a few."

After Bailey was certain Noah was downstairs, she grabbed her phone and called Maisha.

Maisha answered on the first ring and Bailey immediately said, "Why the hell do you insist on not listening? I told you not to call my damn house again!"

"Damn, what has got you in an uproar? I was only calling to check on you. You never answer my phone calls and texts. When I call you at work you're never there. I thought the only way I could reach you was at home," Maisha said.

"Because I don't want to be bothered and you appear not to understand."

"If you weren't ignoring me then I wouldn't have to call you at home."

"Maisha, please spare me the bullshit! I'm not in the mood for that crap today. What do you want?"

"You know what I want. I want you."

"Both you and I know that's not something that can happen. You can't have me and I suggest you move on. Just let go."

"When I called earlier I started to tell Noah about our relationship. Then I thought it might be best if you handled it. So, are you ready to be with me?" Maisha asked.

"You already know the answer to that question. I hate to disappoint you but we don't have a relationship and I don't want to be with you. It was nothing more than sex. I was curious, I tried it and now I'm done," Bailey said.

"I miss you."

"Look, I'm not going to keep entertaining you, your bullshit or this conversation. I'll talk to you some other time. Furthermore, from what I hear you have a man."

"He's just a friend. And why does that matter? You have a husband."

"First and foremost, I'm not stalking and pursuing you, it's the other way around. Second of all, what we had was short-lived and you knew that from the jump. I was curious about being with a woman, I tried it. It definitely was a different experience, I enjoyed it and it's over."

"I hate it when you keep putting me on the back burner. As if you don't have time for me. Why do you keep doing this to me?" Maisha asked.

"I'm not doing anything to you. When I'm nice, you misconstrue it and get everything all twisted up. It appears as though you only understand what I'm saying when I'm being a bitch or being mean."

"I'm so sick and tired of you hurting me. I don't deserve this and you should treat me better than this."

"You're absolutely right. Besides, I'm not doing a damn thing to you. You're doing it to yourself and you're bringing it on yourself. My suggestion to you is that you go and find some woman or man that will treat you the way you want to be treated. You need to find someone that's willing to feed into your bullshit as well as play your games. I'm not the one."

"You are the one for me. No one else makes me feel the way that you do," Maisha said.

"Whatever you say."

"I've been thinking about you all day. I can't stop thinking about you. I thought about the last time we were together and the things we did. I was so worked up that I had no other choice but to play with my pussy. I wish you'd been here for the grand finale."

"And you're telling me this because?" Bailey asked.

"I wanted to share with you."

"You're an intelligent woman when it comes to business. But when it comes to the facts of life, you're dumb as shit."

"You act like you've never been in love before."

"I've been in love plenty of times but I never acted the way you're carrying on. Maisha, it's not love that you're feeling. It's nothing more than lust. I'm sure you can find another woman that can fulfill all of your needs. I'm not her."

"Well, that's what makes us different."

"That is so true."

"I tried to give you some space and some time but you never called me."

"You know what, Maisha, I didn't want to do this. I really didn't but you've forced my hand."

"Do what?"

"I think it will be the best interest of me, my family, and especially my company if you didn't return back to work."

"What the hell is that supposed to mean?"

"It means that I'll have someone pack up your office and send your shit to you. If you show back up in my building, I'll have you arrested for trespassing. I'll give you a letter of recommendation as well as a very generous severance package. But there is no way possible that I can work with you, not like this."

"You can't fire me!" Maisha yelled.

"Oh yes, I can and I did. I believed you when you said you had a handle on the situation. Clearly I was a fool to think that you could continue working for me without any problems. We had this discussion in the beginning and there were supposed to be no strings attached. You agreed to that."

"But shit happens. I can't help it that I fell in love with you."

"And it was never my intention that you would. I certainly can't help it that I don't love you," Bailey said.

"Why are you firing me? You have no grounds to fire me."

"I'm not going to have this conversation with you right now. Continue to enjoy your time off. I wish you the best and I hope that you find whatever or whomever it is that you're looking for."

"Can we meet for lunch or something? We need to talk about this further."

"There's nothing left to discuss. In fact, I'm all talked out. I have other things that I have to focus on besides this unnecessary bullshit with you. I don't know how many ways I can make you understand.

It's over. It was over a long time ago! Hell, it was actually over before it got started," Bailey shouted.

"Okay Bailey, but I guess now you've forced my hand."

"Look, sweetie, do whatever the fuck it is that you have to do. I'm not afraid of you or your threats and you damn sure don't frighten me. So do what you feel like you have to!"

"Okay, you'll see. You fucked with the wrong one."

"I've heard that one before too. Well look, it was nice chatting with you but I have to go. Again, I wish you the best and have a nice life," Bailey said as she hung up the phone.

After the call with Maisha, Bailey tried to get comfortable and relax. But her first thought was telling Noah everything that had happened with Maisha, considering he was so inquisitive regarding her behavior at work. Bailey also knew that it appeared that Maisha was a little unstable and was very capable of doing something stupid. *After I bitched and moaned about his infidelities he'll probably curse my ass out. I should tell him sooner rather than later. I definitely don't want him to be blindsided with this crap. I bet this shit has taught me a valuable lesson.*

Several hours later Noah went upstairs to check on Bailey. As he walked through the door he saw that Bailey was no longer asleep and was working on her laptop.

"Hey babe, I just wanted to check on you, I thought you were asleep, what are you doing?" Noah asked.

"Hey. I'm reading this proposal that Eugene wrote."

"Is that for the new building?"

"Yes and no. It's for a new building, but not for us. This is a building that Brandi will utilize for her foundation," Bailey said.

"Oh, okay. Do you need anything?"

"No, I'm good. Once I'm finished with this I have to order the gifts for Brandi's housewarming party. Then I'm going back to bed."

"So you've decided to leave in the morning?"

"Yes."

"Good, I'm glad to hear that. Is it possible that you won't leave at all?"

"Anything's possible, but right now my mind is dead set on leaving."

"Hopefully by the morning you may change your mind."

"I don't know about that."

"Do you need any help with anything?" Noah asked.

"No thanks."

"Okay. We are sleeping together tonight, right?"

"Um, I don't think so."

"I understand that you're pissed off with me. I didn't know whether or not I had to relocate to another room."

"In all actuality, that might not be a bad idea. There are plenty of empty rooms in this house for you to sleep in. In fact, you always have the option of sleeping in the guest house or the in-laws' house," Bailey said sarcastically.

"Wow, you really don't want to be bothered with me?"

"Noah, can we not get into this again? The conversation was over hours ago."

"Okay, not a problem," Noah said.

"Thank you."

"While you were sleeping I found a couple of marriage counselors. Once we decide on one I'll schedule our first appointment."

"Okay."

"Are you actually going to go?"

"Perhaps. At this point I'm not really sure what I'm going to do. I'm not even sure if this marriage is worth salvaging. However, at some point I will take a look at your list."

"I thought we'd go as soon as possible. I want to fix this and put it behind us."

"That's something you should have considered before fucking someone else."

"You're right, I fucked up. But let me make things right again."

"Noah, things will never be the same between us even if I decided to stay. I'd have to learn to trust you all over again and right now I don't know if I can."

"That's understandable, but I'd be happy if you can just give us another shot."

"Been there and done that and look where that's gotten us. Back to the same place we started. I'm not going to keep going through this with you."

"I'm begging you for another chance to get it right."

"I need to finish working. I can't talk about this right now. My thoughts are all over the place and I'm hurting."

"Okay, I'll let you get back to work." As Noah leaned towards Bailey and tried to kiss her, she turned her head. "I almost expected that to happen, but thought I'd try anyway," he said.

"If you knew it was going to happen then why would you try?" Bailey asked.

"I thought at least I could kiss you, but I see you don't want me to touch you. Well, I'm going to let you get back to your work. I love you," Noah said.

"Okay."

"I guess I'll see you in the morning."

"Maybe."

"Maybe what?"

"I will most likely be gone by the time you get up."

"Please don't."

"It is what it is, Noah."

"Okay."

Before Noah walked out of the bedroom, Bailey said, "Despite what's going on with us, what are you doing on Saturday?"

"I was going to play a couple of rounds of golf with the fellas, why?" Noah asked.

"Brandi and Derick's housewarming party. But you don't have to go, though Brandi is adamant about you being there."

"I'll be there," Noah said.

"Oh Noah, don't think you have to go to keep up appearances. You don't really have to go. Besides, I don't want you to have any false hope."

"I'm going because Brandi is like my little sister. Why wouldn't I go?" Noah asked.

"I'm just saying don't go on my account."

"Whatever you say."

"By the way, so you won't be blind-sided, I am definitely leaving. Tomorrow morning when I get up I'm going to go and tidy up the house in Manassas. I'm going to stay there while we sort things out. You can see the girls as often as you like. I need some time and space to clear my head and think."

"How are the girls going to get to school? Why can't you stay here and sort things out? Can we discuss this?"

"The girls getting to school isn't a problem. I can't stay here to sort things out because I need to get away from you. There's nothing left to discuss. I need to figure out my next steps."

"Your next steps? What the hell is that supposed to mean?"

"I have two choices, am I going to divorce you or am I going to sit here while you cheat on me?"

"I promise it'll never happen again."

"Funny. Déjà vu. I've heard that line before."

"Babe, I tried to tell you about Joi weeks ago. I kept telling you I needed to talk to you but you kept brushing me off."

"You didn't try hard enough. Because you tried to tell me something doesn't justify what you've done. You made a choice and now I need to make the right choice for me and my daughters."

"Okay, Bailey, do whatever you think is best right now."

"That's the plan," Bailey said sarcastically.

"If you want some time apart then fine." Noah said.

"That's exactly what we need, some time apart."

"Good morning," Kya said.

"Good morning, Ms. Lady. How are you?" Brandi asked.

"Blessed!" Kya shouted.

"I know that's right. So what's up with you?" Brandi asked.

"Girl, nothing much, just sitting here watching the girls run around and tear up my damn house."

"Wow. I'd have thought y'all would be still in bed," Brandi said.

"Heck, no. We got up hours ago and went to breakfast then caught a matinee."

"Oh, okay. Where did y'all go for breakfast?"

"Bob Evans."

"What movie did you see?"

"*Girl,* I don't know. It was some Dr. Seuss shit. I slept just about through the whole movie. I wish you could have gone with us."

"Me too but I forgot I had to get this paperwork together and I had to go through the boxes to find it. And thank you for bringing me back home. I felt so bad."

"Girl, it was not a problem. Did you find the paperwork?"

"Yes, I did."

"Okay. Cool," Kya said.

"Why are you up so early?"

"I thought I was going to sleep in, but that didn't happen. Lexi woke my ass up around 6 a.m. and I've been up ever since."

"You really thought they were going to let you get some sleep. Ha ha, you're funny."

"Yeah I know, right," Kya said.

"You got three little divas in the house. They get up every day before the sun rises."

"Right."

"When are they going home?" Brandi asked.

"Girl, the hell if I know. Most likely this evening. Lexi don't want the girls to leave so I need to call Bailey before she drives to my house for nothing."

"Yeah, you might want to call her before she makes that trip."

"I've been trying to call her all morning but her phone keeps going to voicemail. When I called the house phone no one answered."

"Maybe she's getting some much needed rest," Brandi said.

"I hope so. Maybe she and Noah are making up."

"So does that means she and Noah are still together?"

"When I spoke to her last night she didn't say. But I couldn't bring myself to asking that question again. Deep down inside I don't really want to know. Sooner or later she'll mention it. You know how she is. When she's in her thinking mood and focused she doesn't share much info. Once she makes a decision that's when she'll share," Kya said.

"That's a darn shame, I hope and pray that she doesn't leave. I can't see those two apart. I sure as heck hope they'll work it out."

"Well, Brandi, I'd love to see them stay together too. You know Bailey and she definitely don't need our influence or input with making decisions. I'm positive that she'll make the right decision for her and her children."

"I guess you got a point."

"I just hope and pray that everything works out for the best," Kya said.

"I just assumed the girls were still with you because she and Noah were working things out."

"Bailey isn't the reason that the girls are still here. They're still here because they've been having such a great time and Lexi's enjoying their company. Bailey also mentioned picking them up this morning. I'm really surprised she hasn't called yet. She said she would."

"Oh, okay. I guess it's a good thing that they all go to the same school. Just in case they need to stay a little while longer."

"Yes it is. Otherwise I'd be running all over town. But it's all good," Kya said.

"She knows her babies are in good hands so she's not worried. I'm sure they call and text her all of the time," Brandi said.

"They definitely communicate often. However, they had me cracking up the other day."

"What happened?"

"I was taking them to school and TyShae was on the phone with Bailey then Tyanna called her too. Tyanna said that TyShae was taking too long and she wanted to talk to her mom from her own phone. They are hilarious. I don't know who's enjoying them more, Lexi, Steve or me. As long as Tyanna and TyShae are around, Lexi isn't asking about a little sister," Kya said.

"You know sooner or later Lexi's going to ask again," Brandi said.

"I know she is, she's been asking ever since Steve and I got engaged. Girl, she even asked me the other day when was the baby coming."

"Stop playing," Brandi said.

"I'm serious. I told her maybe in a couple of years."

"Are you ready to have another baby?" Brandi asked.

"Hell, no. I know that might be selfish of me but I'm content with the one that I have."

"How does Steve feel about that?"

"He'd like to have one but said he can wait until I'm ready. I'm not sure about that, though. I think he's just saying that to appease me."

"Oh goodness, girl, you better give that man a baby," Brandi said jokingly.

"I will, but I want to wait a little while or at least until I get my new catering company up and running."

"Steve must not know that it may never happen."

"That's not true. It'll happen, just no time soon. I'm just not ready to have a baby right now. But eventually we'll have one. I don't like to see TyShae and Tyanna leave but I know Bailey wants her babies home."

"You haven't even spoken to her so you don't know when they're going home," Brandi said.

"Maybe she'll take them when she leaves your housewarming party tonight. If not it's not a big deal," Kya said.

"Are the girls coming too?" Brandi asked.

"I was going to bring them but my mom wanted to take them out."

"Oh, I thought she was coming too. I did send her an invitation but she never responded."

"She said she has something to do but she's going to drop off your gift when she picks up the girls," Kya said.

"Oh, okay."

"Girl, you know my mom is always ripping and running doing something. She'll probably show up at the last minute. The only thing I can see her doing on a Saturday is shopping. She never mentioned any other plans for today."

"I hope she does stop by at least for a little while. I haven't seen her since she's been back from the Turks and Caicos. Is Steve coming?" Brandi asked.

"Of course, he's going to meet me there. He has to pick his car up from the shop. He also mentioned there was something that he needed to take care of before coming to your house."

"Good. I texted Bailey and told her that I wanted to see Noah here. But if things aren't good between them then he may not show."

"I wouldn't say that. If Noah was invited then he'll be there."

"Okay. I'd really love for him to be here. I owe y'all so much," Brandi said.

"Cut it out, don't start with that."

"No, Kya, you ladies just don't know how grateful I am for all that y'all have done for me."

"Don't worry about it, that's what family's for. We're blessed so we like to share our blessings. Isn't that the way it's supposed to be?"

"Yes but y'all do so much for me. I don't know how and when, but I'm going to pay all of you back."

"Guess what?" Kya asked. "We don't want it back. All we care about it your happiness."

"I'm truly a blessed woman to have good friends like you. I have some special gifts for all of you too."

"Girl, you didn't have to get us a damn thing."

"I know, but I wanted to show y'all how much I appreciate everything that you've done for me," Brandi said.

"We know that you appreciate it. Whatever assistance we provide comes from our hearts. Not because we want something in return."

"I know but I still had to get y'all an appreciation gift."

"Whatever you say."

"Anyhoo, where's your husband? Is he getting prepared for your shindig tonight?" Kya asked.

"Ummm, not really."

"What the hell does that mean?"

"He's not here yet."

"Where the hell is he?"

"His plane lands around noon," Brandi said.

"His plane lands around noon? Did he go on another trip or something?" Kya asked.

"No, he was still in ATL."

"Are you serious? I thought he came home the other day."

"Apparently his meetings were a little longer than he anticipated. So he couldn't leave ATL until this morning."

"Whatever, that's some bullshit. He's been in ATL all of this time, Brandi?"

"Yes, ma'am."

"And you believe that?"

"What else am I supposed to believe?"

"Believe that his story is bullshit!" Kya yelled.

"Kya, just leave it alone."

"I'll leave it alone alright. He's full of shit and you know it, Brandi."

"What am I supposed to do? Am I supposed to think everything he says is a lie?"

"Uh huh. I just don't fucking get it. Maybe I'm tripping or something. But it's okay, everything in the dark comes to light sooner or later. And I can't wait because I'm tired of him playing games with you," Kya said.

"What's that supposed to mean? What are you talking about now, Kya?"

"Because I saw his lying ass this morning while we were at breakfast."

"No, that couldn't have been him. Maybe that was his twin. You know they all say we have a twin."

"No, it was him. I walked past his table and looked right at him. I even spoke and asked when he got back. So don't tell me it wasn't him."

"Girl, you're tripping. You know they say we all have a twin."

"Brandi, I know what Derick looks like. He looked at me and I looked at him. His lying ass even said that he got back a couple of days ago."

"Huh?"

"You heard me," Kya replied. "I don't know who he thinks he's playing with. I'm definitely tired of you being so damn naïve about his bullshit. What's it going to take for you to wake the hell up? Enough is enough."

"Kya, you're tripping, it wasn't him."

"Brandi, I know what Derick looks like, I even had a conversation with him. He was with some man. Don't keep acting like I don't know what the hell I'm talking about. It was him."

"I don't know," Brandi said.

"Well I do. The guy he was with was familiar too but I just couldn't place where I've seen him."

"Why would he lie to me?"

"Because he's a no-good, trying-to-live-two-lives, don't-give-a-fuck-about-you son of a bitch. That's why! You need to get it together, girlfriend! Life is too short and precious to waste time dealing with the foolishness!"

"I know, but I take my vows very seriously. When God tells me my relationship is over then I'll leave. Until that happens I'm standing by my husband."

"I'll make sure I'm not standing by you when the wrath of God comes down. My dear, he's been giving you all the signs for months. You're the one that's chosen to ignore everything that God is placing before you. How much evidence do you actually need? Is it really hard for you to grasp the fact that Derick doesn't take your damn vows seriously nor is he interested in your marriage?"

"I disagree," Brandi murmured.

"Anyway, before I forget, I was calling to check you're all set for today. Is there anything that you need?"

"No, everything's all set. Your staff came by *very* early this morning and started setting up and I finished the daunting task that I was dreading."

"And what was that?"

"I needed to unpack the rest of the boxes upstairs. Ughhhhhh. I'm so glad I'm done with that."

"I know you are. Moving is a pain in the ass. It's the packing and unpacking that makes the moving process worse."

"Yeah, I know. I plan on staying in this house for a very, very long time. I can't do this moving thing again. I hate moving. It takes a lot out of you. But I'm grateful that I had a lot of help to get me through this process."

"Girlfriend, the next time I move I'm going to hire someone to pack and unpack everything. I will only be there to supervise."

"I know that's right, that's something you're good at," Brandi replied.

"By the way, thanks again for hosting brunch. Despite some of the not so good or happy conversational pieces I really had a great time."

"I had fun too. But I think you need to ease up on Deion."

"I'm not saying anything else to her about her sexventures or gallivanting. She's a grown-ass woman, it's her life and she's going to do whatever she wants to. She'll just have to learn the hard way," Kya said.

"You're right. Every action has a reaction."

"Yup and I'm staying out of it."

"We all make mistakes but she's the one that'll have to live with the consequences of her choices."

"I was only trying to help her. I figured if I kept drilling it in her head she'd eventually get the message. But I guess not."

"Maybe she will. We all sit back and think about things when we're alone. I hope she gets it, sooner or later."

"Hopefully."

"The sad part about it is she's never going to meet the right man with her current behavior. Both you and I know what she's doing is detrimental to her well-being."

"That's my whole point. I've been with a no-good-ass man. I'm not going to say I wasted my time but I was with him longer than I should have been. Once I got out of that toxic relationship, look what happened and when I least expected it."

"I know and look at you now."

"If I'd stayed with Jeff then I'd have missed out on this good-ass man," Kya said.

"People don't realize how they actually block their own blessings. Sometimes you have to let someone or something go in order to receive what God actually has in store for you," Brandi said.

"You realize that when it comes to someone else's situation but don't realize your own shit? That's interesting."

"We've moved off the Brandi and Derick situation, Kya," Brandi said.

"Okay, I was just saying."

"Sometimes it just takes longer for some of us to make a decision, that's all. I know my marriage isn't perfect but I'm trying."

"It's not you, it's Derick."

"I'm done with the topic," Brandi said.

"And so am I, for now."

"Thank you."

"No problem."

"I want you to know that I'm happy for you and Steve," Brandi said.

"Thanks, girl. This was long overdue. That man makes me so happy! I'm so glad that I got myself together and I finally let go of Mr. Wrong in order for Mr. Right to be presented to me."

"Ain't that the truth?" Brandi yelled.

"Girl, we've been on this phone for over an hour and I know you have stuff to do. I'll be over as soon as my mom picks up the girls," Kya said.

"Okay, I'll see you a little later," Brandi said.

"Okey dokey. Call me if you need me to pick anything up."

"I think you had enough stuff delivered. We're good."

"Okay. Well, I'll see you a little later on."

Brandi opened her front door and saw Bailey pulling up to the house. "Hey, girl!" she yelled as Bailey got out of the car.

"Hello, sweetie."

As Bailey walked up to the house, Brandi asked, "Where the heck have you been? We've been trying to call you all day."

"I've been so busy today," Bailey said.

"Too busy to return our calls?"

When Bailey reached the front door, Brandi grabbed her and gave a hug. "Is everything okay?"

Bailey looked at Brandi and said, "Don't worry about me. Everything will be fine."

"Come on in the kitchen. Would you like something to drink?" Brandi asked.

"No, I'm good."

"You look fabulous. I love that dress."

"Thank you. You look wonderful. You're even glowing. What's up with you?" Bailey asked.

"Nothing much, I'm just a blessed woman and have every reason to be happy."

"I know that's right," Bailey said.

"I didn't get a chance to ask you but how are Eugene and my assistant doing with your plans?"

"Great. I have a good team and they keep me on my toes."

"That's good. Don't forget to incorporate humor in the midst of your busyness. That's important," Bailey said.

"We definitely do. They crack me up."

"I know I'm early, I wanted to come over to see what you need help with."

"Everything's done. Thanks to you guys there's nothing to do. The caterers took care of everything."

"Okay, then we can sit and relax for a bit."

"Kya should be here shortly," Brandi said.

"Have you spoken to Deion?" Bailey asked.

"No I haven't. I see I have a ton of missed calls from on my phone from her. I didn't even get a chance to call my doctor's office back."

"Why, what's wrong?"

"I had my annual and a consultation about getting pregnant. They're probably calling to give me the results of my tests," Brandi said.

"What tests?"

"The normal tests you get: HPV, STDs, HIV, etc. But I have it set up that they'll email or leave a voice message with the results."

"Oh okay," Bailey said.

"Yes. You have to authorize it though. There's a form that you have to fill out saying it's okay for them to do that."

"I don't know if I want a doctor's office leaving any results on my phone or sending them via email," Bailey said.

"I was like that at first but then I said what the heck. I'll check my messages in a few."

"Yes, please check your messages, God forbid someone had an emergency or something," Bailey said.

Brandi got up to get her cellphone off the counter, and heard someone knocking on the kitchen door. As Bailey walked towards the door, she heard Kya yelling, "Open the damn door!" Bailey opened up and Kya was standing there holding a box and several bags. "Bitch, grab a bag or something. You just standing there looking at me. Do you think the bags are going to jump into your damn hands?"

As Bailey reached for some of the bags, she said, "I love you too, Kya."

Kya walked in the house and dropped the bags on the floor, looked at Bailey and said, "What the fuck ever. You can't return phone calls or texts anymore?"

"I spoke to Tyanna and TyShae."

"I've been calling your ass non-stop. Why haven't you returned any of my calls? What the hell is going on with you?" Kya asked.

"Nothing. I've been busy."

"Yeah right. Busy my ass. Who the hell do you think you're talking to? What's going on, Bailey?"

"Nothing's going on, I needed to get some things in order that's all."

"What things?" Kya asked.

"Kya, do we really have to talk about this now?"

"Yes! I don't know why you're being so damn secretive. What's up with you?" Kya asked.

As Bailey walked to the counter, she said, "I moved out, that's all."

Both Kya and Brandi yelled, "You moved?"

"What the fuck?" Kya asked.

"Yes, I moved."

"Are you serious?" Brandi asked.

"Yes."

"What does that mean? Maybe I'm not comprehending," Kya stated.

"It means that I moved out of the house and into the house we were going to rent."

"And you couldn't call us?" Kya asked.

"Are you okay? Bailey, you should have called us," Brandi said.

"It's fine. There was no need to bug you with my crap."

"I fucking hate it when you act like this. No, it's not fine!" Kya yelled.

"So what does that mean, Bailey? Are you and Noah getting divorced?" Brandi asked.

"We're separated for now. I can't say what's going to happen down the road. But right now I need some time and space."

"That's understandable but you still could have called and informed us. I'm a little fucked up with you right now." Kya said.

"Take a number and get in line. Trust me, you'll get over it," Bailey said sarcastically.

"Eventually. But right now I'm still fucked up with you," Kya said.

"Is there anything that we can do?" Brandi asked.

"No. I've taken care of everything. I didn't have a whole lot to move, just our clothes." Bailey said.

"Okay, but please let us know if there's something that we can do. If you need a babysitter, a shoulder to cry on, vent, anything," Brandi said.

"I will."

"No you won't," Kya said.

"Kya, I will. In fact, I'll need some assistance from time to time with the girls," Bailey said.

"Oh goodness. What are you going to tell them?" Brandi asked.

"I don't know yet. Kya, where are my babies anyway?" Bailey asked.

"With my mom, you would know if you returned my calls."

"Are they coming to the housewarming?"

"Not until later on."

"Ladies, we can have this conversation later. I'm fine and there's really nothing to talk about," Bailey said.

"I like how you're so nonchalant about this shit," Kya said.

"Kya, this is not the time. Besides, Noah and I are good. I just need to clear my head and get my thoughts together."

"Okay, Bailey, whatever you say," Kya said.

"Really, it's all good. I haven't completely walked away from my marriage. Noah would like to go to a marriage counselor."

"And what do you want?" Brandi asked.

"I want to be able to trust my husband. I want things to be normal again. I want him to leave that bitch alone instead of running to her. I want to be with him for the rest of my life."

"Then you've answered your own questions. There wasn't a need to leave your home." Kya said.

"I need some time and space, Kya, to figure all this out."

"It sounds like you're running away. All I know is the two of you love the shit out of each other. Fuck! If the foundation is good then everything else can be fixed. And y'all have one hell of a foundation," Kya said.

"True. But—" Bailey said.

"There are no buts. Get your ass back home, that's what you need to do!" Kya yelled.

"Just put the past and the mistakes that were made behind you. You most definitely have to put the past behind you in order to move forward," Brandi said.

"I'm trying."

"Then try harder," Kya replied.

"For better or worse, my dear. Think about your vows," Brandi said.

"I do. Was he thinking about our vows when he was fucking someone else?"

"I can't speak for him. But I'm sure this is killing him and he understands how bad he messed up," Brandi said.

"We all have flaws and none of us are perfect, including you. I suggest you think about that when you're trying to figure out your next steps," Kya said.

"I know that. I also know I don't want my marriage to end," Bailey said.

"Okay then, there you have it," Brandi said.

"But it's still not that easy. I have some things that I need to figure out."

"Bitch, stop making excuses! Remember, excuses build bridges to nowhere. So you need to cut it out and stop being a fucking narcissistic, spoiled-ass brat!" Kya shouted.

"Just like everything else you and Noah have been through, y'all can work this out too," Brandi said.

"I agree with everything y'all have said. I'll figure it out," Bailey said.

"Just know that the love that you and Noah have for one another is worth salvaging. Yes, cheating is bad, but we all make mistakes. Forgive him and move on," Kya said.

"Thanks, Dr. Phil," Bailey said jokingly.

"Smart ass," Kya said.

"We all go through life's woes and plenty of ups and downs. However, as long as we have breath in our bodies, we must forgive, let go and move forward," Brandi said.

"Exactly. Now I need a cocktail. Y'all making my blood pressure go up. Stressing me out and shit," Kya said.

"Girl, what the hell ever, don't use my drama as a reason to drink," Bailey said.

"I'm confident that everything will be fine with you and Noah," Brandi said.

"I concur," Kya replied.

"Yeah, we'll be okay. So, can we discuss something else? Besides, it's almost time for the housewarming party," Bailey said.

"As of right now there's nothing to do but wait for the guests to arrive," Brandi said.

"Where the hell is Deion?" Kya asked.

"I don't know but you know she'll be here," Bailey said.

"She better," Brandi said.

"I hope she didn't forget. You know how absentminded she can be sometimes," Kya said.

"She didn't forget. I'm positive she'll be here," Bailey said.

"Ladies, excuse me for one second, I'm going to call my doctor's office back to see what they wanted," Brandi said.

"What's wrong, are you okay?" Kya asked.

"Girl, I'm fine. It was probably the recorder calling with my test results. My doctor was also going to give me the name of an infertility specialist."

"Oh, okay. Is Derick here?" Kya asked.

"No he's working but he'll be home shortly."

Brandi walked into the kitchen and dialed the number. "Hi, this is Brandi Knight, someone called me yesterday. I believe it was to give me my test results."

"Hold for one second, Mrs. Knight." As Brandi held the phone and listened to the boring elevator music, she walked to the kitchen door and glanced over her backyard. Within a matter of seconds she heard a familiar voice on the other end of the phone.

"Good afternoon Mrs. Knight, this is Tasha, Dr. Williams's assistant."

"Hi Tasha, how are you?" Brandi asked.

"I'm good and yourself?"

"Blessed, and I won't complain, there's no need to. So what's going on, you have my test results?"

"Yes ma'am, give me one second to grab your file. I know I have it here on my desk. Okay, got it." As Brandi patiently held the phone, she could hear Tasha flipping the pages in her file. "Mrs. Knight, there's a list of negative results. HPV, syphilis, herpes, gonorrhea, chlamydia."

"Okay, that's nice to know. Not that I expected anything to be positive."

"But there is one more thing," Tasha said.

"What's that?" Brandi asked.

"One of your tests did come back positive."

"Huh, which test is that? I thought you said they were all negative."

"Yes, the STD's were but the HIV test came back positive. I'm sorry," Tasha said.

Brandi sat at the kitchen table. So many things were going through her mind. She felt numb and as if everything around her was moving in slow motion. She sat at the table feeling helpless, confused and not sure if she'd heard the information correctly.

"Mrs. Knight? Mrs. Knight, are you there?" Tasha asked.

Brandi's reply was soft and slow. "Yes, I'm still here. Tasha, is Dr. Williams available? I need to speak to her. I'm not understanding what's going on."

"Ma'am, she's with a patient right now. I'm looking at her notes and she'd like you to come in for a consultation, and your husband should get tested as soon as possible."

"Are you sure that you have my file in your hand? How can I have HIV? I'm married. I've only been with my husband," Brandi whispered.

"Mrs. Knight, would you like to come in on Monday morning? You could also get retested if you're questioning the results."

"Yes. Yes. I would like to come in first thing Monday morning."

"I'm so sorry, Mrs. Knight. Would you like Dr. Williams to give you a call when she's free?"

"No, I'll see her Monday morning. What time can I come in?"

"Dr. Williams has an opening at 8 a.m., is that okay with you?"

"Yes, that's fine."

"Okay Mrs. Knight, we'll see you first thing Monday morning."

For the next ten minutes Brandi sat at the kitchen table like a zombie. She put her face in her hands. Her mind was going fifty miles a minute as she tried to figure out the situation. All Brandi felt was confusion and as if she was in a bad dream.

"Brandi. Brandi? Why are you sitting in here?" Bailey asked. Brandi looked up at Bailey with a blank stare. "Brandi, what's wrong? Why are you sitting in here? Your guests have started to arrive. What the hell is wrong?" Bailey asked.

"They said I have HIV," Brandi said softly.

Bailey dropped the glass of wine she was holding on the kitchen floor. She sat next to Brandi and asked, "Who said? What are you talking about?"

Before Brandi could respond, Kya walked into the kitchen. "Excuse me, why are y'all in here? Brandi, some of your colleagues are here."

As Kya walked to the table, Bailey said, "Not now, Kya."

"What the hell's going on, who died?" Kya asked.

"They said I have HIV."

"What the fuck? Who said that bullshit?" Kya asked.

"The doctor. How can I be HIV positive? I don't understand."

Kya and Bailey glanced at each other with the same thought in their head. Bailey put her arm around Brandi and said, "Sweetie, that test could be wrong, they aren't always accurate."

"No, it's right, I know it is. I knew something was wrong. I could feel it in the pit of my stomach. What am I going to do? How did I get HIV? I'm married and I'm not sleeping around. I only have sex with my husband."

"Your husband is the one that gave it to you," Kya whispered under her breath.

"What did you say, Kya?" Brandi asked.

"Let's cancel the housewarming party so you can get some rest. I know you don't feel like being bothered right now," Kya said.

"No. No, we can't do that. We're not cancelling. I'll be okay."

"Sweetie, are you sure? We can tell your guests you're not feeling well, they'll understand," Bailey said.

"No, Bailey, I don't want to cancel the housewarming. I'll be okay. I'm fine." Brandi stood up from the table and walked to the cabinet to get a glass.

"What do you need, sweetie?" Kya asked.

"Kya, what I need you won't be able to help with. I need to know why this is happening to me. Why is God punishing me and what did I do to deserve this? Can you help me with those questions?"

"No, babes, I can't, but we're going to get through this, we're family," Kya said.

"That's easy for you to say, you're not the one that has HIV," Brandi said sarcastically.

Bailey walked over to Brandi and said, "I know you're confused, you're hurting and you have a lot going through your head right now. Just like Kya said, we're a family, we'll get through this and you won't go through this alone."

Brandi started to sob and Bailey hugged her and held her tight. "Sweetie, I love you and I wish I could remove your pain, hurt and confusion. I can't but I can damn sure walk through the fire with you and for you. I promise that you *will* get through this."

Brandi pulled away, wiped her tears and said, "Oh my goodness. Derick."

"What about him?" Kya asked.

"How am I going to tell him? He's going to kill me."

"I wouldn't worry about him right now. Let's just get through the next couple of hours of this party. Afterwards, we'll worry about Mr. Derick," Kya said sarcastically.

"Okay. My guests are here and more are arriving. I have to pull it together quickly. Let me run upstairs and fix my makeup. I'll be back down shortly. I can't let people see me like this."

"Okay, sweetie. Kya and I will entertain your guests. Take as much time as you need," Bailey said.

Brandi started walking towards the steps and said, "Okay, let me freshen up and I'll be quick. Don't wanna keep the people waiting."

While Bailey and Kya waited for Brandi to return downstairs, they repositioned themselves in the foyer so they could greet the guests. They stood there for about forty five minutes before Brandi finally came downstairs. As Brandi walked through the large crowd of friends, family and colleagues she noticed Bailey and Kya standing in the foyer and came over to them.

"Well, here I am," Brandi said.

"Damn, what took you so long?" Kya asked.

"I was fixing my face, I had to fix my makeup. I don't have to look like what I'm going through. Right? More importantly I needed to spend some time with God. When you can't stand anymore you have to kneel."

"I know that's right. A woman that kneels before God can most certainly stand before anyone," Bailey said.

"Not only that, but you can handle and face whatever comes your way. Remember, your circumstances aren't your conclusion," Kya said.

"Preach," Brandi said as she gave Kya and Bailey a high five.

"And it's definitely not the be all and end all. Babygirl, you're going to be fine. Trust!" Kya said.

"I know this is a rhetorical question but are you okay, sweetie?" Bailey asked.

"I'm alright. I mean, I'm going to be all right. I cried about it, prayed and cried some more. But at the end of the day the HIV isn't going to just disappear. Therefore, I just have to deal with it."

"Babes, you're going to be fine. We got your back and we're here for you no matter what," Kya said.

"Thank you. I know I'm going to need all the support I can get."

"You got it, my dear," Bailey said.

Brandi smiled and said, "Okay, enough of that. There are people here and I don't want to tear up all over again. This is a celebration of my new home. We must enjoy ourselves."

"Exactly. You have a house full," Bailey said.

"And did you see the gift table? I had my staff bring in another table to hold all of those damn gifts!" Kya shouted.

"I didn't even pay attention to the gift table. I'll check it out later. Let me go play hostess and mingle with the folks."

Bailey and Kya proceeded to the bar for a refill. While standing there, Kya brought up the subject of Brandi's results again. "I'm not a stupid person but I really can't believe this bullshit."

"I know. It just breaks my heart that she has to go through this. I wish there was something I could do."

"There is. We can be there for our girl."

"Of course. Without a doubt. We most certainly will be there for her. We're pretty much all the family that she has."

"So, I guess we don't have to wonder where the fuck she got it from. When she was talking about it earlier I just wanted to shake the shit out of her."

"Yup. I've been wondering about Derick for a while. Everything with him is so secretive. They haven't had sex in months. He doesn't touch her nor does he show her any form of affection whatsoever."

"Hell, he's never home and he takes these random trips," Kya said.

"Right! When we found those damn books in that trunk, that confirmed it for me."

"I should just go upstairs and pack up his shit my damn self. Why the fuck is he still here? He doesn't want anything from her. He doesn't help with the bills or anything else. And, not to mention, his money is supposedly tied up. That bitch-ass father fucker told her he was saving his money. What real man stacks his money while the wife struggles to pay their bills? What the fuck type of shit is that?" Kya asked.

"Girl, his ass has got to go. I'm hoping and praying he just leaves and gets the hell out of her life. She doesn't need him anyway."

"So true. I can have my cousins come over and put him out. Dookie, MoMo and them would love to kick his stupid ass. As a matter of fact, I'm going to text them right now."

"Girl, no. He's going to leave on his own. This weekend. Trust what I tell you."

"Are you sure you don't want me to call my cousins? I can."

"No, Kya. That's too much damn drama and we're too old for shit like that."

Bailey and Kya were still at the bar talking when they saw Brandi walking towards them. "So are y'all going to be posted at the bar all night?" Brandi asked.

"Girl, we just over here running our mouths," Bailey said.

"She's running her mouth and I'm having cocktails," Kya said.

"This is a pretty nice turnout. Thank you, ladies, for my housewarming party."

"No problem, my dear," Bailey said.

"Anything for you," Kya replied.

"I guess Deion will get here sooner or later," Brandi said.

"I guess the diva is going to be fashionably late as usual. She's probably home taking a damn nap," Kya said.

"She'll be here," Bailey said.

"She better," Kya said. At that moment, Kya saw Derick walk through the front door and down the hall towards the kitchen. "Your man is home," she said sarcastically.

Bailey and Brandi looked around. "Where is he?" Brandi asked.

"He went towards the kitchen," Kya said.

"Oh, okay, maybe he went to the restroom," Brandi said.

Shortly thereafter Chase walked through the foyer. Kya noticed him standing in the foyer adjusting the lime green scarf around his neck. "That's him! That's him!" Kya yelled.

"What? Him who, Kya?" Bailey asked.

"The guy I saw Derick with the other day when he was supposedly out of town."

Brandi looked across the room and said, "Who? John, the guy standing next to Kenny? They work together."

"No, not him, the guy standing in the foyer playing with that bright-ass scarf," Kya said.

Bailey looked across the room and asked, "Who, Chase? I didn't know you invited Chase. I need to go and holler at him."

"Who the hell is Chase? You mean that guy that's always at your boutique? Why the hell would he be here?" Kya asked.

"Chase is my buddy. We started emailing and chatting about eight months ago. He saw my ad in the *Daily News*," Brandi said.

"Why would you be chatting with him?"

"Because I'm a real estate agent and he was looking for a home. Duh."

"What's with the twenty questions?" Bailey asked.

"Did y'all bitches not hear me? That's the guy I saw with Derick. Derick was supposed to be on a damn business trip. Hello, pay attention please," Kya said.

"Nah, maybe it was someone else," Brandi said.

"Brandi, I'm not stupid and I know what Derick looks like. It was him and that guy."

As they started walking to the kitchen, Chase approached them and said, "Hello ladies."

Bailey hugged Chase and said, "I'm going to beat your ass. Where have you been? I've been calling you about some new shit I got in the boutique. I told my manager not to put out anything until you had a chance to see the new stuff."

Chase hugged Brandi and said, "Girl, Ms. Brandi has been keeping me busy with all of these damn houses. I think that's partly my fault, though, I have so many desires and pre-requisites for my perfect home."

"Yes he does. Excuse me, I need to go and find my husband," Brandi said.

"When are you going to stop by the boutique?" Bailey asked.

"Next week," Chase said.

Kya started to clear her throat. It was a hint that she hadn't been properly introduced. "Excuse me, I am standing here," Kya said.

"I'm sorry, darling. Chase, this is my best friend, my boo Thang, my ace and my sister, Kya."

Chase and Kya shook hands.

"You are gorgeous, Ms. Thang."

"Thanks," Kya said.

"I thought you met before at the boutique," Bailey said.

"No, I've never met him. It's nice meeting you though," Kya said sarcastically.

"You too. You sure we haven't met before, you look very familiar?"

"No, we've never met but I think I might have seen you before."

Bailey looked at Kya and rolled her eyes. "We all have a twin," Bailey said.

"Who knows, I get around," Chase said.

Kya chuckled and said, "That's what I hear."

"I'm such a busybody but I'm going to set up shop in DC. Time to settle down. Besides, my body's tired of all the travelling. Not to mention my man misses me so much when I'm gone. Even though he visits me wherever I am, it's just not the same," Chase said.

Kya cleared her throat and said, "That's such a shame. Did your man come here with you?"

Chase looked around the room and said, "Yes he's around here somewhere. He said he was going to the restroom. I don't know where his ass went."

"Anyway, try to come by the shop next week," Bailey said.

"Okay but you know I'd much rather stop by when you're there. Those young girls that work for you get on my nerves. They irritate the hell out of me and they get in my way."

"In other words you want me to be there," Bailey said.

"You got it. Besides, you and I always have great time."

"Okay, just call me when you figure out which day. I'll rearrange my schedule."

While Bailey, Chase and Kya were walking down the hall, Brandi walked towards them, threw up her hands and said, "I don't know where he is."

"Did you check upstairs?" Kya asked.

"No, I'm sure he'll be down in a sec. He's probably changing his clothes."

Chase grabbed Brandi's arm and said, "Now, Ms. Brandi, please show me around this gorgeous home of yours. I see you were holding out on me. Why didn't you sell me this house?"

Brandi chuckled and said, "This house wasn't large enough for you." The ladies walked Chase throughout the house, showing him every part of it. They concluded the tour of the first level and, as they approached the steps in the kitchen leading to the second level, met Derick coming down.

"Hey, I've been looking all over for you," Brandi said.

"Brandi, we need to talk," Derick said.

Chase let go of Brandi's arm and asked, "Wait, y'all know each other?"

Derick stood on the steps and didn't utter a word.

"Of course, this is my husband. I better know him," Brandi said.

"Your *what*?" Chase asked.

"My husband," Brandi reiterated.

Derick walked down the steps and Chase moved closer and stood in his face.

Kya turned to Bailey and whispered, "Bitch, I told you! The shit is hitting the fan right now! This shit just got *real*!"

"What is she talking about, Derick?" Chase asked.

"Chase, this is Brandi. My wife," Derick said slowly.

Chase put his hands on his hips, and asked, "What the fuck are you saying, Derick?"

"My wife," Derick stuttered.

"Okay, clearly I've missed something. What's going on, Derick?" Brandi asked.

"Brandi, can we talk alone?" Derick asked.

"What the fuck do you mean alone? Talk about the shit right here because I need to hear this bullshit!" Chase yelled.

Bailey grabbed Chase's arm and said, "Wait, wait a minute, lower your voice, she has guests. You need to be mindful of that and respect her home as well as her guests."

"Somebody is going to tell me what the fuck is going on. Her husband? What the fuck? So you've been cheating on me?" Chase asked. Derick stood at the bottom of the steps looking like a dog with its tail between his legs. Brandi walked over to the kitchen table and sat down.

Derick followed her and asked, "Can we all just sit down and talk?"

"Bitch, you got me fucked up. I don't have shit to talk about with you. The only thing I got to say to you is come get your shit out of my house and get the fuck on!" Chase yelled.

"Chase, I've told you to lower your voice," Bailey said.

"Oh, this is some bullshit. We've been together all of these years and you're fucking her? And you married the bitch! When were you going to mention this shit? You know what, I don't even want to hear shit your bitch-ass gotta say. I'm done with your tired ass," Chase yelled.

"Chase," Bailey said.

Chase walked to the kitchen door, turned and yelled, "You know what? I'm out of here."

"I think that's a good idea," Kya said.

Chase turned and said, "Brandi, I apologize from the bottom of my heart. I had no idea the two of you were together, let alone married. I'm sorry for disrespecting you and your home. You can have his weak, confused, lying ass. I don't need this bullshit. This shit is crazy."

"I fucking told y'all that something wasn't right. I've been saying it from day one," Kya said.

"Kya, mind your own business, this has nothing to do with you," Derick said.

"Oh no, my friend, that's where you're wrong. Brandi is our business. We are her family and it has everything to do with us," Kya said.

Derick sat beside Brandi and asked, "Can we please talk alone? I really need to talk to you."

As the tears rolled down Brandi's face, she looked at Derick and said, "Whatever you have to say you can say it in front of my family. Better yet, just save it. I don't want to hear it."

Bailey walked over to the table and said, "Derick, maybe you should leave and give Brandi some time."

"No, Bailey," Brandi said. Bailey and Kya walked over to the kitchen counter and stood in the background. They refused to leave Brandi alone with Derick.

"Can we talk alone?" Derick begged.

"Nope," Kya replied.

"So you see, ladies, Derick has given me more than enough. He's given a lot of mental anguish and abuse, false hopes, a fictitious life, fake dreams, a marriage filled with illusions and lies. Oh but wait, what he really gave me that I'll remember for the rest of my days is HIV," Brandi said. She wiped her tears and added to Derick, "Oh no, my dear, you have nothing to say to me that I need or want to hear. But let me tell you a little secret. I knew. I knew all about your gallivanting and sexual rendezvous with other men. I saw you on several occasions going into those damn clubs. See, I was following you. It was like you were leaving all the clues and pieces of the puzzle for me to find. I admit I felt stupid and crazy for staying with you. But I hoped and prayed you'd change."

"Let me explain," Derick pleaded.

Brandi laughed and said, "Are you high or something? Maybe you just don't understand what I'm saying. Let me see if I can say it so you'll get it!"

"You don't understand," Derick said.

"I don't understand? No, *you* don't understand. There is nothing that you can say to me that I really want to hear."

"Let me just say something to you," Derick said.

"Save it for someone that actually gives a shit because I don't want to hear the lies and bullshit anymore!" Brandi yelled. Kya and Bailey looked at each other in shock. They couldn't believe those words were coming out of Brandi's mouth. They'd never heard her speak like that before. But they knew all that Derick had put Brandi through and that she needed to get everything she'd been holding in for so long out of her system. So, they stood patiently with their arms crossed as she vented, yelled, cried and screamed. Brandi stood up and stepped back from the table. She grabbed a paper towel to dry her face. She stood over Derick and yelled, "Get the fuck out of my house . . . *NOW*! You've worn out your welcome and you've got to leave!"

"So we can't talk?" Derick asked.

"We'll talk in court. Oh, that's the other secret. I filed for divorce yesterday, so whatever you think you need to say, tell me in court."

Derick stood up and walked towards the steps.

"Where the hell do you think you're going?" Brandi asked.

"I need to get my stuff."

Brandi chuckled and said, "I got one better. Your shit is in the garage. I packed it for you earlier. And please use the kitchen door because I have guests."

Derick walked to the kitchen door, turned and looked at Brandi and said, "I'm sorry."

"You most certainly are. Oh wait one more thing. Did you know it's a criminal offense to have sex when you know you have a STD? You like dick so much you'll definitely get plenty of that where you're going. Okay, that's all, give me my keys and get the fuck on. You're dismissed!"

Bailey and Kya walked over to Brandi and hugged her. Brandi patted their backs and said, "I'm good, don't worry about me. Let's go party and celebrate. So put on your game faces and stop looking so damn sad. Everything will be alright!"

"Can we drink to that?" Kya asked.

"No! You always find an excuse to drink to something," Bailey said.

"Girl, I was going to get water anyway. I've had enough cocktails for the night," Kya said.

"Sure you were," Brandi replied.

"What? That's a first," Bailey said.

When the ladies walked out of the kitchen Bailey saw Deion standing at the bar with a man.

"Oh I see the fashionably late, nap-taking diva finally made it. Just as the housewarming is ending," Bailey said.

"Where is she?" Brandi asked.

"At the bar."

"Wait, am I tripping? Is that Jeff at the over there by D?" Kya asked.

"Yup, that's him," Bailey said.

"Who the hell invited him?" Kya asked.

"I sure as hell didn't," Brandi said.

"Then what's he doing here?" Kya asked.

"I don't know."

"I'm going over there to find out. I know his ass isn't following me again," Kya said.

The ladies advanced on Deion and Jeff. Without speaking, Kya approached Jeff, pointing her finger in his face.

"What the hell are you doing here?" Kya asked.

Deion looked at Kya and said, "He's with me. Why? I couldn't bring a date?"

"A date! What the fuck? Y'all on a date. You have *got* to be kidding me!" Kya yelled.

"Kya, please don't do this here. Go in the back or something," Bailey said.

Kya acted as if she didn't hear Bailey and continued to ask questions. "Jeff, what is going on?"

"Jeff? Who's Jeff? His name's Jay," Deion asked.

"This trifling ass negro is Jeff. You don't know who you're with. Oh, let me see if I get this right. You met him on your way here, fucked him, and brought him along as a date? You really are a trifling ass nasty ho," Kya said.

"Bitch, fuck you!" Deion yelled.

"No, fuck you! You going to stand here and lie to my face then act like you don't know who the fuck he is!" Kya yelled.

"Kya, take your ass in the back somewhere and y'all talk about this shit," Bailey pleaded.

"Hell fucking no. I want everyone to know about this skank-ass ratchet bitch!" Kya yelled.

"Kya, calm down. Stop acting like a child," Jeff said.

"Can someone tell me why she's acting like the ghetto princess that she is?" Deion said.

"Oh yeah. I'm ghetto? Bitch, this is my daughter's father. If you keep acting like you don't know what the fuck's going on, I'm going to knock the shit out of you!" Kya screamed.

"You're what? You're who?" Deion asked.

"My fucking trifling ass baby daddy. That's who you're with!" Kya yelled.

"I advise you to lower your voice. Don't be coming at me like that," Jeff said.

"Oh my God. I didn't know that. He said his name was Jay," Deion said.

"Like I told you, before you fuck people you might want to learn more about them!" Kya yelled.

"That's it. Take your asses in the den, close the door, and talk about this shit there," Bailey insisted.

"Um, I'm going to stay out here and see my guests out. Bailey, please go back there with them so they don't tear up my house," Brandi said.

"Come on, Kya. Deion and Jeff. Let's go to the den so y'all can discuss this like adults," Bailey stated.

"I don't have shit to discuss. I'm not staying here and listening to this bullshit," Jeff said.

"Man, take your ass to the den and get this shit straight," Bailey said.

In the den, Jeff and Deion sat on the chaise, Bailey stood at the door, and Kya stood at the edge of the sofa.

"Listen, whether you believe me or not I honestly didn't know he was Lexi's dad. I definitely didn't know about y'all relationship. How could I?"

"Kya, she does have a point," Bailey said.

"I might love to shop but I'm not buying that bullshit," Kya said.

"Kya, I don't know how many ways I can tell you this. I didn't know."

"You supposed to be my friend. One of my best friends at that and you're going behind my back fucking him?"

"I didn't know."

"So you mean to tell me that you've never been to my house?"

"Yes I have. What difference does that make?"

"And you've never seen any of the damn pictures of him and Lexi throughout my house?"

"No."

"You are a motherfucking liar! Out of all the men you fuck you just happened to fall on my baby daddy's dick of all people! Bitch, get the fuck outta here!"

"I never paid any attention to the pictures in your house."

"You just going to keep sitting here lying to my fucking face? Bitch, you're scandalous. And this trifling ass fucker ain't any good and ain't worth shit. But you are claiming his nasty ass!"

Jeff got up from the sofa and said, "You know what, D, I'll holler at you later on."

"Wait, don't you think you have some questions to answer?" Deion asked.

"Nah, I don't have time for this shit. What questions do I need to answer? I didn't know y'all were home girls. That's all I got to say. I ain't going to keep listening to all of this shit. Later."

Deion grabbed Jeff's arm and asked, "How the fuck you just going to leave me here? This involves you too!"

"I'm not dealing with this. I got shit to do!" Jeff yelled. As he walked to the door, Deion repeatedly yelled his name. He neither responded, nor looked back. When he got to the door, Bailey opened it and let him through.

"And that's the man you want. What a joke," Kya said.

"You know what, I'm going to let the two of you sit here and talk this thing through. Work this shit out. Y'all are friends for goodness sake," Bailey said.

"Friends don't fuck your leftovers," Kya said.

Deion shook her head and said, "Say whatever you want, I really don't care."

"You know what? I'm not angry, pissed or mad at you. If anything I'm fucked up with your actions and I feel sorry for you," Kya said.

"If I leave the room can y'all talk like two adults?" Bailey asked.

"Maybe," Deion replied.

"I can't agree to that statement. One thing for sure, and two for certain, I say what the fuck I mean and I mean what the fuck I say. With this situation I'm saying what the fuck I feel!" Kya yelled.

"I don't care what you say, Kya, but you are going to respect Brandi's damn house *and* her guests. I understand you're pissed off, but you're a grown-ass woman so act like it," Bailey said.

Kya waved her hand and said, "Whatever."

"I'm going out there to help Brandi, so sit and talk like adults," Bailey said.

As Bailey left the room, Kya got up and walked over to the window. She stood there for a couple of seconds with her arms folded. She then turned to Deion and said, "You and your behavior sicken me to my stomach. I hope before it's too late you'll realize that your reckless behavior equals detrimental circumstances."

"Kya, you can judge me, you can talk badly about me, and you can try to break me down. I didn't know that was your man. How could I?" Deion asked.

"Deion, at this point it really doesn't matter. 'Cause all you do is lie anyway. Talking to you is really like talking to a brick wall. It's your life, your choices, your mistakes, your actions and none of my damn business. I'm going to mind my business from here on out and stay in my lane," Kya said.

"Good, that's what you need to do," Deion said.

"Sweetie, just remember one thing," Kya said.

"What now?" Deion asked.

"You're truly a victim of your own lust. Jeff is not going to do anything but break you into little pieces and tear you down. He's going to use the shit out of you and throw you away when he's done milking you dry."

"Whatever you say. That's not true, he loves me,"

"Is that what he told you?"

"No, but I know he does."

"Oh yeah. Well, actions speak much louder than words. Behind every action is a reaction. I'm willing to bet any amount of money the only action he's showing is how he don't give a fuck about you."

"Okay, whatever."

"D, I know the man, I was with him for over seven years. The only person Jeff loves is Jeff. He's only out for what he can get. And he's a fucking dog that will fuck anything with a pussy."

"Whatever you say, Kya. Just because it didn't work out between y'all don't wish bad luck on our relationship."

"D, y'all don't have a relationship. He's using you, D, I know you see it."

"All I know is this is my man, the father of my child, and we're going to be together," Deion said.

"Wow! And you're pregnant? Are you sure it's his? You do fuck any man you meet," Kya said.

"Fuck you!" Deion yelled.

"Whatever you say. But I'm just keeping it real. You know what, I wish y'all the best and I hope y'all live happily ever after. I'm done with it. Goodbye, my dear."

Deion got up walked to the door and said, "Cool, we're done with this convo. I'm leaving. I didn't come here to be chastised and cursed out."

"In all actuality we're done, period. I definitely don't need fake-ass friends like you. Goodbye. Take care and good luck. Make sure you find out who your baby daddy is. You could always go on Maury, he'll help you out," Kya yelled.

As Deion opened the door and walked out, she turned around and yelled, "Fuck you, Kya!"

"Sorry, babes, I'm strictly dickly and don't get down like that," Kya replied.

After a couple of minutes, Kya left the den. She noticed that the house was now empty and could hear Brandi and Bailey in the kitchen talking. She went to the kitchen and leaned on the threshold.

"Oh well. It's a wrap," Kya said.

"The way Deion stormed out of here and slammed the door, I'm assuming nothing was resolved?" Brandi asked.

"What a fucking night!" Bailey yelled.

"You can say that again," Brandi replied.

"Do you want to talk about it?" Brandi asked.

"No ma'am, there's nothing to talk about," Kya said.

"Come on, Kya," Bailey said.

"Bailey, I don't have anything to talk about. Just leave it alone!"

"Okay then," Bailey said.

"I'm going to kick off these Louboutins, sit back on the sofa and chill out," Kya said.

"Are you ladies spending the night?" Brandi asked.

"Yes ma'am," Bailey said. "We are not leaving you tonight, you're stuck with us."

"Okay, well let's go to the den, kick our feet up, and chillax," Brandi said.

The three ladies walked down the hall to the den. Even though it had been a day from hell they were laughing, smiling and hugging one another. As they all sat down on the sofa and placed their feet on the table Brandi shouted, "Thank you Lord!"

"Yes. *Thank ya!*" Kya yelled.

"That damn girl needs help," Bailey said.

"Thank you for revelations and the uncovered truth," Brandi said.

"I couldn't have said it better myself," Bailey said.

"Seriously, what the hell is going on tonight?" Kya asked.

"It must be a full damn moon," Bailey said.

"You know what, life is like a highway or a journey so to speak," Brandi said.

"How's that?" Bailey asked.

"You look at a map to try and get to your destination. In the process, there are speed bumps, road blocks, a few accidents here and there, detours, twist and turns, standstill traffic and tolls you have to pay. A trip that can take twenty minutes can last more than you planned and expected. But finally, after going through all of that, you've reached your destination. After all of those obstacles you learned a lot about the journey along the way," Brandi said.

"So true, so very true," Kya said.

"What do we do when we're stuck in traffic?" Brandi asked.

"Try to get the hell out of it," Kya said.

"That too. But we try to take short cuts and go around it. Isn't that what life is about? Going over or around the obstacles that we face," Brandi said.

"Yes, ma'am," Bailey said.

"Great analogy, I love it!" Kya yelled.

"Every day that you wake up with breath in your body is another chance," Bailey said.

"I totally agree," Brandi said.

"We also have the power to write our own happy ending," Bailey said.

"I'm not going to let this disease keep me from living the life I was destined to live. Tomorrow I'll get up, dust my ass off and keep it moving! I refuse to give up or give in. I'm not a quitter and I'm not throwing in the towel. God brought me to it and *HE* will bring me through it," Brandi said.

"You better," Kya said.

"It's sad that we spend so much time accommodating others when we should be accommodating the right person, in other words, ourselves," Bailey said.

"Tomorrow is a new day and *all* things will and shall begin anew. I declare that," Brandi said.

"It's been a trying year but I look forward to tomorrow, the next chapter of all of our lives and new beginnings," Bailey said.

As the three of them clasped hands, Kya smiled and said, "It was just another day's journey. But it's okay, we can do this. We got this! We are keeping it moving – together!"

THE END . . . FOR NOW

Reviews

If you enjoyed *Skeletons*, please consider leaving a rating and review on Amazon.

Reviews and feedback are important to an author, as well as other potential readers, and would be very much appreciated. Thank you.

About the Author

Tracey Dowtin, owner and event planner of Tracey Dowtin Events, painter at Abstracts by Tracey, Owner and buyer of Le' EUnique Diva Boutique and is also a business mentor and coach to small business owners and entrepreneurs. Through her mentoring program she is able to assist and mentor entrepreneurs and small business owners with their business plans, strategic planning, marketing and long-term goals for success.

Tracey was born in Chester, PA and raised in Washington, DC where she attended DC Public Schools. After graduating she was eager to enter the "real world" and decided to skip college and join the workforce. It wasn't until years later and working in a not-for-profit organization that Tracey decided to further her education and attend Northern Virginia Community College and pursue her degree in Psychology. Out of all the classes that Tracey took, it was the classes with the writing assignments that she was more interested and seemed to enjoy the most. For her, writing is something that she loves and finds as an easy task.

Throughout Tracey's life, she always loved to write. Whether it was journaling or creating short stories, writing always presented itself as fun, entertaining, relaxing and creative. Being passionate about writing, Tracey decided that she would write a novel. Even with her busy schedule, she was able to complete the novel in her spare time.

Her next goal is to become a motivational speaker, life coach and write many more books. She's happiest when she's extremely busy and helping others succeed. In her spare time, she loves to paint & create abstract art, refurbish antique furniture, cook, shop, travel, learn new things, watch the history channel and spend time with loved ones. She's adamant about showing others that you don't have to settle for where you are in life, and can bring your dreams to pass by tapping into the gifts that God gave you. Tracey resides in Prince George's County, MD.

To learn more about Tracey Dowtin or for information on booking her for a speaking engagement, please log on to:

www.traceydowtin.com

https://www.facebook.com/authortraceydowtin

Twitter: @TraceyDowtin

Acknowledgements

To my family and friends– thank you for your unwavering love and support as I travel through my journey. You've been there from the beginning and have been significant in my writing as well as in all that I do. Without you, bringing my dreams to pass would be useless. I wholeheartedly thank each and every one of you. You all play individual yet major roles in my life and the woman that I am. Words cannot express my appreciation for all you've done. I love you! Blessings to you!

To my team – LionheART Publishing House, Karen Perkins, Louise Burke & CC Morgan, I love you and thank you for all of your hard work, support, guidance and input as I walk through my journey. Without you, I would have been lost. You've guided and assisted me in more ways than one. Your selflessness, tireless efforts and contributions to making my work a success had not gone unnoticed. I wholeheartedly thank you for all that you do and working feverishly on my behalf. I also look forward to working with you with all of my books. Blessings to you!

www.ingramcontent.com/pod-product-compliance
Lightning Source LLC
Chambersburg PA
CBHW071146250626
47159CB00001B/2